# The Witchery

## S. ISABELLE

Scholastic Press / New York

As a play on the *Macbeth* line "By the pricking of my thumbs, / Something wicked this way comes," the witches in this book perform magic by sacrificing blood by way of a thumb pinprick with a needle. This action is described numerous times throughout the novel, and characters cut themselves in other ways before performing spells.

In addition to depictions of self-harm, other content warnings include: blood, violence, gore, death of a parent, and body horror.

All rights reserved. Published by Scholastic Press, an imprint of Scholastic Inc., *Publishers since 1920.* SCHOLASTIC, SCHOLASTIC PRESS, and associated logos are trademarks and/or registered trademarks of Scholastic Inc.

The publisher does not have any control over and does not assume any responsibility for author or third-party websites or their content.

This book is a work of fiction. Names, characters, places, and incidents are either the product of the author's imagination or are used fictitiously, and any resemblance to actual persons, living or dead, business establishments, events, or locales is entirely coincidental.

Library of Congress Cataloging-in-Publication Data
Names: Isabelle, S., author.
Title: The witchery / S. Isabelle.
Description: First edition. | New York : Scholastic Press, 2022. | Audience: Ages 14 and up. | Audience: Grades 10–12. | Summary: Logan came to Mesmortes Coven Academy in Haelsford, Florida, to learn to control her powers, but she soon learns she has a role to play in the ancient curse of the hellmouth—whatever the cost to herself and her new friends.
Identifiers: LCCN 2021050872 (print) | LCCN 2021050873 (ebook) | ISBN 9781338758962 (hardcover) | ISBN 9781338758979 (ebk)
Subjects: LCSH: Witches—Juvenile fiction. | Magic—Juvenile fiction. | Blessing and cursing—Juvenile fiction. | Sacrifice—Juvenile fiction. | Schools—Juvenile fiction. | Friendship—Juvenile fiction. | CYAC: Witches—Fiction. | Magic—Fiction. | Blessing and cursing—Fiction. | Sacrifice—Fiction. | Schools—Fiction. | Friendship—Fiction.
Classification: LCC PZ7.1.I8215 Wi 2022 (print) | LCC PZ7.1.I8215 (ebook) | DDC [Fic]—dc23

10 9 8 7 6 5 4 3 2 1          22 23 24 25 26

Printed in the U.S.A.        37

First edition, July 2022

Book design by Stephanie Yang

For Gabby, forever in my coven.
And for all the kids who ever wished to be witchy.

To be a witch is to be accepted into the world's most exclusive coven. Have pride, for your blood is magic.
—*Grimoire for the Good Witch*, 10th ed.

A prick of a thumb for a spell that is sweet.
A tribute of blood so the dark may speak.
And if one finds that glory comes to call—
Then a witch has the right to sacrifice them all.
—*The Most Wicked Works of Olga Yara*, circa 1860

part one

# the sacrifice

# 1

# logan

*Hallowe'en, five weeks until the Haunting Season*

Logan Wyatt had never known real fear until she moved to this fiendish little witchtown.

Haelsford. A hellmouth, if there ever was one, in the muggy mass of Florida's belly.

Looking out from her window at the top of the Hill, Logan watched the humidity envelop the town in a gray haze. The night was sticky. Summer had long since trickled into autumn, but the humidity had not ceased. Wherever she went, the mosquitoes buzzed near, hungry for her blood.

*Haelsford will eat you alive*, her mother once said.

Logan had tightened her fingers around the handle of her suitcase. Her mother clutched the amber gem at her neck. They were standing in front of the security line at Ontario International. While other families embraced, the Wyatt witches only stared at each other.

Diane Wyatt's parting words were not encouragement, or even the general don't-have-sex-and-die type of *normal mom* warning that Logan would've welcomed. They were words of doubt, of the strangling type of love that convinced witchy mothers to keep their children under overprotective charms. But it wasn't entirely an exaggeration. Born and bred in Wicker, Ontario, Logan was accustomed to the frostbitten peculiarities of the north. She knew of ice-covered homes that creaked and shivered, housing nameless ghouls and their ancient sins. Pale mundanes wandered around in the cold, transfixed by the smell of an oncoming snow. As annoying as it was to live in a household of witches where every single one was powerful but her, she had felt safe.

Heart twitching, Logan picked up the letter waiting on her bed.

A message from Jailah Simmons, Thalia Blackwood, and Iris Keaton-Foster.

They were called the Red Three.

Logan spent her first months at the Mesmortes Coven Academy obsessed with them in the way all the other students were. Not catty, but in *wanting*. Wanting to be looked at in the same way they looked at one another, like each was the most beautiful thing on earth. It was easy to be entranced by them.

While the Red Three often kept to themselves, they didn't operate in the intimidating way of a clique. They mixed and mingled with the freshmen, offering all the sage advice that came with junior year. Each had her individual hobbies—Jailah was part of the Junior Witchery Council, which comprised sociable and ambitious witches who would one day rule the world; Thalia frequented the herbalism lab to tutor those who weren't skilled in greenwitchery; and if Iris liked you enough, she might teach you a thing or two about calling the dead.

Logan couldn't imagine being so unapologetically witchy. They wielded their wands like weapons, wore the blood of their pricked fingers like badges of honor, and delivered textbook incantations as if the words belonged only to them.

4

In a castle filled to the brim with young witches, these three felt so different to Logan, who couldn't heat up her tea with a simple warming spell, and whose wand only ever emitted wisps of smoke instead of brilliant sparks.

But on this Hallowe'en night, she would become one of them.

She didn't know what to wear.

After a frenzy that left her wardrobe scattered around her room, Logan settled on what she was already wearing. Her Mesmortes uniform. White silk shirt, thick socks, and black cape. She opted for the plaid skirt instead of the slacks, her vest adorned with a patch of the school sigil—a severed wolf's head, its howling mouth stretched toward the moon. She liked the hat most of all because it wasn't a comically pointy thing, but more of a top hat— quirky but fashionable. She kept her wand in the vest's inner pocket, resting uncomfortably against her heart.

Logan gave herself a quick look in the mirror. Her pale skin was still adjusting to Haelsford's relentless sun, and she was thankful for the apothecary's sunburn salves. She ran her fingers through her messy blond bangs, though it only made them messier.

A soft yellow light flashed in Logan's peripheral vision and her phone chimed. She picked it up and found two texts.

The first, from her mother:

**Darling, I can see that you are troubled.**

**There is no shame in coming back home.**

And a warning from her older sister, Margot:

**FYI, MOM'S GOT THE LOOK ON YOU.**

*The Look.* Logan was getting better at detecting the super-nosy spell, but she was distracted tonight.

"This is no big," she whispered, ignoring them. "You got this."

She pulled the creamy stationery from its envelope.

Logan Phillip Wyatt, this is your fate!
Your time to shine with your new best mates!
Like Artemis and Apollo, this archer can't wait!
So, find me and fly me, precisely at eight!

She smiled. This note was written by Jailah Simmons, surely. Even without the elegant handwriting or the reference to Jailah's favorite sport, Logan would have known purely from the use of her embarrassing middle name. Only Jailah would've bothered to look it up in the school directory.

Logan ran out of Mesmortes and onto the Hill, an affectionate nickname for the tall curve of land that crested Mesmortes, placing it higher than the Hammersmitt School for Exceptional Young Men, their mundane rivals. Odd looks and giggles from witches dressed like cats and superheroes blurred past her. Logan wasn't quite sure what the trio of witches waiting for her had planned, but she had a feeling that her night would be considerably more sinister than glitter and hot pants.

At the entrance to the archery fields, a bronze statue of Hattie Mesmortes, the academy's founder, waited atop a square of pristine gray marble. Tonight, a real bow and arrow had been positioned adjacent to its bronze twin so that Hattie looked to be wielding both.

The string of Jailah's bow was already nocked back with another string, tied elegantly to Hattie's finger. Logan climbed onto the base of the statue and snipped the string with her teeth instead of her wand, like a mundane might do.

The arrow disappeared into the night. Another letter fell at Logan's feet.

My roses are red.
Your eyes are blue.
You'll find me where the green vines grow.
See you ... soon?
(Jai asked me come up with a rhyme. I made an attempt.)

Heartbeat quickening, Logan jumped off the statue's base and headed for the thick circle of trees that surrounded the Mesmortes herbalism lab. The enormous greenhouse smelled like sweetness and rain. Electric-green vines covered the glass walls in thick tangles, and the moon shone brilliantly between passing clouds.

Logan eased toward Thalia's cubby, careful not to bump into the vials floating freely in the air, the iron cauldrons stacked against the wall, or the jars of witchy ingredients. *Purified toad blood, crushed baby peacock feathers, sap of a weeping willow ...*

A hastily scribbled note was tied to the farthest vial.

The Cavern.
Hurry the fuck up.

Logan swallowed hard. The Cavern was carved into the land at the highest part of one of the many hills surrounding Mesmortes. It was the type of place that served as cover for bodies hastily buried, or nightmares come to life. Witches were hanged there long ago, before Haelsford became a witch-town. A series of tunnels ran under it, once used by witches to escape the mundanes' violence.

*Of course, the friggin' Cavern.* Iris Keaton-Foster had a love of all things dark.

Logan felt the same buzzy cocktail of confusion, excitement, and horror that overwhelmed her last week when the Red Three strolled into home-room. While other witches used the time to gossip or nap, Logan had been practicing *Raiamora*—water to wine—though she had only managed to turn her bowl of water into something that smelled vaguely of cat piss.

When the girls came up to her, she didn't know what to do and tried that smirk Margot always did when she performed a spell for a cute mundane. It fit like an uncomfortable mask.

"What are you working on?" Thalia had asked, pushing up her too-big glasses.

"Ye olde Jesus trick," Logan blurted out. She shouldn't have admitted that, but Thalia laughed and she'd felt comforted.

Iris looked her up and down. It hadn't felt mean, but Logan fidgeted. She'd lived across from the deathwitch for two months now, but it was the first time Logan caught a glimpse of the silver lines peeking out from the hem of her skirt—a horror-film pentagram emblazoned on her deep brown skin. Iris pushed her neat, long braids behind her shoulder and leaned over the bowl. She wrinkled her nose, shot Jailah a disappointed look, and turned away.

Logan expected the three of them to leave her then. But with a smile that soothed her anxieties, Jailah said with a Southern twang, "We should chill sometime."

Standing outside the Cavern, Logan huffed. Sweat dripped down her back. Someone giggled. Logan squinted, but she could see nothing in the black mouth of the cave. "Uh, hello?"

The air shifted. The Cavern air constricted around her, yanking her in like it'd sprouted actual hands. She didn't resist the movement. The dark demanded her cooperation, and then it let her go.

For the first time since arriving in Haelsford, Logan felt cold.

Another witch might've pricked her thumb for *Light*, but the Red Three were watching. Logan avoided performing magic if she could, and especially in front of others.

Sighing, she tapped the flashlight on her phone. The light came, and it showed her a horror. Four walls, no exit. The space around her became a stone box. Perhaps it would become a grave. The Cavern—*the box*—wasn't filling up with water, and the walls weren't closing in, but a stone tomb fashioned by witches could present something much more dire.

*They're gonna leave me here to rot.*

Just as Logan opened her mouth to scream, the ground dissolved beneath her. She fell sharply through the air and was now having trouble distinguishing reality from illusion. She couldn't really be falling through the earth, could she? Was she really here? Was Jailah's arrow laced with essence of blackthorne?

"She's claustrophobic," a voice said.

Logan hit the ground.

"Ow," she muttered. She looked up to find the Cavern reconstructed. There was no box, no high ledge to fall from. Just simple rock—dark, wet, and solid. Torches lined the walls, lit by enchanted firelight.

Two witches stared down at her.

Logan pushed herself up from the ground and wiped the blood from her lip.

Jailah Simmons giggled, the firelight dancing over her deep brown skin and the coils of her glossy black fro. She crunched on what sounded like the last bits of a cough drop or hard candy. "Sorry. We were burnin' fearmonger leaves. Iris's idea. I think she was curious what it'd do for you. Shame she ain't even here to see it."

*Iris didn't show.* Logan didn't know if she was relieved or disappointed.

Thalia rifled through her knapsack. Her usually messy chestnut curls were pulled back into twin braids. She wrinkled her nose, and Logan noticed the smattering of freckles on her light brown skin. A scruffy black dog stood at her side, and he sized Logan up with searing yellow eyes.

"Here." Thalia procured a homemade cough drop from a little canvas pouch. "For the fearmonger."

Logan popped it into her mouth without question. As a greenwitch, Thalia worked in plant magic and healing magic. The candy tasted like lavender and smoke. Logan felt calmer suddenly.

Thalia eyed her. "So. Claustrophobia. That's your thing."

Logan moved the lavender drop from one cheek to the other. "Um. Yeah."

There was a line of black ink on Thalia's wrist. When Logan tilted her head to look at it, Thalia pulled down the sleeve of her shirt. "Why else would fearmonger put you in a box?"

Logan shrugged. Jailah and Thalia stared at her, trying to figure out where the lie was hidden. She wouldn't give.

"Is that it, then?" Logan said quickly. She had so many questions. *Do you do this to everyone? Did I pass?*

Thalia looked to Jailah, and even in the dark, Logan saw fear there. The dog leaned into Thalia's leg. "This is just the beginning. The Haunting Season's almost here. The Wolves are waking up."

Logan tensed.

Jailah threw an arm around Logan. "But first, tonight's Hallowe'en. We're gonna have so much fun!" She glanced at Thalia. "Now, where the hell is that deathwitch?"

Her eager attempt to soften Thalia's warning was only slightly comforting. The Haunting Season—the yearly hex that plagued Haelsford—was just a few weeks away. Monstrous Wolves would soon emerge from the depths of the Swamp with the singular goal of bloodshed.

As they walked back toward the Hill, Logan's gaze drifted toward the Swamp. She couldn't help herself, she had to look. From this vantage, she could barely make out where the beautiful oaks stopped and the corrupted, mangled trees began.

The Swamp was far off, but so heady and full and dark that it felt *close*.

And maybe she was still dazed from the fall, but Logan swore she heard a howl.

# 2

## iris

Iris Keaton-Foster forgot all about Jailah's scavenger hunt and Logan Wyatt, the baby witch she was supposed to be welcoming into her carefully selected group of friends.

Iris had a good excuse. A soul was calling her.

That in itself was not strange. Iris dealt in death. On a normal night, she dipped her toes into the otherworld, allowed souls to tell her their stories, and offered to relieve some of the burdens that darkened their psychic energy. But the restless usually sought her out in subtler ways. The pendulum on her bedroom desk swung, or the lampposts on Twenty-Fifth flickered as she walked by, or a strange message appeared as she typed an AP French Hexology paper, pleading with her to help them find eternal rest. She was used to these things.

It was *what* this soul whispered to her.

*"You've been calling me."*

Outside the enormous oak doors of the Mesmortes main building, Iris stopped suddenly, causing freshman Jenna Prim to run into her and spill pumpkin-spice latte all over both of them. Iris hardly acknowledged Jenna's annoyance. She simply removed her now-sticky knapsack, shook it off, and adjusted the thick grimoire under her arm. She stilled, and she listened.

The voice chuckled. *"Unbind me, deathwitch."*

Iris was supposed to take a left toward the Cavern, but she veered right instead, even as Jenna called out to her, half apologizing, half demanding a new latte.

The little chapel at the edge of campus was Iris's, an unspoken rule of Mesmortes. The chapel was wrecked anyway, with cracked stained glass, half-hanging chandeliers, and splintery pews. As Haelsford's lone necromancer, everyone was eager to give her space. And Mesmortes, like all coven academies, wasn't too keen on necromancy. She learned about death spells in theory-based electives that promoted knowledge of concepts but rarely demonstrated them. If her mother hadn't shown her the depths of her power, she'd hardly be able to call souls at all.

Dust danced across the chapel floor with every step. Iris dropped her grimoire onto the ruined altar and lit the candles waiting there, each of varying heights and scents dependent solely on her laziness in replacing them and what was BOGO at Wax & Wicks. She had a particular fondness for Heretic Red, which smelled like salt and rust and sinister things.

She pulled her braids into a silk hair tie. She drew the pendulum at the center of the altar closer. With her long, thin sacrificial needle, Iris pricked her thumb. From the collection of chokers and pendants tied around her neck, Iris touched her bloody thumb to the sun-shaped talisman that hung from a rusted old chain. This thin piece of gold felt heavier than the others.

*"I Call Upon You,"* Iris said. With her incantation, the pentagram scar just above her knee warmed and warmed, until it burned white hot. The witch ground her teeth. Witchery only required the pricking of a thumb—a

little blood, a little pain, to sacrifice to the earth—but *necromancy* demanded more. She recalled the picture she'd seen at Roddin's House of Souls. The high cheekbones, the blond hair, the thick red scar running straight across the woman's pale neck. *"Madeline Donahue, the Madwoman of Haelsford,"* Iris Called.

Something breathed against her ear.

Iris turned and stood face-to-face with a beautifully haunted apparition.

*"We finally meet, daughter of death."*

Iris almost smiled. Of all the long-dead Haelsfordian witches who she'd tried to contact in the past year, Donahue was the first to answer. Legend said that she cut down ten men with nothing but a dull blade before the hunters brought her to the gallows. Madwoman. Iris didn't care for the nickname. History was always labeling women as mad, whether they were witchy or not.

"I've been calling you for weeks," Iris said.

The ghostly woman wore something between a grin and a grimace.

"I'm just saying, you're dead; it's not like you're busy." Iris held up the talisman. "I have the earthly half of your soul here. With it, you may finally have eternal rest."

The figure offered a wilted hand.

Iris tightened her grip on the talisman. "You died in Haelsford before the first Haunting Season, didn't you?"

Donahue shrieked. *"It was murder! Never quick, always painful! Joy in flames, joy in flames! They burn on and on and—"*

Iris lifted a hand. "I get it. Look, do you know who the Wolf Boy is?"

The ghost expelled a rattling sound. A breath for those who couldn't breathe.

Iris pressed on. "Who is he?"

*"I want rest."*

"Then you'd better find him," Iris replied coldly. Blackmailing a tortured ghost was cruel, but she was desperate.

Last year, the Wolves took their first Mesmortes witch in decades. Amelia Carr, a senior who lived on Iris's floor. Amelia always shared her birthday cupcakes with the whole floor, saving the lone red velvet for Iris. She slipped notices under doors advertising free tarot lessons to anyone who needed to pass History of Divination. She was kind, and she was genuine. Even if Amelia hadn't been a good person, even if she'd been horrible and mean, even if she wasn't a necromancer, too, no one deserved to die like *that*. Like Iris, Amelia wasn't a Haelsford local, but she knew not to get close to the Swamp or venture past the protection spells. Iris still couldn't make sense of it.

Many had tried and failed to break Haelsford's hex. But if the Wolves could take one Mesmortes witch, they could take another. Jailah or Thalia, even Iris herself. If the prophesized Wolf Boy held the key to ending the Haunting, Iris was going to find him. She needed him to tell her the solution. She could end the Haunting herself. But his soul was elusive. Summoning the dead came as naturally to Iris as breathing, but without his face or his true name, she could not initiate a Call.

Unless she had a very unique witch, one with a specific type of magical blood that could stand in for a missing piece.

*His name and his face.* With a proxy, she just needed one of the two.

Iris peeked at her phone. Nine missed calls.

*"You propose a contract, young witch?"*

"You can go places I can't, even with this." Iris touched the platinum-colored mark on her leg. "Find me the Wolf Boy, and you will pass on from here."

The soul drifted from Iris, her face suddenly gaunt. *"A girl touched with death has a heart most black."*

Iris grinned.

The apparition pointed at the talisman. *"Keep the bond between us, and I will tell you what I find."*

Iris gripped it protectively. "You know how to reach me."

A touch of cold, and she was alone.

She called Jailah's phone. "Hey. I know, *I know*—listen—meet me at Roddin's. Bring the baby witch."

In the sudden silence after hanging up, Iris realized her breaths were ragged. She had her work cut out for her. Haelsford, with all its myths and curses, was bad luck for necromancers. They were rare but seemed prone to tragic endings. Iris could count the number of necromancers who graduated in all of Mesmortes history on one hand.

But she welcomed the nervy excitement bubbling up in her. She relished her swift heartbeat. Finally, she felt like she was making progress.

She gathered her things and tucked her bulky *Grimoire for the Good Witch* under her arm. With confident steps, Iris exited Mesmortes Chapel and walked up the path into town, toward a much darker place.

# 3

## thalia

In Town Square, the debauchery of Hallowe'en was in full swing. The cobble-rock walkways were busy with young trick-or-treaters, rambunctious Hammersmitt boys, and thrill-seeking tourists. A man tore open a packet of candy for his small daughter. Thalia looked away, suddenly queasy.

She glanced at Logan, who was taking in Haelsford with a wide-eyed gaze. Town Square might've been plucked out of a Hallmark movie, but the storefronts broke the innocent facade. Vibrant green tendrils of vervain contorted in the florist's windows, pulsing with magic in a way that resembled heartbeats. The chalkboard sign outside the apothecary Brewtiful Day boasted cures for migraines, strep throat, bloodline curses, and everything between. Then there was Hexagon, a general store by day and an eighteen-and-older witchy speakeasy after sundown. And in the middle of it all, Haelsford honored the witches who cursed them. The trio of onyx-dipped statues earned Thalia's first visit when she arrived in town two years earlier. It fascinated her that these witches left an everlasting plague on this town, *and they built them a shrine.*

Thalia once left her own mark on a small town. She'd been running ever since.

"This is so Iris," Jailah said to Logan, trying—and failing—to keep her annoyance hidden.

"Which part?" Thalia offered. "No-show-ing, or demanding we go to Roddin's?"

Jailah threw her hands up. "Both!"

Thalia pursed her lips against a threatening chuckle. Watching Jailah stomp all mean while also smiling at every passerby was entertaining, at least. Thalia's canine familiar, Maverick, kept by her side, easily excited by the trick-or-treaters. "She'll have to wait. I need to grab something from the florist. Go ahead. I'll catch up."

Instead of a door chime, her passing through the front door was heralded by a screech from Suzette's feline familiar. The orange tabby cat promptly hopped off a high shelf and onto the counter to sneer at Maverick, nearly knocking over three mason jar terrariums.

"Easy," Suzette warned, walking in from the greenhouse that extended out the back. She wiped her hands on her apron. "Thalia! Long time, no see." She touched a pot of roses, which were now bending toward Thalia, their petals a more vibrant red than before. "And suddenly, I'm not the most powerful witch in the room."

Thalia felt a tickle of pride. Unlike Suze, who chose greenwitchery as a vocation, Thalia was born with the Gift of the Earth. That was her Pull. The same way Iris's magic favored the dead, and senior Anika Johnson had a way with fire, Thalia had an innate and unbreakable connection to nature. Pulls weren't rare, and Thalia still had to work to cultivate her magic, but she savored the praise.

She scanned the little pots next to the cash register and picked up a pale green plant with red veins and star-shaped leaves. Discreetly, she checked the price. "I'll take this one."

"More fearmonger?"

Thalia shrugged, her anxiety rising. "It's a gift." She pulled her Mesmortes embroidered wallet from her knapsack. She knew how much money she had, and she knew it was enough, but the moment between having the money and handing it over always made Thalia's heart quicken. Maverick, sensing this, nuzzled her ankle.

But Suze waved a hand. "Oh, no, put that away."

Thalia's face grew hot. "I can't just take it."

"Kid, you brought my orchids back to life last month." The fantastically purple flowers were growing near Suze's height behind her. "Also, if you ever want to help out here, I can pay—"

"Thanks, Suzette," Thalia said abruptly. She took the plant and left quickly, Maverick on her heels.

She'd expected Logan and Jailah to be farther off, but the two were watching a trio of Mesmortes freshmen exiting the bakery. Thalia recognized the shocking platinum hair of Morgan Ramirez, who was angling their cupcake away from an eager Jenna Prim. Lilly Han giggled at the sight, her falcon familiar perched on her shoulder.

"I was tellin' Logan about the new tethers." Jai wore an endearing smile. "You think Lilly feels left out?"

Thalia shook her head. "Maybe, but you know tethering doesn't automatically lead to *dating*." There was some teasing there, and Jailah rolled her eyes. Thalia turned to Logan. "You know your tether?"

The baby witch blew up at her blond bangs. "Nope. You?"

Thalia resumed walking. "Nope."

*I've got my own baggage*, she thought grimly. *I don't need to carry some-one else's.*

Logan walked next to her. "My aunt once told me about two witches in Quebec. So, like, they grew up together, went to the same coven academy. Problem was, he thought she was annoying, and she thought he was stuck-up, and they despised each other all throughout school. But the day before graduation, it just *happened*. They tethered."

"I'm guessing they learned to love each other and lived happily ever after?" Thalia muttered.

"No. They couldn't deal with each other long enough to let their magic work together. They moved to opposite sides of the world, started families, and never spoke again. Imagine having your tether be the one person in the whole entire world that you can't stand."

Jailah shot Thalia a pointed look. "There are worse tethers to have."

The three continued through and past Town Square, the cobblestone path spitting them onto Ole Roddin Way. There was one dilapidated shop at the end of the road.

Necromantic Emporium and House of Souls.

The windows were cracked and the paint was chipped, but Thalia was most offended by the dry potted plants lining the porch. She pricked her finger and dropped a bit of blood onto the soil. The dying marigolds immediately stood taller, their petals a perfect orange.

Gleefully, Iris appeared from behind the moth-eaten screen door. "Finally!"

Jailah shook her head. "Nah, I'm not going in there."

Iris looked at a frowning Logan. "Don't piss your pants over the haunted house vibes, baby witch. She's not the wicked old lady everyone says she is. Roddin's rough around the edges, but that's it."

Thalia snorted, sarcasm hiding her own fear. "I'm sure she wasn't hex-bound for shoplifting."

Iris didn't buy it. "Relax, T. She won't bite."

Logan shivered. "You call her Roddin? Like, the street she lives on?"

"I mean, I never asked her name, she's not exactly a social person, and she doesn't trust anyone—whatever. Stop stalling and get in!"

The Emporium walls were covered in shelves stocked with oddly colored mason jars of different sizes, some even taller than gangly Thalia herself. Snake eyes, shark tongues, ground armadillo fingers. Candles were scattered about. There was an old gramophone in the corner, dead flowers strung up on the walls, and dirty glass cases of witchy antiques. Unnaturally thick cobwebs covered every surface, presumably from the baseball-sized spiders perched in the corners of the ceiling. It was a picture of the type of magic that most mundanes probably thought witches practiced. The haunted, wicked kind.

"I don't like this," Logan whispered.

Jailah squeezed her hand. "Yeah, this place is creepy."

"I know!" Iris replied cheerily. She picked up a salamander tail and waved it in Jai's face.

Thalia watched her friends dutifully, the way they navigated the shop and one another's space. Iris was the only one who looked at home here—no surprise since she'd become something of a mentee of the strange hexbound witch. Jailah, however, inspected her surroundings curiously, not entirely trusting, poking things and squealing when they poked back. Logan was fixated on an antiques display, her brow furrowed in concentration.

Thalia couldn't resist. She peeked over the baby witch's shoulder.

The display held crescent-shaped rubies for protection against vengeful ghouls, earrings made of sapphire to boost waterwitchery, and a set of cracked opal rings that belonged to the old Haelsfordian Coven Troupe. She read the label: *Before the Wolves took half of the 2001 company and the Troupe disbanded, members were given a single opal ring to mark their initiation.*

"Hexed jade," Logan whispered to herself.

Thalia pushed up her glasses to read the description of the crystalline necklace below her. *Combats the Seeing Quartet: The Feel, The Seeker, The Sound & The Look.*

Thalia pulled the little star-shaped plant from her knapsack and nudged Logan. "Hey. For you."

She took it without asking what it was. Thalia didn't like new people, but she felt oddly endeared to this one, if only because she held the pot like it was a precious thing. Logan read the label still taped to it, eyes widening. "Fearmonger? Like what you used in the Cavern?"

"Yeah, just wait until it's fully grown," Thalia said with a smirk. "It'll let you know when you're in danger."

Iris appeared suddenly with a tray of vials, each filled with liquid gold. "Let's play a game!"

Thalia stepped back. She knew what this was, and she wanted no part of it. "Roddin's cool with this?"

Iris shrugged. "She *likes* me, it's fine. Now, pick your poison." She brandished the tray like a game show assistant. "Three are honeysuckle sap. One's essence of alítheia."

"I pass," Thalia said, heart thrumming. Her voice leaned playful, but her eyes were serious.

"Alítheia?" Logan paused, clearly riffling through mental flash cards. "Truth-telling serum?"

"It'll make you admit your most embarrassing secrets," said Jailah, lifting a brow. "Like the fact that Iris reads Wolf Boy fanfiction."

Thalia guffawed, but Iris wasn't bothered. "It's *research*. Come on, Logan. Take a sip."

While their eyes were on Logan, Thalia opened up the lining of her thin green jacket. She felt like a snake-oil peddler in an old film, but it was worth it to have her arsenal of serums on her. She fiddled with a vial of a thick green liquid, the very one she sipped from each morning and steadily refilled once it was empty. Sevdys, a serum to combat alítheia.

But it wasn't needed. Roddin appeared from a back room, swooping in behind Iris to pull the tray from her grasp. Thalia was unexpectedly relieved to see her. The Roddin Witch had pale, sun-damaged skin and wild green eyes, twitchy fingers and dark hair. She placed the tray on the glass counter and pulled her long gray robe tighter around herself.

When she found Thalia's eye, Thalia flinched. When she looked at Roddin, she saw what her life might become. The unwitch had been banished so long ago that it wasn't clear what she'd done to deserve it, though there were rumors.

Roddin locked up the vials. "Not my alítheia, dead girl. I don't need the Witchery Council sniffing around here, saying I gave truth serum to kids."

Iris frowned. "We could call it payment for Donahue. That's one less soul in your charge." She winced suddenly. "They're *really* loud today. I can rest a few more, you know."

Thalia's eyes drifted to the trinkets swaying above her. She shivered. *House of Souls.*

Roddin waved away Iris's comment. While she was unable to use magic, she apparently could still hear the souls. Roddin turned her focus to Logan. "New blood."

"Look closer," Iris whispered.

Roddin touched her fingertips to Logan's temples. The trinkets swayed faster, their chimes a sweet melody.

Thalia felt an anxious thrum in her chest. She didn't know what to think of Logan. Iris was convinced that she could help them sever the hex that was the Haunting, but she and Jai had their reservations. For one, could the Haunting even be ended? And by a bunch of juniors, at that? It wasn't like people weren't trying—every year, witches from around the world strolled into Haelsford, convinced they were powerful enough to go into the Swamp, find the heart of its malice, and kill it from within. Seasoned old women with decades of training. Young, arrogant men, convinced they were Chosen Ones. Greenwitches, deathwitches, witches who had done nothing but research Haelsford's traumas. Every year, the Wolves spat them out in pieces.

Thalia looked at Iris, and Iris looked at Jai, and Jai gave them both a pointed look. Thalia thought of what she'd said to them both, just last night.

*If we get hurt, everyone will think we deserved it.* "Oh, those girls were dabblin' in some dark, dark magic, tryna end the Wolves and shit." *But somethin' happens to her?* Jailah's Alabama twang had come out strong. *You know what people will say.* "Last time I saw sweet, innocent Logan Wyatt, she was runnin' with those three Black witches."

The trinkets stopped swaying, and the room was still.

Roddin smiled. "You found a proxy."

24

Iris smirked.

"You don't understand." Logan stiffened, shaking her head. "I can't—"

"I need candles," Jailah interrupted, brown eyes beaming.

"And sage," Iris added.

Roddin nodded toward that dark room in the back.

Thalia threw her arm over Logan's shoulder. This next part would be fun. "Do you want to hear a story, Logan?"

# 4

## logan

The four young witches sat around Roddin's creaky old prayer table. The elder unwitch watched intently from the corner. Light came from a bowl full of short candles that smelled like honey and herbs. Pop music played softly from Jailah's phone, an oddly fitting choice. They were witches, yes, but teenaged girls all the same.

"Is this a scary story?" Logan asked, and felt childish for doing so despite being their same age. Most witches received their blessing at thirteen, but Logan's came late, at sixteen. She wasn't like Jailah, so composed and wiser than her seventeen years and the bubble-gum-flavored gloss on her lips; or Thalia, introspective and brilliant and slightly haunted; or Iris, the type of girl who said *I won't bite*, but only ever meant the opposite.

Thankfully, Iris didn't laugh, call her *baby witch*, or brush away her fear. "Scary? It's awful."

The Red Three pricked their fingers and spilled their blood over the candles. They wriggled their wands at the flames while whispering a sinister, melodic chant. The smoke followed the rhythm of their wands, spooling around them like dark threads for knitting.

Iris used those threads to build a miniature landscape atop the table. Though Logan knew it was Haelsford, it was all wrong. The shops, the walkways, and the schools were missing. Nothing but the Swamp and the Hill. The details were there in the blades of grass and the mucky slush of the River Lea.

"Did anyone ever tell you how the Swamp was made?" Thalia asked.

"Dark magic. Selfish witches. Murderous mundanes," Logan replied. That was the title for Haelsford's entry in Fodor's *Supernatural Locations You Have to See to Believe!* Logan had it bookmarked on her laptop from back when she decided she couldn't become a witch in a boring place like Wicker, Ontario. "I've heard bits and pieces."

"Once upon a time," Jailah started playfully, "there were three witches: Adelaide, Mathilde, and Sloane." From the smoky Haelsford miniature, Jailah twisted her wand to make those three cloaked figures and filled the town with people.

"The Strigwach Sisters," Logan said. "From the statue in Town Square." She hated walking past the thing. The iron figures were cloaked in a lacquered onyx that somehow seemed to move in the wind. Though hoods concealed the figures' faces, Logan always felt like their gazes would be cruel.

"Before it was Haelsford, it was a small village that belonged to witches. There was peace, harmony, magic, all that good stuff," Jailah continued.

"What witches can do when not disturbed by mundanes," Roddin added from the shadows.

"But it was taken from them," Thalia said softly. "A traveling caravan of mundanes tortured and hanged witches every winter, calling it the Hunting Season. They put blackthorne in our wells and fed it to the animals we ate. They wanted to show that no devil-given power could save us from their God-fearing hands. They took the land and called it Haelsford."

Logan bit the inside of her cheek. She knew the history of witches and how much they suffered, but as a newly born witch, she hadn't had time to think about what all this history really meant to her. How easily Thalia said *we* and *us*, like she'd been there. Logan still felt weird calling witches her kind.

Even in a silent vignette of black and gray, the smoky figures did not lack the violence of Thalia's words. Logan felt both the agony of the witches and the bloodthirsty delight of the mundanes.

"But three sisters escaped," Jailah said solemnly. "They were weak and spent days digging through the earth with their hands and what little magic they could conjure up to create an escape route under Haelsford. They made a vow that no mundane would harm a witch here ever again."

Logan had an idea of what came next, but it was fiercely satisfying to hear Iris say it. "Each Strigwach had a loyal wolf familiar, and from them, they made Wolves."

In the smoke, those three Wolves became a pack.

Jailah continued, "They were patient. They watched the town for months, planning out how they could take it back. They infiltrated Haelsford, using *Shade* to pose as mundanes, and when the moment was just right . . ."

The Wolves howled. While they were miniatures of smoke, Logan still flinched.

". . . they sent the pack into town."

"Why did the Wolves start hunting witches, too?" Logan asked, shivering.

"Dark witchery," Thalia added. "The Strigwachs broke every law of nature to create Wolves from the originals, and they got rebellious creatures in return. You can't just steal from the earth."

Logan considered this. "Professor Ahmed said that greater things than blood have been given up to perform the darkest spells."

The Roddin Witch stepped out of the shadows, her mouth upturned with wicked amusement. "And what else did your professor say?"

Logan swallowed. "Anything needing more than a prick of a thumb would be too much for any young witch to control."

Roddin's smile grew. "The greater the power, the greater the risk. You could sacrifice yourself. You could sacrifice one another."

In silence, the young witches flitted curious looks among themselves. Sweat dripped down Logan's neck. "What could the Strigwachs have sacrificed to do this?"

Jailah shook her head. "We don't know."

"Or maybe *we* are the sacrifice, every year," Iris added.

"And what will it take to break it?" Thalia whispered, clutching the crucifix at her neck.

The hooded figures cried out silently for mercy from their own creations. The Wolves did not obey.

Jailah cleared some smoke, leaving only a ghostly picture of a land surrounded by a marsh. "A few mundanes survived and returned to Haelsford when the Wolves retreated into the Swamp. They set out to find witches who could cleanse the corrupted earth that the Strigwachs left. While no witch has been able to end the Haunting, mundanes began to offer up sacrifices in exchange for protection. Soon enough, Haelsford was a witch-town again, and this time, there was a common goal between us and them. To protect the town from the monsters."

"But the Strigwachs may have left us with a protection of their own," Iris said. A figure rose from the Swamp. She made a great Wolf next to him, along with vicious cubs at his feet. "The Wolf Boy."

Logan felt drawn to him. "Before the Strigwachs died, one of them turned a boy into some kind of cure, right?"

Iris nodded. "The youngest, Mathilde. They say she got all mushy at the end and wanted to forgive the mundanes, so she hid a way to end the Wolves in the one place her sisters wouldn't think to look—a mundane."

"He's the only one who can stop the Wolves," Jailah said softly. "For all and forever."

"But," Logan started, "he's already dead, so the power's dead with him."

The witches pulled their wands away, and it all dissolved with a glittery gleam.

Iris was transfixed by the dissipating wisps of smoke. "Yeah, well. I'm gonna Call him."

Logan furrowed her eyebrows. The calm way Iris spoke of her Pull like it was an everyday hobby surprised her. If Logan were a deathwitch—the type of witch Haelsford seemed particularly determined to devour—she'd never practice magic at all.

"And this is where you come in, proxy."

Logan's heart twitched.

"You know what you can do, right? What your blood can do?" Thalia asked.

"Of course she does!" Jailah exclaimed. She glanced at Logan. "Right?"

Logan nodded. "I am a cheat code."

She was *supposed* to be able to do great things. Margot said being a proxy was like being ambidextrous. A little uniqueness in her witchery. A neat party trick. Proxies made up for what witchery might lack. Her blood could replace bee venom in a love potion, or a lock of her hair for the fur of a fox in heat spells for the winter—both of these she knew from actual trials that Margot and her mother put her through. Logan wasn't supposed to even need a wand to draw out the magic in her blood. But none of these things worked for her. Her hands never glowed when she pulled her witchery forward like they were supposed to, and a drop of her blood or a lock of her hair just ruined spells.

"How did you guys even know?" Logan asked. "I haven't really been advertising it."

"I like secrets," Thalia replied softly, as if the admission was a secret itself.

"She can help with the Call, right?" Iris asked Roddin. "I can only Call with a name and a face, but a proxy could substitute for one of those." She was excited, hardly breathing between her words.

Roddin nodded slowly. "If the witch is worthy."

*Worthy.* Logan couldn't tell them that her blood was weak and her magic was weaker, not when they looked at her with the most promise she'd ever seen. She touched her thumb to her eyebrow. She felt the unmistakable bite of an anxiety headache coming on.

"Mm-kay, that's enough deathwitch talk. Come on." Jailah grinned and fluffed her fro. "It's Hallowe'en. Let's go hex some boys."

# 5

## trent

In a town that called itself home to witches and Wolves, the mundanes of Haelsford held their own. They possessed a fraught sense of pride that wouldn't let them abandon a town that no reasonable person, magic or not, should want to live in.

Worst of all were the boys of the Hammersmitt School for Exceptional Young Men. One was trouble enough, but the back room of the Battlement was full of them. It was Haelsford's bougiest bar, and the boys propped their feet up on the nice couches, leaned back against the floral-papered walls, stacked towers of empty beer cans and toppled them over. The floor seemed to bend under the weight of their self-importance.

Trent Hogarth arrived late, purposely so. He hadn't wanted to spend more time here than he needed to. He scanned the room and found a dark-haired boy holding a quintet of cards in his hands.

A freshman relinquished the spot beside Mathew Beaumont, but Trent shook his head to say *We're not staying*.

Carefully, Mathew revealed his hand to Trent.

*Bloody royal flush.*

Mathew effortlessly wore a look of distaste, but he belonged here. You knew it by looking at him: his pale skin, his neat clothes, his messy hair, his always-bored eyes. Mathew did all the things Trent imagined the heir of old money should. He rode horses, ate caviar—*enjoyed* caviar—and spoke like an upstanding suitor from the 1800s, all politeness and ardor. He worked part-time at the small café in town, but that was more a character-building thing assigned by his father. In truth, money was his vice, his virtue, his namesake.

Most Haelsfordians couldn't smell the wealth on Trent. They couldn't tell by his $900 Jordans or the clipped endings of his South London–accented words. They bristled at his dark brown skin and his kinky Afro fade. Trent would never fit in the way Mathew could, and he had no desire to. He was only biding his time until graduation—charming the locals, ignoring the bullshit, taking refuge in his barber's chair in the next town over.

Haelsford had been his mother's hometown. It was where she'd found her coven. There were secrets here that he'd intended to dredge up.

Blond, sunburned Anders Osnes squeezed Trent's shoulders. "So, what are we sacrificing for the Haunting, bros?"

The room quieted. The Wolves were perhaps the only thing that made these boys feel vulnerable. They didn't care who your parents were or if they got blood all over your favorite loafers.

*We're running out of time*, Trent thought grimly. Only a few weeks stood between this town and the hungry, howling Wolves. Every year, the list on the memorial in Town Square grew longer, the names etched into the obsidian columns by the tip of a witch's wand.

The mundanes were busy prepping their yearly sacrifices. All around town, mundanes gifted riches, antiques, and favors to their witchy neighbors in exchange for protection. Even the mayor's office would deliver something rare and expensive to the Haelsford Witchery Council, like solid-gold cauldrons or bushels of whatever coveted out-of-season plants were needed for their spells. In the past, the protection spells for the schools on the Hill were done by a family of witches who lived in town. But this year was different. The Mesmortes witches decided they wanted to do it themselves, asked for the honor, and their headmistress agreed. For the first time in their history, the Hammersmitt School for Exceptional Young Men would sacrifice to the witches of the Mesmortes Coven Academy.

Like the exceptional young men that they were, they'd procrastinated.

Mathew said, "Trent and I are looking into something, as promised."

That was an understatement. Trent had the damned thing on him.

The diamond-shaped rock had come from the cellar at Beaumont Manor. It was just *there*. No lock on its porcelain box. How could it be dangerous?

The first night that Mathew left the box open, he told Trent he'd dreamed of bloodred rain and burning himself alive.

Another day, when Trent strolled into Matty's room for some loose-leaf paper, a bout of thunder shook the dorm violently enough to make the lid of the box shift. Mathew found him in the corner, whispering frantically of witches and death and the Wolves that were coming for them all.

There were other things. Things that gave them nightmares and night chills, things that twitched in the corners of their eyes and skittered in the dark.

At first, they wanted it gone. Then they thought, *What a potentially perfect Haunting gift.*

Mathew played his hand.

The boys whooped, all except Peter Haelsford. Conceding a pair of aces, he said, "Maybe the Wolf Boy will save us all."

Trent sucked in through his teeth. Placing hope in a story as good as myth undermined Trent's and Mathew's ability to *handle it*. Peter was just that type of boy—pretentious because no one ever told him to quit it, and his ancestors claimed to have founded the land they lived on. How a white kid thought he could possibly have any ancestral claim to land here, Trent didn't understand.

Peter grinned. "Loosen up, Matty."

"It's *Mathew*," Beaumont snapped, rising from his seat. He tolerated that nickname from Trent only. "It's Hallowe'en, boys. Don't get into trouble."

Hogarth and Beaumont ignored the pleas to stay. Their real interests for the night lay in the ramshackle shop outside of town, a ten-minute ride on their skateboards.

····◦❂◦····

Roddin's Necromantic Emporium and House of Souls seemed to bend slightly to the right. Trent wondered if the chipped gray paint, destroyed shutters, and cracked windows were aesthetic choices. He couldn't imagine a house of souls looking like a trendy little boutique. The nicest thing around was a pot of brilliant marigolds.

*I'm shittin' it.* He wished he'd brought along his mother's small antique knife. It could protect him in more ways than one. But he also lived for things like this: staring up at a haunted house, the dark sky full of heavy clouds, his instincts warning him that this might end in his death, and—

*Howls.*

35

Mathew attempted indifference with his crossed arms and skeptical brow, but he looked more *unpleasant dad* than *nonchalant suave*. "I don't know about this—"

"Nah, don't start." Trent leaned his skateboard against the house and pushed Mathew through the front door.

"Welcome."

The voice was so sudden that Trent nearly knocked over an hourglass full of crushed python bone. The Roddin Witch was behind a glass counter, her fingers splayed atop it. He understood that their kind lived much longer than mundanes, but Roddin seemed older than Haelsford itself. Trent knew her story, or, at least, the little that everyone else knew. He'd heard it from his brothers, who'd all graduated from Hammersmitt before him, and from Mathew, whose family was longtime Haelsfordians. He knew that banishment was the worst punishment a witch could get.

"Mundanes," Roddin mocked. She counted off on her withered fingers. "I don't entertain tourism, voyeurism, or playful curiosity. I offer no vengeful promises to bring you back as a ghost to haunt your enemies, nor can I preserve your dead pets' souls, cleanse your haunted houses, or brew you an illegal love potion. Understood?"

Mathew pointed to himself. "Hi. I'm Mathew Beaumont." Then to Trent. "This is Trenton Hogarth. We go to Hammersmitt on the Hill."

"And?" she said, bored already.

"And we heard you were a necromancer," Trent said quickly.

Mathew shot him an annoyed look.

Trent ignored him. "Weren't you?"

The Roddin Witch pulled up her sleeve and showed them a faded scar in the shape of a pentagram.

*Wicked.*

"My skill has been stolen from me . . ." Her voice trailed off. She squeezed her hands into furious fists.

Trent would never know what it was like to be a witch, but he knew what it was like to have something special taken from you. "So, you can't talk to the dead?"

She relaxed her hands. "Ah, you should've asked my deathwitch Foster."

Mathew raised a brow. "Foster?"

"She'd have you for lunch. You are so . . . *soft*. If only you'd come earlier, wouldn't that have been fun!" The Roddin Witch lifted her head toward the trinkets swaying from bronze hooks in the ceiling. "I can no longer initiate Calls, but souls do talk to me when they please. There are some things no binding hex can take from a witch. Death will always be in me."

Her fingers were suddenly on Mathew's wrist.

She grinned. "And it seems death is in you, too!"

Mathew pulled away. He didn't have to speak for his skepticism to be made clear.

Roddin turned to Trent and touched his face. He leaned into it.

"Witchy blood, hm?" The trinkets above them chimed, and Roddin nodded her head in agreement with their song. "We see your mother," she sang playfully. "Oh, the rush of water!"

Trent's face contorted with grief. Everything had shifted from something dark and whimsical to dark and threatening. Though Roddin only had a few fingers on his cheek, he felt like she'd reached into his chest and took hold of his heart. He could hardly breathe with the worry that this was a mistake.

She bent her head toward him, their foreheads nearly touching. She smelled like incense and teak. "You were promised to her, Trenton, and she'll be back, so dark and so bright that not even hell will have her!"

"She'll be back?" Trent asked wistfully.

Mathew pulled him away. "I think that's enough."

Hands shaking, Trent pulled the heirloom from his pocket. "She's legit, Matty."

"Trent, anyone could have read about..." Mathew shook his head incredulously. "Your mom—"

Trent cut him off and pushed the porcelain toward Roddin. "We don't know what this is, but we know it's powerful. Would it make a good Haunting sacrifice?"

She considered the heirloom. "Why don't you two just"—she ripped off the lid and touched the stone—"chop off a few fingers, or—"

Swiftly, she was thrown back into the wall with a sickening crunch. Glass rained down as vials and jars crashed around them. Sharp violence, sudden quiet. Trent scrambled to replace the lid. Mathew, breathing hard, stepped around the counter and extended his hand to Roddin. She turned away from him and pulled herself up with a hand on the slick counter.

She took a shaky breath, then *laughed*. "How did you acquire this?"

Mathew coolly picked a piece of glass from his hair, though his face was red with worry. "What is it, exactly?"

Her laugh grew. She seemed pleased. *Energized*. "Depends on who you ask. A battery, a weapon, a curse, a drug. It's an amplyfyr."

"It amplifies witchery?"

"In an amount like this, undiluted..." Her hand hovered over the porcelain. "It does more than that. It *feeds*. On your soul, on my soul, on all that are weak, and all of us are. There is highly skilled magic here, and the sanctifum box was made to keep its power locked up."

The boys shared an uncertain look, and Roddin clicked her tongue impatiently. "This is the most powerful thing you could ever give a witch! A *true* necromancer could raise heathens with it." Her gaze darted between them. "It could have a nice home here in my shop."

Ensuring that the box was sealed tight, Trent slipped the heirloom into his pocket. "Thank you for your time, ma'am. We appreciate it."

She frowned. "It's awfully rude to use a witch for her knowledge without supporting her small business."

Trent left with a deck of playing cards depicting different decapitated witches as the face cards. Mathew bought a pack of gum infused with calming elixir. Roddin watched them go, curiosity coloring her face.

"So, we know it's witchy, powerful, possibly terrible, and probably dangerous." Mathew slapped the mosquito brazen enough to land on his arm.

Trent smiled wickedly. He was amazed that the awful and exciting thing they'd stumbled upon seemed exactly like the sort of awful and exciting thing that a Haunting sacrifice should be.

Mathew frowned. "Do you even know any Mesmortes witches?"

"Maybe we should get to know them." Trent waggled his brow.

"That's not what I meant."

"Matty. You know how art always ends up in the wrong hands after war? Cultures get looted and shit."

Mathew scratched the back of his neck, a predictable sign of discomfort.

"Come on, we both know that your great-great-greats probably stole this. The heirloom doesn't belong to your family; it belongs to *witches*."

"It's not like I want to keep it for myself. You're not worried about what could happen if the wrong witch got ahold of this? Did you hear her? Weapon, curse, drug?"

"Well, I ain't cuttin' off my fingers, mate."

Mathew chuckled but quickly furrowed his brow all serious, and Trent already knew what he was going to say: *You shouldn't have asked her about necromancy,* or *That wasn't part of the plan,* or, *Trent, you can't bring your mother back from the dead.*

Mathew would never understand. There were strange things about Lourdes Hogarth's death that kept Trent up at night, and he was going to find a way to bring her back, not just because he missed her fiercely but because he needed answers.

# 6

## mathew

It probably seemed strange to outsiders that Hallowe'en in a witchtown was so full of mundanity—candy, costumes, and carved pumpkins. But in Haelsford, so much of the year was reserved for actual horrors.

The Box Chant was a two-story parlor between the end of Mesmortes land and the start of Hammersmitt. It was the one thing that the mundane boys and the witches could agree upon for a night like *this*, a party where everyone was invited, their rivalries forgotten.

Fun, before the Wolves.

The giggles of witches and Hammersmitts pierced the air like knives. Witches read tarot in one corner, beckoning mundanes with their alluring gazes. The scenery changed with each passing moment: first an old-school disco, then a Western saloon, then an extravagant ballroom right out of *Beauty and the Beast*. The air was rife with music, the crushing of red cups, and whispered sweet nothings.

*I shouldn't be here.*

The thought lingered like the sticky Haelsford air on Mathew Beaumont's skin. His soda had gone flat, and his patience was equally withered.

In fact, Trent promised that they would go trick-or-treating in town like they were nine, avoiding all the witchy houses and forgetting the sacrifice. Of course, Trent talked him into throwing on one of his nice white shirts and taking off his pants. He kept patting the pocket on the front of his shirt to make sure he hadn't lost the heirloom. He hadn't wanted to leave it back in their room now that the Roddin Witch knew about it.

Trent looked him up and down, a cherry stem hanging from the corner of his mouth.

Mathew let his vintage Wayfarers slide down his nose. "You said fifteen minutes or one drink, whichever came first. It's been an hour, and that's your third drink, Hogarth."

"Yeah, well, Tony Azoff challenged me to a duel, and I cannot leave until I've won."

*"Duel?"*

Trent sighed dramatically. "He said he could get more numbers than me! Witchy ones! But whoever gets a witch to kiss them automatically wins. Anders says Azoff's already got five numbers. Five! It's because he's dressed as Thor while I'm all Time Lord." Trent adjusted his heavy knit scarf. "Maybe Eleven would've been sexier," he muttered.

Mathew had no idea what he was talking about. With the scarf and the wide-brim hat, he thought Trent looked ridiculous, but Trent possessed the easy confidence to pull it off. "You've got the accent; that gives you the edge."

"According to Pops, it's gone all transatlantic." Trent laughed.

"Good luck convincing a witch to kiss you."

Trent scoffed. "Bruv, I've already kissed three. I just want the numbers, too."

Mathew groaned.

"I think you're supposed to high-five me."

"I'm just glad to see you get over Rixton, the prick."

Trent fidgeted slightly. Mathew didn't think the wounds were still raw, but he immediately regretted mentioning Trent's ex-boyfriend. "Anything left in the flask?" Mathew asked quickly. "If I'm gonna be here any longer, I need something stronger."

Trent pulled the golden flask from his pocket. They angled away from the parents and volunteers who were failing to enforce the no-alcohol rule. Mathew let Trent pour until his Diet Coke touched the rim of the cup.

He drank deeply and grinned. "Go get 'em."

"I swear, we'll leave in a few!" Trent winked at him before he was swallowed up by the mob on the dance floor.

There was a girl next to Mathew suddenly. He recognized her as a Devereaux School of the Arts student. His sister attended the mundane private school in the next town over. He wished he'd seen her approach so that he could find a swift exit.

"It's incredible, isn't it?" she said.

A tattoo of a red-and-black helix snaked up her pale arm. She was only his age, maybe a bit younger, but Mathew didn't think it looked like ink from a gel pen. "I'm not interested in hexeating."

"We call it warlocking," she scoffed before leaving.

Whatever. It was the same thing. Hexeaters were vultures, sniffing around for witchblood. Though they mostly kept to online message boards to preach witch worship and swap conspiracy theories, a town like Haelsford was bound to attract a fair few. Some even believed that a daily shot of witchy blood could make a mundane magical. The thought turned Mathew's stomach. Or maybe it was the rum.

Witches weren't his thing. He wasn't witch-averse, not like those protesters who came around every summer screaming unholiness and throwing red paint on the Hill. Mathew just didn't like things he couldn't explain, and the umbrella of *magic* often left him wanting. Witches made him anxious. He could deal with it if he had to, like with Roddin. He'd even exchanged pleasantries with three different witches tonight and survived.

Mathew decided that standing by the drinks might look less pathetic than standing alone in the corner. He grabbed a handful of cheese puffs, spotting Rebecca on the upper level gossiping with other Devereaux students. He couldn't tell what his twin was dressed as. It was a colorful mishmash—she'd taken bits and pieces from several different costumes and stitched them all together in the living room. She saw him, and in no desire to be yelled at to *stop brooding*, Mathew quickly turned to the Cinderella pouring a drink next to him.

"Hi, nice costume," he blurted out.

The girl was clearly caught off guard with the sudden conversation and nearly spilled Sprite all over herself. "Crap." She turned to him, blushing. "Uh. Thanks."

Mathew hesitated. He hadn't expected that her blue eyes would have that witchy glow. You could tell a witch by the way the air shifted, the thickness of it, like walking toward a campfire. But in a room full of witches, the air pulsed with their presence.

He patted his pocket. The amplyfyr was safe.

She looked down at his bare legs. "Um, what are you?"

"*Risky Business?*" He cringed, thinking of how strange he appeared to someone who wasn't into '80s flicks. He sipped some liquid courage. "You go to Mesmortes?"

"Mhm! I'm new."

"That's why I have no idea who you are. Mesmortes students keep to themselves."

"I shouldn't be talking to you." She laughed.

"Why not?"

The witch smiled, smug and relieved, like she was happy to have to explain it to him. "It's the first rule of Mesmortes. No Hammersmitts."

Mathew chuckled, wondering how many numbers Trent had accrued by now. "What are you drinking?"

"Pineapple juice and Sprite."

"I've got rum and Coke, want some?"

She sputtered, "We're underage!"

"Yeah, but I go to Hammersmitt. I was born to break rules." He leaned down, cutting the space between them. "It's not like Mesmortes, only for *good* witches."

"Wicked ones, too," a voice said.

Another witch. This one tilted her head, haughty amusement glowing in her gaze. Long, thin braids framed her deep brown face. Her ears were lined with studs and hoops, her neck adorned with too many chokers and chains to count. She was dressed like a vampire, thick red eyeliner smudged around her dark eyes.

The Cinderella witch waved. "Hey! This is, uh—"

Mathew pressed his hand to his chest and opened his mouth to speak, but the vampire witch ignored him. "Baby witch, Thalia said you promised her a dance."

The Cinderella witch smiled meekly at him as if to say *good luck*, before maneuvering through the dancing bodies to a girl with glasses, dressed like a hippie.

This left Mathew Beaumont facing his fifth witch of the night, one he couldn't look away from, fang-toothed, short-skirted, and red-lipped, spiking his pulse with just a glance.

Unsure of what to do, he tried smiling.

She stepped back. "Why are you looking at me like that? Ew . . ." She put her hands on her hips. "Wait, you think I sent her away because *I* want you."

Mathew glanced over his shoulder because, surely, she was talking to someone else.

"No. *You.* Girls don't act like that in real life, asshole."

A flicker of anger sparked in his chest. "You don't even know me."

She rolled her eyes. "Do all pretty rich boys study lines from the same script?"

Mathew cocked his head at her, grinning like a criminal. "Shit, you think I'm pretty?"

She scoffed. Was she annoyed? Amused?

Mathew decided he didn't care. "It must be tiring, being so mean to strangers."

"Meanness is my lifeblood, actually."

He backed away, remembering his manners. "Enjoy your night."

She glided past in those too-high heels, slightly brushing against him, grazing his hand with hers—

His flesh burned, his stomach roiled.

The entire world changed around him.

Everything was gone. The Box Chant, the people.

*Rebecca. Trent.*

In unending darkness, there was a mirror filled with wires of light instead of glass. The vampire witch stood on the other side of it, biting her lip, her brow furrowed in concentration. Even in this unfamiliar realm of the supernatural, Mathew could feel in the pit of his stomach that something was wrong.

In the mirror, he saw a horror.

The witch looked at him, confused. *Furious.*

A trickle of her blood and a twitch of her wand, and they were pulled back, as if someone had simply flipped a switch. No one seemed to notice. It'd felt like a few minutes in that . . . whatever that was but had only been a second in the Box Chant.

Mathew's stomach lurched. He wondered if she'd seen the same things he had. Then he thought, she must've. Yes, she had to know. She stared at him, black holes for unblinking eyes. It was an angry look that made him think, *What did I do?* when he hadn't done anything at all.

She was gone before he could think of anything to say.

Mathew stumbled to the bathroom. He knew he looked like a lightweight. Or at least people would think that. Thankfully, the Box Chant only had single-use restrooms, so he was able to lock the door, lean over the sink, and try to get his breathing under control.

He closed his eyes.

*Bodies.*

He couldn't explain the mob that reached out from that mirror of light. The souls scurried to him like moths to a match. He saw melted faces, bruises, and exposed bone. No one who died peacefully would ever be trapped in a place like that. Worst were their tortured and desperate moans. Mathew could taste the iron and smoke in the air still, as if it were unraveling before him again.

The heirloom had done that. Despite the porcelain, somehow, it had given this witch the power to open up *something* that had frightened even her. If she had it in full . . .

*No*, Mathew thought suddenly. *Not her.*

*We can't give it to* her.

# 7

## iris

Iris was hungry, she was starving, *she needed more*. A touch of his skin, that power. Her witchery demanded it.

Outside, she opened up the channel in her mind. She squeezed the talisman around her neck.

A voice slipped into her thoughts. *"Breathe, dead girl."*

Iris gulped down frantic breaths, struggling to understand what had just happened.

*He opened the Chasm.*

*No . . . I opened the Chasm.*

*But he made it happen.*

Her stomach turned. As a necromancer, she was allowed entry, but her mother always taught her to stay away, to not let them touch her. These tortured souls were so much harder to handle than the ones she usually communicated with. These souls wanted to keep her.

*One moment, you're just listening*, her mother had warned, *and the next, Death has wrapped its claws around your heart.*

But it wasn't just the Chasm's opening that shocked Iris. The Hammersmitt had also given her a brief surge of power like nothing she'd ever felt before, as if all the energy in the world belonged solely to her. Like she was *unstoppable*. It scared her because it was the same word Morgan Ramirez had used to describe their tethering with Jenna Prim, the two of them loving the attention everyone gave them in the middle of the mess hall.

Morgan had taken Jenna's hand in theirs. *It's like, together, our power is unstoppable.*

"No, no," Iris muttered. "This is impossible."

Donahue was still in her head. *"Remember the land you stand on. It breeds impossible things."*

Those words were the only thing that made sense right now, because Iris Keaton-Foster had found her tether right here in Haelsford.

A mundane.

A *Hammersmitt*.

She didn't even know his name.

Iris was a rarity, and she'd expected that her tether, wherever the witch was, was one as well. You couldn't learn to be a necromancer; you were born one. A rich white mundane boy with dark hair and a stupid smirk was not special. He had no witchery, so why should he be able to access her witchery as he pleased, like a tourist? Haelsford was full of tourists, and Iris hated them all. They didn't know her and only saw a stereotype, the Black girl with a scowl and an attitude. They called her intimidating; they called her *mean*. Hadn't he? She let them think what they want. They came to gawk at the witchtown like it wasn't real, but an attraction. Iris was certainly real. She'd given enough blood to prove it.

What was his sacrifice? What blood did he give?

"The night is young, deathwitch! Where're you going?" Jailah called out to her from the Box Chant, moonlight glinting off the golden spires of her headband. She was dressed as the literal sun.

Iris shook her head. "I'm tired! Going to bed!"

Jai frowned but didn't press on. She knew Iris well enough to know when she didn't want to be bothered.

That night, Iris didn't get much rest. She lay in bed and saw it all again, an excruciating replay. The flash of white light. Total darkness. The mirror. The Hammersmitt's mouth open in slight terror.

*It can't be him*, she thought, wanting to believe it. He was nothing to her, and she'd just experienced an unexpected surge in her necromancy at the very moment that they touched.

*A fluke.*

In the morning, she told herself that there was only one boy who deserved her attention—the one who could end the Haunting. But at noon, Iris found herself on the sidelines of field hockey practice trading essence of greenthorne for info about the damn Hammersmitt boy.

She pointed at the vial. "Don't waste it. Thalia Blackwood grew that greenthorne with her own blood."

Freshman Lilly Han took a long draw from her bottle of Gatorade. "Which boy are we talking about again?"

A quick ball whizzed near them, and Iris swiftly slid herself and Lilly down the bench and out of the way. "One of the Hammersmitts. We spoke at the Box Chant."

"Like, seven feet tall, dark hair, super delicious?"

Iris ignored Lilly's giddy smile. "Please. Five nine at most. He was the one in his underwear—"

"Ooooh!"

Iris groaned, but she gave Lilly a secret wink. Lilly's falcon, Jang-Goon, circled above them, keeping a watchful eye on his witch.

"I think it was Becky Beaumont's brother," Lilly said, smoothing back a few wayward strands of black hair.

"I don't know her."

"She's mundane, goes to Devereaux with Anika Johnson's brothers. His name is Mathew. You'll find him at the stables, and sometimes he works at Soma Café— Hey, you owe Jenna a latte, by the way."

Iris chuckled. "The girl holds a grudge."

"I broke her favorite pen during orientation, and she still brings it up." Lilly swirled the mint-green liquid in its vial. "Essence of greenthorne. How is this going to help my Demonology presentation?"

Iris stood. The witches were coming off the field now, scabbed and grass-stained and out of breath. "Stir a few drops in a *Vie* potion, add a cursed artifact, and watch as it reveals its secrets. But make sure Jenna and Morgan are with you, okay? Don't do it alone. Demons are never kind. And hey, if you find out anything else about that boy, let me—"

In the distance, from somewhere deep in the Swamp, a howl cracked the air.

For a second, everything was still.

Someone dropped a hockey stick. Grass crunched beneath skittish feet. The howl continued. An underclassman looked back to Iris, the grip around his hockey stick tightening. Iris was the only upperclassman around. And then they all looked to her.

Jang-Goon squawked loudly above them, a troubled cry.

Iris stepped in front of Lilly and pulled out her wand. "Get behind me!" she yelled, and the others sprinted to her.

*It's too early.*

Iris's thoughts were frantic with horrible scenarios. There were nine witches other than her. The protections wouldn't go up for another few weeks. If this time was different, if the hibernation pattern somehow changed, a Wolf could run out of the Swamp and onto the field in minutes.

Then the howl stopped. Like the whisper of a spring wind, every witch sighed at the same time.

"Haunting's soon," Lilly said plainly.

And Iris was wasting her energy on that Hammersmitt boy.

She felt a soft thud in her head, like someone knocking on the door to her mind.

Madeline Donahue's voice seeped in. *"What would you do to keep yourself and the others safe?"* she asked.

"Whatever it takes," Iris whispered.

*"Good. You will need it all."*

# 8

## jailah

**Four weeks until the Haunting Season**

Most Haelsfordian families ran generations deep. Either their ancestors were witches or witch burners, and whether witchy or mundane, none wanted to give it up, Wolves and all.

Jailah Simmons was one of Haelsford's transplants. She was the first witch in her family in nearly thirty years. Her mundane parents shipped her off from their home in Alabama so she could attend one of the finest, oldest, wealthiest coven academies in the world. Haunting be damned, she was thankful for Haelsford, for Mesmortes, for Iris and Thalia, who understood the fraught intersections of being Black and witchy.

She was lucky to be supported and loved. Her father didn't understand a damn thing about witchery, but he had bought Jai the fancy cauldrons with rubber-padded feet, leather-bound spellbooks, and an expensive wand with a retractable sacrificial needle. Her mom was less concerned about her magic than she was that Jailah was behaving herself at school. But Jai's mom was a doctor and her father was a lawyer, and it was expected that she'd graduate from Mesmortes as the best witch the school had ever seen.

Jailah had passed around the petition to do the Haunting protections. She was the reason Mesmortes would get their first sacrifice. It made her giddy. Mesmortes didn't do class rankings—with Pulls and tethers, there were too many variations in witchery to judge one against another. But Jailah was powerful, with a terrifying amount of ambition bubbling up in her. Best of all, she knew how to charm. She wanted the world. She was born with an insatiable desire for something greater than attention or success, something that good grades, money, and leadership positions couldn't buy.

It was hard to put a name to it, but *glory* came close.

The curse on Haelsford was a consequence of sinister magic performed in response to sinister crimes. The magic needed to break it would likely be some truly sinister spellwork. Sacrifices like no other. And if they succeeded? Glory like no other.

Jai was the first to arrive at the Mesmortes auditorium. Instead of wooden or metal bleachers, cascading rows of obsidian jutted out from the walls to form a half circle around the dais in the center of the room. Sunlight shone through the glass dome lined with thick greenery— peonies, ivy, radiant violets, bright marigolds. An intersection of darkness and light.

Jai greeted the incoming witches with cheery pleasantries. A smile and nod for Rowe Adler, who had just transferred from Hammersmitt. Rowe had a pin with a blue-pink-and-white flag proudly displayed on her Mesmortes knapsack, and Jai was impressed with how quickly she formed her cool little Goth crew. The five of them entered the auditorium like a badass biker gang. Jai offered personalized handshakes for the archery team and hugs for the Junior Witchery Council. She went through the motions with utter genuineness and thought nothing of it until Logan Wyatt stopped before her and asked, "Do you personally know everyone that goes here?"

Jailah smiled. "Not yet, but I'm working on it." She put a hand on her shoulder. "You good?"

Logan's hair was a mess of frizzy locks and disheveled bangs. She attempted a smile, but it didn't reach her eyes. "I was practicing. It didn't go well."

"What were you working on?"

*"Azuamorraille,"* said Logan. "I was trying to levitate my grimoire."

"It'll get easier once you reform the spell."

Logan's helpless sigh nearly broke Jailah's heart.

Reformation was the true witch's way to do it. It was a way to make your witchery your own. With proper focus, skilled wandwork, and painstaking repetition, a witch could dwindle a mouth full of mumble from a spellbook into an easy phrase. *Azuamorraille* could simply become *Up.*

"Isn't it easier to just remember things and recite them?" Logan asked, not even trying to hide her hopelessness.

"Are you scaring the baby witch?" Iris's voice cut like an arrow through the noise. She and Thalia were among the last of the students who came trickling in. "She looks terrified."

"She's just been studying real hard." Jailah led Logan up the glossy black steps and into the top row. Thalia and Iris squeezed into the row in front of them.

"Is this everyone?" Logan looked around at the chattering witches.

Jailah nodded. "All seven hundred and twelve of us."

"Here comes the headmistress," Thalia whispered.

Headmistress Westhoven was a short, curvy woman who could either quell your anxieties or send you running with just a look. She had dark skin, a round face, and piercing brown eyes. Her dress was high-collared and black, her lips were glossy, and she wore her gray locs piled atop her head in a neat bun. Stoic Professor Circe, head of the Defense and Protections courses, followed behind her, a full head taller, not a swipe of makeup on her pale skin or a dollop of product in her flat, knee-length red hair. As always, she looked like she'd rather be hiding behind the stack of books in her office than in front of the students.

The headmistress waited until not a single fidget could be heard throughout the auditorium. "Afternoon, dearest witches." Her voice rippled through the air without a microphone.

"Afternoon, Headmistress," the students replied.

"One month now." Westhoven smiled. A chill ran down Jailah's spine. "Just like that, another Haunting Season is upon us. As you all know, we will be receiving the first sacrifice in our history from our esteemed neighbors, the Hammersmitt School for Exceptional Young Men."

Someone wailed an "Ow! Ow!" to a rush of scattered giggles.

Westhoven acknowledged this with an amused nod. "As distinguished witches of Mesmortes, it is imperative to our reputation that we accept their offerings with thanks, admiration, and grace. This is the start of a new era for all of us, mundane and witch alike." She unclasped her hands and held them out to the students. "To prepare for the Haunting, you will each be assigned a captain who will help you review the protection charms to be performed. The freshmen captain will be Jenna Prim, Freddy León for the sophomores, juniors with Jailah Simmons, and seniors will report to Anika Johnson."

Jailah flashed her girls a wide grin. "Who, me?"

Thalia chuckled. "Surprise, surprise."

As Jailah made her way down the steps to some polite applause, she heard Iris sing, "There she is, Miss Americaaaa—"

Jenna invaded her personal space the moment Jailah stepped onstage, but Jailah didn't mind. "This is so exciting!" the freshman said, face beaming.

Jailah looked over at Anika, who'd taken the time to greet and thank the elder witches individually. *Damn it.* Jailah took her lead, Jenna followed, and, finally, an anxious Freddy León.

"There are three spells to be performed, as outlined in the materials you all received last month." The headmistress turned to Anika. "Let's start with Johnson."

Anika stepped forward, sure-footed, her thick box braids swaying. The wash of gold shimmer across her eyelids made her brown skin glow. She acknowledged Jailah with a polite smile. This was no competition—they were demonstrating, not dueling. But with the entire student body gathered around them, it was practically an arena.

Jailah liked Anika. She was witty, studious, and an enormously talented witch, and she'd been Jai's orientation group leader. Anika was something of an older sister to her, even teaching her an arsenal of hair spells, ones that could take Jai's glorious fro into glorious microbraids in mere minutes, or a silk press without heat damage. But she couldn't wait for Anika to graduate and leave the Junior Witchery Council in her hands. It was all she wanted.

She used to joke about it with Veronica, her ex.

*First, JWC. Then High Witch of the actual Council.*

*Nah*, Vero had chided her. *Then—the world.*

Anika stood at center stage, and the headmistress placed a supportive hand under her elbow. "Have you practiced the first spell?"

"Yes." Anika pricked her finger. She exuded a cool confidence as she recited the incantation. *"For Our Blessed; Against Sharp Claws and Snarling Teeth."*

Jailah relished the concentration on Anika's face. She loved magic, whether it was hers or another's.

Anika's spell brought up the temperature. An orb grew around the stage, pulsating with a faint orange sheen.

"Good," Professor Circe said, satisfied. "León, the second spell, please."

Freddy pushed up his sleeves. His voice was deep. *"For Our Mundanes; Against Red Fur and Hex-Given Strength."*

The orb grew hotter, a blanket of blue air growing above the orange.

The headmistress opened a palm toward Jenna. "And the third, Prim."

Jenna considered her newfound witchery as an exciting game to be had, not something to second-guess. She puffed out her chest and incanted loudly, *"For Any Living Creature in Haelsford; Against Any Wolf Who'd Dare Cross This Threshold!"*

A crash of static rose above them. The final spell sheened green. It settled into place, and the heat became a soft comfort.

"Lovely, just lovely." Professor Circe turned to Jailah. "Simmons, your turn."

Jailah stilled. There were only three protection spells.

"For last year's MidWinter Celebration, you had flocks of bluebirds flying in the sky and swans dancing in the pond. You used *Suffitiomorrai*, correct?"

"Yes, Professor."

"Very impressive. Do you think you could make a Wolf or two?"

Jailah's breath caught in her throat. Conjuring birds out of smoke wasn't hard, nor were the miniature Wolves she'd made at Roddin's. But a full-sized Wolf? Or two? There were pictures and drawings of the beasts that they were all shown every year in Professor Circe's classes. Yet she'd never seen one up close before.

But she said, "Of course, Professor."

The other witches stood back. The audience chattered excitedly but hushed once Jailah raised her left hand.

She stuck her thumb with the little retractable sanctified needle under her wand. She raised her empty right hand, too, to steady herself.

*"Suffitiomorrai."* She drew a breath. *"A Hexed Wolf of Haelsford."*

Red smoke from her wand leached beyond the protective barrier and settled just off the dais, in front of the section of the auditorium where her girls were.

Her witchery welled up in her chest. She felt the heat extend to her hand, drawn to the wand held in her fingertips. She pushed it outward and closed her eyes.

In the darkness, she drew up the shape of the Wolf. It was like a tracing of a picture, correctly colored in. Massive paws, long crooked claws, messy tufts of crimson fur, rows of rotting teeth. A few gasps started around her. She took that as a good sign. But that wasn't enough. An ugly, feral animal didn't make a Wolf.

Now, behavior. She reached for something monstrous within to give this beast of smoke. Bloodlust and anger and a need to win.

The Wolf ran around the auditorium, snapping its jaws and growling hungrily. Smoke billowed in its wake. Jailah imagined a real Wolf would be much faster. But someone in the audience screamed when it got close, and that was good enough for Jailah.

*I really did that, huh.*

From the seats, Iris shouted, "That's my fucking girl!" Which prompted Professor Ortega to emerge from the shadows and call Iris down for a talking-to.

"That's good," Professor Circe whispered. "Just beautiful. You're a natural."

The headmistress addressed the assembly once more. "This is what the Swamp holds. Wolves that would do anything to cut into your flesh—"

Freddy León screeched suddenly and dropped to the floor.

Jailah's Wolf had bolted for the protection. Though it was only made of smoke, those rows of teeth were terrifying. It hit the spells and exploded in a plume of vapor.

Westhoven shot Jailah an approving look. "As you can all see, the protections we put up are vital to our safety. As we are gracious witches, we now hold the safety of over a thousand mundanes in our blessed hands. And a real Wolf isn't made of smoke."

As the headmistress moved on to curfews and safe practices, Jailah's gaze drifted. She found that the students not focused on the headmistress were focused on Jailah herself. She fed on this—the awe, the fear, maybe a touch of jealousy. She ran in debutante circles back home and was taught that there were certain things that a girl shouldn't be. Attention-seeking. Cutthroat. Desperate to be loved, but okay with being unlikable. She used to feel bad about it. That was before Vero.

Jailah didn't look like the Chosen Ones in books and movies. She'd been given the support to succeed but had never been told that she was destined for legendary greatness. There was no prophecy placed on her head, no witch who foretold her future to her parents on the night of her birth.

No swords to pull, curses to break, lore to be fulfilled.

So, she'd make her own.

Jailah imagined the Wolf once more. Those snarling teeth, those blood-thirsty eyes. She would give anything to make her town whole again.

She would do anything for that glory.

# 9

## logan

Logan looked around at the atrium, which seemed plucked out of a haunted mansion.

*I don't know if this place is for you*, Margot had said a few months ago, stretching out the Mesmortes informational packet. Margot hadn't meant to insult her, but it stung.

Now Logan thought, with a tinge of condescension, *You were wrong. Here I am.*

Even if her wand was still in her pocket. Even if beads of sweat pooled on the back of her neck as she followed Iris and Thalia down the steps for practice. Though Professor Ortega had extended the size of the auditorium, their corner was a popular one. That was the thing about being with the Red Three. Others always wanted in.

Jailah approached with confident grace. "Please tell me one of you got a video of me bein' real witchy with those Wolves."

"I got it," Thalia said, waving her phone. "I even added those cat ears you like so much."

"How did you do that?" Logan asked Jailah. "That was amazing."

"I practiced," Jailah said, like it was that easy.

The headmistress's voice rang out again, instructing the witches to begin practicing the protective charms.

Logan sucked in a breath.

While the auditorium grew loud with the incantations, she leaned toward Jailah and whispered, "I haven't been practicing. I forgot about it."

She left off that her forgetfulness was a direct result of her actively stuffing the little spellbook she was given under her mattress, along with other neglected schoolwork. She knew the words. She just couldn't perform them.

Jailah nodded. "Okay. No big."

"I got her." Wand clutched in one hand, Thalia circled Logan. With her free hand, she waved Iris and Jailah away. "Witchery isn't just about blood. It's about intention. Think about the kind of witch *you* want to be."

Logan flexed her fingers. "I want to be the type of witch that doesn't second-guess her spells. I want to be a true proxy." She swallowed. "I wanna help you guys save Haelsford."

Thalia smirked. She pushed up her glasses and rolled up her sleeves. "All of that starts here."

Logan drew her wand, trying not to dwell on how heavy it felt.

Thalia lifted her own wand. *"For Our Blessed; Against Sharp Claws and Snarling Teeth."*

A vibrant orange light seeped from the wand, adding to the colors that were growing all around them, produced by other witches.

"Feel your witchery inside of you? Call it. It's okay to fail here. This is just practice."

*"For Our Blessed; Against Sharp Claws and Snarling Teeth."* She'd said it slow and quiet, but her magic seemed to hear. She felt the flame flicker in her chest, something that should've felt familiar and comforting but only

made Logan's hand tremble. The wand tugged at the heat, and Logan, jaw clenched, willed it to follow.

Her own orange spell grew next to Thalia's, encapsulating them both in glowing twin orbs.

"Holy crap," she muttered. "It's working."

Thalia grinned. "Keep going."

Logan concentrated on the heat in her chest, simmering hotter with every breath. *"For Our Mundanes; Against Red Fur and Hex-Given Strength."*

The blue light grew with a vibration. It shimmered under the sunlight pouring in from above. Logan felt like an awestruck mundane. It was her magic, something created from her blood and her words, but it mystified her all the same.

Thalia glanced over her shoulder at Iris, laughing. "Told you. You owe me!"

The deathwitch scowled.

As Logan's neighbor, Iris had good reason to think that Logan wouldn't have been able to pull off the spells. She'd probably heard her late-night study sessions full of frustrated curses and failed incantations. Perhaps she'd noticed how Logan kept her fists closed and her wand in her cape. Though Thalia had bet on her, the fact that they were betting at all made her uncomfortable and a touch angry.

"Logan?" Iris said tensely, eyes focused past her.

The glittering blue-and-orange orb had become a mess of gray smoke, billowing from Logan's wand in thick puffs. The air smelled like a fire. The other witches noticed, and the whispers began.

Frantically, Logan drew her wand away and immediately regretted it.

With a sizzle and a pop, the plume exploded, the force knocking a few witches off their feet, sending others tumbling, and covering everyone nearby in soot.

Only Logan remained standing. She would've done anything to have a spell to send her straight back to Ontario right then and there.

Groans and whimpers and murmurs grew loud. Iris brought herself to her feet with a huff. "Damn. Save the fight for the Wolves."

Thalia fared a bit better, only being taken down to a knee. "You got a name for that spell?"

"I don't even know what that was," Logan replied quietly. She wasn't sure if it was better or worse to let others think she had done it on purpose.

"My new blouse!" Jenna Prim shot Logan a contemptuous look. It quickly went apologetic—Logan sensed Jailah over her shoulder, giving Jenna a glare. "Whatever. It'll wash."

Jailah's dark curls were dusty, and she paused to blink ash out of her eyes. "Whoa, where'd that come from?"

"I didn't—"

"It was amazing!"

"Amazing?" Logan was still shaking. "That was horrible!"

"Nah, it was *magic*!"

Professor Circe approached, heels pattering atop the soft layer of soot. She shooed the onlookers away, but the Red Three didn't budge. Maybe they thought they were being good friends by standing with her, but it only made Logan feel worse.

Professor Circe considered Logan with narrowed eyes. "You're supposed to be practicing the trio of protection spells, not . . ." She gestured around herself. "What fire spell is this?"

"I don't know." Logan sighed.

"Well, what did you incant?"

"Nothing. I was doing the protection spell, and this happened."

Her eyes narrowed further. "What is your name?"

"Wyatt. Logan Wyatt."

Logan could pinpoint the *aha* moment. She was sure the professors talked about her and her uselessness with a wand, the same way the young witches gossiped. "Perhaps you should take a break. Get some rest; eat a snack." Professor Circe pursed her thin lips into a line. "And practice harder."

Those final words slapped Logan in the face. She felt the heat in her eyes and in her cheeks and spun on her heels. It was silly to think that a nap and a snack could fix Logan's issues with magic. *She just wants you gone so you don't mess up practice for everyone else.* Maybe it was a blessing. She wouldn't have to suffer through her own magic either.

Footsteps followed Logan out into the courtyard, and she was content to ignore them until Iris grabbed her knapsack.

Logan yanked it back. She sloppily wiped her face before trying to walk ahead.

Iris threw herself in front of Logan. "Didn't you hear me calling you?"

Blood pounded in Logan's ears. "You heard the professor. Nap and rest and some more practice. Hopefully, I don't choke all of Topthorne House to death."

"Wouldn't be a total loss. Wesley Morris keeps blasting country music until three a.m., so yeah, take care of her for me, won't you?"

Logan rolled her eyes.

"I'm kidding. Obv."

"Well, congrats. You bet right. I'm a crappy witch."

"It wasn't about your magic; it was about how long you were going to last here—"

"Oh, that makes me feel *so* much better."

Iris shook her head. "I mean here, as in, *with us*. You don't even know us, and we took you to Roddin's and started scheming about ending the Haunting. I thought it would've scared you off, but you're still here. Why?"

"I guess I don't scare that easy."

"Exactly, which makes you perfect for what we're going to do."

Logan stilled. "You found the Wolf Boy?"

"Not yet. But I know that when the time comes, I can count on you."

Maybe Iris really believed that, but Logan was having trouble believing it of herself. "You don't need for me to be good at magic." She drew her arm, pushing her sleeve back. "Just take my blood. Find his name or his face, or whatever."

"That's not how it works. We can't create out of nothing. Your blood can't just give me his name."

"Fine, but once you find it, you'll just need my blood to stand in for his face to call him, right? Take it now."

"No."

"Well, why the hell not?"

"What kind of person would I be if I let a baby witch lose her way?"

"That's not your job. I've got remedial classes; the professors are supposed to fix me."

"Fix?"

"You guys don't have to help."

"Maybe not." Iris fiddled with the hoops in her ears. "But I have a vision of us. You and me and Jailah and T. We save Haelsford."

"A vision?"

"Maybe a daydream." Iris smirked. "Was that really unintentional back there?"

Logan huffed, blowing up her bangs.

"Sorry, I just gotta know—what does that feel like? I mean, it's easy to get spells mixed up, but I've never had *that*—" Iris paused, clearly looking for a way to say what she intended without further insulting Logan. "Does it hurt?"

Logan shook her head. "No. It felt like . . . I could feel my witchery growing, but I couldn't stop it. It's like trying to turn off a faucet, but the handle keeps spinning and spinning, and the water is fire, and I think the fire might hurt someone." She quieted. "But it's also the only time I feel witchy, so I almost don't want it to stop."

Slowly, Iris's mouth inched into a chilling smile.

Saying nothing else, the deathwitch walked back toward the atrium, leaving Logan more curious than before.

# 10

## trent

Paper targets littered Trent's bedroom. They were scattered across the floor, covered his desk, and lined the windowsill. He'd pinned them up on any space of the white wall that was free and had been too lazy to throw them out when they were all cut up. Mathew, who'd come in just last week with spackle and a scowl, was bound to give him a proper scolding.

Trent attached yet another target to the wall. Knife throwing was usually his favorite form of release, but his sour mood wouldn't budge. He'd just spoken to his father on their monthly phone call, and Damien Hogarth was unimpressed with Trent's perfect grades. The patriarch had spent more time singing the praises of Trent's older brothers: Prince had sat in on his first tumor removal of med school, Kendrick excelled at his concerto, and Troy—the oldest, the golden boy—landed the latest *Forbes* cover. As the fourthborn son, Trent simultaneously felt invisible and endlessly scrutinized.

It was also his turn to babysit the heirloom. Mathew wanted eyes on it at all times. The porcelain box sat on Trent's desk, untouched by the barrage of targets.

Feeling suddenly stifled, Trent opened up the window. He poked his head out much farther than others on the tenth floor would.

"Talk to me, Mum," he whispered.

Trent was a freak of nature. *The invincible boy* he called himself, and not for nothing. When his mother drove the two of them off a cliff, from sixty feet up and into freezing water full of jagged rocks, she died and Trent did not. At the very least, he should've been severely hurt. If not then, then maybe last year when his tire blew out on I-95 and he went hurtling toward oncoming traffic, or last week when the chandelier in Raver Mess Hall fell, and Trent, suddenly clumsy, tripped out of the way. His life was full of near misses. He had a keen curiosity for unexplainable things and supernatural phenomena because he truly believed he was one.

Trent twirled his mother's favorite knife. Red handle, gold inlay. He flipped it into the air and caught it effortlessly. She'd passed it down to him along with her talent for blades. Whatever attempts his father made to keep carny blood out of his boys failed with Trent. While a member of the Haelsfordian Coven Troupe, Lourdes Hogarth specialized in weapons— shooting antique guns and blasting herself out of cannons and swallowing knives. She was best with blades. She wasn't the woman standing with an apple atop her head; she was the one taking aim.

She'd grown clingy in the weeks leading up to their trip to Brighton. It didn't feel weird, considering he was leaving for Haelsford. He asked the same thing every year around August: *Why Hammersmitt if you're not coming with?* And her response was one he'd frequently heard around Haelsford. *Living with Wolves will make you fearless.* Even if his mother refused to go back to the town that gave her throwing knives and a family of outcast witches, she wanted her sons to be made of the same stuff she was.

*Talk to me.*

Trent took the rigorous shaking of the branches as a response. He'd been reading up on witches lately, focusing on defensive spells and anything like *dead witches protecting their children from the beyond.* The librarians were starting to give him odd looks in response to his charming smile and long lists of rare titles. It was all useless—he couldn't find anything that made sense, and it didn't help that Trent's mother rarely practiced her magic around him or his brothers while she was alive.

But Trent wouldn't stop until he reached her again. He had to know why she'd whispered *You were promised* right before she sent them flying off a cliff.

It was perhaps the only real secret he had. He'd tried convincing himself that he was misremembering, but a part of him knew that he wasn't, and that he really had seen her turn the wheel sharply and press down hard on the accelerator. He remembered the Jaguar, clean and expensive. The opal ring around his mother's pinkie finger. Her neck, the paisley Burberry scarf around it.

*Because Lourdes Hogarth wouldn't be caught dead in last season's wear.*

Trent laugh-sobbed and immediately put his head in his hands.

If only he could talk to her.

If only he were a witch.

*If only I was a necromancer.*

His phone beeped. A text from Mathew:

**Hey. So. We should think about
sacrificing something else.**

Trent rolled his eyes even though Mathew wasn't there to see it.

bruv, what??? have you got
another awesomely horrifying
witchy thing that
you're sitting on?

We don't even understand
how it works.

AND???
that's exactly why it's the
perfect sacrifice!!!!!!!!!!!

I'll come up with something.

what happened last week? you've
been acting weird af ever since

Three cascading dots, and then nothing. And then: **Nothing happened.**

Trent didn't believe him. Something went down at the Box Chant. He knew from the constant airiness of Mathew's gaze, like he was trying to remember a faded memory. There was a rumor going around that Mathew had hooked up with a witch, which realistically meant he'd probably just stood near one. Whatever it was, it'd changed him.

Trent fired off six furious red-faced emoji and grabbed his skateboard. Before heading out, he strapped the knife to his leg.

It was very unlike Trent to skate down the Hill at this speed. Normally, he hugged every curve expertly and cautiously as Mathew kicked the pavement faster, faster, *faster*. Trent watched for stray rocks and sharp cuts of wind. Mathew watched the world blur by.

But right now, Trent had no one to pretend for.

Just the wind. Even that seemed resistant, thick, urging him to slow down.

*Make me*, he thought, and crouched down on his board, gathering that dangerous speed.

So, it did. Just as Trent caught a crosswind that threatened to send him barreling into the library's solid granite wall, something like suction pulled him back, forcing him slow, saving his skull from a concerning fate.

Trent cackled as he was thrown from his board and into a soft thicket.

--- ⬢ ---

Trent brushed a few stray blades of grass from his curls as he walked into the Haelsford Public Library. The line was long. Trent didn't mind. He liked people-watching, and the public library always brought out a diverse assortment of folks. A few Devereaux girls, chatting about homecoming. The couple who sent sweets to his dorm room after his mum passed. A Mesmortes witch cleaning her glasses with her cape.

"Name?" The librarian kept her head down, eyes on her keyboard.

"Morning, Mrs. Lopez."

The woman looked up at him from behind bright pink frames. "Trenton."

He brandished his worn-out library card. "I think I have three this time."

"You have eight." She pulled the titles from the shelves behind her. "I'll get you a tote bag. They're purple this month."

Trent flipped through the first book as the librarian went to the back workroom: *Grimoire of the Chasm: Actions in the Afterlife.*

"Why is everyone in this town so obsessed with death?" a quiet voice said.

Trent turned his head and found a witch girl peering over his shoulder. She smelled like a forest fire.

She was, in all forms, a regular girl. Brown skin, slightly lighter than his, gray eyes, loose chocolate curls, big glasses. She had a soft gaze, a round face, and eyebrows that readied to connect in the center. There was that light behind her eyes—or maybe it was a darkness—that simultaneously put him on edge and piqued his interest. Unlike most Mesmortes witches he came across, her plaid slacks were rolled up at the ankles, the color of her cape was washed out, and her top hat seemed a bit too big for her head.

Trent closed the book. "I've got a Witchery Defenses quiz next week."

She laughed with condescension. "Listen to me, these are the only defenses you need to know: Never piss off a witch, never cheat a witch, and never annoy a witch. Basically, just do whatever we say, and you'll be fine."

Trent scanned the books she carried. *Aurora Xie's Most Protective Spells*, *Fighting Omens and Hexes*, and *Bountiful Fruit for Bountiful Sight*.

"Oh, and never make a bloodpact with a witch."

"Bloodpact?" he asked.

"You know, anything that involves, like, relinquishing your firstborn child to a crone in exchange for beauty and wealth or whatever."

"Huh. Thanks." He stuck out his hand. "Name's Trent."

"Thalia," she said softly, as if she didn't want him to hear.

Something howled outside. High-pitched and cruel.

Neither spoke, but their eyes stayed locked on each other. A stranger might just be a friend when faced with the snarling teeth of a Wolf.

A second line opened up, and the librarian there waved Thalia forward.

A bit awkwardly, Thalia placed her stack on the desk. "Hey, what are you boys getting us for the Haunting?"

Trent smirked. "A dozen cupcakes."

"I like coconut almond with vanilla frosting."

Trent took her in once more. How uneasy her body language was, though her eyes hardly left him. An examination from a girl who rarely trusted.

Mrs. Lopez returned. She scanned and packaged Trent's books quickly, but he walked away at a deliberately slow pace. Thalia caught up with him as he reached the exit.

"One more thing," he said, holding the door for her. "Do you know a girl called Foster? She must go to Mesmortes."

Thalia's jaw tensed, which was an answer on its own.

"She's a necromancer, right? Like"—he lowered his voice—"can she raise up the dead?"

"Uh, why are you asking me this?"

"I have something that would interest her."

"Really? What?"

"I'd like to chat with her myself, if that's okay."

"Unless it's about the Wolf Boy, it's useless." Trent raised a brow, but before he could prod further, she gave a sardonic laugh. "Don't waste your time."

It was drizzling, and Thalia pulled her cape over her books. The mundanity of it instantly endeared her to Trent.

He caught the flash of lettering on her inner wrist. "Exodus 22:18?"

Thalia smiled mischievously. "Thou shall not suffer a witch to live."

# 11

## thalia

When Thalia reached the cabin in the clearing along the swampy mud-slush Haelsfordians called a river, a prayer bloomed in her throat. She choked it down. She wasn't the praying type anymore, but *old habits*.

She scanned the area first, though all she wanted was to run inside and breathe the familiar incense-scented air. But she pricked her thumb, waved her wand in a slow circle, and whispered, *"Clarity."*

The air pulled toward her in a colorful gust, all zoomed in. When the earth went still and she saw that there was indeed no one hiding out in the forest to truss her up and carry her away, she breathed out.

The cabin was as she left it. Messy, but untouched. The vines raged all around, giving the walls a vibrant green color. Iris's and Jai's presences were evident as well; the deathwitch had left behind a tube of black lipstick at some point, and a single falsie of Jailah's rested on the bathroom sink. Thalia's desk, next to the unmade bed, was piled with vials and little potted plants, loose screws and scrap metal. She shuffled them away and placed her stack of library books there.

Thalia inherited the cabin from the elder greenwitch who used to live here, and she kept it so she had a place to be alone. It smelled like incense and rose, just like home before her father chased her away.

Her mother's rosary hung from a crooked branch protruding from the wall. Thalia never got rid of it, though her mother's God, the saints, and every angel had turned their backs on her.

"Don't look at me like that," Thalia whispered, glaring at the Virgin Mary's delicate face carved into the thin piece of metal. "All pious." Thalia ran her thumb over the black beads. "I've been good."

Shaggy fur brushed against her leg.

Thalia pressed her palm atop Maverick's head. "No one sneaking around?"

The scruffy little mutt only blinked at her, but she felt his affirmative response.

She'd chosen Haelsford for her new home, not just because of Mesmortes but because it was a witchtown, governed by a witchery council. They had a mundane mayor, but everyone knew that was just to placate the non-magical population. Most importantly, *no cops.* Her hometown had a sheriff and a small police department that, before Thalia's spectacular fuckup, dealt mostly with traffic violations, drunken fights at the one bar in town, and the occasional slashed tire. It was the type of town where people said, *Nothing like that would ever happen here,* whatever *that* was. If it were anywhere else, they'd have put her on a list, her face flashing every half hour on national news. Thalia often imagined seeing herself on old-school Wanted posters, with sinister eyes and a violent scowl. It'd have her true name.

*Talullah Turner.*

*Wanted for Murder, Witchcraft, and Crimes Against God.*

But Annex, Arizona, kept things in-house. The sheriff was prideful, and that was a lucky thing for Thalia because he never put out an APB on her. He, and likely her father, wanted to bring her in themselves.

*Not that they'll ever get the chance.*

Thalia looked out the window and toward the Swamp. She could just make out the moldy tree limbs and the decaying leaves. She was becoming a better greenwitch and could feel her connection with the earth growing stronger with every lesson, every spell, every shrub picked for a potion. She was beginning to feel the Swamp, too. The life that once was, calling her for mercy. Like an itch she couldn't scratch, a lingering presence on her witchy senses, oil on her skin.

Thalia unfastened her damp cape and placed her top hat on the window-sill next to her backup wand. It was uglier than her main one, with its splintery, unfinished wood and crooked handle. But she didn't need it to look nice. She just needed it if someone took her everyday wand away.

She cleared off a spot on her desk and texted Iris:

**there's a hammersmitt looking for you.**

A text came in from her own curious Hammersmitt, Anders Osnes, whose name was saved in her phone only as a green leaf emoji.

**wuts good, o fearsome witch?**
**just checkin in on my herb**

Thalia glanced over at the potted plants lining the windowsill in the tiny kitchen. She called it martyr's touch, which was just a cross between foxglove and chaste tree. It did nothing on its own, but when soaked in an elixir to ease the mind and touched with *Dreamdaze*, what mundane would know?

Selling fake weed made her feel a little slimy, but Thalia wasn't like most Mesmortes witches. Even her friends couldn't relate. Jailah's parents were rich as hell, and she never batted an eye at purchase totals displayed on keypad screens. Iris's tastes weren't quite so flashy, but Thalia got the sense that the deathwitch wanted for nothing. Her parents had left her more than enough for her comforts, whatever the story was there, though Iris still liked a good deal on fresh candles. Thalia knew from obsessive googling that Logan Wyatt was a legacy witch. Apparently, her family were local celebrities in her little Canadian town, stemming from her great-great-grandfather—Logan Phillip Wyatt I—saving a school during a killer snowstorm, with skilled waterwitchery. Thalia couldn't imagine what it was like to know the name of every witch who came before you. Logan might've been having trouble with her magic, but all her belongings were drenched in that pleasantly *new* smell. At least in her family her witchiness was expected.

It was Thalia's mother who had instructed Aunt Nonni to smuggle her out of Annex. Somehow, that trip was the happiest she'd ever been. It wasn't exactly fun; she was taller than Nonni but still got relegated to cramped back seats, her legs folded like origami. Sometimes their driver had really bad BO, or chickens in the back seat, and when they passed the wayward traffic stop, Thalia had to crouch down just in case her father had put out an AMBER Alert.

But it was amazing, truly and fantastically so, because she'd escaped Annex with her life, drove through seven states, found a flea-ridden dog at a truck stop, and was greeted in Central Florida by eleven witches with starlike white hair and little green plants growing out of their skin. All had the Gift of the Earth, like her. The Coven of Flowers of the Southeast took pity on her and paid her Mesmortes tuition.

And though her mom sent what she could, Thalia's side hustle was a low-effort way to supplement the money she made from being a resident assistant. Plus, her favorite cauldron had a crack in it, and she wanted a new, non-thrifted uniform. If she'd taken a job with Suzette, the elder witch would've tried to get to know Thalia. Anders Osnes only ever asked her where to meet, and how long until the next batch.

She texted back: **Saturday, dawn, the chapel.**

Her finger hovered over the next text down, the one she was trying to ignore.

**I know it's risky, but I miss my girl.**

Her mother was persistent.

Thalia's mind raced. She loved her mom, but their relationship was strange. They were less mother and daughter, and more partners in crime—Thalia, a fugitive. Fiona, a double agent. The responsibilities had flipped, too. Thalia should've been the one begging to see her mother and being talked down from those desires, reminded that things were still too dangerous. Instead, it was Thalia who constantly snapped Fiona back to reality. It was Thalia who was putting money aside to get them a safe place away from her father. Once she graduated, once she'd become a stronger, more experienced witch, she could keep them both safe. But until then, they had to be careful.

Swallowing hard, she texted back.

**It's too dangerous.**

Her heart racing, she lifted her rusty old cauldron onto her desk. She dropped in crow's foot from the campus apothecary, maiden's hair from the herbalism lab, devil's ivy from the vines growing all around her cabin, and just a droplet of perfume from Jailah's dresser, for comfort. From the locked wooden box in the corner, she found a familiar blue vial and poured a few drops of its thick red contents into the cauldron.

*"An Abomination,"* she whispered, tapping it with her wand.

A green plume of smoke grew from the cauldron. Thalia inhaled.

Though thousands of miles away, her father appeared before her, pacing the cabin floors with a hardened face. He was talking in that animated way that made people believe his words, whatever they might be. The people of Annex went to church every day, and he was their favorite vessel for the word of God. He'd gone gray. His pale skin was tough and wrinkled, perhaps as much the sun's fault as his age. She wondered how he could've grown so old in just two years.

"I hate you," she whispered coldly, knocking the cauldron away in a fit of anger. It hit the floor, the crack at the top growing deeper. Abraham Turner's presence vanished, leaving only a faint trickle of smoke in the air.

Her father was a good man. That's what people always told her. Good enough for them to overlook his Black wife, for a time. God-fearing, charitable, and insistent in keeping Annex a bleedbay, a city that still had its witch-killing laws. It was one of fifteen remaining across the country. She wondered if he missed his old shotgun, the one that was currently hidden under Thalia's bed, chamber empty, the safety locked into place by unbreakable vines. Another souvenir. She'd taken it not only so he couldn't use it on her, but to be petty. She knew it'd make him furious.

They made each other promises, Thalia and her father. He promised that for the death and destruction her magic caused, he'd stone her, for God told him so. Thalia promised him the same thing Jesus described when Lucifer was banished from heaven.

*I will see you fall like lightning.*

She realized someone was knocking at the door.

"Thalia?" the voice said, small but spunky. "You in there?"

She opened the door to Morgan Ramirez bouncing up and down on her porch.

"I'm so sorry. I know you don't like us to come here, but there's an emergency!"

Though Thalia made a point to know everything about all of her residents, Morgan stood out to her from the moment they first met, pronouns written in all caps on their name badge. She had so much fondness for this young witch who navigated the world on their own terms.

"Emergency? Morgan, stop that." She pressed her hands to their shoulders to keep them still.

"Katie and Delaney want to switch roommates because Delaney accidentally knocked over Katie's last vial of dove droppings, so Katie was all, Screw off, Delaney! And Delaney was all, Well, screw you, too! And I was all— Thalia?"

Thalia's thoughts had drifted to a plot of land in a little desert town. She refocused. "Huh?"

"Now Delaney insists on sleeping on me and Jenna's floor, which is not going to work! You have to tell them to make up!"

Thalia chuckled. This was her home now, this land, the school, and witches like Morgan who lived on her floor, always looking up to her. It was Iris and Jailah and maybe new girl Logan, and her wand, always sure in its sparks of life. "All right, let's go talk it out."

She led Morgan back toward the Hill, her thoughts settling into a plan. She ran her fingers over the Gothic font on her wrist. Thalia couldn't take back what she'd done, but perhaps she could find forgiveness in another way. Rectifying the life she took by breaking the curse on Haelsford.

It was a goal that gave her purpose, which all of her Catholic upbringing told her was a necessity in life. Maybe they'd give her sainthood, the Girl Who Healed the Swamp. That was real atonement. For all she'd done to turn her back on the God who turned his back on her, she couldn't shake her fear of heaven's closed gates. Her mother used to say that Catholic guilt grew like weeds. *By the time you realize it ain't a harmless shrub, it's too late.*

But Thalia felt in her deepest witchy instincts that even if she ended the Haunting, there were others who wanted her head, worse than Wolves because they didn't operate in the supernatural but in money, and whiteness, and privilege.

Thalia knew that her story would end in one of two ways—with her death, or her father's.

# 12
## logan

**Two weeks until the Haunting Season**

Dusk was breaking all around Mesmortes.

Formative Protections was Logan's last class, and though she usually got out before the first dinner bell, Professor Ahmed had held her back for a chat about her *interesting abilities*.

According to the professor, Logan's unpredictable magic was nothing to fuss over. It was, as she put it, *perfectly normal for a new witch*, which just made Logan feel worse. Not only was Logan terrible with a wand, but she wasn't even special in her awfulness.

She skipped dinner and walked back to her room. She thought a school like Mesmortes was what she'd needed to snap her magic into place. A bit of exposure therapy, like delving into a tank of spiders. Mesmortes had promised her this with the pamphlet that arrived at her door in a lush black envelope. *Come to Haelsford. Let us show you the witch you were born to be.*

Logan rubbed her eyes. *If the professors can't help me, then who can?*

She wasn't sure why, but her thoughts drifted to the Roddin Witch, who had inspected her with interest and curiosity. It was fleeting. Just imagining herself walking into the Emporium made her palms sweaty.

Logan changed into her favorite pajamas, turned on the dehumidifier, switched off the light, and pulled the sheets over her head. She fell hard into the type of sleep reserved for high fevers and the haze of the meds taken to break them.

The dream came to her all at once.

She saw a brown-haired boy sitting on the porch of the old general store, watching the men and their horses go by. His pale skin was nearly sunburnt, his green eyes wide and curious. The preacher's daughters went past, their hands over their faces to shield their delicate complexions. The boy tilted his chin down, an acknowledgment of their presence, something small and respectful. Nothing to earn him the stern look of their father, who did nothing in his life but preach chastity and witch aversion. The preacher did love a hanging. A burning. A stoning. The man of God had hands as bloody as the butcher's boy.

Logan could feel all these things like she *was* him, like she knew these people and had lived this life. She even felt the nerves lurch in the boy's stomach as tangibly as if they were her own.

It was autumn, and the land was ripe with its last usable pickings. People spent the days greeting everyone they met with warm smiles and happy words, like it was Christmastime. It was *not* Christmastime. It was the Hunting Season.

Another year, another festive massacre. It'd come so soon. The boy was still scarred from the last year. He remembered her—and so Logan did, too—the witch they'd tied to a horse and dragged on the Oak Trail, winding through town. Her screams haunted him every night, a lullaby of horrors.

All he'd done was watch. But he was seventeen now. He couldn't hide anymore.

Hysteria exploded at the town square. Something startled the horses, and their riders desperately yelled out commands. The boy stood, stepping up the stairs to get a better look.

Men shouted to clear the way, pushing against the crowd that gathered. Before they blocked his view, the boy saw the girls.

*New victims*, he thought instantly. But they didn't look much like witches.

There was a girl's voice in the fold. Small and frantic, she cried out for help. It chilled him. The boy moved closer but was immediately pulled back by a grisly man who smelled of dark beer and fresh tobacco.

"Go fetch Father!" the man said.

When he let go, the boy fell to the ground. "Has there been an attack?"

"Get off your ass!" His brother raised his hand sharply, and the boy flinched. Logan twitched in her sleep.

He forced himself away, even as the cry of one girl became that of three.

They brought the girls to his father's living room floor. They were sisters, and they shivered even in the heat.

The boy's father put his stethoscope to their chests. He listened to their pulses and examined their pupils. The boy pressed cool cloths to their foreheads. His brothers waited in the kitchen, arms crossed. They were tall and mighty, and the two of them together suddenly made the space feel smaller.

Something tugged the boy's sleeve. It was the youngest girl, deathly pale. "There's something in my throat," she whispered hoarsely. "Might I have a glass of water?"

The boy fetched the water. The men watched as he handed it to the girl. She gulped it down.

She was halfway through when she cried out. Something sludgy slithered from her mouth and into the glass. The boy jumped backward. The water turned black as she vomited up sludge-like tar.

"She's been touched by a witch!" one of the other girls screamed out, holding her own throat.

The boy backed up against the wall, wide-eyed and frozen.

It was too much. He was not built for this.

"The witch cursed us," said the other. This one was less frantic, her words an utterly unnerving type of calm. Bleak and unemotional. "*All* of us. We're doomed to burn in hell."

The boy couldn't focus. He only saw the girl's black-slicked mouth, the fuzz lining her teeth.

He turned away and—with frightening reality—looked directly at Logan.

His brow twitched in confusion. He opened his mouth to speak—

Logan woke abruptly, wrapped up in a cocoon of sweaty sheets. Her mind was a blur. This wasn't a normal nightmare. The delirium didn't break once she jolted awake. The world she saw *clung* to her.

She couldn't shake the feel of the boy's eyes on her.

She forced herself out of bed and splashed cold water on her face. Hands clenched against the sides of the sink, she looked at her reflection. Logan opened her mouth wide to make sure there was nothing sprouting in her throat. She was sure she'd felt something there.

As she reached for a towel, there was a flash of gold.

Logan could do nothing but gape at her sunshine-tinted fingertips. A sudden energy bubbled up within her. Light. Power. Witchery.

She proxied.

The last time this happened was just a few months ago. Logan was in the

Mesmortes auditorium with fifty other baby witches. Most received their blessing at thirteen, and so at sixteen, Logan was the oldest in the room. She'd been told that receiving such a late blessing wasn't completely uncommon, but sitting with the others like this? Logan was acutely aware of how much she stuck out.

Professor Circe had been testing Pulls, and as Logan expected, nothing called forward her magic. Not the single clover growing in a glass orb, not the flame, the water, the flecks of skin, the piece of a weathered bone. Until Professor Circe undid the clasp of the golden, egg-shaped trinket in her hand.

"Last thing—" She revealed a small heap of glittery white powder within the trinket.

Logan went tense all over.

"This is ash of an amplyfyr. You only need to press your finger against the ash, Wyatt."

When Logan touched the dust, it was like she was hit with a painful yet euphoric punch in the face. A deep breath, and suddenly, witchery drowned her.

It was over in a flash, but Logan's fingers still pulsed with yellow light.

Circe did a double take. "You're a proxy!" She looked through Logan's file. "Why didn't you tell anyone?"

*Because my witchery doesn't work.* "I didn't think it was a big deal."

And she truly hadn't, until now.

A nightmare had come to her, and she proxied.

Her breath quickened as she considered what she'd seen. Three strange sisters who stumbled into Haelsford speaking of witchery. A kind boy, hesitant to hurt witches.

Could it be?

*The Wolf Boy. The Strigwach Sisters.*

"Holy crap." She swallowed hard. She didn't know what the Strigwachs looked like, or if the Wolf Boy was more than a hopeful tale. But she knew in the pit of her stomach that this wasn't a regular dream. And if that gut feeling wasn't enough, the light brimming through her fingers was surely a sign that something special was happening.

She wanted to tell the others. She wanted to go screaming into the hallway, knock on Iris's door, and show her. *I proxied! And my power brought me a dream that might help you.*

But then what? Even as she stood there thinking about what to do next, the light in her fingers subsided.

When she tried to harness this unfamiliar wave of witchery, she felt like the entire room was going to go up in flames.

# 13

## mathew

Mathew Beaumont pulled off his riding cap and shook the sweat from his hair. It was always hot, but it was too hot for this—watching Basil Haelsford and the rest of the freshmen attempt to goad their mares over the hurdles.

Basil was nice, eons less insufferable than his older brother, but Mathew disliked him because he was lazy, easily frustrated, and couldn't understand that horses weren't cars. He couldn't just buy Mountain, advertised as the fastest horse in the South, and expect her to comply. You had to forge something from mutual respect first, after hundreds of hours toiling in the mud, rain, and heat, with tempers flaring and leather reins biting your palms.

*And what kind of name is Basil anyway?*

The freshmen riders were in a sorry state, but Mathew couldn't bring himself to care. His head hurt from thinking too much about other things.

He let the rumor mill spin that he'd been some sort of charming rogue, expertly flirting his way to the attention of a witch. The truth was, he was terrified . . . and a little drunk that night. It wasn't like him to actively attract a witch's gaze. That was Trent's thing, staring down witches like, *Hex me, I dare you.* Mathew was more like, *Please don't look at me.*

Atop Ruby, Mathew blew his whistle. "A truly awful showing, people.

All right, bring 'em in." Sasha, the new stable hand from town, hurried over and took Mountain's reins. She gestured for Ruby, but Mathew shook his head. "It's okay. I got her."

Blushing, Sasha led Mountain away.

"How do you do that?" Basil asked, sucking in a breath through his teeth.

Mathew stroked behind Ruby's ears. "Do what?"

"Get girls to blush like that."

Mathew blinked. "Basil. Go get some rest."

He led Ruby into her stall and filled her grain trough. He patted her, planted a kiss on her neck, and whispered, "Good girl."

One of the nearby buckets hanging from a stall swung ominously. Movement flashed in the shadows. Ruby reared and whinnied, all spooked and skittish. And there was that heat. Different from the Florida sun, bending the air around him.

*She found me.*

"You kissed your horse," the witch said plainly, flipping her braids over her shoulder.

Not what he expected her first words to be. The simplicity of them amused Mathew, but he didn't smile. "I did." He got the brush out, humming sweetly as he stroked Ruby's hair. He kept his hands steady, even as his heart thrummed and his palms went clammy.

She drummed her fingers against the strap of her knapsack, the sunlight glinting off her numerous gold rings. "Am I scaring her?"

"You are."

She leaned against the stall door. "Am I scaring *you*?"

"No."

She smiled like she could sense the lie.

Mathew backed away to resume his work. "Her name's Ruby. You can pet her if you want."

She examined him with the darkest eyes he'd ever seen, a frown growing on her glossy red lips. "What's your deal? It seems like everyone knows who you are."

"Everyone but you, apparently."

"I don't care much for Hammersmitts."

He grinned through the tension. "I'm honored to be your first."

Her face twitched, resisting an eye roll. "Hallowe'en night. Because of you, I saw the Chasm."

Mathew looked her up and down. She didn't know about the heirloom; she . . . she thought it was something in *him* that caused what happened on Hallowe'en. Was that even possible?

Mathew leveled his voice, made it hardly bothered. "I don't know what the Chasm is."

"It's a purgatory that traps restless souls." She matched his cool tone.

Mathew inhaled sharply. "You're a necromancer."

*Roddin's* necromancer.

*Deathwitch Foster.*

She laughed a little. "Uh, duh."

*Like it's no big.*

She was a witch; she was literally magic. Mathew got that, but he couldn't understand necromancy being this casual thing. Shaking his head, he grabbed a stool from the corner and placed Ruby's hoof in his lap. Delicately, he picked away at the dirt in her horseshoe.

Abruptly, Ruby bucked forward, showing teeth.

Mathew hadn't noticed that the witch was in the stall until her hand was outstretched, her fingers wrapped around his bicep. He didn't move, but he met her stare with one of his own. He wondered if she could feel his pulse pounding through his skin.

They both waited in silence.

Seemingly unsatisfied, the witch released him. "Your turn."

"My turn?"

"Touch me."

He couldn't resist a smirk. "Oh—"

She clicked her tongue. It sounded like a warning. "Whatever you were gonna say, keep it."

He bit back the chuckle. Shoulders relaxing, he touched her arm gently. The witch slowed her breathing, as if that might trigger the chaos that happened the last time they spoke. He knew this was all useless. The heirloom wasn't on him.

"You're not a witch," she whispered.

"No."

"Parents? Siblings?"

He shook his head. "Not a witch in either of my parents' lines." She didn't need to know that that was precisely why they'd gotten married. "I'm Mathew," he said softly, for no other reason than it felt weird to be sitting there with his hand on her body without telling her his name. "Beaumont," he added.

"Yeah, I know," she replied, pulling away. "I'm Iris."

"Foster, right?" he asked.

"Keaton-Foster." She blew out a breath. "Don't freak out, but I need some of your blood."

His brow shot up. She'd said it like she needed to borrow a pencil. He would've laughed if she didn't look so serious. "Uh. Am I allowed to ask why?"

"I just need to know what you are." She drew a needle. "Don't worry—it's self-sterilizing."

He fidgeted. "Look, I don't know what happened on Hallowe'en—"

Her gaze softened. "Please?"

No was the rational answer. Who knew what a witch could do with his blood, and a deathwitch at that, one who seemed overly familiar with the Roddin Witch. But the slight discomfort in her posture and the desperation of her gaze had him thinking irrationally.

Holding on to that hint of her vulnerability, he extended his arm to her.

She placed her hand under his. He flexed his fingers. She was close, and he found himself examining the small mole near her eye, her dark lashes, the smoothness of her deep brown skin. Her eyes flicked down at him suddenly, and he looked away.

"Do you need me to count to five?" she asked.

He shook his head, his lips curling into a smile.

The witch—*Iris*—collected a few droplets of blood from his thumb into a little vial strung around her neck, adding it to the collection of trinkets already there.

"Thanks," she whispered, hardly audible over the whistling wind. Before he pulled away, she pressed her thumb against his and pointed her wand. *"A Stitch."*

He rubbed his forefinger against his smooth thumb, then pointed at the vial necklace. "Does this mean we're going steady?"

Iris bit the inside of her cheek. There might've been a smile. "Careful how you speak, Beaumont, to a witch who has your blood."

Mathew swallowed hard. There was something unsettling about hearing his name on her tongue, like her saliva turned to venom around it. "What are you going to do with it?"

"Nothing bad. Scout's honor." She showed him a viper-like grin. "Hey, have you been asking around about me?"

"No. Thought I'd steer clear of the girl who called me an asshole."

"Hm. I just thought you might be as curious about me as I am about you." Iris shrugged. "My bad."

If it were anyone else, he might've thought she was flirting.

"You've heard of the Wolf Boy, right?"

"Of course."

"Do you believe any of it?"

Mathew wouldn't dare laugh. Her face was sharp in its seriousness.

"I'm looking for him." Before he could answer, she twirled her wand and said, "Well. This has been incredibly disappointing. See you never. *Take Me Away.*"

She vanished, suddenly there, and then suddenly not.

Mathew felt the curiosity wade up in him, but he pushed it away. Visions of ghosts and blood and possessive stones were not worth his time, not when he couldn't make sense of it, and especially not if it meant dealing with girls like *her*.

He closed his hand around his pricked and stitched thumb, clutching his fist to his chest.

"I'm so done with witches," he said to Ruby, then sighed.

Because even saying it aloud wasn't enough to convince him of it.

# 14

## thalia

**Two weeks until the Haunting Season**

Thalia couldn't concentrate on Professor Fournier's lesson. She was looking out the window toward the Swamp. Every day brought them closer to the Haunting Season, and she could feel the corrupted magic of the Swamp growing.

She wasn't in the mood for lessons, thoroughly distracted by the most recent letter from her aunt Nonni, burning a hole in her Mesmortes-branded knapsack. Thalia had one rule: Do not initiate contact with *him*. That's it, and she felt like it was fair, but Nonni had decided to be brazen.

While Thalia's mother, Fiona, remained in Annex as a way to keep an eye on her father's plans and, in turn, keep Thalia safe, Abraham Turner did not know that it was his own sister who smuggled Thalia across the country. Thalia had asked that Nonni keep her distance from him, lest she accidentally give something up. But Aunt Nonni, for some reason, had written her to say: *I think I could get through to him.*

Thalia had sent two words in response. *I don't.*

Jenna Prim's laughter brought her back to class. She could feel

Professor Fournier's eyes on her as she circled the room with a ruler.

Thalia poked the potted plant in front of her. Immediately, it bristled with life.

She liked school. She worked hard and got good grades, but it was difficult to find anything exciting when she once lived in a coven of elder greenwitches who'd shown her how to be one with the earth. Besides, she had other things to worry about. Little things, like, *Keeping my location from an entire village of people who want to see me burned*. She was more concerned with what would happen after school. Next year after graduation, would she go back to Annex? Would she face them?

"Yours is looking a little short," Jenna muttered, admiring her own healthy cypress.

With a chuckle, Thalia straightened her crooked glasses. "Not for long."

She pressed her hands to either side of the pot. Jenna looked on eagerly, as she always did. *Nerd*, Thalia thought fondly. A freshman in a junior-level class. Jenna had no Pull to greenwitchery; she just worked on her magic with tireless devotion.

Thalia pricked her finger and stuck it into the soil. The plant bristled. She felt the life of it thrum against her skin and pulse in her veins. *It's like playing God, Talullah*, one of the elders of the Coven of Flowers had once said, her voice sweet.

She raised her wand, and the plant grew and grew, wanting to reach her touch. By the time Professor Fournier came around, it was the tallest one in class. The professor didn't bother with the ruler, she only winked at Thalia and moved on.

"You don't even need an incantation," Jenna said in breathless admiration. "So cool."

The lesson was interrupted by a sudden high-pitched alarm. Jenna groaned, and Thalia brought her hands to her ears.

"Another drill?" Layla Marks whined from behind them.

An image of their headmistress appeared in the center of the room like a ghost.

"WITCHES OF MESMORTES, THIS IS A DRILL. WOLVES HAVE BROKEN THROUGH THE PROTECTION BARRIER AND HAVE INFILTRATED THE HILL. SEEK SHELTER IN YOUR DORM'S HOLLOW ROOM."

Many of the students hurried out of eagerness to ditch class early. Professor Fournier only sighed and shooed them away. "We'll resume tomorrow!"

Thalia filed out of the greenhouse. She made for Bramblewynn House, Jenna on her tail. Others marched to the other dorms: Topthorne, Laarsen, and Terrywood.

The headmistress's warning blared through the halls once more, and though it was annoying, Thalia was happy for the distraction from her own thoughts.

"Go to the hollow room," she instructed Jenna as they made their way through the crowds of ambling witches, none of them taking this very seriously. "I'll meet you there for roll!"

Thalia was sticking the key into her room door when Jailah popped up out of nowhere and scared the shit out of her.

"Jailah! *God!*" Thalia shrieked.

"Oh, my sweet T, so jumpy!" Jailah twirled her curls with gentle fingers.

Thalia huffed. "It's been a rough day."

Jailah eyed her curiously. She knew not to ask for details.

Jai was the only Haelsfordian who knew about Talullah Turner.

They'd been freshmen, and they were trading secrets, about themselves, about each other. Back then, they'd only known each other through Iris and were in that weird stage where they never really hung out without her.

Jailah had nervously nibbled on her pen. "I like girls."

Thalia bit her lip. "I'm on the run."

She hadn't revealed the whole story. Thalia couldn't bear parting with the secret of her crimes, so she kept the inciting incident vague and focused on the journey that brought her to Aunt Nonni, the Coven of Flowers of the Southeast, and, finally, to Haelsford.

In Annex, she was a child with blood on her hands.

Here, she was a revelation.

Thalia hoped one day to be so powerful that her hair would turn white and she'd have sprouts popping up out of her flesh.

Then she'd return to Annex.

She couldn't remember why she'd told Jailah all of this, only that it felt like a grave mistake and a great relief at the same time. Thalia looked at her now, never more certain that she'd done the right thing, even if Jailah annoyed her sometimes.

"I'm sorry for scaring you," Jailah said, batting her eyelashes. "I'm gonna bake you a cake!" She was the type that wouldn't ever rest if she thought someone she loved was angry with her.

"You know what I like," Thalia muttered, opening the door. "Give me a second."

She hung her cape and top hat on one of the countless curved branches growing through the walls. The sheer amount of green throughout the room made it look abandoned, like a tree house that hadn't been attended to in years. If not for the clothes on the floor, the books on the desk, and the vials floating around, it would've looked unlived in. Just how Thalia liked it.

As the floor RA, she needed to go to the hollow room. But she also needed a minute alone. She timed it perfectly—when the headmistress's voice rang out once more with the alarms, she let out a frustrated scream.

*Your father is not here.*

Thalia breathed in through her nose.

*He is in Annex. You are in Haelsford.*

Straightened her back.

*Your mother loves you, and Aunt Nonni would never betray you. You are safe.*

She slipped out of her room and flashed Jai a small smile. "Okay, I'm good."

With Jailah in tow, Thalia opened the hollow room door to a gaggle of chattering freshmen.

"Roll," she said, and the witches calmly counted off and spouted green sparks from the end of their wands.

The sixth-floor hollow room was between 27 A and B. It looked like a safe—wide and silver and cold. The tall candles in each corner were always lit. The windows were covered with thick drapes, and when everyone was inside, the door sealed itself shut.

Jailah wrapped her arms around herself. "The one on my floor in Laarsen House has a TV."

"I never got around to decorating," Thalia muttered.

The headmistress appeared again. "THIS IS A DRILL: WOLVES HAVE BEEN SPOTTED ON THE MESMORTES CAMPUS. TAKE SHELTER. REMAIN CALM."

Jenna snapped selfies next to the apparition. "This is boring!"

"Let's do trust falls!" Morgan Ramirez said, and they looked to Thalia for approval even though their tone didn't imply that they were asking for permission.

"Be careful," Thalia replied.

She and Jailah sat against the wall. The younger witches formed a circle. Giggling from the middle of it, Jenna Prim pricked her finger and sent Lilly Han into the air with a levitation spell so lurchy that she almost hit the ceiling.

"Careful!" Thalia and Jailah shouted at the same time.

"I got it!" Jenna said, smirking.

Her wand wavering a little, her face furrowed with concentration, Jenna drew away her hand.

Lilly fell from the ceiling with a cut so sharp, the others shrieked. But Jenna stopped her just before she could crack her skull against the floor.

Thalia watched them put their lives in one another's hands. She rubbed at her tattoo. "We gotta help Logan. She should love her witchery like this."

Jailah nodded. "You got a plan?"

"Yeah, I got a plan."

If there was one thing she remembered about the day she told Jailah her secret, it was that they were ferociously close in that one tense moment. It was the indescribable kind of friendship that no one had given Thalia until then, the kind that she never knew she ached for.

# 15
## logan

**One week until the Haunting Season**

The Everglades were on fire. The archery fields smelled like smoke from the acres of land burning up just fifteen miles away. The homegrown Haelsfordians seemed unbothered. Apparently, these fires were common, and what could really scare anyone who lived with Wolves in their backyard every winter?

"You got this!" Iris shouted. She had one arm hooked over the stone arm of Hattie Mesmortes, and she swung from it gleefully.

Jailah cupped her hands around her mouth and shouted encouragements that Logan could barely hear over her own ragged breaths. Thalia stood in front of Logan, gray eyes glinting in the moonlight, her bloody thumb pressed against the thin skin of Logan's inner elbow. Smoke hovered in the air from Logan's shitty attempts at the Haunting protection spells.

"It's okay. We'll keep trying," Thalia whispered. She was trying to be soothing, but Logan could hear the fatigue in her voice.

"Can't you give me something?"

"What, calming elixir?"

"No, like, something to make me stronger, like when we got tested for Pulls—"

"An amplyfyr?" Thalia frowned. "Your magic is clearly strong already. You're trying to learn it, to control it, not multiply it."

"At this point, I'd try anything." Logan drew her hand away.

Jailah joined them. "Good job!"

Logan gritted her teeth. "I didn't do anything but contribute to Haelsford's poor air quality index."

"But you tried! That counts for something, right, Iris?"

Iris was unfocused. Her gaze went distant, as if she'd forgotten where she was.

"Hellooooo?" Jailah waved her hand in front of the deathwitch's face.

Iris didn't seem to see her. She stretched slowly. Her palms angled outward, her braids splayed out in the air, and her feet lifted a few inches off the ground.

"Oh, here she goes." Thalia wiped her glasses on her cape. "Who is it this time? Murder victim need you to avenge them?"

"Nah." Jailah smirked. "Hot ghost boy looking for his deathwitch bae."

They laughed.

When Iris spoke, she had two voices at once. One was her own, but the other was richer and much older. "Yeah, yeah, y'all are *sooo* funny."

And the laughter stopped. Logan's own fear surfaced as Jai's brow furrowed and Thalia took a step backward. Whatever they'd seen of Iris's death magic in the past, this was different.

Iris's body kept still except for her mouth. "Guys. Meet Madeline Donahue. She's going to help us end the Haunting."

The night was warm, but Logan shivered.

"Oh!" Jailah reached out and touched Iris's cold hand. "You're a legend! I'm Jai, I'm sure Iris has told you about me, about us, we're her friends, nice to meet you!"

Thalia's disposition was less sunny, though she seemed relieved. "What have you found?"

Iris's fingers twitched. *"It is not what I have found, but what you must find. Four witch girls here, so four answers I will give. Then you and I will both be free."*

"Who is the Wolf Boy?" Iris asked immediately, in her own voice.

And she answered in another. *"His name has been scrubbed away. He is blessed and he is cursed."*

"Where is the Wolf Boy?" Jailah asked.

*"His bones remain in Haelsford, like so many of the Wolves' kills."*

Iris's hand opened toward Thalia.

Thalia crossed her arms. "What do we need to end the Haunting?"

*"The boy holds your absolution. It can only end after it has begun. The Wolves must be awake to be put to sleep."*

Logan forced out the words. "How can I help?"

*"You are the anchor."*

The answer was worse than she could've imagined.

Her heart thrummed. "What? How?"

Iris breathed out, her body rattling as she floated to the ground. Every bit of her personality was restored as she immediately launched into a spiel about the Wolf Boy. Jailah and even skeptical Thalia joined her, theorizing on what these messages meant.

Iris gleefully threw her arm around Logan. "See, I told you! You're a part of this. We're gonna save Haelsford, baby witch."

Logan attempted a smile. She wanted to be excited with them, but Madeline Donahue's words only made her more uncertain of her witchery.

Things had changed since Hallowe'en. She hadn't felt quite right since that time in Roddin's shop. More not-right than before—everything still blew up around her, her potions went sour, and the cactus she was looking after for Remedial Herbalism died within two days, to Thalia's horror. She was used to these things.

But when she slept, she dreamed in fragmented clips of the Haelsford she'd never lived in, that place the Red Three showed her in smoky vignettes. She didn't want to hide this, but she couldn't tell them, not until she felt like she could be the witch that they wanted her to be. Whenever these hallucinations came to her, her witchery surged. Was that what the Madwoman of Haelsford meant as she spoke through Iris? The anchor. As a proxy, was she meant to bring everything together?

She imagined going back to her family with her own legendary accomplishment: *I helped break the curse of Haelsford. I played a part in ending the Wolves.*

⋯⋯➤ ✪ ◀⋯⋯

She had visited Roddin's in the early morning, knowing what she needed from the unwitch. She was tired of waiting for dreams and hallucinations, or for magic to come to her.

To find the Wolf Boy in her dreams, she would have to scry for him.

Logan had never attempted it, but she had once seen Margot scry. Perched over her sister's shoulder, Logan had felt Margot's skin grow pale and cold. At first, Margot had wept tears of joy, for the vision she'd chosen to relive was one where their father had never left them. But when Margot grew lost in the finger-length sliver of scrying glass, their mother had to rip the glass away from Margot's bleeding fingers. Logan had never seen her so furious, or so terrified.

*Never again*, Diane Wyatt had said.

In the shop, Roddin had prodded Logan. "You are not scared of being taken by it?"

She hadn't answered. "How much?"

Roddin's eyes softened. "Repay me by keeping your wits."

And when Logan eyed the necklace of hexed jade on her way out, Roddin let her have that, too. Logan had slipped the heavy chain around her neck and felt the soft heat of her mother's *Look* subside.

Now in her dorm room, she lifted the scrying glass. It'd been the ugliest one in Roddin's shop. With jagged, sharp edges, it looked like a star, but as if the angles were done without care. When she looked into it head-on, her left eye and a slice of her chin were missing. But it fit well in her hand, the edges effortlessly melding into the space between her fingers.

"Show me the Wolf Boy, the boy from my dreams," she whispered.

He came to her in a haze of smoke. He brought old Haelsford with him, and suddenly Logan saw a whole world in the piece of misshapen glass. It was even more real than in her dreams, though she could feel the wooden floor of her dorm under her crossed legs, grounding her to reality.

She enjoyed magic like this. The type that didn't ask for her wand and a mouthful of words. Just some blood, a thought, and a look. If only all witchy things made use of a magicked object like scrying glass. The glass showed her Mesmortes Chapel, pristine and pure, nothing like the haunted thing it was now.

"There were three witches that attacked us!" one of the sisters said from the altar. Sloane Strigwach, Logan wagered. The middle child. Her pale cheeks were flushed as she fueled the congregation's fury. "They flew onto our farm and declared their love of the dark prince. They killed our father first, then our mother, and tortured our little brother! Will you hunt them down?"

The men in the pews shouted in bloodthirsty affirmations.

A dark-haired witch appeared like a wraith from behind Sloane. Adelaide. Her green eyes burned with anger. "Find our attackers before they set their sights on others! Before they come here!"

*And this is how they do it*, Logan thought. *This is how they enraptured the town. With love and bloodlust.*

In the pews, the youngest sister turned to the boy next to her. Mathilde placed her silk-gloved hand on his. He looked at Mathilde, and Logan knew that look even if she'd never felt it before. The town might have loved the girls for stoking their gruesome need of witchblood, but the boy had fallen completely for this one alone.

Logan pushed away a stupid flit of longing.

Suddenly, the vision melted into another.

When all the hunters left town with their guns and knives, with their maces and rope, the Strigwachs called their Wolves.

Logan watched in silent awe. Twenty enormous Wolves bloomed from the black muck of the Swamp, their copper fur covered in the filth of it. With sharp teeth and crooked claws, they stepped onto solid land. Red sludge leaked from their eyes like they were weeping blood, and Logan forced back the bile that rose in her throat. None of the stories had prepared her to see the beasts in all their wretched glory.

They howled. Logan thought it sounded like a chorus of human screams.

Then the Wolves crashed into the unguarded town.

Logan released a choked gasp at the Wolves' unrepentant violence. They ripped apart the weak mundanes who were left behind from the Hunting, their teeth furiously burrowing into their flesh.

The vision shifted once more. The boy was running, and even in the near dark, Logan knew that he was in the Cavern. He was being hunted, but not by a Wolf.

"Wait!" a voice cried out. It was so sharp that Logan was surprised to see frail Mathilde. "Don't run from me!"

An explosive flash of light from her wand illuminated the Cavern. Guarding himself from it, the boy stumbled into a corner of rock.

The Strigwach stood before the boy, wand raised. Even as she cornered him, he had that look of love.

"I will save us all," she said, teeming with love herself. "And you, my little wolfboy."

As she began to incant, the Wolf Boy turned to Logan, eyes wrenched in desperation. "Help me!"

It jolted Logan out of the vision so forcefully that she fumbled the glass.

"No!" Logan shrieked as the scrying glass shattered.

She put her hands over the pieces, then dropped them uselessly into her lap. She knew she couldn't fix the mirror, and likely would've just set it all aflame.

Logan closed her eyes and breathed deeply. She didn't know his name or what Mathilde did to him. But her hands were warm. The sight of her witchery glowing like sunlight in her shaking fingers convinced her that the dreams and visions she'd seen were true. Her magic was doing it for her, even if she wasn't the one to call it.

And she felt so, so, so *witchy*.

# 16

## jailah

**The Night of the Haunting Season**

Jailah Simmons breathed out.

The arrow flung from her bow: sharp, exact, tight.

As if rigged with magnets, the arrow found the target—a scarecrow marked HAMMERSMITT with great red letters.

She owned it all. The archery field. The humidity slicking her grip. The touch of dirt on her contacts. Jailah wasn't team captain—she had no time for it on top of Junior Witchery Council and classes and the Haunting. She *knew* she was the best of the best. But Hardy Schrader, with her trembling hands, had seniority and wanted it so badly.

*Please, Jailah, just drop out of the race. I need this. You'll get it next year.*

"Haven't seen you like this since Veronica was on the team." Layla Marks said this sweetly, but anyone with a lick of sense knew she was taunting. You didn't bring up a hexbound ex-girlfriend without questionable intentions.

Jailah sent another arrow toward the hay-stuffed Hammersmitt. It went sailing overhead, a rare shot missed. "Layla, honey, you're blocking my light. Scooch a li'l, won't you?" she said.

"You must miss her, no? The girl who got you into all this."

There was a slight hush. The other witches had turned up to witness Jailah's golden arm, but now on the agenda was a little fun, the type to gossip and giggle about later.

"Miss her?" Jailah's sweet Southern tongue spun sugar around her words. "You say that like I have time to! You'll know what that's like when you've finally made varsity."

Layla reddened, clear as day on this darkening night. Hardly looking, Jailah sent her last arrow into the strawman's skull.

She slung her bow over her shoulder, leaving the arrows for some freshmen to pluck out, in awe of the inconceivable prowess of Jailah Simmons. "I'll see you all later. Get your game faces on. We've got a town to protect."

Never mind Layla Marks's little taunts, or the fact that Jailah went into town that morning to buy her favorite shade of lipstick and saw a girl watching her. Tonight was important. It was December 1 and the Wolves were waking up.

The girl wore a snapback and had smudged purple eye shadow all over her eyes like someone Jailah once knew. Though they stood a road apart, Jai could see that her skin had a sickly glow, the kind that came from having your witchery hexed into metaphorical shackles.

The girl wasn't supposed to be seen, clear from the way she jerked back when Jailah met her eye. The unwitch tried to keep steady, those eyes meant to be intimidating and cruel, but Jailah smiled and blew a kiss. It said, *Tell Vero I said hey.*

Jailah shook off those thoughts. Vero was in the past, and tonight was about the future.

She ran up to her room in Laarsen House to shower and change. She looked like a dream come true—flawless skin, massive fro, glossy brown lips. Her smile was staggering, her batted eyelashes a charm. Dressing up made her feel just as good as nocking an arrow and watching it fly. When their histories told of the first time the Mesmortes Coven Academy protected the mundanes of Hammersmitt, she would not be a footnote. Her name would be distinguished in the history books.

The others were waiting at the bottom of the Hill. Thalia, with her always-slanted glasses, played fetch with Maverick. Logan watched, her hair a mess, her smile soft and shy. Iris had her hands on her hips and a scowl that softened once Jailah flashed her a grin and asked, "Y'all ready?"

Together, they walked toward the Box Chant.

"A few reminders." Jailah counted them off on her fingers. "No hostility. We can be a little smug, but not mean. Whatever they give us, we need to be gracious."

Thalia made a tree move aside its low-hanging branches with just a touch to its trunk. "Any last bets?"

"It's gonna be something boring, I'm telling you," Iris muttered, kicking a moss-covered stone out of her way with more force than necessary. "Like some sanctified candles or new cauldrons."

Thalia perked up. "Like, those brass ones? I'd take 'em."

*Does it matter?* Jailah thought. "I'm just happy we're all here, doing this. What a night." She turned to Logan. "How ya feeling?"

"I feel like I shouldn't even be here," Logan admitted. "You guys are the ones who convinced the Witchery Council to let Mesmortes protect the Hill. This is your thing. And, uh, about tonight . . . there's no way I could single-handedly screw up the spells? Like what if I do something wrong, and the protection doesn't go up the right way, and the Wolves—"

"Chill. That's not gonna happen. Look, when this is over, we'll work on some spells, okay? You'll have my undivided attention."

Maverick whined suddenly, his eyes trained on the sky.

A black cluster of crows circled above them, each one flapping to the same haunting beat. Maverick nudged Iris with his nose. A bird dropped a piece of parchment onto the brim of her hat.

"It's Roddin," Iris said, her eyes not leaving the note. "It's urgent."

*The audacity.* Jailah said, "Roddin can wait. We have to meet the boys, *hello*, the sacrifice!"

Iris waved the note. "Apparently, the boys have come to us."

# 17

## iris

"Roddin!" Iris strode into the empty Emporium yelling. "Familiars are great and all, but what do you have against cell phones? They are perfectly reliable!"

"*Hey*, I take offense to that," Thalia said with a tight smile, scratching Maverick behind the ears. "How else would we create *melodrama*?"

Even with the touch of amusement in Thalia's voice, Iris noticed the way she kept smoothing her hair with her fingers, her own tell of discomfort. It stung. Iris had spent enough time at the Necromantic Emporium to grow fond of it. When she was bored, she visited the cranky old woman here, the only other deathwitch in Haelsford who understood her Pull. Iris always offered to rest any of the spirits that were trapped in the appropriately named House of Souls, though Roddin seemed to think she wasn't ready to free the loud ones in the trinkets above them. Iris felt like she and the shop were made up of the same stuff, and if Thalia didn't like the look of the possessed antiques, then what did she think of Iris, who could *speak* to spirits?

"Hi," said a cool voice. A Hammersmitt stepped out of a dark corner. "Thanks for coming."

Iris and her girls sized him up. He appeared to enjoy it, comfortable in his backward baseball cap and sneakers. The ease with which a mundane could occupy this space and speak so casually while outnumbered by witches was admirable. Iris could give him that.

"Trenton Hogarth, Your Graces." He bowed, sly in his grin.

Thalia gave Iris a pointed nod.

He was clutching a white paper bag, which he smoothly passed to Thalia. "Coconut almond, as you like."

Thalia snatched it quickly, as if that would make everyone else oblivious to the gesture.

"I'd like to make you a deal," he said.

Jailah looked Trent up and down. "The sacrifice happens at the Box Chant."

"The sacrifice that we have planned now is, well, meh. You deserve more, and trust, you want this."

Iris raised a brow. When he said *you*, he said it right to her. She looked over his shoulder and found the Roddin Witch watching silently. "I thought you hated mundanes, and now you've got one gallivanting around in your shop."

*"Gallivanting?"* Trent frowned. "I like to call it a saunter."

Iris narrowed her eyes. Logan chuckled. Thalia and Jailah groaned.

"This one won't leave me alone. Better that he bothers you from now on instead," Roddin said.

"Awesome," Iris responded dryly. "God. The suspense is totally killing me."

Trent presented a porcelain box.

"A jewelry box?" Iris looked to Jailah. "Told you. Boring."

"No, it's what's in it that's the sacrifice," Trent said.

Logan angled forward. "And what's in it?"

The door chimed.

Another Hammersmitt entered the shop, his hair disheveled, his eyes gloriously furious.

Iris braced herself. What happened on Hallowe'en could happen right now.

"Matty . . . hey . . ." Trent said tentatively, much like a kid caught with his hand in the candy jar.

Mathew Beaumont looked around. "Hi. I'm Mathew, and I'm late. Apologies. What have I missed?"

"Nothing, yet," Logan said, still eyeing the box.

"What the hell is going on?" Jailah asked.

"I'll leave that to Trent. Any other questions?" Mathew pointed to Thalia, who was licking frosting off a cupcake.

"Pass," she grumbled.

"Ooh, me next," Iris said. "Why is your shirt so tight? Don't you need to, like, let your chest breathe?"

"He likes to show off, don't you, Matty?" Trent guffawed.

Beaumont grimaced. "Serious inquiries only, thanks."

"I'm always serious," said Iris.

Beaumont clasped his hands together. "I'm in perfect health. I appreciate your concern. Trent, this is a terrible idea."

Iris raised a brow. "Wait, I love terrible ideas, you have my full attention now. What is it?"

The boys exchanged a look that she couldn't decipher.

Iris stepped forward, took the box, and ripped the top off. Trent and Beaumont tensed up.

She hovered a finger over one of the pentagrams on the diamond-shaped rock.

"Don't," Beaumont pleaded.

"Why not?" She touched the stone with a childlike poke. And when nothing happened, she poked it again with an amused annoyance. "How boring—"

With one cold movement, Iris dropped the rock and abruptly slammed Mathew hard against the wall, her hand on his chest, his shirt balled up in her fist.

Iris couldn't breathe. The surge of power blindsided her. It wasn't like Hallowe'en night, when she'd apparently tethered with Beaumont and opened the Chasm. That had felt like a slight moment of hysteria, a *mistake*, but something she could eventually control.

This was something that wanted to control her, like a hand had forced itself into her chest and taken away her ability to function, a puppet to an almighty puppeteer.

Above her, the trinkets cried out in an unintelligible, painful song.

"Hey!" Trent screamed, but he didn't approach her. Carefully, he pulled the rock into its box.

But Jailah didn't hesitate. "Iris, get off him!"

With one hand still propping Beaumont up, Iris pointed her wand at Jailah, stopping her short. It was wrong, but it *felt* right. Her mind was muddied with dark thoughts.

"You gonna hex me?" Jailah asked severely.

Iris swallowed hard. "I kinda want to, yeah . . ." Her voice trailed off as the power subsided. With a cruel look at her own hand, Iris set Beaumont free.

Mathew, red-faced and out of breath, smoothed out his clothes. "This is a new shirt."

She would've laughed if she wasn't so perplexed. Teetering, she moved away to rest against the wall.

Thalia's hand hovered over Iris's back, like she was afraid to touch her. "Are you okay? You need an elixir?"

Iris couldn't even look at her. Shame burned in her cheeks. "How the hell do two mundane boys have an amplyfyr?"

"An amplyfyr?" Jailah flexed her fingers, as if considering if she wanted to go next.

Logan said, "That's what they used to test our witchery."

"Sort of," Thalia continued, pushing up her glasses. "They use amplyfyr dust, ground up so it's diluted. This stone is all that power in full."

Iris pointed at Roddin. "I want confirmation."

"I've already confirmed," she spat, and shut herself away in her prayer room.

"We've been here before," Beaumont said casually.

"So, this is the sacrifice?" Iris didn't smile, and she felt a little off, but this brightened her spirits, even though the amplyfyr was the very thing to darken them.

"It's a trade. I'm assuming Trent would like to speak to his dead mother, right?"

Trent grumbled affirmatively.

Iris looked at the stone once more. "Yeah, you're not the first. What, did she cut you out of her will?"

Trent's coolness broke momentarily. "Could you bring her back with this?"

"Back?" Iris glared at him. "You don't mean—" But judging from Trent's stupid hopeful expression, he *did*. She laughed. "Bringing back a dead person would cross the line of even the darkest witchery. You can't give life without a cost. A high one. This, *this*"—she opened her arms, gesturing to the world around them—"this is not sacrifice! Witches receive gifts every Haunting Season, so we'll protect you, but it's an exchange. You'll know a real sacrifice when you see it; it's way more painful, and you'll wonder what you ever got in return."

Mathew stepped between them. "Ten minutes to talk to his mother, that's it."

Iris considered this with a sharp exhale. "How do you have this amplyfyr?"

He shrugged. "We found it in my basement. I didn't know. I still don't know."

A bit of anger sparked in her chest. He was a dryblood—he'd told her himself, and Iris had inspected his blood, examining his ancestry for magic. There was none. But there were mundanes who had come to possess witchy artifacts and decided they owned them. To collect? To keep from witches? Iris didn't care what the reason was; it infuriated her. Maybe that was why she'd attacked him under the amplyfyr's influence. Maybe a part of her was angry to be connected to him.

Jai began to pace. "The Wolves are coming. We have to get back to school for the protection spells."

With a small sigh, Iris whispered, "Ten minutes with your mother."

"Twenty," Trent dared.

"Don't push it." She cupped the porcelain in her hands. "Meet us at the Box Chant after we put the spells up. We'll be done before curfew starts."

"If the school finds out we have a pure amplyfyr, they'll confiscate it," Jailah added, ferocity in her voice.

"Maybe they should." Thalia shrugged. "Maybe we shouldn't be handling it at all."

Jailah looked back to the box, and Iris knew what she was thinking. *All that power.* Jai could look sweet when she wanted to. It wasn't a lie; she really was the most caring, and sweet, and soft person that Iris knew. But she was also merciless about protecting herself and the power within her, and she would rip the world in two before letting anyone else have it.

"We're keeping it, but we're not gonna, like, *use it*. Fair?" Jailah asked. The witches agreed. "What'll we tell the others? We need a sacrifice to present."

"The Oak Trail," Mathew offered. "It's yours again."

Iris blinked. "You can do that?" She, like other Haelsfordian witches, had never set foot on the famed trail that led directly from Mesmortes to the Green, a massive garden of witchy herbs. It ran through the land where Hammersmitt was built, sparking the current tension between the student bodies. This sacrifice was a vanity gift of sorts as there were other, albeit longer, ways to the Green. It was also an undeniable olive branch.

Mathew nodded. "Trent and I spoke with Principal Chandler. Any Mesmortes witch who needs to get to the Green can take the shortcut through Hammersmitt."

That these boys had convinced the Hammersmitt administration to now allow Mesmortes witches to cross through their campus softened Iris's heart a bit, and judging from Thalia's eager eyes and Jai's impressed brow, she wasn't the only one into it.

Iris's stupid feeble chest tightened. She *hated it.* "Fine," she spat, and stomped out the front door.

But Mathew sped up to walk alongside her. "That's why the Chasm opened up on Hallowe'en," he said. "I had the amplyfyr in my pocket."

"Oh," Iris said, shrugging off the uncomfortable disappointment. The amplyfyr had felt vastly different from the power surge of Mathew's touch. But it made more sense than him being her tether. "That explains that."

"Why did you think it could've been me?"

"It doesn't matter now."

"Right, you have the Wolf Boy to find. Will the heirloom help?"

Iris had forgotten she mentioned the Wolf Boy to him and was surprised he remembered. "I don't know. I really shouldn't be messing around with it. I think it's cool because it's a freaky witchy relic, not because I wanna be using it." She gestured back toward Roddin's. "You can imagine why. Sorry, uh, by the way."

He shrugged. "Maybe there are other witchy things in my basement. I can check it out."

There was that anger again. Iris wanted to *scream.* He could've been living with an entire collection of valuable witchy antiques and not even known it. "Careful, I'll end up slamming you into a wall again."

"Oh?" Mathew strode ahead of her, walking backward so that they were face-to-face. He looked down at her from beneath wayward strands of dark hair. "Is that a promise?"

Reflexively, Iris dug her nails into the meat of her palms, distracting herself from the heat crawling up her neck and into her cheeks. She was grateful that her dark skin never visibly reddened. "I thought you wanted nothing to do with witchery."

"It's to make up for Trent annoying the hell out of you."

"You mundanes are all the same. You get one taste of witchery, and it's not enough."

"I'm no hexeater, Iris."

"No, you're just a Hammersmitt that likes hanging around Mesmortes girls. It won't end well."

He raised a brow. "I'm game." Without another word, he broke off for Hammersmitt.

Trent and the girls had caught up with her. Trent followed Mathew, waving at Iris like he'd known her forever, leaving the four witches standing in an awed silence. They looked at the porcelain that Iris still held. "I don't love the feel of it," she said.

Jailah offered to take it, and Iris felt her chest loosen once it was out of her grip. There were voices and vibrations, loud and terrible, and Iris knew that her girls heard it, too, and that they felt the same.

For a brief moment, each witch wanted all the power that the amplyfyr promised.

# 18

## jailah

Howls sang through the air.

As Jailah led two lines of junior year witches toward the Swamp, eyes followed them from behind Hammersmitt windows. A few watched from the roof. Some were brave enough to step out in front of the school and lean against the brick, sleeves rolled up, whispers abounding. Word was already spreading that the witches could use the Oak Trail again, thanks to the Red Three.

"You're eating this up," Iris said from behind.

Jailah grinned. "Hell yeah I am."

Sharp gusts of wind sent Jailah's cape whipping around. Jailah took in the dark sky. A storm was coming. She turned back at the lines of juniors following behind her. They looked like superheroes. Maybe a bit more sinister with black uniforms and sleek top hats, but that only made it better.

Before she could give herself a last internal hype-up, she found herself staring into the dark mouth of the Swamp. A mess of gnarled tree trunks and exposed roots. If she moved just a few feet forward, the grass under her loafers would be brown and mushy, the air thick and rancid.

Jailah turned. Iris and Thalia stood with her, but most of the other witches waited back several feet. She beckoned them forward. "Come on up! And spread out until you're touching toes with the sophomores and seniors!"

Logan moved up first. The baby witch gave Jai a shaky smile, and the others finally followed suit. Jailah grinned. They formed a line, each witch standing three arm's lengths apart from another. Jailah heard Anika delegating to the older witches farther down, and every few minutes, a professor swept by to observe, encourage, and chastise the freshmen breaking dress code even though they weren't in class.

Jailah rolled down the waistband of her own skirt. She went to Thalia, who was staring at the Swamp with an odd, wistful look. "T? You ready?"

Thalia nodded absently.

"What are you thinking 'bout? You look like you're far away."

Thalia ran her teeth over her bottom lip. "I'm trying to find the beauty in the ugliness."

"I don't think there's a bit of beauty in there. 'Less you think Wolves are pretty."

"It's just something my dad used to say."

Jailah nearly choked. Thalia rarely spoke of her father in a way that wasn't dripping in anger and hate.

Thalia sighed. "I can barely look at it, it's like . . ." She fluttered her fingertips. "I can *feel* the earth suffering under the Strigwach hex. I wonder if there's a way to heal it." Thalia shook her head. "I don't know. That sounds stupid."

"Not stupid. Who else could do it but you?" Jailah took Thalia's arm.

The headmistress came around and gave one last inspiring speech. Jai appreciated the hell out of the rousing words of encouragement, but she wanted to get on with it. The magic in her was abuzz. She was ready to make her mark against the most powerful hex she'd ever seen, one that withstood nearly a century of attempts to bring it down. She had a bit of odd respect for the Strigwachs. They were dead, but their magic terrorized Haelsford still. Jailah just couldn't help being impressed.

Even before the headmistress instructed them to, Jailah raised her wand. *Showtime.*

Together, the witches of the Mesmortes Coven Academy started the spell to save themselves, and so many others. Jailah recited it with fierce glee. *"For Our Blessed; Against Sharp Claws and Snarling Teeth!"*

As the light exploded from her wand, she looked at the line of witches around her. Their spells fused with one another's, creating a glorious wall of protective magic from the hands of over seven hundred teen witches.

*What a night*, she thought. She was part of it yet thoroughly awed by the power.

A voice interrupted her thoughts. "Cover me."

Jailah turned to Logan, whose wand was stiff in her hand at her side.

"What are you doing?" she hissed. "Get your wand up."

"I can't do it—"

"Yes—"

"Look, don't say *Yes you can*, like you always do. There's a time and a place for the encouraging speech, but maybe now, when we're trying to keep out murderous Wolves, isn't it." Logan looked over her shoulder. "Do the spells for me, because if I screw this up, someone could die,

126

right? This is the most important magic any of us has ever done."

Jailah was pretty sure that the headmistress, faculty, and Haelsford Witchery Council weren't going to simply let the teen witches do the protections without some serious checking and reinforcing, but she understood Logan's point.

Logan was smart. She *was* doing magic—a crude version of a basic flare spell to emit a blue haze from her wand—in order to keep her lack of participation from being too obvious. Even if Logan wasn't totally skilled with a wand yet, Jailah could appreciate that.

"I got ya," Jailah said, pulling Logan closer. "Do the movements with me."

When the barrier had been cast, the glee of the witches was boisterous and triumphant.

It didn't last.

The howls grew into a thunderous roar.

The Wolves never woke quietly, but since this was their first time putting up the protections, these young witches had never been this close to the Swamp when it happened. Those who Jailah had eased forward to the barrier were quick to move back.

Jailah resisted the urge to slap her hands over her ears. "They're just being dramatic!"

But as she stood there, she imagined a Wolf bounding toward her hastily with its wild fur and glowing eyes. The sound of its horrible panting growing with its hunger. Nothing like her *Suffitiomorrai* Wolf.

Finally, Jailah retreated. When she daydreamed of how this night would end, she thought they'd be holding their heads high as they turned back to Mesmortes. Maybe some laughter, a few middle fingers aimed at the Swamp. Iris shouting, *Screw you, Wolves*, as a nightcap.

Instead, her witches seemed a little scared, very sweaty, and too tired to smile. Jailah and Logan walked up the Hill in near silence. When they caught up to Iris and Thalia, Jailah found them both wearing scowls.

"Shit," Iris said sharply. "I'm gonna use the amplyfyr."

Jailah's mouth popped open. "We *agreed*—"

"I've changed my mind."

"What, in the whole hour since we got it?"

"Desperate times, right? That was cute and all, but we all know that *real* protection means ending the Haunting."

Jailah couldn't argue with that. She knew that feeling well and had acted on it. She had felt it twice now: once before she gave Vero up to the Witchery Council, and now, thinking about the amplyfyr.

Thalia shook her head. "I already tried to talk her out of it. Your turn."

"Would it be that bad?" Logan chirped. "What's the worst that could happen?"

"If this were a movie, that's the line that gets us killed, Logan," Thalia replied. "She attacked Mathew!"

Iris rolled her eyes. "Did he die, though?"

Jailah looked around. No one seemed to be paying them any attention, but she lowered her voice anyway. "Okay. What's your plan?"

Iris cracked her knuckles. "Madeline Donahue said that the Wolf Boy was buried in Haelsford, right? That's something I already guessed—I spent a week last year in the graveyard calling for someone to answer. I got silence, mostly, except for the pervy spirit who insisted that I'd be a great vessel for his ghost children."

Thalia wheezed a laugh.

"Not funny. I tried again this week and got nothing. But maybe the amplyfyr supercharges my necromancy so that I can find him. Or maybe it brings me his name, his face, I don't know! But what the hell do we have to lose?"

"Your control over your own body?" Jailah whispered.

"I can handle it."

Jailah wiped sweat from her brow. "We don't even know if the amplyfyr is gonna help you do what you need to do. Can we at least sleep on it? Besides, you need to focus on our new friend Trent, remember?"

Iris relented with an affirmative grumble.

Jailah clasped her hands. "Y'all ready to watch Iris talk to dead people?"

"I need to change first," Logan said. She lifted her top hat and shook her damp hair. "The humidity's killing me."

Jailah nodded. "We have time. Let's meet back here in half an hour."

As Thalia and Iris walked on, Logan pulled Jailah back. "Thanks. For the spells."

"No prob, babe."

Logan gestured toward Iris up ahead. "Do you really think the amplyfyr would hurt her?"

"I don't know for sure that it wouldn't. Seems a good enough reason to play it safe." She waited until Thalia broke off the path toward Bramblewynn House and for Iris to slink into Topthorne. "I think you should take it."

Before Logan could finish sputtering a disagreement, Jailah pulled the porcelain box from her knapsack, the lid reinforced with pink satin hair ties.

Swallowing hard, Logan took the box. "You trust me with this?"

"Yeah," Jailah said plainly. "I trust you."

*And if Iris came looking for it, she'd never think that I gave it to the baby witch.*

Jailah looked up at the dark sky. "Go get ready. We've got to be back before the Wolves come out."

# 19

## logan

*Desperate times.*

Logan stood alone in the center of the Topthorne House hollow room. With the safe room being used only for Haunting drills and emergencies, she figured it would be the best place for a little privacy, and a little more space than her dorm room. After changing out of her uniform, she'd come with the intention of attempting to scry with the broken glass. Instead, she'd spent the last fifteen minutes looking into the canvas pouch that held the glittering pieces. Carefully, she picked up a piece, examined it, and sighed when no image came to her. She tried again, and again, and once more until the glass finally nicked her finger. Even then, with her blood dripping into the satchel, there was nothing.

She plopped down on one of the many velvet couches. Logan heard that Amelia Carr had decorated the space last year, wanting her witches to be comforted even if in fear. The abundant candles smelled like lemon and cherries and vanilla. There was a lush chaise in the corner, just beside the bookcase that was filled with grimoires and spellbooks. A white lacquered cauldron rested atop a pink rug on the floor, filled with calming elixir. Logan had placed the fearmonger plant that Thalia had given her on the windowsill—her own room never got enough sunlight, and the leaves were beginning to wrinkle and droop.

She placed the amplyfyr on the coffee table, next to a copy of *Gifts of a Proxy* that she pulled from the bookshelf. In it, High Witch Ciaran said that magic was a flame, always burning up in a witch. But to a proxy, magic was a raging wildfire.

It felt true. Every time Logan called her witchery, it became a burst of pressure building up in her, ready to destroy everything around her, and maybe her, too. But she was sick of being embarrassed, of asking the Red Three to bail her out, of having everyone pity her.

*Open me*, the stone seemed to whisper.

Heart thrumming, she slipped off the hair ties.

Logan paused. This was the thing that had made Iris attack Mathew. It didn't amplify her power; it took control of her. If the deathwitch could be vulnerable to whatever had manifested in that stone, then what would it do to Logan?

*But why shouldn't I get to experience power? Why shouldn't I feel strong, too?* She flipped the lid open, thinking of that testing day in the auditorium. Her witchery had flowed out of her in a delicious surge. Curiosity could be a dangerous thing, but Logan couldn't bear it anymore.

Trembling, Logan touched the stone.

Her world froze, every color and light brightened in a vibrant flash. Speckles of golden stardust formed an aura around her. Finally, it wasn't hiding from her. Her magic was real, and it was *alive*.

"*Aza. Ozo. Aye,*" she whispered. The finding spell that she'd never reformed, though she felt confident she could try some reformation now.

She felt like she could do anything.

*"Aza. Ozo. Aye. The Wolf Boy of Haelsford."*

The world shook. She blinked through the flashing images.

A town. Three sisters. A picture of a boy. A headstone.

Even larger than Mesmortes, Hammersmitt, and Town Square was Haelsford Cemetery. The pieced-together remains of Haelsfordians that saw the first incarnation of Wolves were here, six feet under, in this massive graveyard.

The headstone was simple, and like most others, it was unmarked. A fraught sense of ownership swooped into her chest. She found him. The Red Three may have started this, but Logan *found* him. She was the anchor.

She touched the headstone. "Hello, Wolf Boy."

It was easy for Logan to detach herself from the heirloom's grip. It wasn't like with Iris, all violence and horror, maybe because as a necromancer, those things were already in her. Or maybe it was Logan's ability to proxy that protected her.

*Maybe I'm more special than even Iris.*

This is what a proxy truly was. Holding the power to manipulate magic against its own rules, and it was hers. All hers.

Logan's mind reeling, she fantasized about how the Red Three would react when she'd tell them what she'd found.

They would love her for this.

It was all she ever wanted.

# 20

## jailah

When Jailah got the text from Logan to meet her at Haelsford Cemetery, she didn't think twice. She'd simply messaged the boys, pulled her hair into a sleek bun, and headed out.

Now, standing in front of what was apparently the Wolf Boy's headstone, she had questions. Firstly—

"Logan, what the hell?"

"Don't think you're supposed to say that in a graveyard," Thalia quipped. She kept a good few feet away from the headstone, twirling a strand of grass around her finger.

Iris, however, was leaning—practically sitting—on it. "Trust me, the dead don't really care."

Jailah turned to Logan. She had admirable determination on her face, and the amplyfyr in a tight grip without the safety of the sanctifum. Jailah hadn't expected this when she gave the stone to Logan. She didn't know whether to feel guilty or proud. "You said the stone brought you here?"

Logan nodded. "I did a finding spell with it."

"That's not how a finding spell works," Thalia interjected, brow in a skeptical furrow. "You'd need his blood."

"It's different for *me*." Logan's face was painted over with the resolve of a more powerful witch, one who wouldn't let fear shake her. It made a fierce difference in her posture, her gaze, the way she spoke.

Thalia turned her concerned eyes to Jailah.

"What's his name?" Iris asked bluntly.

Logan hesitated. "I don't know."

"Then I need his face."

Iris pushed off the headstone and pointed her wand at the grass. *"Dig Up the Bo—"*

"What are you doing?" Thalia demanded, lunging forward. She looked like she wanted to smack the wand out of Iris's hand, but stopped herself, and simply reached for her own wand instead.

"This is the second time today that one of us has raised her wand at another," Jailah said, her own wand at her side.

"I was possessed," Iris seethed. "Come on, T. What's your excuse?"

"You're not supposed to disturb the dead!" Thalia hissed, jaw tense.

"I'm a necromancer!"

"You've only ever messed around with souls and helped them find rest. This is *different*."

"Hey, can we talk this through?" Jailah attempted diplomatically. She moved to Logan, who still seemed so fixated on the headstone. "Iris needs the Wolf Boy's name and face to call him. We have neither, but Logan could use her proxy skills to make up for one or the other, right? So . . ." She looked at the dying grass. "Do we have a choice?"

Thalia's eyes widened. "You're cool with digging up this grave?"

Jailah shook her head. "I'm just saying, if we're not trying to end the Haunting, then why are we here?"

"We don't know if it's him! The Wolf Boy is a legend—he might not even exist!"

"It's him," Logan asserted. "You'll know it's him when we call him." The eerie lilt to Logan's voice made Jailah shiver.

Thalia backed away as Iris pricked her finger and made a slashing motion in the air over the grave. *"Dig Up the Bones."* With every slash, a sizable chunk of dirt flew up from the ground. She looked to Jailah. "Little help?"

Jai grimaced. "Uh, hold on." She pulled out her phone and opened up the PocketSpells app.

"It's *Lahara-Nys-Noxia*," Iris muttered.

Jailah pricked her finger. "A'ight, don't look at me like that, deathwitch, I never needed this spell before." She incanted, slashed her wand, and cringed at the dirt hitting her boots.

Still keeping her distance, Thalia said, "We have guests."

Jai turned and found the Hammersmitt boys looking reasonably disturbed.

"Er," Trent started, shooting Mathew an uncertain look.

Mathew considered Logan, then looked to Iris. She was utterly consumed by the job in front of her, so he turned to Jailah. "Why are you digging up this grave?"

Jailah sighed. "We're digging up the Wolf Boy."

"*We're* not; you guys are," Thalia added, pointing accusatory jabs at Iris and Jailah.

"What?" Trent asked no one in particular. "I thought we were going to call my mum. I thought—"

"Your mommy issues can wait." Iris rolled her eyes.

Jailah gave Trent an apologetic look. "We will, Trent. This is just . . . well, it's urgent."

He nodded. "All right, but you gotta fill us in on this shit."

As Jailah gave a final slash of her wand, the last of the dirt flew from the grave, and Iris stepped into it without hesitation. Thalia held her wand at her side. Her brow was still furrowed in concern.

Trent watched expectantly, looking at Jailah with his arms open, like, *Well?*

Jailah stepped to them. "Boys, it's time to make a decision. *This* is witchery. Sometimes it's simple—a spell to make your eyes clearer, to calm your allergies, or give ya a good night's rest. But other times, it's digging up the Wolf Boy's grave on a Saturday night. You can leave now, if you want. We made a promise to you, Trent, so we can reschedule." She smiled sweetly. "Or you can stay."

Jailah realized now that her girls were tuned in. Iris had one hand on the lacquered casket but was watching the boys over her shoulder. Thalia, anxiously fiddling with her wand, stopped to consider this moment, and Logan smiled a little, a break in the intensity, like she was genuinely happy to expand her circle of friends.

"I'm in." Trent winked.

That didn't surprise Jailah at all. But Mathew, on the other hand, was focused on the grave. He ran his fingers over his lips, thinking something that made his eyes narrow.

"You look worried," Jailah said, a teasing edge to her voice.

He turned to her with a sardonic grin. "I wouldn't be here if I didn't want to be here. So I guess I'm in it now."

"Good," Iris said. "Because this next part's gonna suck."

Iris turned to Thalia, and even before she spoke, the greenwitch furiously shook her head. "I know what you're gonna ask, and the answer is no."

Iris pointed to the blank headstone. "Without his name, I need a face to call. Doesn't it feel like fate that you're here, the most talented greenwitch in Mesmortes? I can try to *Mend*, but it wouldn't be as good as yours, and this is too important to mess up. Give me his face, and Logan's blood can make up for his name."

Jailah heard Trent and Mathew conversing quietly about *witchy math* and would've laughed if she didn't feel so uneasy. She eyed the grave, her stomach turning as she imagined what decay they'd find if they opened it up.

Thalia crossed her arms. "I won't touch a corpse!"

"You're my best friend—"

"And you're mine, so don't ask me to do this."

Logan stepped between them. "Or maybe I can make up for both parts with the amplyfyr. Like, it already brought me here. Maybe it'll make my magic stronger and we don't need his name or his face. I mean—" She gestured toward the ground. "We have his bones! Doesn't that help?"

Thalia frowned. "You shouldn't be messing around with the amplyfyr."

"It's fine. I feel strong."

"But we can't tell if it's you talking, or the stone," Jailah added. "But fine. Let's try it this way."

Iris didn't argue.

"And if it doesn't work?" Thalia asked softly.

"Then the Wolves live on." Iris stepped out of the grave and dumped out her knapsack. The contents ranged from appropriately mundane to completely odd: a pair of sunglasses, a golden pendulum, a jar of something muddy and slick, two bunches of red weeds, a tampon, a compact, sage wrapped in plastic, six tall candles, and several jars of coarse salt.

"Bloody Mary Poppins," Trent whispered.

"Everyone, sit around Logan and me," Iris commanded, pulling Logan to sit with her in front of the grave.

They did as they were told, and Iris steadied the pendulum between herself and Logan. She handed each person a jar of salt. "Make one big circle of salt behind you. No gaps. We don't want anything slipping out."

Mathew fidgeted next to Jailah. "She knows what she's doing, right?"

"I can hear you!"

With her wand, Iris arranged the candles, one in front of each person. The sage came next, a sprig for each. Iris sang *Will You Light My Candle?*, which Jailah always found sweet, but decided that this was probably not the best time to try and harmonize.

"Now, hold hands. I'd like everyone to think of everything they know about the Wolf Boy. The legends you've heard in town, the whispers of your odd witchy neighbors, the things your parents warned you about. Think about the Wolves and what they've done to us. Beg him for help." Iris turned to Logan. "I need *you* to think really hard. Focus all of your attention on him. Help us wade through the souls for this *one* spirit. And give us your blood."

Logan pricked her finger, letting her blood drip into the ground between them. There was a stark hush as she uncovered the amplyfyr, like they were all holding their breath in anticipation of something terrible. But when Logan touched the stone, the only change was the brilliant gold in her hands.

"Close your eyes." Iris took Logan's free hand in her own. "The winds have turned to us, its feeble callers, to awaken this soul so pure. A few words to be given, a few to be had. Tonight, we summon the Wolf Boy of Haelsford. Loved by all but one. He is blessed, and he is cursed. The key to ending the Haunting for all and forever." Iris's voice hitched into a lower octave. *"I Call Upon You, the Wolf Boy of Haelsford."*

Mathew fidgeted again, and Jailah peeked an eye open. He seemed uncomfortable, but okay. Trent, however, looked ill, so different from the confident boy just a few minutes earlier.

Wind blew through the cemetery. Jailah saw that Thalia's eyes were also open. She shook her head, her dark brow wrinkled.

"Is that you, Wolf Boy?" Iris demanded. "Swing the pendulum for yes!"

The pendulum swung frantically.

Iris's voice went so low that it didn't even sound like her. "I'm here, Wolf Boy!"

She began to chant, her voice going hoarse.

The only part Jailah could make out was: *winds turn, rains change.*

As the wind gusted violently around them, Jailah had only one thought. *This was a mistake.*

# 21

## mathew

"HAIR IS GOOD, BLOOD IS BETTER, FLESH IS BEST!" Iris's head angled toward the heavens, her throat undulating as she spoke.

Mathew's eyes watered from the cold winds. It was hard to look at her. Her veins were bright and black, like she'd been pumped with an electric tar.

"What . . . did she . . . just say?" Trent wheezed.

Mathew turned to Trent and found him slouching over. "Trent?"

His hand went limp in Mathew's. He muttered something before passing out and slumping against him.

Mathew looked around frantically, and he saw that Logan was still. Her lips were pursed in concentration, her eyes gleaming.

*"Iris!"* Jailah shouted. "What's happening?"

"WINDS TURN! RAINS CHANGE!" She was standing, her feet lifting off the ground. One hand was still in Logan's. And the other—

Thalia screamed out in agony. Iris, or whatever had hold of her, dug her nails into Thalia's shoulder. Thalia's blood ran steadily into the ground, which shook violently beneath them. Suddenly, a black vine the size of a tree sprouted from the dirt.

"I'm not doing it!" Thalia cried. The vine bled a dark, greasy liquid that smelled of oil and rust. "Jai, help!"

Cursing, Jailah broke from the circle and extended her arms to Iris.

With just a blasé wave of her hand, Iris sent Jailah flying backward. Her foot caught some of the salt, creating a perfect break in the circle.

Mathew swallowed hard, Iris's warning echoing in his head. *We don't want anything slipping out.*

The air shook with rippling magic. Iris and Logan were possessed, Thalia was hurt, Trent had fainted, Jailah was *gone*, dark magic whirled around them as it pleased, and Mathew flinched because there was something brewing in him. Suddenly, he felt electric, and the power was a spark in him, running from his chest outward, like his veins were made of light.

Iris chanted on, but Mathew could feel her pulling to him. He felt stupid. He was not a witch, so what was this? Was it her? Had Iris somehow freed herself from this force and was using him to pull herself out?

Something hitched in his chest. A wheel turning and clicking. He imagined himself turning this wheel with all his strength. It vibrated rapidly within him, but he gritted his teeth, forcing himself to bear it. None of this was of his own volition, but he had no other choice than to try *something*. He reached out and grabbed her wrist—

A small part of him wasn't surprised when the world went dark and he found himself standing before the mirror of light once more.

This time, Iris was not on the other side. She was halfway in the mirror, dipped into the threshold of light. Beyond her, Mathew saw the ghostly souls racing around her, their cries growing loud.

Iris huffed, pained and desperate. But her words were angry as they echoed around the dark. "I don't need your help."

"I know you don't." Mathew lowered his fingers to her hand. She didn't pull away, even though she still looked annoyed by him. "Let me help you anyway."

He started to pull back, but Iris only planted her feet. Her dark brown skin was illuminated by the crackling blue light of the Chasm. *"Don't.* I'm fine—"

He shook his head. "You told me what the Chasm was. I know that if you go in, you might not get out." He tugged a little. "Come back. Come back to us. To me."

Suddenly, the anger on her face turned into fear. Her eyes were tearing up, her mouth pursed. "I didn't . . ." Iris exhaled sharply. "I didn't mean to."

Mathew wasn't sure what she meant, but he pulled again, and she moved toward him. And only now as she stepped out of the threshold to the Chasm in full did he realize why she hadn't wanted to come with him. It wasn't that she *couldn't.* It was that there were two pale hands wrapped tightly around her other arm.

Iris looked into Mathew's eyes. "But he won't let go."

And suddenly, they were in the graveyard once more, hands still clasped together. Iris floated back toward the earth, and while there was no one clutching her arm, Mathew felt an odd heaviness in the air.

A blur moved in the corner of his eye.

"Jailah!" Mathew screamed, but before he could stop her, she tackled Iris so hard that the two of them skidded viciously into a headstone with the type of force that would've broken a mundane.

Thalia sucked in a breath and clamped down on the three dark wounds Iris left in her shoulder.

"Oh!" Logan exclaimed as the magic was severed. She dropped the heirloom, and Mathew noticed her reluctance as she placed it back in the box.

Trent breathed softly, his eyelids finally twitching open. "What . . ." he muttered dreamily. "What just happened?"

Mathew helped him to his feet. "I'll explain later."

Jailah, teeth bared and mud-covered, dragged a limp Iris Keaton-Foster back to the ruined salt circle and dropped her hard into the middle of it.

"Ow! It's me," Iris said weakly.

Jailah pointed her wand at her. "Prove it."

Iris stayed down. "You, Jailah Simmons, are perfect at *everything*. Baby witch likes strawberry fraps. Thalia's still crushing on Dustin Fulham, even though he graduated—"

Thalia scrunched up her face. *"Hey—"*

Iris stretched her hand over her head and pointed at Trent, whose face was as clammy as hers. "This is filthy rich Hogarth. And . . ." She swallowed hard. "Beaumont. He's got a horse named Ruby."

Mathew half smiled. He wiped sweat from his forehead.

Jailah sighed. "I broke the circle. The salt. I was trying to help you; you said something might slip out—"

"It doesn't matter," Iris muttered. "It's too late."

Thalia trembled. "Too late for what?"

The casket began to rattle viciously, the feeling reverberating through Mathew's soles.

"Oh." Iris sucked in a breath. *"Shit."*

The casket door flew open, and two pale hands grabbed at the edge of the grave they'd dug up. A boy climbed up.

As the witches and their mundanes stared into the eyes of a boy once dead, the Wolves howled. So started the Haunting Season.

part two

# the wolf boy

# 22

## thalia

There was a dead boy in Jailah Simmons's bedroom.

The circle of girls looked down at him, waiting for . . . something. Anything. But the boy merely sighed. Eyes closed, breaths shallow.

Thalia's heart hadn't stopped thrumming in the past hour. They had successfully levitated the boy through the halls under an invisibility spell. But even now, safe in the confines of Jailah's room, she couldn't catch her breath.

Even as she watched his chest rise and fall, she couldn't believe her eyes.

It seemed wrong that he could come back from death and be so beautiful. A red ribbon tied up his perfect brown curls. Even without a *Mending*, his skin was youthful and flushed, nothing like the decayed face they'd imagined. The boy was dressed in tattered clothes that must've been nice once, a thin white shirt, brown pleated pants.

"What do we do?" Iris whispered, glowering at him like she expected an answer.

"We?" Thalia's own angry scoff surprised her. "This is *your* mess."

"*I* didn't do this!" Iris exclaimed. "I only wanted to find the Wolf Boy, but holy shit, this is *wild*. I don't even know how resurrection works. It's not something you can just fucking google!"

"Then how did this happen?"

Iris pointed an accusatory finger at Logan, who flushed red. "Me?"

"Yeah, you! You and the amplyfyr! Why did you even bring it?"

"You didn't care when it was going to help you Call him, did you?" Logan snapped. "You said you wanted to use it yourself! Desperate times!"

"*We* did this," Jailah added quickly.

Thalia shook her head. Why weren't they getting it? She had no part of this dark magic. "No, *I* did not."

"No? Then why did a giant stalk just happen to appear out of nowhere after your blood was given to the earth? I don't know the ingredients to resurrection either, but I'd place good money on it involving fresh black-thorne grown from a greenwitch. Y'all, *we* did this. It doesn't matter if the amplyfyr was behind it. If this gets out, do you think the Witchery Council will care?"

Thalia felt the wind knocked out of her. She was stunned silent for a moment. The ache in her shoulder where possessed-Iris had dug her nails into her flesh throbbed in response.

"No one can know," Iris said suddenly, her voice urgent. "Think of the consequences."

"Banishment," Thalia forced out. As much as the resurrection had discomfited her, it had happened. It was real. There was no use dwelling on who was to blame.

Logan squealed. "I can't be banished. I only just got to be a witch!"

"No one's gonna find out," Jailah muttered, a threat tucked into her words. "Not a goddamn soul. Thalia, do your thing."

Thalia suppressed a yelp, but she didn't argue. He was alive now, wasn't he? She wasn't touching a corpse, she was kneeling beside a living, breathing boy.

*God help me.*

Her gray eyes went milky white when she pricked her finger. He stirred as she pressed her wand to his chest.

His heartbeat thrummed in her.

"He's . . . he's very much alive," she said. "Heart rate a little fast, temperature a little high, but nothing worrisome. It's like he just played a game of soccer, not rose from the dead. I think he fainted from the shock of everything." And suddenly, her fear became curiosity. "He's. *Healthy.*"

"Why's he so fresh? He's, like, a hundred years old," Jailah questioned. "I mean, he looks a li'l underfed, but shouldn't he be all maggot-eaten?"

Iris's eyes widened. "It's like someone was saving him for resurrection. Some sort of preservation spell."

"Mathilde?" Thalia asked, rising to her feet. Her tone became hopeful. "She's the one that gave him the cure, right? What if everything was leading to some Haelsfordian witches finding him, bringing him back, and ending the Haunting?"

Logan inhaled sharply. "Guys—"

Suddenly, the Wolf Boy twitched. He muttered incoherently, his voice growing louder with every word.

"He's waking up!" Thalia waved her hand at Logan. "You talk to him."

"What? Why me?"

"Hello?" Iris pointed at herself, then Jai and Thalia. "Hundred-year-old white boy, duh!"

"Mhm." Jailah tucked a threat into those two exaggerated syllables. She twirled her wand. "And if he says somethin' slick, best believe I will not hesitate to—"

The Wolf Boy jolted awake.

"Oh!" he cried, scurrying backward into Jailah's fluffy pink beanbag chair, which startled him even more.

Logan put a hand up at him and said, "Just relax!"

He glared at her, muttering disjointed sentences of fear and confusion.

"You are safe here," she said slowly.

"Where am I?" he whispered fearfully.

"Jesus," Iris muttered somewhere in the background. Thalia knew then that she was not the only one alarmed by the clearness in his voice, the beautiful velvet in his tone. He truly was *alive*.

"Who are you?" he asked, hazel eyes dropping shyly to the floor.

"We're friends," Logan replied. "My name is Logan. This is Iris, Jailah, and Thalia." She drew in a slow, testing breath. "And we are witches."

"Witches?"

"Do you know what witches are? What we can do?" asked Jailah.

He brought his knees to his chest. "God save me. Is this hell?"

Iris bit the inside of her lip hard to keep from sputtering out a giggle. Thalia hit her arm softly.

"What's your name?" Logan continued. "What do you remember?"

Thalia fidgeted. The way Logan looked at him—eyes gentle, cheeks red—felt too intense, like Thalia was intruding on something intimate.

"My name is Theodore Bloom." His eyes darted left and right, searching for familiarity. He put his fingertips to his head and winced. "I remember the cold. I remember the dark. Nothing *here* is familiar. How did this happen?"

"You were preserved by magic through death," Iris said gently. "They say you know about the Haunting."

"Haunting?" he choked out.

"Yes, the Wolves—"

*"The Wolves?"*

Theodore Bloom lunged at Iris and managed to briefly graze her neck before being levitated into the air.

"Poor thing," Jailah whispered, all amusement and malice. With a wave of her hand, she drew him to the middle of the room, and the witches converged around him as he thrashed in the air.

"You will burn for this!" he spat. "Ruination will befall you and your bloodsisters!"

"Calm yourself," Thalia said. She wiggled her fingers in front of his face. "Or I'll do it for you."

Bloom bared his teeth. Then his features softened, and all the cracks of sadness and desperation became visible through his anger. "Let me go!"

He looked to Iris, and she returned his gaze with one unnaturally dark, even for her. "You smell of death," he shouted, eyes wild. He thrashed again, all flailing limbs and futile grunts.

Thalia decided she'd seen enough. She pressed her wand to his chest. *"My Words Are a Lullaby."* He began to calm with every syllable in her incantation. *"Aren't You Tired, Theodore Bloom?"*

He fell into a sudden sleep.

Thalia let out an exhausted huff before plopping onto Jai's bed.

"I think we all deserve a chamomile tea!" Jailah clapped her hands together, but it lacked her usual spark.

"Sixteen missed calls." Iris tinkered with her phone. "I need to update the boys. They're probably freaking out."

"We need to figure out what to do next," Thalia urged.

Jailah cut in while she brewed the tea. "I know, but Trent and Mathew are as much a part of this as we are now. We can't keep them in the dark. We need to know what they're thinking."

Logan said the obvious aloud, curling her shaking hands into fists. "They're liabilities."

Iris turned to Logan. "You okay?"

"Yeah."

"The amplyfyr's intense, and I didn't hold it like you did." She pumped her brows, impressed. "You're a strange witch. I mean that in the best way."

Jailah slipped a warm mug between Thalia's hands. She hadn't realized that she was trembling. "Where is the amplyfyr anyway? Last I remember, Logan had it."

"It disappeared," Logan replied, shaking her head. "I was holding it, and then it turned into ash in my hand, like the resurrection spell used it up and destroyed it."

Jailah made a sound that Thalia couldn't quite place as happy or disappointed. "That's probably for the best."

Iris nodded. "I'll be right back."

She left, and the room went silent.

Thalia sipped her tea, the undead boy dreaming in front of her.

# 23

## iris

"Beaumont," Iris said weakly into her phone. She leaned against the stone wall of the stairway, all the night's horrors catching up with her.

"I've been trying to reach you," Mathew replied tersely.

"I know what you're gonna ask, and everything's okay. How's Trent?"

"He's fine. He's asleep." His voice went cold. "Iris. Are *you* okay?"

Iris ran her fingers along the walls. "Yeah," she whispered, trying to keep her voice steady. "I'm fine."

A tight knot wound up and upon itself in Iris's chest, right between her lungs. Not a metaphorical one; she felt no whimsical nervousness or butterflies or clammy hands, but rather the actual sensation of a ball of string winding in her.

She thought of the Chasm, how an irresistible voice had called, claiming he was the one she was looking for. Iris had known deep in the pit of her stomach that the Chasm was not to be entered, but she had found herself walking toward it, *wanting* to. And before she could stop herself, she dipped her hand into the other side and felt the soul latch on to her.

"What happened tonight?" she asked. "What did you see?"

He released an exhausted sigh. "I'm coming up the Hill."

"Curfew starts in a few minutes!"

"It'll be quick. Meet me out here, please, Iris."

Iris hurried steps down the stairwell. Her phone still pressed to her ear, she broke into the humidity, crossed the courtyard, and waited at the bottom of the Hill. Aside from a few tinny howls, the night was quiet.

And there he was. Close enough that she knew it was him, but far enough that she couldn't quite read his expression.

Mathew's mouth moved. She heard it through the phone. She felt it reverberate in the knot in her chest. "It's going to sound ridiculous."

"Not to me," she replied.

He approached with slow, soft steps. "I don't know how it happened. We were in the graveyard, and you were—" He fumbled for the words.

"Possessed?"

He nodded. "Everything happened at once. I reached for you, and it was like Hallowe'en. Suddenly, I was in the Chasm, and"—he rubbed his chest, right above his heart—"it was like I was reeling you in. Like you were the catch and I the line. I could feel you at the other end, and suddenly you were a weight connected to my soul . . . Uh, that sounds—"

"Corny."

He flashed a smile. "I know. But wherever you were, it didn't matter." His voice went low, and though she tried to resist, it made Iris shiver. "You were coming back to me."

She could see his face in full now. Brow wrinkled, the gray tinge of fatigue under his eyes. He was finally close enough for them to tuck away their phones.

Iris rubbed her eyes, wishing for clarity. "Why do you keep doing this?"

"Doing what?"

"Being you," she said. "Doing nothing but confusing me. The mundane boy who can open the Chasm." Her voice was calm, but Iris was horrified. She didn't feel like herself. She looked down at her hands and didn't recognize them. *A resurrection.* Her power did this. And she hadn't meant to. Her mother had warned her against opening the Chasm, against attempting a resurrection. Iris had to end the Haunting now—it was the only way she could make this awful mischief worth it.

"You're an unknowable one, Beaumont," Iris said finally.

And there was that smug smile she loved to hate. "The feeling's mutual."

Iris looked to the Swamp. "This is the last Haunting. I know it. In the past few weeks, a Haelsfordian ghost spoke to me about the Wolf Boy. I met Logan, and she found his grave. Trent brought us the amplyfyr, and now he's alive." *And you, my mundane tether.* "It can't all just be a coincidence. Also"—she took a deep breath—"accident or not, resurrecting someone is the worst thing a necromancer can do. I keep waiting for the heavens to fall, or for, like, a biblical flood. The end times, hell-raising shit. But there are other, more mortal repercussions. If the Witchery Council finds out, us witches would be banished, and god knows what would happen to you two."

"There's a lot on the line." His voice was steady and cool.

"Yes." She shifted her weight from one foot to another. "Could we borrow some clothes for him? Old shit you don't want, or—"

"Yeah, of course. I can, uh, drop them off tomorrow?"

"Thanks."

Mathew looked down. "So. I know that ending the Haunting is very important to you. But. Couldn't we just . . . get rid of him?"

Iris release a surprised chuckle. "What?"

Mathew shrugged awkwardly, keeping his shoulders up for a second too long. "He was already dead, I mean. Right?"

"Oh, Beaumont," Iris muttered, still laughing. She finally turned back toward Mesmortes. "You're just full of surprises."

Only very specific things made Iris's eyes fill up with wonder. She had a collection of books given to her from her dead mother, and as a largely self-taught necromancer, that mad fit of curiosity only appeared while Iris flipped through those gilded texts, craving something that she hadn't seen before.

She didn't know that people could do that, too.

# 24

## jailah

Jailah couldn't shake the fogginess in her head. It was hard to get a solid eight hours after witnessing a *goddamned resurrection*.

Slowly, she walked up to an abandoned industrial center an hour away from her muggy little town. The lot had been transformed into a skate park of horrors, with pavement-sheared loops and hills, tunnels, and dangerously thin bridges.

*And why not?* Jailah thought. *What else could you do with this life?*

Veronica Dominguez had loved magic. She used it for everything, no matter how simple. She didn't open jars without her wand or walk into the rain without forcing it to fall around her. Vero's parents had spoiled her completely. She could have had anything she wanted from them, but she craved the one thing that they couldn't give her.

"I want to be free," Vero whispered to Jailah one night, the two of them lying across the grass on the Hill. Jailah hadn't understood what she meant at the time, and yet, she ended up becoming the very person that took so much of that freedom away.

Graffiti covered the walls. Jailah's eyes lingered on the symbol left clean in the center: a fleur-de-lis engulfed in flames.

On top of it, in spray-painted letters: BIRTHRIGHT & ANARCHY.

*Adorable*, Jailah thought cuttingly. A sigil for a coven of unwitches and a motto that vowed revenge. Both were so typically Vero.

Jailah popped her bubble gum. Her purse dangled on the edge of her wrist. Her kitten heels clacked noisily against the pavement, daring someone to come by and tell them to quiet, and her waist-length microbraids swayed behind her. A hurricane of a witch dressed like a pretty sun shower.

A boy sat on a metal beam above her. He whistled low.

A girl bounded out of one of the concrete tunnels on a skateboard. She rode so close to Jailah that her ankle was almost snapped by the board.

Before Jailah could tell the girl to watch herself, others shot out of corners and from behind walls, crawling out of the earth like insects. She wasn't sure where Vero had found all these hexbound and hexeaters to make her unwitchy gang, but knew she'd do the same in her position.

*You get kicked out of your community? You make your own.*

Suddenly, Jailah felt a presence behind her.

Veronica Dominguez was wearing red lipstick that looked distressingly close to blood. One side of her head was shaved, and thick braids flowed from the other, green and black. They were once pink, Jai's favorite color. Her deep brown skin was slightly lighter than Jai remembered it, as if Vero hadn't seen the sun in months. She was dressed plainly, a dark sweatshirt and ripped jeans, but still, even with her current unwitchiness, she shone like a beacon.

Veronica tilted her head. Her smile was ravishing, and her delight, dangerous. Hatred brimmed in those wide brown eyes. "Jailah Simmons." She clicked her tongue. "Thought I heard a rat."

Jailah lifted her chin. "Nice to see you, too, Vero. Can we talk?"

Vero shrugged. "We are talking. What do you want?" Her little crew watched them both intently.

"I need your help with something."

"What could a magicless girl like me offer to a powerful witch like you?"

Jailah closed her eyes. Everything about this hurt. She eased kindness into her voice. "I didn't come to fight. I just need essence of alítheia."

Veronica keeled over with laughter, braids swinging, her humor spreading into giggles in the others. When she rose, she wiped her mouth, smudging her red lips. "Can't you get it yourself, Queen Jailah?"

"I'm not twenty-one. No one will sell it to me; you know that."

"Nah, the Jailah I know has endless strings to pull." Vero circled around her, stopping at Jai's back. She leaned in, her breath tickling Jai's ear. "Or are you still afraid of getting into trouble?"

"I wouldn't be here if I had any other choice." Potions that altered people's minds, like alítheia, were heavily regulated and hard to come across. Jailah needed enough for weeks, maybe months, and she couldn't get her hands on that kind of supply without raising some eyebrows. While Vero could no longer make potions, she could still deal the more valuable ones under the table.

And . . . she'd wanted to see her again. At least now she had an actual excuse.

"Find someone else to do your dirty work for you," Vero spat.

Jailah clenched her fists and spun to meet her gaze. She inhaled sharply—she'd landed closer to Vero than expected. There was a familiarity in this closeness, and Jai pushed back the nostalgic tenderness softening her heart. "You're my tether, Vero."

"Aw," Vero said with a smug look of pity. "I'm not your tether. Not anymore. *You* did this."

Jailah caressed her wand, a force of habit.

Vero stepped back, her eyes wide with amusement. "Oh! Are you going to enchant me? You gonna *make me*?" Every word was hardened by a hatred fostered only by a teenaged girl scorned.

Jailah knew exactly what had made her that way. She knew her part in it. She knew how easily this could've been her, wandless and shunned to the point of living in a repurposed industrial complex. But it didn't make Jailah feel better to know where Vero's anger came from. It made her feel worse.

"Tell me what you want."

Veronica glanced over at one of her henchmen. Immediately, the redhead skated away into the playground's main tunnel. "I want you to admit your sins."

Jailah looked at her phone. "Only if we make it quick."

Vero winked. "Ooh! I haven't heard that in a while."

The red-haired girl came back with a small clear flask, a pale gold liquid sloshing around slowly in it.

"I'll need more than that."

Veronica grinned. "This is the price." She held it out to Jailah.

Jailah didn't think. She just took one long swig and felt it creep in. The alítheia became an oddly satisfying fire burning up in her. It was like being drunk and lowering your inhibitions, without the dizziness or the sick, or like anything could be said and everyone would forgive you. Suddenly, Veronica Dominguez, the only girl in the world who might want to see Jailah suffer, looked like her most trusted confidante.

"Ask me what you want," Jailah said, her sweet voice taking a harsher tone.

"First," Vero said, pointing upward, "up there."

⸻•••✦ ✪ ✦•••⸻

Balancing atop a thin metal beam a good sixty feet from the unforgiving ground, Jailah took a deep breath.

Vero looked up at her, eyes searing with hate.

Jailah sometimes wondered what they would be now if Vero hadn't sought out that ugly little book, inscribed with the name of one Olga Yara. How many kisses they'd have racked up, or how many arguments. Maybe they'd be making junior prom plans. Maybe they'd have broken up. Regardless, Veronica would have been her tether.

If only she hadn't asked Jailah to cast *The Culling* with her.

If only Jailah hadn't stabbed her in the back.

The truth potion thrummed in her, oiling up her jaw. Below, the others jeered loud and cruel.

She knew Vero's game. A witch like Jailah could potentially fight it if she concentrated hard enough, which was quite difficult considering she was spending all her willpower on not splattering to the ground beneath her. She dripped sweat, and her calves burned.

A girl yelled up at her, "WE CALL THIS TRUTH OR DIE!"

"Least she ain't chicken shit!" another voice mocked.

*I know that's right.*

"Who's the potion for?" Vero asked.

Jailah exhaled. The words were ready to spill out, promising a wave of bliss if she'd just let them free.

"A boy!" she said between gritted teeth.

"A *boy*?" Veronica stepped away from her friends, a speck in Jailah's peripheral vision. "What boy's got you all hung up?"

Jailah watched another fat drop of sweat hit the beam. She forced herself to bite down on a little sliver of her tongue. Her mouth filling with the taste of iron, she built up a wall of witchery, reinforcing the parts of her that the potion tried so desperately to limit. Concrete blocks stacked up in a moldy wall of wood.

*"Jailah . . ."* Vero sang.

Jailah groaned, searching for a truth. "A boy you've never met!"

She felt Vero's ferocious eyes on her. "Oh yeah, what'd he do?"

Jailah's mind slipped briefly toward the pain shooting up her legs. *A truth. Any little truth.* "He's alive!"

There was someone else in the distance. One of Veronica's sentinels. Jailah could just barely see her.

Hurriedly, Vero cupped her hands around her mouth. "Hey! If you had to choose one of your girls to throw into the Swamp, who'd it be?"

Jailah tried to shut her teeth against it, but a word slipped through the cracks. "Thalia!"

She fell from the beam.

Her gasp catching in her throat from the shock. It happened so swiftly, Jailah hadn't realized that it wasn't her leg that gave out. She'd been knocked down.

She stopped abruptly, just a foot from the concrete ground.

"Remember trust falls?" a voice said plainly.

It wasn't one of Veronica's sentinels. It was one of Jailah's.

Vero's crew scattered. None wanted to get caught too long in the gaze of the witch who, unlike Jailah, came in wand blazing.

162

Thalia glared at Veronica. "Give us the alítheia. I'm not Jailah. You won't find me hesitating."

Veronica stuck out her tongue, sunlight glinting off the black ball pierced in the center of it. "You're hesitating right now."

Thalia pointed her wand between Veronica's eyes. "Have some dignity, unwitch. Don't make me take it from you—"

"I'll talk to the Haelsford Witchery Council," Jailah said suddenly.

Both Thalia and Vero turned to her. "What?" they said, with *very* different inflections.

"I have an internship with High Witch Lucia this summer, and I think I can convince her to end your punishment early."

Vero hesitated. "You're just saying what you think I want to hear. Your word means nothing to me."

"I'm on alítheia."

"You're a snake. Alítheia or not, I don't trust you."

Before she could stop herself, Jailah cut into her thumb with the sacrificial needle embedded in her wand. "What about a bloodpact?"

"Jailah!" Thalia shouted roughly. But she ignored her.

"I will try my hardest to unbind you, Veronica—"

"Leave it," Vero said, pulling a flask from her back pocket and shoving it into Jailah's hand. "I don't want your bullshit bloodpact. I've only got five years left; I'll survive. Find some other way to clear your guilty-ass conscience."

"Was that so hard?" Thalia mocked.

Vero stalked off, not giving either of them another look.

"Seriously? *Seriously?*" Thalia shouted at Jailah. She walked off in the other direction, her dismissal like a slap in the face. Thalia didn't say another word until Jailah drove them into the roundabout before Mesmortes.

"I can't believe you offered her a bloodpact, Jailah! If you couldn't come through, she'd own you."

Jailah couldn't hold it in any longer. "You know . . . I only told the Witchery Council about Vero's plan to cast *The Culling* because she was a threat to me, she was stronger than me, and when I saw the opportunity to take her down, I did."

"I know."

Jailah shook her head, unable to process Thalia's nonchalance. "I'm a terrible person."

"*The Culling* could've killed you both! Jesus, thank god the Council got rid of that Olga Yara book."

Jailah bit the inside of her cheek. Olga Yara was taught to young witches as a cautionary tale for pressing the limits of witchery. The old witch had gained notoriety for sacrificing great things for powerful spells and sealed her fate after murdering six children in a healing spell to save her dying baby. Her magic worked, but when the baby cried, it was in the voices of the ones Yara had killed. She couldn't stand it, so she buried the baby, got banished for it, and was hanged by mundanes.

*The Culling* was supposed to strip the magic of nearby witches, and that power would be given to the ones casting the spell. But it was tricky to pull off; the incantation was about six pages long, and if it wasn't recited perfectly in one go, it cast a death spell instead. The heretic witch had an awful sense of humor, as if she wanted to test the strength of any witch who dared use her spells.

It was best that Thalia didn't know that the ugly Yara grimoire was in

Haelsford at this very moment, hidden in Iris's chapel with a collection of equally forbidden books that her mother had given her. Iris was glad to have it, and Jailah had relished that curious look in the deathwitch's dark eyes.

"There's nothing wrong with looking out for yourself. You could've been hexbound for years. Can you imagine?"

Jailah didn't like to think about it. She parked the car, her hands trembling. "You know why I chose you, right? To throw into the Swamp?"

Thalia didn't look at her. "You had to choose one of us. The elixir demanded it."

"It's because you should be dead by now."

Thalia fidgeted, as if anticipating Jailah's next words.

"I mean, *I* probably would be. There are twelve hundred people in Annex, and they all want to see you hanged. What's a Wolf to a town that wants you dead? You endure, babe. You're the only person in the world who could wade into the Swamp and come out with a cute sweater of red fur. All that corrupted earth, all that hexed nature. If there's anyone in Haelsford who could survive it, it's you."

"Damn, you're good at that." Thalia smiled.

Finally, Jailah felt calm. "Ain't nothing but the truth, T."

# 25

## logan

Theodore Bloom sat on the plush couch in the middle of the Topthorne House hollow room.

On the coffee table was a brass teapot full of hot black tea and a Cuban sandwich from town. He ate. He drank. He still looked a little pale and gray, like the death he was touched by wanted to make itself known.

The Red Three stood by the fire, discussing what to do with him. Logan tried to pay attention and offer whatever help she could, but it was a lost cause.

For one, she was *baby witch*, forever doomed to follow and not lead.

Secondly, she had lied to their faces about the amplyfyr and wasn't sure if she could do so again. It hadn't disintegrated last night. She'd managed to slip it into her knapsack while the others were distracted. But with the amplyfyr back in its sanctifum, all her confidence disappeared. She no longer itched for her wand, and she didn't want to try any magic without the stone.

Thirdly, she couldn't look away from the undead boy. Logan sat across from him. Whether the others noticed, she didn't know, because she didn't turn back.

His hand resting against his forehead and his eyes to the floor, Theodore didn't look up at her. His thin shoulders were hunched over. Mathew had dropped off some clothes and the Hammersmitt sweatshirt was loose around Theodore's frail frame. Logan examined the pale skin of his sharp collarbones, savoring it the way she would've if this were still in her dreams.

*I found you.*

Logan topped off his tea. "Hi."

His eyes flitted under his hand.

*I scryed for you.*

"Are you feeling okay?" she asked.

*You asked for my help.*

He shook his head. All the hysteria from the night before had become a quiet despair.

*And now you're here.*

"You're going to have to talk at some point."

"I did not ask for this," he whispered shakily.

"I know." Logan dropped her voice. "I know about a lot of things. I know you loved Mathilde."

Finally, he lifted his eyes, sadness intensifying their beauty. But his words were cruel. "You won't say that name to me again. I would rather cut off my own ears than hear it."

"But you did love her, didn't you?"

Logan watched as he struggled against the alítheia. Whatever he was remembering of Mathilde now, it was something pleasant. She was surprised to see that smile, how full and young he looked with it. It was the first time she'd seen him purely without pain since his resurrection.

Maybe it was just the truth potion, but she wanted it to be an effect of her presence.

She leaned in. "But she betrayed you."

"Unsurprising." Something Logan couldn't quite place flickered in the Wolf Boy's hazel eyes. "I take it you've never been in love?"

Logan held his gaze, trying to decipher that mystifying look.

He leaned in just as she meant to look away, as if he didn't want to relinquish the hold he had on her. "Avoid it. I'd hate to see a sweet girl like you burdened with all that pain."

Logan's hands curled into fists. It wasn't an insult, but she couldn't stand the presumption. Baby Witch. Sweet Girl. It was all the same.

Theodore looked her up and down, his features softening. "I mean no offense. I feel awfully lucky that the first face I saw in this new life was one of a girl so kind."

*The first face I saw.* That, Logan liked. She watched as he silently questioned why he'd kept talking, the alítheia in full effect now.

"Logan. That's your name?" he asked. Her name on his tongue was both comforting and unnerving.

"Wyatt. Logan Wyatt. Logan Phillip Wyatt."

"Did your father expect a baby boy?"

She shrugged. "No. But my *parents* liked the name, so that's what they named me."

"Logan Phillip Wyatt." He mulled it over, taking care to languish on every syllable. "What is your talent?"

"My talent?"

"I can feel your auras." Theodore looked over at the auspicious group debating in the corner. "Jailah. She's got more power than you. Iris, my savior, is a grim reaper of a girl. Thalia has her magic touch and healing heart. So . . ."

"I'm not special," Logan said, rising from her seat.

He stopped her with a gentle touch on her knuckle. "Then why do I recognize you?"

She exhaled sharply. She felt the peculiar anxiety of being caught doing something she shouldn't have been.

"How? How could I know you?" Theodore examined her face.

"I don't know," Logan said quickly, pulling her hand away. This wasn't the time. The Red Three were drawing away from the fireplace.

Jailah ran her fingers over the delicate teapot. She said it belonged to her grandmother, and Logan wondered if she ever thought it'd be used to loosen up the mind of the resurrected Wolf Boy. The thought floored Logan because it still seemed so inconceivable that this was real life, that this was happening. But there he was, sitting right across from her.

*I brought you back.*

"Before we go further," Jailah interrupted, "we just wanna say that we're huge fans. Aside from, you know, what happened last night." Her tone was sweet, but Logan thought she looked like she wanted to flip the table over.

Bloom leaned back. "I don't understand."

"Well, I'd explain it to you, but the last time we mentioned Haelsford's unfortunate li'l affliction, you tried to attack my girl."

Iris rolled her eyes. "We're gonna need you to not do that again, okay?"

Bloom looked down. "I'm sorry. That was horrible of me. You mentioned the Wolves and I just . . . I don't know what came over me."

Iris nodded. "So, you can end the Haunting?"

"I—I don't understand," he answered.

"But you knew the Strigwach Sisters, right?" Thalia asked.

Theodore swallowed. "Yes. Mathilde, Adelaide, and Sloane. They wanted to slaughter every innocent soul in our village."

"Innocent?" Jailah sneered. "You stole the town! You hunted witches for fun!"

"No. I never took part."

"That's right. He didn't," Logan added.

They all looked to her.

She bit the inside of her cheek. "Alítheia. Remember?"

Iris considered this with a small nod. "I have to be sure." Her voice wavered. Logan imagined she'd expected an actual god, not a boy who looked too frail to wield any sort of power against the monsters of the Swamp. "Look, you're supposed to be the Wolf Boy. You need to tell us everything."

"I know nothing of anything that could help you. But I *heard* you, death-witch. You've been calling me. There was a light that led me toward your voice, and then . . . I woke up." He paused. "She called me that once," Theodore muttered shamefully. "*My little wolfboy.* I don't know what it means."

Thalia stepped forward. "I can help you remember. Well, maybe. I've never done this on, uh, a dead person before."

She pulled out her wand, and Theodore bucked away.

"Back away, witch!" he cried.

Logan grabbed his hand. He didn't pull away. "It's okay, Theodore. We're good witches. We just want to end the Haunting, and you can help us. It's not gonna hurt."

He looked at Thalia, still wary.

Thalia lifted her hands. "I'll be pulling some memories. Stay calm, keep breathing, and you won't feel a thing."

Logan held her breath as Thalia recited a spell of her own making. *"Show Me Your Memories."* She twisted her wand near Theodore's right temple and wound smoky purple puffs like cotton candy around the tip.

Eyes closed, Theodore clenched his jaw.

Thalia inspected the smoke closely. "They're fractured. His memories . . . *break*. Here—" Thalia swished her wand, and the memories filled the room around them, as if playing on multiple projectors.

Black smoke tinged the purple. Theodore's eyes began to twitch.

"There he is," Logan whispered.

Images flashed, showing pieces of who Theodore Bloom was in his past life. He helped an old woman with her pregnant dog and planted seeds in a garden. He dropped a dish and was smacked by his father for it. His brothers ridiculed him for not taking up arms against witches.

As the Strigwach Sisters came to town, Iris and Jailah gasped. Logan looked at the confusion on the Red Three's faces as they tried to parse the quick-moving images. None of this was new to her, though Adelaide's angry green eyes still made her flinch.

"There!" Jailah shouted suddenly.

The room went dark for a moment, but a flash of light revealed a figure standing in curves of wet rock.

"Is that the Cavern?" Iris asked.

Darkness, again. The corrupted memory played like a video that wouldn't fully buffer. But the sounds were clear—howling Wolves, and Theodore Bloom's frightened voice.

"What do you want with me?" His voice echoed around them.

The figure stepped into a sliver of light.

Jailah gasped.

"Holy shit," Iris whispered.

"Mathilde," Thalia said, breathless.

It was like seeing through a foggy window. Logan's dreams were much more vivid, but the Mathilde here was still entrancing. Her eyes screamed determination against her pale face. She brandished her wand and parted her lips to speak—

*"My little wolfboy."*

Theodore cried out suddenly, his body twitching, his face contorting in pain. Logan went to him, and for a moment, considered holding him. Instead, she turned to the others. "Uh, guys!"

Her wand still outstretched, Thalia dropped to her knees. She grunted. "It's like he's fighting me!"

"You gotta hold on, T!" Jailah shouted over Thalia's whines and Theodore's grunts.

But this memory broke and melded into another. Thalia's and Theodore's breaths calmed as the room went dark again.

And when the images appeared once more, drenched in purple smoke, each witch found herself staring at her own awestruck image as they looked down into the Wolf Boy's grave.

Thalia pulled off her glasses and exhaled hard. "That's it. That's all he's got."

"What?" Iris's disbelief was touched with anger. "How can that be it?"

"Sorry, do *you* want to try?"

"I just mean—" Iris's expression softened as she turned her attention to

Theodore Bloom, who sat sheepishly on the couch. Logan felt for him. That look from the deathwitch could stop hearts. "What do we do now? How do we end it?"

Theodore sat slumped over with his hands in his hair. "I don't know," he choked out.

"What happened in the Cavern? What did Mathilde do to you?"

Thalia shook her head. "Iris, you don't understand. *That's it.* Everything we saw is everything he remembers."

Her words threw the girls into a stunned silence. Iris's mouth popped open, and her hands were outstretched toward Jailah as if expecting a solution, or a miracle. But Jailah wore a rare expression of helplessness. Thalia merely rubbed her eyes and sighed. With all that had happened not even twelve hours earlier, no one wanted to believe that there was yet another mystery to discover. This was just the beginning.

Jailah finally broke the silence. "This was never gonna be easy, was it? There's gotta be something we're missing, but until we figure it out—" She nodded at Thalia. "Go to Hammersmitt. It's time for the boys to chip in. He can't stay here."

"Then what?" Logan asked, so quietly that she could hear the fire crackling over her own voice.

Silence fell again. The witches looked to the Wolf Boy. They'd expected a warrior, not a teenaged boy wrapped up in anxieties and one of Mathew's oversized sweaters. Finally, they understood how it felt to be thoroughly disappointed by their own witchery.

Logan had never felt closer to them than she did now.

# 26

## trent

Trent's eyes flew open, bedsheets tangled all around him like vines. He gasped for air. Outside, the newly awakened Wolves were howling in the Swamp.

He held his head in his hands. Thalia had given him a potion to take care of his post-fainting nausea. Not only had it knocked him right out, but it also gave him wicked nightmares.

His heart pounded. No . . . they weren't nightmares at all. Last night's horrors came to him at once. The wind, Iris's possession, the boy in the grave.

A voice bombarded his thoughts. *Blood is better, flesh is best!*

Like a knife, a thought cut through the drowsiness. Before the graveyard, before the resurrection, there was a spellbook.

He had gone to visit the Roddin Witch alone.

Mathew hadn't known, and though it wasn't meant to be a betrayal, it had felt like one. But he needed to know.

"What if . . . I wanted to bring her back?"

Roddin released a dark burst of laughter. "You can't raise the dead as you please. Think of all the madness that would be done if any witch could go on reanimating souls. That's why there are so few of us touched with death. Even after all the terms have been met and all the blood has been spilled, after the winds have turned and the rains have changed, the earth must see it fit."

It wasn't a satisfying answer. So, when he pressed on about resurrection, she pulled a fat book from a rickety shelf. The ink on the pages was faded. Trent ran his fingers over the words.

"The book is bound with human skin," Roddin had said plainly, before riffling through the pages.

Trent yelped and drew his hand away. With a clawlike finger, she pointed to the terms for revival.

Trent's eyes widened at the archaic handwriting. "An amplyfyr, fresh blackthorne, elixir of the fallen?"

"Hair is good, blood is better, flesh is best."

The thought of carrying around a piece of his mother's decayed body turned his stomach. "A soul's circle, candles, and—" He squinted at the text. "Wait, *what*?" Trent's blood ran cold. He read the curvy text of the last ingredient once more before looking up at her. "You're shittin' me."

The Roddin Witch cackled as she pressed her hand to his shoulder, nails digging into his skin. "Raising the dead. Did you really think it would be easy?"

⸺⸳⸳⸳•➤ ✪ ◀•⸳⸳⸳⸺

"Matty!" Trent yelled suddenly. He yanked off his satin bonnet and clumsily grabbed his mud-splattered jeans from the floor. He pulled his phone out of the pocket, and an icon of an empty battery taunted him. "Oi! *Matty!*"

Mathew didn't answer. He must've been at Soma Café.

Trent scrambled for the charger coming out of the wall under his desk. An agonizing minute passed before the phone booted up and allowed Trent to place one very tense voice mail in Mathew's inbox: *WHEN YOU GET THIS, CALL ME! AND STAY AWAY FROM THE WITCHES, MATTY!*

He texted a similar thing with ten exclamation points before jumping into the shower.

Underneath the steaming water, Trent cursed himself for getting involved with the witches. Instead of spending last night doing stupid Hammersmitt things, he witnessed a full-fledged resurrection. Trent would've thought that was cool just a few weeks ago. But after seeing the boy climb up from the grave, and knowing what he knew about the last ingredient to the resurrection spell . . .

Trent clutched the bar in the shower. He felt dizzy, he felt sick. But he had to find Matty, and the two of them needed to leave Haelsford. Maybe for good.

After he pulled on clean clothes, there was a knock at the front door. He ran to it, his still-damp feet slapping against the floor.

Trent flung the door open, and his heart went wild.

"Hey!" Thalia Blackwood beamed at him. "Um, how are you feeling?"

*You twit. Mathew wouldn't have knocked; he has a bloody key.* "Fine," Trent said, the sound more a stutter than a word.

She had a thermos in hand and extended it to him. "I brought tea!"

He took the thermos, careful not to touch her hands. He didn't want her to feel them shaking.

She cocked her head. "I wanted to talk to you about last night."

*Calm down. She'll know something's wrong.* "Come on in."

Thalia took a seat at the marble island in their kitchen, marveling at it. Dark circles lined her eyes. "Hammersmitt is even bougier than I thought."

Trent forced a laugh. He chanced a look to his bedroom, where his mother's knife rested on the windowsill. Quickly, he angled a glass jar of cocoa clusters at Thalia. "Matty's sister made them."

"Don't mind if I do," Thalia said cheerily. She treated herself to two clusters while Trent took a few nervous sips of his tea. It warmed him up immediately, the heat spreading through his muscles.

"Feeling better?" she asked.

He rubbed the back of his neck and stretched. "Yeah." Much better, actually. He could feel all the tension slipping away from him. *You can't be alone with her*, he thought, even as he considered divulging everything to her. *You need the knife.*

"What are you thinking about?" she asked.

*You can't trust her.* "I need to go grab—"

Thalia put her hand on his. "I'm sorry. You and Mathew are part of this now, and part of *us*. I can't go around trusting everyone I meet, but with you guys, I have no choice. Trent, have you told anyone about the Wolf Boy?"

A warmth crept up his throat, demanding to be released. "What? No."

"Is there anyone that you want to tell?"

Trent shook his head furiously.

Thalia leaned back and pulled her messy brown curls into a loose bun. "And if it were ever to come down to us, the witches, or to you and Mathew, who do you choose?"

He didn't hesitate. "I choose us. All of us."

Thalia's eyes widened. She'd looked older in the past minute or so, but as a stream of sunlight from the kitchen windows touched her face, she relaxed. "You are too good." She removed her glasses and rubbed her eyes before replacing them. "I'm sorry I had to do this."

She shuffled in her knapsack for something, and when she lowered her head to rummage, Trent felt that heat throughout him once more. It was killing him not to speak. "I'm scared."

She looked up at him, now holding a small vial of an oily green liquid. "Of what?"

*Don't.*

"Of you," Trent choked out. Every time he thought, *Stop talking*, the words seemed to place a heavy heat on his tongue, like he was swallowing smoldering coals.

Thalia's expression changed from curious to concerned, a transformation so quick that Trent flinched. "Why would you be afraid of me?"

Trent's short-lived resistance dissipated. "The last ingredient in a resurrection spell is the blood of a murderess, which means one of you killed someone. Is it you?"

The warmth slipped away, and with stark clarity, Trent looked down at his tea.

He looked up and found himself staring straight at the point of Thalia's wand. Her thumb bled. "Does Mathew know?"

Trent raised a hand reflexively. "No!"

"How did you find me?"

"I didn't find you! I just read about resurrection from a book in Roddin's— Thalia, put the wand down!"

"You won't forgive me for this," she said coldly.

And Trent found enough viciousness to throw himself at her. They fell to the floor hard, and the wand spun out of Thalia's grasp. Trent pushed himself off her quickly, desperately, but as he made for the wand, he heard her say something indistinguishable and surely witchy.

Where she got another wand from, he didn't know. He lurched back. "Thalia, no!"

A blast of black smoke rushed toward him.

Trent went slack. He could feel a voice chattering through his memories like a surgeon's tools, picking away for something meaningful . . .

"Trent! Hello?!" Thalia waved her hand in front of his face.

He was standing in the middle of the kitchen while she sat on a stool, holding a handful of chocolates. Something about this seemed dreamlike, though the solidity of the floor beneath him couldn't have been faked.

Had he invited Thalia in? Yes.

*Yes*, and he'd offered her the jar of chocolates that Becky made.

"You were asking me about the Wolf Boy," Thalia whispered, leaning over the counter. She was close. Trent could count her freckles. "His name is Theodore Bloom."

*Yes.* She'd come to check on him, and he asked her about the boy who'd risen from his grave.

*That sounds right.*

*That* is *right.*

Trent's head hurt badly, but he smiled. "What are you planning on doing with him?"

"We think he should stay here. It's way too risky to keep him at Mesmortes with other witches. You guys can pass him off as a friend, or a transfer student . . . Where is Mathew anyway? He came by to drop off some clothes. Have you seen him since?"

"Mathew?" Trent reached back into a clouded mess of memories. "Probably Soma Café. I haven't seen him all morning."

And Trent continued to reach and reach and reach, like he was looking for something that he'd never seen before.

"So, it'd be okay?" Thalia asked, snapping him out of it. "For Bloom to crash here?"

"Yeah." Trent shrugged. "Totally."

He popped a cocoa cluster into his mouth, suddenly content.

# 27

## thalia

Talullah Turner wasn't sorry. She was sick of being sorry.

Her blessing arrived in the worst place for a preacher's daughter that it could: in the middle of Mass, during her father's sermon. She was thirteen years old.

Witchery theory stated that blessings came when the witch was most vulnerable. In a physical sense for most, and that usually meant while they were sleeping. They'd find themselves floating above their bed, awoken by that terrifying sense of falling, or from scratching their face on a popcorn ceiling, or bumping their head. A bit of fear, maybe a bit of blood. That would have been preferable.

With a hallelujah on her lips, Talullah felt an ungodly heat creep up her spine and spread throughout her. It came from within, like she'd swallowed a flame, and her terrified heartbeat only made it stronger. She turned to the pews of worshippers, analyzing them with a critical eye. Her witchy senses were coming in like baby teeth. Suddenly, her surroundings felt questionable. Was she safe? Mrs. Marsters, her second-grade teacher, was looking at her kind of funny. What was she thinking?

Witches were more than just mundanes who could manipulate magic and wield wands. Their entire beings were augmented. Instincts were heightened, senses reinforced, bodies made more durable. Not infallible or invincible, but whatever you believed gave witches their power—the earth, evolution, the devil, or an all-seeing being—it equipped its chosen with almost-feral tools needed to outlast centuries of violence against their kind.

Talullah thought she was having a panic attack.

Her mother touched her hand. "Are you okay?"

Talullah looked up. Her mother's dark brown skin was lined with worry. The burgeoning witch drew in a shaky breath. "I don't know." Her body felt like it was on fire. "I think I'm gonna be sick—"

Her eyes snapped forward as the organ resounded, the blare of "Ave Maria" vibrating through the church. The worshippers stood for their song, and when Talullah picked herself up, she found that her feet weren't touching the ground.

She opened her mouth in shock, but the scream she heard wasn't her own. It was her mother's. Then one scream became a chorus of cries, replacing what should've been joyous song.

It wasn't possible. Talullah's parents' bloodlines were clean, and witches were born of Satan's hellfire, not to a pious couple living in Annex, Arizona.

*Please, God, not me.*

She floated higher into the church, powerless. The congregation looked up in silent horror. She looked down, ashamed.

Talullah fell, drenched in the piercing red light of the stained-glass windows.

The impact drew gasps, but it didn't hurt much. The sharp pain in her skull seemed more related to stress than hitting her head against the church floor.

She closed her eyes, wishing this was a nightmare to wake from.

When she opened them, her father stared down at her with a hatred reserved for the most depraved sinners. Brows furrowed in disbelief, pale face red with shock.

She should've run then.

Abraham Turner was an exquisite liar. "We will always love you," he said later that evening. "But you are an abomination."

Talullah wrung her hands. "Why is this happening to me? You said that God looked at his children with love and forgiveness. Why am I being punished?"

Fiona Turner pursed her lips into a thin line. "Your tone, Lullah."

For all of Talullah's devotion, the one thing she could never get behind was God allowing suffering. She bothered her parents about it incessantly. *If God is so good, then why are people hungry? Why is there murder, war, death?* Talullah was never satisfied with whatever verse they spat at her in response.

"Tell me," Talullah said, a bit angry. "Why me?"

Her mother approached. She stroked Talullah's hair. "Resist the pull of the devil's witchery, and you will find God's love. Give in, and you will only find damnation."

Talullah spent weeks under the keen eye of not only her parents but the entire population of this little town. It infuriated her. She knew in her heart that they'd just been *waiting* for her to fuck up. Even if Talullah shared her father's gray eyes, height, and ever-curious expression, her light brown skin and loose curls were of her mother. That was all they saw, and finally, they all had an excuse to judge.

It was okay at first. Talullah could handle her father's sermons, always pointed toward her, taking on more violent themes. She ignored the taunts at school and learned that even without a wand, a raised hand and a murmur sent them all running. It didn't last long. The others realized that she was never really going to do anything. She didn't have a wand, and worse, she didn't have the courage.

*I deserve this*, she thought. *I am an abomination.*

But her power begged to be released, no matter how hard she tried to ignore the spark. When she ran away from bullies after school, the trees bent toward her like they meant to embrace her. An exposed root that Talullah easily jumped over tripped several of the others. And the way the wind sang and the willows whispered, beckoning her . . . it didn't sound like the voice of Satan.

After a month of restrained curiosity, Talullah locked her bedroom door and sat cross-legged with her laptop, a half-filled bag of Doritos, and one of her mom's famous coconut almond cupcakes. She typed *how to be a witch* into Google.

Outside, the wind gusted in approval.

At three a.m., eyes burning, Talullah dialed a familiar number.

The voice on the other end was frantic. "Lullah? What is it? What's wrong?"

"I need a wand," Tallulah whispered.

"That's why you're calling me?" Aunt Nonni paused. "You need a wand?"

"I can't get one myself. There aren't any witchy shops here, and I can't just order one!" She had to feel the weight of it. She had to let the wandmaker pull her blood into the wand and hitch the connection between the wood and her heart.

Nonni sighed. Talullah could hear Maria, Nonni's wife, chuckling on the other end.

"There's a wandmaker in Phoenix," Talullah whispered excitedly. "I looked him up. He has good reviews. So I can come visit you, right, and you can take me?"

"Oh, your parents would just love that."

"*Please*, Nonni."

Nonni sighed again. "I have next weekend off. If they'll let you visit, then maybe. We'll see."

"Yay!"

"I said *maybe*."

In the end, she got the wand.

She only practiced when her parents were out. That didn't happen often since her mom ran a bakery from home, but on Saturday nights when they went out to dinner, they left her behind, believing her when she claimed that her witchery might act up.

Talullah twirled her wand. She dripped her blood into her father's violets and watched them shiver. She wrote down spells from open-source grimoires on the internet and learned about incanting from a YouTuber named NotYourMothersWitchery. She pricked her thumb with her mom's sewing needles.

But she needed more. Herbs, a cauldron, a sanctified needle . . . she needed to be around other witches. She needed to go to a school for kids like her.

Nonni agreed. "Your father will never talk to me again, but you can't stay there."

Talullah didn't like the tension in those last words, like there was more to fear in Annex than her parents' disapproval.

Abraham and Fiona never found the wand. They never looked through her diary of scribbled spells or attempted to unlock her laptop and scan the browser history. Nonni never snitched. No one would've ever known that Talullah was a practicing witch if not for Oliver, Raina, and Michelle, sophomores at St. Christopher's. The prodigal offspring of the affluent Warner family did nothing but terrorize the younger citizens of Annex. Talullah had never been a target since Abraham held so much sway.

That was over now.

She'd felt the grating wrongness of her walk home from school, but the baby witch didn't yet know how to respond to it.

Her eyes burned when they pelted her with blackthorne-steeped water balloons. She thought her skin was going to fall off; she thought she was going to go blind. The Warner triplets were in their perfect black convertible but leapt out once she was on her knees, gasping for breath.

Raina kicked her hard with a heeled boot, and Talullah felt the cruel warmth of blood spread over her face.

"We're just preparing you," Michelle said sweetly. "They torture witches in hell. Get used to it."

Talullah stayed down, even as her body pleaded at her to get up and run away.

Another kick to the head, this time from Oliver, and her skull rebounded off the sidewalk so hard that her vision was dotted with little white spots. Her witchery couldn't protect her now.

Or could it?

It was risky to take her wand to school, but Talullah couldn't bear to be away from it. As the Warners trotted toward their car, she pulled it from the waistband of her pleated skirt. Her vision still blurred, her mind still reeling, she pushed her magic hard against the watered-down blackthorne that was trying to subdue her. Talullah aimed at Raina texting in the back seat.

*"Azuamorraille,"* she whispered.

She'd just wanted to scare them. Lift Raina into the air and dangle her there until she wet her pants. Maybe she'd cry, and apologize, and they'd never mess with her again.

But it wasn't just Raina that levitated.

The entire car lifted with all of them in it, and in Talullah's horrified shock, she swung her wand and sent the car crashing violently into the side of the high school.

Talullah was frozen. It was the most awful thing she'd ever seen.

The sidewalk was soon full of jaw-dropped passersby, scrambling and screaming and looking at Talullah like she was the devil incarnate.

*God, no,* she thought, realizing that so many people had seen her.

Then she felt anger like she'd never known before. They'd all seen *everything* and chose to stand around and watch. Nothing mattered until their own were hurt, never mind the witch bleeding on the pavement.

Like vultures, they converged on her, and Talullah knew she could either run away or stay here, take responsibility, and die. She hadn't known then that she'd killed Oliver, but even if they'd all survived, she knew what the consequences would be.

In that one moment of selfishness and self-preservation, she was changed forever.

This was why Thalia Blackwood could understand every bit of Jailah's thought process in betraying Vero, and why Jailah understood her. Even so, Thalia didn't tell her about altering Trent's mind. There was a standing moral code of witchery. Thalia never intended to break it. She didn't *like* messing around in Trent's head. But if the last ingredient of a resurrection spell called for a murderess's blood, then no one could ever know that she was the one to supply it.

This was for survival. If her own father could lead the witchhunt to her with torches and blackthorne-loaded guns, then a Hammersmitt she barely knew surely could, too.

An icy tremor inched up her spine. Thalia knew herself to be needlessly paranoid, but she couldn't deny that outside of the Wolf Boy, if there was anyone with the power to bring them all down, it was the Roddin Witch. She knew too much about their interest in the Wolf Boy, and she had a book with the spell for bringing up the dead.

Standing in front of her cabin, Thalia called Maverick. *Come on, lazy-bones.* He appeared from behind the window first, then popped through the doggy door and ran to his witch.

Thalia touched the top of his head.

*Keep an eye on her. But don't get too close.*

He barked in agreement.

*I mean it. She was once a deathwitch. And she's done something horrible. Let me know what you find.*

Thalia pulled her hand and her thoughts away. She didn't need him to sense this last bit—

*She's the only person in Haelsford I'm afraid of.*

# 28

## mathew

In the living room of Beaumont Manor, the young heirs exchanged a secret code of eye rolls and smirks while their parents tried their hardest to discredit each other.

Mathew's parents were tense, the two of them surrounded by beauty and wealth but neither feeling like they had anything particularly valuable in their lives. Mathew was already annoyed that he'd spent hours rummaging in the basement for witchy things and come up empty. His parents' squabbling only amplified the headache in his skull.

He was *bored*. Just a few days ago, he watched a boy pull himself out of his own casket. And now that undead boy was at Helios Dorm, probably riffling through his protein bars, or summoning the devil, or whatever magical zombie boys did in their spare time. Mathew hadn't known what to think when the witches brought him over, but now he considered himself unimpressed. The witches seemed to agree, judging from their annoyed expressions, and he felt that whatever Iris imagined she'd have to do to end the Haunting, Bloom was not what she'd envisioned.

Rebecca cleared her throat and shot him a questioning look. He only sighed, unable to hide his lack of interest.

"Your father thinks it'd be best for you to go with him to Orlando after the divorce is finalized," Frances Beaumont said, looming over Rebecca. The way she said *father* made Mathew roll his eyes.

"I'm not going anywhere," he muttered.

"Neither am I," Rebecca added.

"Why? It's not like either of you are witches." Ainsley Beaumont poured more bourbon into his coffee.

"Not yet, at least," whispered Rebecca.

The adults grimaced.

Mathew grinned.

"You're almost eighteen," Mother and Father said simultaneously, their witch aversion the one thing they agreed on.

"I hear witches are getting their blessings later and later these days," Mathew said.

Rebecca stretched out her arms, wriggling her fingers. "Oooh, you know, lately I've been feeling a bit *weird*, like I told you, Matty."

"I bet we'll be witchy by next week!"

"You know the first thing I'm gonna do?" Rebecca turned slowly toward her parents. "I'm cooking up a love potion like you've never seen." Her tone went faux jolly, like a disgruntled teen forced to play elf at the mall in December. "We'll be a family again!"

*"Enough,"* Frances growled. "My family has lived in Haelsford forever. We've raised you here so that you would learn to stand tall in the face of witchery, not to cower at it, and certainly not to dabble in it."

Ainsley scoffed. "Never mind that you might get mauled by a goddamn Wolf." Dear old dad was starting to stink of liquor.

"We've only got another year left of school," Mathew retorted.

"Exactly," his father replied. "*Just* a year left. Would it hurt to move somewhere new before Yale?"

*Yale.*

Mathew finally stood up to leave.

Rebecca tapped three times on the mahogany coffee table. *Don't leave me.* Hammersmitt was a boarding school; Devereaux was not. Mathew had an escape, a home away from this big, lonely house. Mathew had insisted on a dorm for this reason.

"Is it time to leave for the luncheon, Matty?" she said in the terse way of a threat.

Mathew looked at her with one raised brow. *I said I wasn't going.*

She crossed her arms. *I'm not going alone.*

*You have Mom and Dad—*

Her last look veered toward *you may be my twin, but I will end you*, and that was how Mathew Beaumont ended up at the Haelsford house in his very best dress.

He was being a godawful guest. As his parents wore their fake smiles and toasted their crystalline glasses, he just watched. Mathew avoided all unnecessary interaction, aside from allowing Anders Osnes's inebriated father to lean on his shoulder and ask him what his body count was.

"Because you know . . ." the man sputtered, "when I was your age, I had a new girlfriend every—"

"That's nice," Mathew said plainly. Skillfully, he adjusted his shoulder and let the man's hand drop. As Osnes stumbled, Mathew slipped away. He could only just tolerate bro talk, an explanation for his absence from the garden, where other Hammersmitts were getting drunk on liquor more expensive than a semester's tuition. If Trent were here, he might be able to bear it.

A chorus of excitable voices pulled Mathew from the sitting room to the foyer, where a line of witches strode through the front doors. Gini Haelsford greeted them warmly, or at least as warmly as a mundane descendent of Haelsford could.

The other guests navigated the Haelsford house with ease, but none more than Jailah Simmons. She delegated to the witches who followed her in, pointing out the refreshments, the important adults, and the bathrooms. "I'm here if you need me," she said, and sent them on their way.

Mathew had never felt so relieved. "Jailah? Hi."

She slumped forward, as if she'd been walking on her toes for the past hour. "Oh, thank god." She peeked over her shoulder. "Did you know that there are four thousand bee variations in the country?" Then, angrily, "Did you know that Mr. Azoff can list them all by heart?!"

Mathew laughed. "I normally tune out around *Augochloropsis anonyma*."

"Bah." She adjusted the headband pushing back her fro, and, using Mathew to steady herself, she peeled off her heels and pulled a pair of flats from her purse. Mathew could feel the fatigue in her. Her eyes were hazy, her voice worn out. She even stood with an awkward tension.

"I didn't know you knew the Haelsfords," said Mathew.

"I'm here on behalf of the Junior Witchery Council. Gini Haelsford's on the city board, and we need to convince her to let us turn the town into a winter wonderland for the holidays. Normally, it's a given, but since I'm a new Senior Witch, I thought it'd be nice to schmooze her up a bit. I wanna do it big, real big, and we need more of your much-appreciated taxpayer dollars for that."

"Understandable." He threw a look over his shoulder before continuing. "So, how long's Theo—"

"Don't mention him here," she replied, smiling wide. "Just in case. How are you not dying from the heat?" She petted his jacket.

"It's Florida. I'm used to it."

"No, this is . . ." She flexed her fingers and exhaled slowly. "Something's wrong here."

"What is it?"

She pressed her palm to her cheek. "You really don't feel that?"

Mathew shook his head.

"There must be magic in the walls. It's a protection spell, something strong. I can't place it."

"It's the book." Rebecca approached, and after saying these words, which were very strange to both Mathew and Jailah, she proceeded to stare at them like she'd said nothing at all.

"What book?" said Jailah, sizing her up.

With a Twizzler hanging from the side of her mouth, Rebecca said, "So, I might have convinced Peter and Basil to break into their moms' super-secret wine cellar last week." She removed the Twizzler from her mouth and used it to point into the hallway. "But it was full of books. Turns out the Haelsfords aren't as witch-averse as their ancestors. They might even be hexeaters. Like, why else would you own so much witchy shit?"

Simultaneously, Jailah and Mathew spun around to look at the lovely couple, who were currently making their Chihuahua greet guests in high-pitched voices.

Rebecca continued, "We were rummaging around some of the things and . . . there was this book, and it was the worst of all of them."

Jailah tutted. "What was in it?"

"Nothing. The pages were blank."

"How was it the worst one, then?"

"Didn't you just say you could feel it?"

Jailah rolled her shoulders uncomfortably.

Rebecca shrugged. "I feel it, too."

"Why can't I feel it?" Mathew asked.

"Maybe it's a witch thing," Jailah whispered.

Rebecca drew back, and her tone was venomous. "I'm *not* a witch." She stalked off, haughtily pulling mimosas from a server's tray, one for each hand.

Jailah put her hands up. "Whoa. Okay. Did I say something wrong?"

"Our parents would have a fit if we were witchy. Mom used to say that being born mundane was the only thing we ever did right."

"One, offensive, and two—is she seeing anyone?"

"You should probably stay away from her, and I mean that for *your* sake. Jailah"—Mathew tapped his fingers on his chin—"we should steal the book. Because, one, it's shitty that a family of mundanes have it, and b, because I'm bored as shit."

"That—no—you messed that up."

Mathew loosened his tie. "I've had two Manhattans. You ready? Let's do this."

Jailah's big brown eyes popped open. "No! I'm not doing anything—"
The two composed themselves as Dana Haelsford hovered, nodding at them curiously. Mathew had seen Jailah's sweet disposition before, but the way

she turned it on was an enviable gift, even for him. Her smile was perfect and polite even as she said, "You're on your own."

"I just need you to unlock the door with your witchery powers."

"You can just say *witchery*." Jailah chuckled. "Okay, I'll bite. We're doing this because we want to return a witchy artifact to witches, right?"

"Yes."

"And because you're hoping it'll be something that you can impress Iris with."

"Right! Wait, what? No—"

Jai's grin was genuine now. "Uh-huh."

Mathew rolled his eyes. "You'll have your winter wonderland, real big. I'll get Gini to approve the budget."

"Yeah?"

"You're a Mesmortes girl, so maybe it isn't clear, but being a Beaumont means something on this side of town." He frowned. "Okay, even I can objectively hear the privilege in that."

Jailah smirked. "I'll unlock the door and stand watch, but if anyone comes around, I'm throwing you all the way under the bus."

"Well. Damn."

"Honey, you're a rich white dude. I have so much more to lose." She checked her phone. "I've got a Council meeting to go to. If we're gonna do this, let's do it now."

They waited for an opportune moment to sneak into the hall, and Mr. Osnes drunkenly careening into the refreshments table seemed good enough.

Mathew watched Jailah prick her thumb with a little needle protruding from her wand. "Practical," he said.

Jailah winked at him. *"Throw Away the Key."*

The lock clicked open.

"That was easy," Mathew whispered.

"You should hear the unlocking spell before it's reformed. Takes about three minutes to recite. All right, remember what I said: in and out, quick."

Mathew braced himself. His phone giving light, he stepped carefully down the creaky steps, feeling uncomfortably like the next victim in a horror film. He wondered if Rebecca had been creeped out when she'd talked to Peter and Basil down here. Maybe the boys were frightened, but she probably would've said something like *Don't be a fucking baby,* and that was if she'd decided to censor herself.

It was too quiet. Mathew's steps made no sound. His breaths, faster now, were hushed.

Shelves lined the curved walls. He held up his phone and started reading spines, flipping through them cover to cover, looking for the blank witchy book among this strange collection of grimoires and relics.

Holding his phone between his teeth, Mathew used two hands to pull out the books and scan their covers, trying to move faster, racing against Jailah's warning, in awe of how many witchy books the Haelsfords owned, the frightening and sudden realization that this was wrong, that it was too late, and *what was this darkness in him—*

Mathew was sitting on the floor. The book was hard in his hands. Like stone. But the cover was soft. Like satin. Like *skin.*

He rose, a newfound violence in him.

When he thought of blood on his hands, it felt warm and right.

# 29

## iris

At Mesmortes Chapel, Iris sat in a Soul's Circle of low-wicked candles and fresh sage. For the tenth time, she whispered an incantation of utmost mischief. Blood dripped freely from her thumb. She didn't know what else to do. They had the Wolf Boy, but apparently that wasn't enough, and the well of Haelsford lore had run dry. So, Iris tried another approach.

*"I Call Upon You, Mathilde Strigwach,"* she said, her voice echoing through the empty chapel.

Iris had her name, and her face—her *true* one, not a drawing scribbled in a dead townsman's journal, but a real, moving image.

But the only answer to her calls were her own ragged breaths. She wanted to scream in frustration.

She bit down on her lip. *"I Call Upon You—"*

A candle went out. Iris's breath caught in her throat, but the draft that followed was not the usual slippery, thin feel of a ghostly breath. It was the humid breeze of the air outside. Iris stood, turned, and found herself slamming into Mathew Beaumont.

She was prepared to hurl a sarcastic insult at him, but a blistering force of decayed magic against her witchy senses shocked her speechless.

Mathew viciously flung a book at her, but the moment it left his finger-tips, his hard, merciless expression changed.

"Oh." He sighed, slumping into a pew.

He was a pale, sweaty imitation of the Beaumont boy who could spar with Iris. This was a boy who had his heart sucked out and replaced with something soul-eating and cruel.

She stepped away from the book that had landed by her feet.

"Did I just throw that at you?" Mathew huffed, horrified. "Shit, I'm sorry."

Iris unclenched her jaw. "Beaumont, getting possessed by weird ancient artifacts is *my* thing. Get your own. This town's not big enough for the two of us."

A hint of a smile appeared on his face.

"I attacked you, remember?"

"Hm, must've slipped my mind." The smile became a smirk, unraveling her.

Mathew peeled off his jacket. He undid the top three buttons of his nice shirt; he pulled off his tie. He tried to stand, but Iris forced him back down with just a slight touch on his shoulder. In the light hitting him from a stained-glass window, she examined the rough edges around this too-clean boy. The slick skin. The messy hair. The shallow breaths.

Iris levitated the book, inspecting its black pages and the strange color of the binding. She cringed as its heady magic wafted toward her. Suddenly, she felt annoyed, and dizzy, and heavy with fatigue. The other-worldly effects only made her more curious, but she didn't feel confident in fighting back if it was something like the amplyfyr. Or something even worse.

"Where did you find this?" asked Iris. "Please don't say your basement."

"Not *my* basement. The Haelsfords'."

She winced. "I need a sanctifum for it, but for now . . ." With her magic, Iris dug into the chapel floor. She made a bed of burnt sage, placed the book atop it, covered it with more sage, and sealed the floor together. Tendrils of its muted power still seeped into the air. "I'm gonna leave it alone. I mean, think about what happened on Hallowe'en with the amplyfyr in your pocket."

Mathew nodded. "And hell, that was in its porcelain."

Iris did a double take. "It was in the sanctifum?"

Beaumont clearly didn't understand the bombshell he'd dropped. "I didn't just walk around with it loose in my pocket, Iris."

She sat backward in the pew in front of him so that they were face-to-face. "Then it wasn't the amplyfyr that opened up the Chasm, Beaumont!"

He shook his head. "What? I just thought maybe you were so powerful, and so was the heirloom—I don't know, some witchy stuff!"

She placed her hand, soft and dark, over his.

She pulled out her needle.

Iris didn't have to say a word, and she was thankful. Mathew pulled up his sleeve. His fingers were rough and calloused. Iris pricked his thumb and shook his hand over the Soul's Circle.

When she pricked her own thumb, the pentagram scar on her thigh burned. "I'm Calling Mathilde Strigwach."

He raised a brow, impressed.

"Don't get excited, it's never worked before." She sighed. "*I Call Upon . . .* Hey, say it with me?"

His eyes softened. "Okay."

Their voices merged as the drops of their blood seeped into the cracked rock. *"I Call Upon You, Mathilde Strigwach."*

A beat.

Nothing.

"Never mind." Iris drew away from him, and the world exploded beneath her.

She was knocked back into the pew as a horrible screech grew from the ground. Flashes of light burst all around the chapel, like lightning striking from the ground up. As Iris struggled to get her bearings, the world spun, and a voice taunted her.

*"Deeeead girrrrrrl."*

The air sang to her, but not as invitingly as any other soul that had called to her before. This cloying voice was as terrible as it was cursed.

"Iris!" Mathew helped her to her feet and tried to pull her away from the destructive magic.

"Wait!" She pushed past him and toward the flashing sinkhole forming in the middle of the chapel. The book lurched against the floor violently, like something was alive and trying to pull itself from the pages.

The voice seeped with corruption. It no longer taunted. Now it demanded.

*"WHY DID YOU BRING HIM BACK?"*

Iris fell into a crouch. The physical and emotional strain of the spirit bore down on her, and she couldn't take it. She held back a few screams of her own. The voice was unbearable, like suffering made solid. Weeping children, screeching souls, the hungry howls of Wolves.

Iris's heart stopped. "How do you know what I've done?"

So much louder now: *"WHY DID YOU BRING HIM BACK?!"*

Iris could do nothing but try to breathe. The night of the resurrection returned to her. The strangling darkness, the Chasm, the fear of being dragged into it. She pushed herself to fight it. "To end the Haunting!"

*"KILL THE WOLF BOY, KILL THE WOLVES! LET THE BEASTS DEVOUR HIM WHOLE!"*

Tentatively, she opened her eyes. Fighting an invisible resistance, Iris forced herself to crawl closer to the book, even as the weight of the manifestation crushed against her. She sat next to it, the wicked heat rising. The white light pouring out of the book grew brighter and brighter.

With a quick slash of her wand, Iris shouted, *"Show Me Your Soul!"*

Sighs against her skin.

The whispers of pages brushing past.

Iris saw them turn and turn and turn. What were once blank pages were now littered with flickering text, as if illuminated by a dying lightbulb. The first page bore one line.

*All I want is for the slaughter to end.*

Sweat rolled down Iris's back. The book was both protected and corrupted. She could feel the protective charm on it, old but stubbornly strong, as well as the hex put upon it to erase its contents. The dueling sets of magic irritated her own witchery. "Come on," she whispered. "Tell me more."

It showed her the same Haelsford they'd seen in Theodore Bloom's memories, but not from his point of view. A hopeful realization hit her.

"Iris?" Mathew whispered fearfully from somewhere behind her.

She'd forgotten he was there. From his startled expression, Iris imagined what she looked like—face ashen and sweaty, her hands trembling, her eyes wide and optimistic.

"Don't be afraid." She smiled, and the fear in his face only deepened.

"Thank you for this, Beaumont."

He replied with something disapproving, but she turned back to the book and the dark magic seeping from it.

The pages spoke to her in tense whispers.

*Sloane used to teach us forgiveness and love in the face of witch aversion, but she grows weary every day. I think Adelaide might have her ear, and Adelaide has only ever wanted blood for blood, I think she might be . . .*

Iris's breath caught in her throat. *She might be what?* Desperately, she flipped through the pages, searching for more. Like Theodore Bloom's memories, the diary seemed incomplete, chunks missing from the narrative. As Iris read, she felt the destructive hex causing the heat to rise to searing heights.

*They have cut up the witches of the Vox Coven like animals. They littered their parts down the Oak Trail so that any witch that passed might see . . .*

*They call it Haelsford now, and the mundanes have made a sport of witchhunting.*

*Adelaide made a strange potion last night. She seemed mundane, not even the aura of a witch on her! Her blessing was hidden. I don't know what she plans to do with something like this . . .*

Distantly, Mathew called Iris once more. He was worried, but Iris ignored him. Her witchy intuition told her to *stay and see*. Without looking at him, she stretched a hand out behind her. Asking no questions, he simply placed his hand in hers.

The book twitched. Iris's mind filled up with cries of anguish.

*The mundanes are not of this earth! They are monsters, every last one! I have cried so much that I can barely see. How cruel can God be? He blesses us just to bring us to the pyre!*

"'Adelaide just wants the slaughter,'" Iris read aloud, her voice shaking. "'She just wants *to* slaughter . . .'"

*. . . all of them! Death favors those whose souls are lined with black, and hers is the blackest of all.*

*Adelaide has taken an interest in the swampland that surrounds the town. She has commanded our wolves to wait there, to wait for our call. I miss Zara desperately, but even a mundane would know a familiar if they saw it. I asked Adelaide to greet Zara for me, but she only ever says to come see her myself. I am too scared . . .*

Without warning, black flames erupted from the middle of the book. The hex was winning, growing faster than Iris could read.

She clenched her jaw. She smelled burning flesh. Her skull felt like it was on fire. It came so quickly that Iris could only glimpse at the final lines.

*I cannot let Adelaide do this.*

*I offered an alternative, that we could Forge their minds into forgetting the Hunting. My sister will not listen . . . She has become hysteric with power—*

*"Iris!"* Mathew screamed again.

Face dripping with sweat, Iris read the final lines.

*A bloody death for the wolfboy! A bloody death for the wolves! Together, the way the earth tied them up!*

Iris was yanked backward against Mathew, narrowly missing the sudden explosion that devoured the book inches from where her face had just been. Mathew's hands were on her shoulders, her back was up against his chest.

"Why did you do that?" Iris said hoarsely, scrambling away.

Beaumont shook his head in disbelief. "It was gonna melt your face off! I told you to move, and you wouldn't listen!"

She heaved with adrenaline. Her thoughts were a jumble, but she plucked out one vital piece. "Kill the Wolf Boy, kill the Wolves."

Mathew stared at her, awestruck. "The witchy book told you that?"

Iris looked upon the pile of ash with wet, tired eyes. "It wasn't just a witchy book, Beaumont. It was Mathilde Strigwach's diary." She paused, looking back at him. "Theodore Bloom has to die to end the Haunting."

# 30

## jailah

The Junior Witchery Council meeting had just begun, but Jailah was regretting not calling in sick. The morning had been stressful enough, with the gathering at the Haelsfords', and Mathew Beaumont's strange exit, and the Wolf Boy's enduring existence. Every day that he was alive was another day that put them at risk.

Jailah normally relished the quarterly meeting with the elder witches. She liked how different they all looked, the way they sat in a line with their wands in front of them. The room was decorated in gold and black velvets, encased in high windows, and the table alone was worth cherishing. It was legendary, cut down and crafted by mundanes after the agreement to make Haelsford a unified town. Apparently, the dark stains in the cracks of the wood was Wolf blood, though Jailah never dared asking if that was true.

This table was revered because, through a century, only important people were invited to it. Jailah usually baked for the occasion. Her brown-butter banana bread always won her points with Senior Witches Maxima and Eleanor, even if High Witch Lucia thought it was too sweet.

She wished she could brag about securing donations from the Haelsfords for Winter Wonderland, but her priorities had changed so quickly. Her world had been flipped on its head. Meetings and party planning and special events seemed so trivial considering the undead boy she knew was holed up in a Hammersmitt dorm. She trusted Trent and Mathew, as strange as that was to think, but didn't imagine those boys would ever take the blame for him if they were found out. Still, she was relieved to have gotten him out of Mesmortes, even if part of her didn't feel right about letting him out of her sight.

High Witch Lucia rapped her long red nails on the table. Jailah looked up and found herself staring straight into Lucia's dark eyes. The elder witch raised a brow. "I know you're sitting right in front of me, but it's customary that we take roll—"

Jailah shook her head. "Sorry." The other young witches giggled. "Here."

As Lucia continued calling attendance, Anika Johnson leaned to Jailah's ear. "Your cape's inside out."

Jailah looked down. "Oh. Thanks."

Jenna gave her a sideways glance. "And you've got a hair sticking straight up—"

She patted it down. "Shh, pay attention."

High Witch Lucia finished taking roll. She nodded toward Eren Gates—now Senior Witch Eren—the newest addition of the seven-member Council. They cleared their throat. "First on the agenda—a mundane has a complaint about a witch's apple tree growing over his side of their fence."

Jailah resisted a sigh. The Council always wore kid gloves during the meetings that the JWC sat in on. She was curious about the types of issues they discussed behind closed doors. Peacekeeping, banishments, illegal use of love potions.

*Unintended resurrections?*

And that was why Jailah had to come. She had to see if the Council gave any hint that they knew what happened on the night the Haunting began. Perhaps the bursts of protection spells throughout the town had given the group some cover.

"Next on the docket"—Senior Witch Maxima rolled forward a dusty old gramophone—"the Roddin Witch thanks us for our protection once more."

Jailah's eyes grew heavy with fatigue.

"Simmons," Senior Witch Eren said suddenly. "You wanted to talk about the Winter Wonderland festivities?"

Jailah folded her hands. "Um. It's. Great! It's going great."

They looked over at the rest of the Council. "Is that it?"

*Come on, girl. Get it the hell together.* Jailah smiled. "As always, the Vasquezes will enchant the snowfall. Soma Café's doing a twenty-four-hour karaokefest—it's open to everyone, but mostly for our blessed that have been rejected by their families. The streets leading up to Town Square will close at seven a.m. for the Holiday Parade, and, um . . ." There was a knock at the chamber doors, and Jailah rejoiced internally. "It should be fun."

Senior Witch Amalah opened the door with just a curl of her finger.

A young boy, maybe only eleven, ran into the meeting. Jailah did a double take. The little witch's pale face was drenched in fear. Breathless, he shouted, "Help, quick, a Wolf!"

A gasp caught in Jailah's throat, but she didn't hesitate. As the High Witch and her Council made quickly for the door, Jailah was the first of the students to follow.

The Council members walked toward the protection barrier. A crowd had formed, mundane and witch alike. Someone told her to stay back, but Jailah didn't move until she saw the body.

Jailah turned and stumbled away from the scene. She gagged from the ripe scent of blood, heaved twice, and choked out her meager breakfast.

The elder witches quickly formed a barrier, shooing away the crowd. *You should've stayed back*, Jailah cursed herself. The image would stay with her. The bent limbs, the swollen, near-unrecognizable face. She knew it was Mr. Finn from town, the owner of the bakery, solely from the blood-soaked uniform. The first kill was always jarring, but this was the first time Jailah had seen the aftermath.

"Do they usually do that?" Jenna asked, suddenly next to her.

Jailah lifted her heavy head. "What?"

"Leave enough of the body? Like, you know, intact?"

Her head was thudding, and Jenna's high-pitched voice wasn't making it any better. She whispered, "Jenna, I need a moment—"

"Ugh, the Wolves are so scary. I wasn't here last year, obviously, but I heard Amelia's body never came back."

"Jesus, for five seconds, shut up, Jenna!"

Jenna flinched. Her freckly cheeks went red, and her mouth opened in shock.

Jai shook her head. Chiding Jenna was like screaming at a puppy. "*Sorry.* I'm not feeling too good. I need a second." She plopped onto the grass. "What were you saying?"

Jenna shrugged. "Nothing. I don't know." Suddenly, she got choked up. "I'm just scared."

Jailah's heart pounded. She tried to calm herself with every slow-breathing technique she could think of. "It'll be okay. I know this is your first Haunting, but it'll be fine. It comes every year. Don't you worry one bit."

Jailah was bad at hiding her emotions, and she could see that her answer wasn't good enough. But Jenna nodded and turned to return to the others without a word.

Jailah slipped toward Mesmortes. She sent an urgent message in the group text.

She needed answers from Theodore Bloom.

# 31

# thalia

Trent brought Bloom to Thalia's cabin five minutes early. Of the two—the rich boy and the dead boy—only one made her nervous.

Maverick let out a suspicious bark. He looked at Thalia like, *Really, you're bringing them here?*

"Don't start," Thalia muttered. "And get a good whiff of the pale one."

Trent was his usual carefree self. He wore a bright purple snapback that matched his sneakers. As he placed one foot on the first step, Thalia's heart pounded. She waited for him to say something, anything to reveal that he knew what she'd done to his memory.

Instead, he moved in for a hug.

She let him. He smelled like fabric softener and the comforting mustiness of the Haelsford Public Library.

He pulled away. "You good, love? I know this week's been mad."

She nodded.

Trent flashed his perfect, warm grin. "Are we the first ones here? Pathetic."

"This isn't a party," Thalia said, forcing a laugh.

"Don't limit yourself. Anywhere can be a party if you try hard enough."

He finally stepped inside and left her face-to-face with the Wolf Boy.

Theodore's eyes were downcast. Still a perpetual ball of anxiety. Thalia couldn't help but sympathize. She waved a little. "Hi again. I'm Thalia, remember?"

He looked up, his soft brown curls falling between his eyes. "I remember. You're the greenwitch."

"Yes."

He shivered. Thalia sensed that though he was nervous, he wasn't clueless. He had an idea of why he was here.

He attempted a polite smile and stepped inside anyway.

Of her girls, Logan arrived first. Though Haelsford was getting cool enough for the locals to start sporting obnoxious coats and scarves, Logan dressed lightly. A casual yellow dress and high-top Chucks.

"You look cute. Is that lipstick?" Thalia offered.

Logan blushed deeply. "It's just lip balm."

Bloom opted for the corner of Thalia's bed. Logan leaned against the windowsill. There was quite a bit of space between them, but their bodies were turned to each other.

Trent rummaged through Thalia's empty cabinets. "Oi, not even a granola bar."

"Keep going through my stuff and God help you, Hogarth." Thalia jabbed a finger toward him.

Jailah came stomping through the mud-slush. Maverick ran out to her, and she caught him in her arms.

Thalia chuckled at the sight of her, all flustered and unkempt for once. "What happened to you, O High Witch?"

Jailah got closer, and Thalia stopped laughing. She'd never seen such fear in her brown eyes. Maverick licked Jai's hand, the one comfort he knew how to give.

Thalia dropped the playful tone. "Jai? How was the meeting?"

Jailah breathed in and straightened her back. "If the Witchery Council felt the resurrection spell, they didn't mention it. I think we're okay." She looked to Bloom. "How are you feeling, Theodore?"

He folded his fingers together. "I'm well." He looked at Trent. "I appreciate the hospitality."

Trent winked, totally unbothered. "Don't mention it, s'cool, even if you did eat all of my Hobnobs."

A ghost of a smile appeared on Theodore's lips. It softened his already-gentle face, but was gone before it could truly be appreciated.

Jailah was all business, though Thalia could see that she was trying so hard to be sweet and polite. "You said that there were things you remembered about your past. Mathilde had called you her little wolfboy, right?"

"Yes."

"And we saw what Thalia showed us in your memories. But we didn't see much about the Wolves. What do you remember of them, exactly?"

Thalia fidgeted. She shot Trent a quick look that he didn't seem to notice before sighing. "Like I said before, we saw everything."

Jailah clicked her tongue. "Uh-huh. I wanna hear it from him."

Theodore's lip twitched. "Mostly, I remember my life before the Strigwach witches came to town. I lose everything when I try to think of the night the Wolves attacked."

Jailah's fists clenched. "A'ight. What about the spell that kept you all fresh and clean in that grave? You and Mathilde met in the Cavern after the

Wolves were born. What else did she do to you? What did she tell you about ending the Haunting?"

The words were like a splash of cold water. Bloom cringed, and Thalia didn't miss the quick look he gave Logan before answering. "I don't know. I'm just as lost as you."

"Then why are you here?" Jailah spat. "What makes you so goddamn special?"

Logan looked to Thalia, urging her with her gaze. Thalia knew she should say something, but she didn't exactly disagree with Jailah.

"Do you know what we've risked to bring you back? What we're risking now by keeping you around?"

Jailah drew her wand.

Trent stepped forward and Logan moved to Theodore, but Thalia finally spoke up. "Whoa . . ." she started. "Let's wait for Iris and Mathew to get here, yeah?"

Jailah ignored her, and now Thalia could see that her eyes were welling up. "If you can't tell us what we need to know, then I'm taking it from you."

She was too fast to block. Jailah hit Bloom with *Night-Night*, and the boy flopped backward onto the bed.

"Hey!" Trent yelled, throwing up his hands.

Logan stood, furious as Thalia had ever seen her. "Jailah, what's going on?"

Jailah exhaled. "There's been an attack."

Thalia's hand went reflexively to her rosary. "Already?"

"I saw it, T," she whispered. "I saw the body."

"Who was it?" Trent's voice was gentle.

"Mr. Finn, from the bakery."

Thalia looked away. It felt like too much to cry for someone she hardly knew. Though sinfully, she was relieved it wasn't someone she was close to. "He knew better. I don't understand."

"The pull of the Swamp?" Logan offered, her voice shaky. "Even I've heard the whispers that there's something in the Swamp that calls us—"

Jailah waved a hand. "Whatever it is, it doesn't matter. We're ending the Haunting." She refocused on Theodore Bloom. "Thalia, we need more memorywork."

Finally, Trent turned to Thalia.

Pulling Bloom's memories in the relative privacy of the hollow room was hard enough, but with Trent here? She felt exposed, like he could see into her heart and her past, though she was the one to make sure he couldn't remember knowing either.

Trent crossed his arms. "You're just gonna, what, like, hack his mind?"

The guilt wasn't a soft-rolling wave. It crashed into Thalia at once.

Her wand was stiff in her hand. She tried not to sound stricken. "I don't know. I'm just a beginner greenwitch."

Jailah scoffed. "What? You've done it before—"

"You've done it before?" Trent interrupted, his eyes wide.

"Not like this." Thalia avoided his gaze. "He allowed me in last time, but the memories were all broken up."

"You'd said he was fighting you. Maybe this way, we get his memories whole." Jailah shrugged.

"It feels wrong," Logan said, shaking her head.

"We can't just wait around for him! We've got the Wolf Boy in the flesh, and someone's already died."

As Jailah and Logan spoke tensely, Trent moved to Thalia's side. "The hell was that?"

"Trent, he's fine. He's just knocked out."

Trent scoffed. "I mean, yeah, but isn't there a witchy code of ethics? What the bloody hell is the difference between using your wand or drugging his drink? Or a bloody chloroform handkerchief?"

Thalia rolled her eyes. "You know that's not the same."

"How? Jailah just knocked someone unconscious, and he couldn't even defend himself. He wasn't attacking us. He wasn't doing anything. He was just sitting there! And taking his memories like this? You wouldn't do that."

"You don't know me," Thalia said harshly.

"Thalia—"

"And you don't get to judge me, mundane."

Trent stepped back. Jailah and Logan stopped squabbling and turned to them.

Thalia didn't know where it came from. She wasn't the type to get all high and mighty on her witchery, but every bit of fear and disappointment in Trent's sanctimonious words took her back to Annex. She pictured the faces of those clamoring for her death. It didn't feel far from how Trent looked at her now. The fear of witchery in Annex nearly killed her. The only difference now was that Thalia could choose not to cower.

She waited anxiously. The memorywork she'd done on Trent couldn't be broken unless she undid it or another piece of magic severed it. But she didn't relax until he walked back over to the corner, arms crossed, his usual comforting aura gone.

As the rush wore off, Thalia felt sick. Trent was right. She was dangerous.

She'd broken the moral code. And he *could* judge her because she'd done it on him.

*You had to do it, to save yourself.*

She closed her eyes.

*This is who you are now.*

Maverick barked anxiously at the door as Iris and Mathew walked in wearing similar expressions of unease.

"Y'all," Iris huffed. "We found something."

# 32

## trent

"Well, technically *I* found something," Mathew said dryly.

Trent scoffed a laugh. The arguments had caused the room to become stifling, and Mathew being there helped Trent remember to breathe again. He thought that he'd carved a space with the witches, but the last ten minutes had made him feel utterly alone.

Mathew, maybe sensing this, looked to Trent. He raised a brow, and Trent angled his head toward the unconscious boy slumped back on Thalia's bed.

Mathew looked, sighed, and stuck his hands in his pockets. "What happened here?"

"They wanna look into his mind. He didn't have much of a choice," he replied.

"But we'd rather not." Thalia shook her head at Jailah. "I've never retrieved a memory like this before. In class, we practice on live, *willing* subjects. It probably won't even work, or I could damage his memory permanently. It's too risky."

Trent wondered if that were true, or if maybe he'd managed to change her mind. He tried to catch her eye, but she wouldn't look in his direction.

She sat on the table by the window, plucked a stray ivy leaf from Logan's hair, and seemed to want to hide from this conversation.

*Mundane.* It wasn't an insult, really. The world was still very much on the side of mundanes. But he couldn't shake the icky feeling when he thought of her eyes when she said it, the *way* she said it. She seemed to resent him in that moment. Maybe he'd overreacted. Jailah had warned him that being part of this meant seeing that some magic wasn't kind.

Unlike Mathew, Iris didn't seem to register that she'd interrupted something tense when she walked into the cabin. She gave Ted Bloom a casual look—a little confusion, a little annoyance. "He's gotta die."

Logan made a choking sound. "Wait, what?"

"I mean for the Haunting to end. He has to die."

"You could've led with that," Jailah said skeptically. She seemed calmer, and her voice dripped less venom. "He was *already* dead."

Iris groaned. "Guys! I just read about it in Mathilde Strigwach's diary."

Logan shifted her weight from one foot to the other. "You have her diary?"

Iris said, so quickly that it was almost unintelligible, "Yeah, Beaumont brought it to me."

Trent wagged a brow—*there was always time for teasing*—which Mathew vehemently ignored.

Iris closed her eyes. "The Wolves just took their first kill. We saw—"

"Yeah," Jailah interjected. "We went over that."

"What else did the diary say?" Logan asked.

"Mostly stuff we already knew—that the sisters made the Wolves from their familiars, and that Mathilde didn't want to go through with it in the end, she wanted mercy for the mundanes."

"And you believe it?"

Iris bit her lip. "I think so. There's one way to know for sure."

Trent looked at Ted. "Go on, wake him up."

Jailah brought him back with *Wakey-Wakey*. Whatever the spell was, it didn't leave him groggy or tired. Trent watched as he opened his eyes and sat up. "Sorry, I . . ." He looked at Jailah. "I don't know anything about the Wolves."

It was bizarre, the way he just snapped back into the conversation, like he'd been *paused* rather than put to sleep. Trent found it unsettling for reasons he couldn't quite articulate.

Ted looked at Iris and Mathew, and Trent could see the confusion settling in.

"Hi, Theodore," Iris started. "So. The Wolves just killed a man."

Theodore wrapped his slim arms around himself. Trent felt like he was always condensing, trying to make himself smaller and smaller.

"*And* we found a diary that belonged to Mathilde Strigwach."

At this, Teddy flicked his eyes upward. He peered at Iris, but between his soft face and wringing hands, there was no bite in it. "Did she speak of me?"

"You could say that," Mathew added bluntly.

Iris continued, "Mathilde wrote down everything she felt about the Hunt, her sisters, this town, the Wolves, and how she changed her mind about what she wanted for Haelsford's fate. It matches everything we've heard about her, but really, you're the only true witness we have. I get it, you don't remember much, but does that sound like Mathilde to you?"

"Yes," he answered. "Mathilde was different from her sisters. I didn't really understand until now . . . I suppose it makes sense if she didn't want to go through with the Wolves and they did."

Iris nodded. She looked back at the rest of them. "Say we're Mathilde and we want to end the Haunting, yeah? We've got to be stealthy. If anyone knows us, it's our sisters, and they're the ones who absolutely can't find out that we're doing magic to stop them. So, what do we do? We put the key to ending the Haunting in the mundane we're kinda in love with."

Red crept into Ted's cheeks.

Logan narrowed her eyes. "Wouldn't that be the first place they looked? It'd be obvious that she'd confide in the guy she, uh, loved."

"Nah." Iris's lips curved into a smile. "Because he doesn't know shit. The key is hidden because it isn't a word, or a spell, or a code. It's doing the thing they'd least expect. It's in *killing* the mundane she's in love with."

Thalia mulled this over. "It works in a few ways. If Adelaide and Sloane suspected anything in Theodore, they'd enchant him, or give him truth serum, or *mindhack*"—she glanced at Trent, finally—"but there'd be nothing for him to give up."

"And if they just decided to be done with it and kill him, well, that'd end the Haunting anyway, so Mathilde still wins," Mathew said. "It's foolproof."

"No," Jailah added. "Smart as hell, but not foolproof. Somethin' went wrong on the night of the Haunting, or else it wouldn't still exist."

Iris nodded at Theodore. "How did you die last time?"

He frowned. "I don't know. I'm sorry, I'm sure you're tired of hearing me say that."

Jailah looked like she might touch his shoulder, but thought better of it. "Well, we know you definitely weren't ripped up by the Wolves."

"And that's the problem," Iris said. "You died, but not in the right way. To end the Wolves, uh, we have to give you to them. They gotta devour you whole. I'm guessing Mathilde thought that would've been the way her sisters would choose to do it."

Theodore regarded them all with heavy eyes. Trent felt the guilt settle in the air as they spoke of this boy's death like they were excited to do it.

"Is that what she said?" Theodore asked.

"'A bloody death for the wolfboy, a bloody death for the wolves, together, the way the earth tied them up.' Mathilde's words, not mine." Iris shrugged. "This is awkward."

"I see." He rose from the bed.

Immediately, the group tensed.

Trent ran his boot over the knife strapped to his ankle. Jailah tightened her grip around her wand. Thalia straightened off the desk, and Logan watched Teddy with curious eyes. Iris held her ground, and Mathew moved to stand closer to her.

But Theodore only sighed in his soft, desperate way. "I've died before. I can do it again. Perhaps this time I'll get some peace." He hardly looked disturbed. "When do I have to do it?"

"An old witch said the Haunting can only end after it's begun. It always ends on the full moon of February, so the twenty-seventh this year," Iris explained. "But . . . considering someone's *already died* . . ."

Theodore nodded. "I understand."

"What was it that you said you wanted?" Jailah asked suddenly.

Trent raised a brow. Shock registered on Iris's and Logan's faces. They clearly hadn't considered that Bloom might want something in return for his life. Trent knew that they'd been giving him doses of truth serum—which Trent didn't love but understood. He studied the way Jailah looked at the undead boy and tried to imagine what she was thinking. *He might be forced to tell us the truth, but he's thinking his own thoughts. And if he's thinking on his own, then we can't control him.*

"I won't spend my new life trapped," Theodore whispered. "I want . . . time."

Thalia narrowed her eyes. "You're asking too much. We could be banished."

He looked down at his hands. "I won't leave Haelsford, nor will I tell anyone about what happened. I just want to be able to live again, even if it's only for a little while. Let me have until the Haunting's last night, and I will give myself up."

Even if they hadn't spiked him with the truth stuff, would they think that these were lies? Trent had felt the marks of solitude in everything Theodore did, like the careful way he spoke and the delicate way he moved, like trying not to upset someone fragile. How could they take away the last bit of life that he had left?

"God has given me a second chance." Theodore sighed.

"Nah, I did," Iris grumbled.

"Let's talk it over," Jailah said, and without hesitating, she put Teddy back under.

"Really?" Trent threw his hands into the air. "Hey, I say we give him what he wants."

"What?" Thalia exclaimed. "He's living proof of us performing a resurrection!"

"He's a person!" Logan snapped.

"He's a *liability*."

"Aren't we all?" Trent asked.

"Not if we can trust one another," Thalia said.

Logan groaned. "Sometimes you guys talk about him like he's nothing, just something to use up and throw away!"

"Calm down," Iris seethed. "He's not even supposed to be alive!"

*"All right,"* Mathew cut in. He rolled up his sleeves. "None of us wants to get caught, but how far are we willing to go to protect this secret? He says he'll go. That has to be the truth, right?"

"The truth can change," said Thalia. "When it comes to future actions, alítheia presents what a person truly *believes* will happen. So, no, we don't know for sure that he will."

Mathew considered this. "He knows that the Wolves are dangerous, and it's not like he's got a family here to go home to. But think about it—if we keep him cooped up, maybe that changes his truth. Suddenly, he resents us, and when it's time for him to go, he decides fuck them, let the Wolves go wild. Who do you think he'd rather die for, the people who gave him the chance to live again or the ones that raised him up only so the Wolves could tear him apart?"

"That's right, Matty boy," said Trent.

"We don't need him to agree to it, Mathew," Jailah said.

Trent turned to Jailah and shrugged. "You're volunteering to push him into the Swamp, then?"

Jailah quieted.

Matty looked around. "Any other takers?"

They were all silent until Trent asked, "Shall we vote?"

Iris sucked in through her teeth. "Why should we? I'm the one with the most to lose. That was my resurrection spell. This isn't time for the rah-rah, *we're all in this together* shit! If we're found out—"

"We all go down, love." Trent gestured toward Mathew. "We've been the ones hiding him out."

Mathew looked at Iris with big, pleading eyes. "Iris, it's the smarter move."

She turned away from him. "I vote no. We could end the Haunting *today*. Why wait two months? How many people will die if we wait?"

"I'm with Iris," Thalia added immediately.

"Same," said Jailah. "And Logan's with us, so that's that."

But Logan said nothing. Her silence was concerning enough for Jailah to furrow her brow.

"Logan," Thalia said gently. "You're with us, right?"

Logan wrung her hands. "I think the boys have a point. Even if I wasn't worried that treating him like a prisoner would start his, you know, villain origin story, I think, just, that he deserves some kindness. Two months seems long to us, but it's everything to him."

Jailah looked Logan up and down, and sensed the resolve there. "I guess the vote's tied."

Trent jabbed a finger toward Theodore Bloom. "Doesn't his vote count?"

He almost regretted saying it. Disagreements immediately filled up the room, and even Thalia's dog took cover under the bed. Amid the squabbling, Trent wasn't sure what else he could say. Theodore Bloom wasn't his friend. If he died—*when* he died—nothing in Trent's life would really change. But the last few weeks had altered Trent's once-naive view of magic. Between the resurrection, today's kill, and this, the very magic that once enraptured him had soured. Advocating for Bloom made him feel less slimy.

He looked at the girls differently now. Perhaps he should thank Bloom for interrupting what was supposed to be a séance for his mother. If these were the consequences of necromancy, then it had to have been for the best.

"Fine!" Iris conceded finally, breaking up the shouting. Without waiting for further arguments, she snapped the spell off Bloom. The boy barely took a breath before Iris was kneeling in front of him, fire in her eyes. "You get until the last night of the Haunting Season. Then we give you to the Wolves."

"Could've put that gentler," Trent said. He tried to be light and funny, but it came out exasperated.

"It's okay." Bloom chuckled sadly. "And *thank you*. This world is overwhelming, and yet, I want it all. I want to make the most of this brief new life. But I would give it up to finally end the Strigwachs' tyranny. I would do it gladly."

# 33

## logan

Mr. Finn's death had hung over Haelsford like a dark cloud, but just like one, it soon passed. Logan was surprised at how quickly the town moved on. After his name was etched into the memorial and his family packed up his house, his name was hardly spoken. There was less grieving and more about wondering who would be next.

On the last day before winter break, Logan Wyatt went to the Hammersmitt dorms.

She'd been strategic about it. Iris was in her calc midterm, Thalia had pre-break RA duties, and Jailah was already on a plane to Alabama to see her grandparents. It wasn't like the Red Three told her she couldn't see him, but the general theme was Don't Get Attached. Logan hated that Theodore wasn't always within immediate reach. Her dreams were gone. She wanted the real thing.

The moment Trent opened the door, he said, "Love, he ain't here."

Logan blushed. "What?"

He had a packet of M&M'S in his hand and flipped one into his mouth. "You heard me, baby witch."

"Ugh, you don't get to call me that."

He chuckled. "My bad, I thought it was cute."

"I'm tired of being *baby witch*."

"Isn't that what school's for? Aren't you all baby witches? You've just got to learn, right?"

"I think I'm a lost cause."

"Then you need these more than I do." He handed her the packet of candy. "Maybe share 'em with our friend Ted."

"Well, where is he?" She hated how eager her voice sounded.

"He said he wanted to see if finding the old places he used to hang out might trigger his memories. He usually comes back within an hour or two."

Logan's eyes widened. "You've been letting him leave? Jailah would kill you!"

Trent shrugged. "I don't like him being all cooped up in here. He went by the lake, said he wanted a swim. And now you get some alone time, *you're welcome*."

Logan huffed. She pulled out two beaded bracelets from her pocket. One was the same shocking purple of Trent's favorite sneakers. A little wolf emblem dangled at the end of it. "Merry Christmas."

Trent grinned, his brown eyes wide with wonder. "What! I didn't know we were doing presents!"

She smiled up at him. "No worries. It took two seconds." She pulled out another one—blue, to match Mathew's eyes. "Give this to Matty for me. I might miss him before I leave for break."

Trent saluted her, and she was off to find the Wolf Boy.

⋯•⟩ ✪ ⟨•⋯

The Green deserved more than its name. The lush garden seemed too lively and beautiful to share the same land as the Swamp. The air smelled like lavender and honey. Every bush burst with life. Roses, posies, sunflowers, and witchy herbs like foxglove, butcher's broom, and snapdragon. Each individual plant here grew like the soil was perfectly attuned to its needs.

The live oaks converged overhead, crowning a canopy over a path. The very same trail that Logan and the Red Three had bargained for in Roddin's shop. Before everything changed.

Theodore Bloom stood on the embankment, shaking water from his long brown hair. The dark jeans he'd borrowed from Trent were cuffed at the ankles. He had Mathew's light sweatshirt balled up in his hand. He stared absently in the distance, and Logan quickly followed his gaze for what he could've been staring at, if only for a reason to look away from him and all his . . . *glistening shirtlessness.*

She watched his movements in quiet bliss for a few moments. Everything gave him pause, from the red finch diving toward the surface of the water to the leaves rustling in the wind.

Logan stepped on a twig, and Theodore jumped. He turned, meeting her with that strange beauty that somehow bested death. There were boys like Mathew, stately ones, faces with sharp angles made for brooding. And there were boys like Trent, touched with a gentler, friendlier face and a smooth tongue.

Theodore seemed to be their opposites. His softness made him captivating in a different way. He screamed innocence, even when his wild hazel eyes were narrowed with distrust.

He calmed at the sight of her. "Logan Phillip Wyatt." Her name sounded comfortable on his lips, like it belonged there.

"Sorry. Didn't mean to scare you."

"Most things in this new world scare me. But never you." Slowly, he pulled the sweatshirt over his head and sat on the embankment. Logan perched next to him. She offered him the M&M'S, and his eyes widened. He popped one into his mouth and savored it. "Why do you even bother with other food?"

Logan laughed. "How have you been, Teddy?"

He raised a brow. "Teddy?"

Logan's face warmed. "Uh—"

"It's okay. You can call me that." He looked away, but not before she caught his smile. "I've been well."

He couldn't lie to her, but some part of her didn't believe it, unless his definition of *well* when dealing with impending death was much more optimistic than hers.

"Do you come by here a lot?" she asked. "Trent mentioned that you like to explore."

Teddy shot her a chastised smile, ducking his eyes. "Will it upset you to know that I sometimes go into town? No one notices me anyway, but I have a feeling that the other witches wouldn't be happy to hear it."

She shook her head. "You're right; they wouldn't. But they don't have to know. I mean, what would be the point of bargaining for time if you were just going to hang out at Hammersmitt?"

"Thank you," he whispered. He dipped his toe into the water. "I wish I could put it into words for you to understand, Logan, how strange it is to be home and recognize nothing you see."

"I understand. I pictured Mesmortes very differently. I thought, *Who couldn't be made a witch in a place like this?*"

Teddy extended his arms, his long fingers curling into fists. "You can feel the magic here like it's alive."

"Sometimes I can't stand it. It's like I never left home. Every person in my family is an awesome witch, and I'm the only one who doesn't belong."

"I know how that feels."

"I know you do," Logan said, heart thrumming. "You were the only one who didn't want to kill witches."

He paused. "How could you know that?" He scanned her face. "And why do you seem familiar to me? It's like I know you somehow, but that can't be possible."

"I saw you in my dreams, before you came back, before we looked into your memories. That's how I knew that you loved Mathilde." She inhaled sharply. The feeling of finally revealing something she'd been sitting on for weeks was equal parts terrifying and relieving.

He moved closer to her. "I don't understand."

"I never really knew what I was seeing. I guessed it might've been you, but I didn't know for sure until, *you know*."

"Until I came back."

"Yes, but . . ."

Logan's voice trailed off. Her fingers pricked with warmth.

A dull yellow light grew in her skin, shining through her veins, glowing under her nail beds. She knew it wasn't tethering—there was no foretold lock snapping into place, or the pull of a knot tightening in her chest. *She was proxying.* It happened with him. In her dreams, and here, face-to-face.

"What's happening?" Teddy asked, eyes widening.

"My magic. I would say don't worry, but it has a mind of its own."

"Show me."

*And there it is.* That moment Logan always dreaded, where she had to explain, *I can't.* Not at will. Not without the amplyfyr. Logan would hate to see the curious expression on Teddy's face be replaced with disappointment.

"It's okay," he said suddenly, shaking his head. "I'm sorry. You don't have to." Gently, he placed his palms under her glowing hands. His thumbs rested atop her wrists, her pulse thrumming against them. He looked at her hands with awe, held her like she was precious. "You should use your magic how you'd like. Or . . . not at all."

These were words she didn't know she craved. She felt like he was seeing her completely.

Logan stared, looking for the flaw in him. Goose bumps lined her skin. She bit her tongue against what she wanted to say, fearing it would be too much. *You don't know what it means to hear that. Not even my mom ever said that. Or my sister, who's supposed to be my best friend. And definitely not the Red Three.* "My magic doesn't feel like it belongs to me. I can't call it properly. It's either weak or it's too much to handle. Nothing ever goes the way I want it to."

He flipped his hands over so that their palms touched. "You lied to me."

Logan's heart thrummed. "I did?"

The Wolf Boy looked up at her with the first wide smile she'd seen from him. "You told me you weren't special. But your magic brought me here."

*Don't get attached.*

Logan pulled away, if only because the nervy buzz in her stomach was growing. She felt so at ease at his side. His smile was hard to look away from. She placed her hands in her lap. The lingering feeling of his fingers on hers was painful.

Teddy's cheeks were red, and he rose to his feet, suddenly restless. "All right, I'm going back in."

Logan found a daisy to poke at as Teddy stripped off his shirt. She only looked up when he splashed a bit of water at her from the middle of the lake. He was visible from his pale collarbone up, and he raised a brow.

"I know what you're asking, and the answer is no!" she called out.

He shook his wet hair out of his eyes. "Well, lovely, because my question was if you were planning on spending this beautiful day without a swim!"

She laughed, mostly to buy herself some time as she frantically considered her outfit. She wasn't about to strip down, even though she was pretty proud of her matching Sailor Moon underwear. But the leggings under her plaid skirt were thick and dark, and the band tee she'd taken from Margot was light enough to not weigh her down.

She thought of what Margot would say. *Get in the damn lake, Lo. Or you might as well let Mom put* The Look *back on.*

Logan wasn't used to the side of Teddy that wasn't overwhelmed by shyness and dripping with fear. She didn't want to lose it. And she wanted him closer. So, she stripped down before she could stop herself, and didn't look his way until she was neck-deep in the water.

He laughed as she swam to him. "I never thought I'd swim in this lake again, much less with a witch!"

She smirked. "Lucky you!"

He was so close that she could count the beads of water clinging to his lashes, the droplets running down his bare shoulders. "Do the others know about your dreams?"

She bit her bottom lip. "No."

"Why not?"

"I don't know. I guess I just wanted something to myself."

"Then it's *our* secret, Logan. And I have to thank you. I've noticed that you're the only one of the witches that stands up for me."

And suddenly, he wasn't the Wolf Boy and she wasn't the baby witch. They were just a boy and a girl, doing something that Logan felt had been plucked from a movie. For the first time since coming to Mesmortes, she felt like she was enough as she was.

It lasted until they crawled out of the water, threw on their clothes, and started back toward the Hill. The moment Logan saw Mesmortes up there, cradled in sunlight, she remembered that this would end in two months' time.

Standing at the edge where the Green ended and the Hammersmitt land began, Logan turned to Teddy. "You'd really die for Haelsford?"

"I'm out of place here. Everyone who lived when I did is dead." He gave her a curious look. "And what do I have here to stay for?"

"Sometimes I wonder the same thing."

# 34

## iris

As a Christmas gift to Haelsford, the Wolves took their next kills: two mundane frat boys, visiting from a university a few hundred miles away. Screenshots of their comments pledging to livestream a night in the Swamp circulated quickly online. Their fathers blamed the Witchery Council and threatened lawsuits, but they would fail. Everyone knew the rule: Enter at your own risk. The boys were just another tragic part of the town's memories now. Besides, everyone was eager to move on to other, more festive things.

Iris genuinely loved Christmas.

It was more about the season than the religion; as an *involuntary spark to a resurrection*, she wasn't feeling too keen on Jesus at the moment. She just liked cinnamon and eggnog and the look of Thalia's wreath nailed to her door. Ghoulish black ivy and poisonous red berries.

Most of all, Iris liked having the school to herself—alone, in a comfortable, quiet room that smelled like incense. She promised herself a reprieve from the whole Haunting business during winter break. The Wolves could howl as loudly as they wanted to; Iris wasn't going to think about them.

As she opened up a dog-eared page in *Incurable Hexes and Enchantments*, she heard voices coming from the hall. She recognized both, though one was muffled by the distinct static of an electronic device.

*Boys.* Iris narrowed her eyes. *Hammersmitts.*

He was just outside her door now, and before there was a knock, Iris shouted, "NO ONE'S HOME!"

"Iris."

She pulled the door open. Mathew Beaumont wore a blue sweater and black slacks, somehow looking both well put together and exceptionally nervous, which Iris appreciated. In one hand was a tin of cookies, and the other held a phone showing a beaming Trent Hogarth.

"IKF, my favorite necromancer!" Trent said, accent thick. "Happy Christmas! *Hey*"—he held up his wrist to show the electric purple bracelet that matched Mathew's blue and Iris's red—"twinsies."

"Beaumont, Hogarth," Iris said, more amused than angry. "What a horrible surprise."

Mathew smirked. "I brought cookies. Snickerdoodle, homemade by a girl who looks just like me." He nodded at her. "Nice sweater. Are those unicorns?"

"How did you even get in here? You don't have the witchblood to pass through the campus charms."

"You underestimate the Beaumont charm, Iris, and you should know better."

Trent wolf-whistled. "Mates, I'm still here."

"Night, Trent," Mathew said. He ignored Trent's protests and ended the call. "Ari Hannigan. She's a—"

"Sophomore. I know her."

"Her dad plays golf with mine, and she held the door open for me. How are unicorns Christmassy?"

She pointed at the silver lines on her green sweater. "They're running through tinsel."

His smirk softened into something pretty.

Begrudgingly, she stepped aside for him.

Iris's room was lit by candles clustered in each corner, three large mason jars stuffed with fairy lights on her desk, and a giant pink neon sign that read xoxo hanging over her bed, her favorite thing Jailah had ever given her. It was a weird scene—girlish and morose—with both boy band posters and tattered Demonology texts. Though her desk was neat and her bed made, there was a little chaos in the eerie way everything looked.

"It's very you," Mathew said politely.

Iris nodded, satisfied. "Thank you." She sat cross-legged on her bed.

Beaumont stood awkwardly, staring at a jar of quick-moving tadpoles.

"Sit," she said, a little mean because she didn't know how else to say it.

He had a brow raised as he sat beside her. It was an odd moment. He kept one leg hanging off the bed; probably for the best—*he was just so tall.*

He passed her a cookie and left the tin open. "Where are the girls?" he asked.

"Jailah's in Alabama, Logan's in Canada, and Thalia's up north near Orlando. Trent's in London, right?"

"Yeah. So why are you here? What do you do alone for two weeks?"

"You sound like Jai." She was pleased that he knew Jailah well enough to laugh. "Having a few weeks to talk to no one but myself and a few ghosts is my idea of a vacation. It's nice."

"Sorry for ruining it, but that's what friends are for."

"I wouldn't call us that."

He leaned back and closed his eyes. "What do you call two people that travel into underworlds together?"

"Two people that just happen to know each other and occasionally frequent the same space."

"And the same bed."

She nudged him away with her elbow. What . . . was this? She had a Hammersmitt on her bed. And he was utterly content to be there, listening to her speak. The wheel in her chest turned. Iris took a moment to drink him in.

Eyes still closed, he said, "I see you. Checking me out."

"Every time I think you can't be more annoying—"

He winked at her. "I mean, it's fine. You like my face."

"Ergh, shut up." She lay back next to him, her eyes firmly trained on the ceiling above her. She was hyperaware of Beaumont staring at her now.

"How do you feel about this whole Wolf Boy sacrifice thing?" he asked.

Iris sighed. "I want to say that it's nothing, and that he was already dead."

"It's not *nothing*. He's alive now."

She touched her middle finger to her thumb, which was tender from being pricked often. "The Wolves need to end, and I would do anything to do it, but it's still sad, I guess. He'll be killed in two Haunting seasons."

"But witchery demands sacrifice," said Mathew, offering up her own words.

In truth, Iris felt guiltier than she let on. Jai and Thalia weren't exactly excited about killing Theodore Bloom, but they had such steely, resilient attitudes about it. *It's him or us*, Iris reminded herself.

"So, uh. No family you could be with?" Mathew asked curiously.

*The boy's persistent.* "You're not with *your* family."

"I take any chance I can to get out of that house. All they do is fight."

He was wearing that face, the *you can trust me* face, and Iris wanted to, desperately. But this was something she hadn't even told her girls, and it seemed like a betrayal to confide in this boy she hardly knew. Even if he was her tether. Even if the cog in her chest loosened into a reassuring thread.

"I was raised by ghosts," Iris said finally. "You know how kids believe in the tooth fairy and Santa Claus? When I was a kid, the silly thing I believed was that fathers only appeared in the daytime and mothers never grew old."

Iris never noticed the supernatural sheen of her mother's face, the odd perfection in her movements and features, how static and lovely she always looked, as if suspended in time and space. Her father only ever appeared in reflections, only spoke through enchanted electronics—a radio announcer's voice, the newscaster on TV—but she could feel his touch. A leaf caressing her cheek, or a gust of wind picking her up when she stumbled over her first steps.

"There's a town called Sun Harbor on this little island by the Keys," Iris explained. "There's nothing there anymore but an old mansion that's falling apart, and that's where they are."

"How did they die?" Mathew asked gently.

"My mom was a thief." Iris smiled, and it made Mathew smile. It felt good even though her heart ached.

Iris explained that Sage Foster was once a woman on the lam, persecution looming because she was the worst kind of witch: powerful, unrepentant, un-banished. She was a witchy book collector turned witchy book bandit. A vigilante, of sorts, taking what was stolen from witches and sharing the texts among her coven. Her power was self-taught and wild. She vowed to hurt any mundane who would try to restrain her.

Enter Mortimer Keaton, a coroner, who'd caught her among the bodies, *talking* to them.

Enter Iris, their baby girl, touched with death.

Enter a town of angry mundanes, their guns loaded with blackthorne, their hearts full of hate. Even as they approached the cemetery, uninvited, on the day of her wedding, Sage promised to keep them all together until the baby on her hip knew enough to take care of herself.

"The apparitions are strongest in the summer, during the anniversary of their deaths. I visit them every June. They flicker in and out during the rest of the year. It's hard to see."

*You can't keep us forever,* her mother always warned. Alive, Sage had the power to preserve them, but she couldn't put herself and her husband to rest now. Iris had to do it; she knew she did, but she couldn't. Not until she knew for sure that she could go on without either of them in her life. Iris could live with that guilt, but she couldn't live without them.

It was Beaumont's turn to take her in now. But to her relief, there was a knock at the door. She didn't know what she might do if he kept looking at her like *this*.

She opened the door to a tear-soaked and shivering Morgan Ramirez.

"What's wrong?" Iris frowned, suddenly worried.

"I think . . . something . . . bad happened . . . to Jenna." Morgan spoke between sniffles.

Iris's heart sank. "How—"

They shook their head, impatient and frustrated. "Trust me! It's a tether thing."

Iris couldn't argue with that.

"I came to check first, just in case I was wrong, but she's not in her room, and she's not answering her phone!" Morgan cried.

"What do you think happened?"

The little witch burst into tears. "She's in the Swamp. I *feel* it. Iris . . . I think the Wolves got her."

Within ten minutes, she was in her car. Iris had Mathew white-knuckled as she sped to the marshland, and though they were still safe behind the barrier of witchery, he clearly wasn't comfortable with a host of things here.

"What if . . ." He paused, considering what to say next. "You hear about that woman who died a few years ago? Patti Wells? She told a neighbor that she could hear her daughter crying to her from the Swamp, even though her daughter was in Miami on a field trip. Maybe the Swamp was calling out to Morgan through the form of Jenna."

"But they came to us instead of going into the Swamp. And besides, it's not worth it to stay home if there's a possibility that Jenna's out there." Iris slowed down a bit, easing them onto a worn-out trail of slush, the water here covered with a thin green film. "They're tethers. It's. A thing."

Beaumont lifted a brow.

Iris spared him a split-second glance, her heartbeat quickening. "I'll explain later."

"Maybe we should call someone?" Beaumont suggested through gritted teeth.

"We can't, Mathew. The Witchery Council won't risk sending a party into the Swamp for someone who might not even be there. It's shitty, but they just wait for the bodies to turn up."

He said nothing at first. Then, softly, "You just called me Mathew."

Iris became attuned to everything. The slowness of his breaths, the soft way he took them in. The fidgeting in his fingertips, rested against the dashboard, like he was resisting the compulsion to reach for something. The way the moonlight surrounded him, forcing him all aglow. It was unknown territory, and she was deep in it. In this moment, he could say anything and unravel her completely. She hadn't meant to give him that power.

"That's your name," Iris snapped. Her wand rattled in the cup holder as she sped forward.

"You don't call me that. You call me Beaumont."

Iris pressed down harder on the gas. "Yeah, well, I'll call you Beaumont, then!"

Slowly, his hand drifted toward her. Iris frowned at it, but he just clutched the steering wheel tightly, right under her own grip.

"Do you feel that?" he whispered dreamily.

She shook her head. Mathew had moved his hand once more, leaving one finger hooked on the wheel while the others rested on her knee.

Mathew wasn't looking at her anymore. He seemed far away. "It's colder."

"It's the Winter Wond—"

"*IRIS!*"

Something fleshy hit the windshield, and in Iris's frantic lurch to steady the speeding vehicle, a wheel hit a wayward boulder, and she sent them flying instead.

Iris instinctively reached for her wand and felt it brush her fingertips before it skittered away.

The car flipped once, twice, three times before finally stuttering still.

⸺⸺⧕ ✪ ⧔⸺⸺

The world was upside down. The air smelled like gasoline and blood.

Iris pressed her hand to the open wound on her head.

*My wand.*

She turned, and the sight of Beaumont dangling lifelessly in his seat punched the air out of her. She reached for him, but a fresh wave of dizziness forced her still. "Mathew?" she said weakly.

Iris quieted. She heard voices, her blood running cold.

*I am past the barrier of protection. I'm in the Swamp.*

Her parents called her name. The sound nearly entranced her, but the car lurched suddenly. There was something above them. It snarled.

Iris clenched her fists, willing herself to be still. *Silly*, she mused. If it was what she thought it was, it could already smell her blood.

There wasn't time to look for her wand. She reached for a jagged piece of glass instead. She figured she might get in one good swipe at an eye or its nose before it bit into her neck, and the chances of even that were minimal. Tonight, she would likely become another unfortunate story of death-witches in Haelsford. At least she could say that when faced with imminent death, she refused to go out like a wimp. If the beast wanted her, it would have to put some effort into it.

Iris felt the metal lurch down on her, then release. Her heart pounded.

Two giant paws stepped out in front of her window. Slowly, like the thing had enough mind in it to be sadistic, it lowered its head and peered at her.

Iris wanted nothing more than to shut her eyes against the snarling black teeth, the misshapen face, and, worst of all, the beast's wet red eyes.

She tightened her grasp around the glass, even as it threatened to break skin.

The Wolf lunged. It hit the window hard, but it didn't break. It lunged again, slamming into the glass with such fury that its own dark blood smeared across it. It didn't seem to notice, slamming once more with a growl.

"I . . . Iris?" Beaumont asked faintly.

"Mathew, find my wand!"

She kept her eyes on the beast. The Wolf struck again with a loud crack of its own bones. A thin fissure formed in the glass.

Iris felt Beaumont's frantic movements as he hurried to gain purchase on his surroundings.

The Wolf thrashed against the glass again, widening the break, rocking the entire car. Glass cut into its flesh, ripening the air with a sour iron smell. It chomped at the air, its red eyes hardly wavering from Iris's face. She lurched as far backward as possible, but she still felt its coarse fur against her neck. It wanted her, and it would eventually claw its way to her.

In a burst of adrenaline, Iris slashed at its exposed snout. The Wolf whined in shock, but only pushed its head farther through the glass—

She felt a twitch in her chest. Instinctively, before Mathew could shout her name, she opened her palm and felt him drop her wand into her hand.

The Wolf broke through just as Iris let out a scream. *"Burn in Flames!"*

The beast was blasted backward in a plume of red fire. Iris rarely used the destructive fire spell and didn't know if the Wolf was dead or alive. She had no intention of finding out.

She pointed her wand at the base of the car above her. *"Up!"*

The car righted itself into the air and onto its wheels. Shakily, Iris pointed her wand back toward Mesmortes. She sent them barreling through the protection before the wrecked vehicle stuttered to a stop.

Iris and Mathew sat motionless for a few moments, dazed. Neither of them said a word as howls grew louder from the Swamp behind them. The

243

lights of Mesmortes and Hammersmitt twinkled perfectly in the distance, and Iris felt like she was a world away.

"Shit," Mathew said uneasily. "We're safe now."

But Iris didn't feel safe. The air smelled rusty and warm and felt like danger, as if the night was saying, *I am not done with you yet.*

She squinted into the darkness. There was something ahead, a shadowy bundle in the high grass. "What is that?"

With her wand, she ripped away the mangled door. The two of them staggered toward the bundle.

Grief slammed into Iris's core.

"Fuck," Iris choked out, dropping to her knees. "Please, *no.*"

There was a body before her, mangled into pieces.

# 35

## thalia

Christmas made Thalia's skin itch.

In her nightmares, she wore a green dress that touched the ground and her curls were pulled back from her face. Her father was up at the altar working the congregation into a fury. Her mother maybe touched her hand, as if willing the word of God to take, and maybe it would've. Thalia always wondered what she would be if her witchery never came. Would she have grown up like her mother? Holding a respectable, nonthreatening job, bearing a child, and spending days adhering to both God's will and the will of her husband?

*Bleh.*

It was almost worth it, in some ways, that she murdered a boy in a Maserati. At least she never had to answer to the pressures of her family ever again. A little dramatic, but effective. She told herself that, even as the guilt grew.

Of course, this secret meant spending Christmas alone.

She didn't need Iris or Jailah or Logan to see her like this, huddled up in the corner of her cabin, wand ready, protective spells like a cage around her. So she told them all she was spending break with the Coven of Flowers, the witches that always welcomed her back with open arms.

She tried to remember what her father looked like when he was happy, but could only make out bits and pieces. The picture wasn't complete. Raised brows. A hearty laugh. But every time Thalia tried to hold on to it, she only felt her father's fear and anger as he called for her death. *That*, she could remember clearly, and how anxious she'd felt in the attic as her parents bumbled in the house below, just after Thalia had sent the Warner triplets flying.

Her phone pinged with an alarm alert. It was 7:30.

Thalia trudged over to her desk, and instead of pulling a vial of her father's blood, she pulled the one of her mother's and added it to the cauldron.

It would've been easier to forge a connection with a piece of enchanted jewelry, like *The Look*, but having her mother purchase such a talisman was too risky. With her mother's blood, there was no trace of magic once the connection was severed. But Thalia was running low on the blood, even with their infrequent meetings. If they didn't re-up, they'd have to resort to burner phones and texts.

Thalia breathed in the smoke.

Her mother appeared, wearing a thin smile. "My girl."

"Mom."

Fiona Turner blinked. Thalia wasn't sure if there were tears in her mother's deep brown eyes, or if it was the glistening sheen of the spell. "You look so thin. You eating well, baby?"

Thalia didn't know what to say. She was so rarely attended to in such a way. Only in these meetings did Thalia realize how badly she missed being fussed over and loved in that unconditional way that was different from the way she loved her witch girls and they loved her.

"I'm fine," she managed softly. "You look well."

It was true. Where Abraham Turner had looked worn down, Fiona was radiant as ever. Her smooth dark brown skin showed only a few new wrinkles, and it glowed.

Fiona smiled. "I don't have long. Grades okay?"

Thalia nodded. "Good enough."

"Good enough?"

Thalia blew out a laugh-sigh. "I'm a greenwitch. I have the Gift of the Earth; I'm pretty sure that's, like, automatic acceptance to any college-level healer program in the country. If. You know. College—"

"Of course, college," her mother interjected, wringing her hands. "Yes, I forgot about your, um—"

"My Pull."

Fiona smoothed out her pristine green blouse. She was trying her best, Thalia knew that. But growing up in a place like Annex and bearing a witchy daughter still had its hold on her, it seemed. Old habits. Thalia always wondered if their relationship would be the same if she'd been a necromancer instead.

Her mother turned slightly, listening to her surroundings. "Look, I . . . I was thinking. This summer, maybe, I could come see you."

Thalia's heart dropped. A flicker of anger grew in her chest. "What, and lead *him* right to me?"

Her mother's voice dropped to a tense whisper. "You know I would never, ever put you in danger. You know that."

"No," Thalia said sharply. "It's too risky, *you* know that."

"I haven't seen my daughter in almost three years. Can you blame me?"

Thalia could not stop the fracture that grew in her heart. She blinked hard. If she cried, her mother would likely begin to sob. "I miss you, too. It's not like I don't wish we could—"

And suddenly, Fiona's face changed. A wide smile grew on her face as she yelled over her shoulder, "Coming, honey!"

Thalia exhaled through her nose. She could see the sadness in her mother's eyes, even as she forced that smile.

Their time was up. Fiona winked. Thalia nodded. And she pulled back the spell.

With an iron weight in her heart, Thalia rolled up the gray beaded bracelet that Logan had given her and picked off a messy piece of fruitcake. Nonni's baking was not spectacular, but she loved it anyway, out of principle. It was the only gift she ever got from someone in her old life. Maverick kept watch at the window, eyes alert, tail calm.

"Forgive me, Father, for I have sinned," Thalia whispered as she paced. "Killed a boy, would like to see my father dead, and I am a horrible daughter to my own mother. To rectify my crimes, I will say ten Hail Marys and rid Haelsford of its hex." She wiped her eyes and laughed to herself, if only to keep from bawling.

Her phone blasted a twangy tune. Thalia looked at the name, considered ignoring it, but found herself picking up. "Jai?"

"Juuuust checking in."

"I'm fine. I'm—"

"Still in Haelsford. Thalia, what kind of friend would I be if I didn't know when you were lying?"

Thalia flopped onto her bed. "I'm fine," she repeated.

Jai's voice was a soothing balm. "I know you are, babe. You're the strongest person I know. But some days are tough. Christmas is always tough for you. I wish you'd text Iris. The two of you all alone, I hate it!"

Thalia relaxed her clenched jaw. *Jailah just cares*, she reminded herself. *You knew this would happen when you told her.*

There was a creak outside. Thalia sat up, and Jailah sensed something, because of course she did. "T? What's wrong?"

Maverick hopped off of the windowsill. He didn't growl, but Thalia felt the wariness in his eyes and wagging tail. He puttered toward the door while watching her, as if to say, *You need to see this.*

Thalia opened the door, half expecting her father and a bullet.

Not this.

Never this.

She clamped her hand to her mouth. The deathwitch looked so small and delicate while leaning against Mathew Beaumont, who had his own injuries to deal with.

"Jenna," Iris whispered. "The Wolves killed Jenna."

# 36
## logan

Logan bounced on her toes outside Soma Café, her feet crunching in the fake snow. She held her phone a few inches from her ear, and still, Margot's voice boomed.

"I CAN'T BELIEVE YOU!" screamed the elder Wyatt sister.

Logan looked through the window at Teddy, who was sipping his latte with trepidation. "I'm sorry, Go. I didn't mean to miss my flight, and every other one has been canceled!"

"YOU ARE LEAVING ME ALONE WITH MOM ON CHRISTMAS!"

Her heart fluttered with guilt. "No! Aunt Marjorie will be there, and Auntie Louisa, and Aunt Carolyn—"

"I fully support you severing *The Look*, but not coming home for Christmas is a really big deal."

Logan touched the jewel at her neck. "I know."

"A few months ago, you were begging me to let you come home! It doesn't even snow in Florida!"

"Actually, the witches have turned Haelsford into a winter wonderland. It's even kinda cold; it's pretty neat."

"That doesn't count! Pop-Pop can't call us Go and Lo without the Lo! You're missing mini apple pies and lamb roast."

"What do you want me to do? I didn't cancel the flights!"

"No, you just missed yours!"

A couple glanced at her on their way in, and Logan dropped her voice. "Well, you should be glad! The weakest Wyatt witch won't be there to ruin the fun."

Margot sighed tensely.

"You have no idea what it's like to sit there and watch the rest of you use your magic like it's the easiest thing in the world, while Mom and at least three cousins whisper about you, and your pathetic witchery, and how you've abandoned your home for some hellhole three thousand miles away! I'm sick of it, Go, I'm sick of being the pitiful one!"

For a few moments, Margot said nothing. Logan could only hear the faint holiday jingle in the background, and Go's tense breaths.

"So," Margot said quietly. "You missed your flight, huh?"

Logan's heart fluttered with guilt. "Yeah."

"Look, I'm sorry that—"

"It's fine. *I'm* fine. Never mind. Merry Christmas."

Margot scoffed. "Whatever. Merry Christmas."

Logan hung up. For a few moments, her thumb hovered over Margot's name. She knew she should call and apologize, but she was too stubborn and too excited to have Teddy to herself on Christmas.

Soma Café was dim, thankfully. If Mathew decided to come in on his day off, he would not have seen them. Not with the lighting, and not among the enthusiastic decorations that had taken over the café. Actual snow fell from the ceiling, the windows were covered prettily in ice, and a beautiful fire crackled in the front of the room, which smelled like evergreen trees and sugar cookies. The air was flush with love. Couples and families and friends gathered at each table, chattering away happily, like a pack of murderous Wolves weren't waiting in the distance. Logan had the same thought she'd had so many times before: *Haelsford is so friggin' weird.*

Dressed in one of Trent's leather jackets and cool blue jeans, Teddy took one look at her and said, "That went poorly."

"Yes, it did."

"I'm sorry."

"What could you possibly be sorry for?"

"You missed, um, your flight, because of me—"

"No, Teddy."

"Because I had too many questions about the flying machine, and you were trying to explain it to me."

With a laugh, she crossed her arms on the table, which was entirely too small. Teddy's arms were everywhere. He had them draped across the length of it, his long fingers grasping the opposite edge—*Logan's* edge—like he was trying to keep steady. His hair was wispy, and though he kept trying to push a wayward curl behind his ear, it always flopped back onto his face.

There was a karaoke stage set up at the far side of the café, and the next person took it to some light applause. The woman held the microphone, and the twinkling beginnings of "All I Want for Christmas Is You" played over the speakers.

Teddy sipped his latte. She was happy to see his bracelet dangling from his wrist, the same deep green as his hazel eyes.

"So?" Logan asked.

"It tastes like a pumpkin pie."

"Exactly! How do you like the music?"

He grimaced. "It's very strange. A lot is happening."

"Don't let Mariah hear you saying that." The front door chimed, and Logan casually flipped her hair over her face.

Teddy lowered his voice. "Logan, if you think the others wouldn't approve of us being here, maybe we should go."

She frowned. Even though Logan *had* been worried about what they might think, hearing Teddy say it out loud just annoyed her.

He smiled apologetically. "I just don't want to cause any—"

"Don't worry. Everything's fine."

The table was too small. If either of them leaned in any closer, she would be in trouble. She turned in her seat and watched the woman finish up her song, which led to two witches' strangely haunting rendition of "Last Christmas." When Logan turned back to Teddy to ask him if this was more his style, she found him gazing at her, his head resting in his hand.

She blushed. "How about this one?"

"This what?" he asked softly.

God, it was impossible when his voice sounded like that, all dreamy and low.

"This song." Slowly, Logan arranged her arms back within his little barrier.

"I wasn't paying attention."

"It's still going."

"You make it very hard to focus." He wrapped his hands around her elbows, his thumbs resting in the upside of them. "At first, I thought you reminded me of her."

Logan didn't have to ask to know that he meant Mathilde.

"But now I see that I was wrong. There has never been anyone in the world quite like you."

She shook her head. "You barely know me."

"But I *feel* like I do."

It was absurd, but she felt the same way. So comfortable in the presence of a boy she'd spent so little real time with. "And I can't even do magic," she whispered.

He tilted his head at her. "Well, I don't care."

He couldn't have known what those words meant to her. She felt burdened by her so-called blessing. She was inferior before it because she had no witchery, and then after, because she was weak. Not once did anyone ever say that it was okay to not be an Iris, or a Thalia, or a Jailah, a Margot or a Diane. She never felt that she was fine just the way she was.

Logan couldn't stop herself. She leaned in and kissed his cheek. If he saw the tears in her eyes, he said nothing of it. Not knowing what to do with her hands, she quickly wrapped her fingers around her mug of hot chocolate.

He placed his hands atop hers. "I want to live, Logan. I wish I could lie and say otherwise."

But he couldn't; it was impossible. Everything they gave him had been saturated with alítheia. Logan felt a bit gross about it. Even if lying wasn't exactly a good trait to have, everyone did it. Stripping it from him was just another form of control. Even so, she was comforted by the fact that everything he said was true.

"Why would you want to?" Logan muttered. "When we first met, you told me that you didn't want this, that you never asked for it."

He looked at her, hazel eyes deep with affection.

It was a dangerous thing, to look at someone like that, or to be looked at like that. Logan glanced down at her shoes. She'd already kissed his cheek; she didn't want to know what she might do next.

"Things have changed," he whispered.

Gently, he slipped his fingers under her chin. She was drowning in his eyes, drinking in his scent, buried by the feeling of his touch.

Logan's thoughts wheeled frantically, a plan forming.

"You have to die for the Haunting to end," she said. "How do we make you stay?"

He brushed her cheek with his knuckles, an electrifying touch. "I promised that I would end the Wolves. I cannot go back on my word."

"You really mean that? You would just die again? For what? For Haelsford?"

His brow furrowed in confusion. "Isn't that what you want? This is your home."

Logan let it slip, the shame that had been burning in her since she moved to this town and let it chew her up. "No, it isn't. I don't know what everyone else sees in Haelsford, but it isn't my home. I wouldn't give up my life for it, and neither should you."

She hadn't seen this look on Teddy's face since his first new day. Complete and utter shock. It softened into innocence—reddened cheeks and a meek gaze. "Oh, you've made me so selfish."

The sounds of sirens broke the holiday atmosphere. The café quieted.

"What's that?" Teddy asked.

Logan shook her head, though she had a feeling. Everyone else in the café seemed to think the same thing. Haelsford didn't have cops; it had the Witchery Council. There wasn't a hospital; there was the town infirmary staffed by greenwitches. Sirens only rang out for kills.

She looked up at Teddy. "We should go."

···•» ✸ «•···

Back at Mesmortes, Logan quickly slipped Teddy into the Topthorne House hollow room. She went to her room and rummaged in her messy desk for her wand. She frowned at it, then pulled a thin green book from under a stack of unread self-help books that Aunt Marjorie had sent her.

She returned to the hollow room and found Teddy wringing his hands. "Someone died tonight, right?"

She bit the inside of her cheek, wishing he hadn't asked the one question that made it difficult to ignore the consequences of her plan. "Yes. And the other witches are definitely going to want to send you into the Swamp, like, immediately."

She placed the book on the coffee table. *The Magical Modifications Handbook.* She'd stolen it from Go's arsenal. There was a picture of a witch changing an apple into a banana on the cover, which felt too juvenile for the spell Logan knew was inside.

She turned to Teddy, who looked tired and desperate and scared. "There's a spell. If I can do it, I could hide you in plain sight, just until after the Haunting, and then we can explain to the others that you deserve to live again."

"We?" Theodore whispered sweetly.

"We're kind of in this together now." Logan shrugged, though she felt a lump in her throat.

"You're sure about this?"

Logan couldn't bear to hear the doubt in him, too. She eyed the ominous fearmonger plant on the windowsill, remembering Thalia's voice. *It'll let you know when you're in danger.* To her comfort, the thick, star-shaped leaves were healthy and full. She tugged at a leaf, just to be sure. It wouldn't come free.

"How kind do you think they'll be when they learn you've helped me escape?"

"You're not going to escape; you'll be right here. And I don't need to answer to them. *I* brought you back."

Theodore closed his eyes. "Why are you doing this?"

"You know why."

Teddy was very good at finding the right places to touch her. His fingers grazed the inside of her wrist, and a breath hitched in her throat. She thought it unfair that he could do that to her, with just a touch. She hated how it excited her, and she loved it all the same.

"I'm a wreck," Teddy whispered suddenly. "A boy with two lives lived. I'll bring you nothing but pain."

Logan chilled, but he was on her before she could properly think of why those words unsettled her. A touch, so simple, his fingers to the corner of her mouth, and she couldn't see straight anymore.

He kissed her so suddenly that Logan felt dizzy, and light, and heavy all at once. Electric and on fire. Like she was exactly where she needed to be.

He looked at her, mouth parted, eyes wondrous.

She felt no shame as she pulled the amplyfyr from her bag. She'd been too paranoid to keep it here in the hollow room, or in her own room, or anywhere but on herself at all times. Carefully, she drew back the porcelain top. *Just this*, she thought. *I do this, then I'm done. Forever.*

Theodore stood by her, his hand resting on her waist.

The heat of the amplyfyr took her immediately. It hit her, and she felt *strong*. There was nothing in her head but the singular thought that she was right to do this. No guilt, no repercussions. Just her, the magic, and the beautiful boy.

She rose her wand to Teddy's face. "Hold still," she said, in a voice that was not totally her own.

From the windowsill, a single fearmonger leaf fluttered to the ground.

# 37

## jailah

Jailah's dress was black and plain. She slipped into dark leggings and ripped out the pink tie in her silky-straight hair. Her dark tresses fell around her face.

Reluctantly, she looked into the full-length mirror. She hated who she saw.

There was a soft knock at the door. "Jailah?" Mathew's voice was gentle on the other side of it. "Iris is calling again."

Jailah tittered with her hands. "Say you never saw me."

Mathew Beaumont's nondescript bedroom was the perfect place to hide. Jailah couldn't bear being at Mesmortes. Covenhood was the least appealing thing to her at the moment, and Hammersmitt was the only place in Haelsford where she could get away from it all. She was too exhausted to be angry, too distraught to be gentle, and too numb to fake otherwise. It was a foreign feeling to her. Her best days were total highs, and she let herself sink into bad days with impunity.

It wasn't even like this last year, when she watched Veronica walk out of the Witchery Council trial screaming, her witchery snuffed out like a flame. There was guilt, but whatever *this* was, it was capped with helplessness.

*Because last year, you made your decision and you knew you'd have to live with it. You acted anyway. This time, you didn't act at all.*

Jailah hadn't seen Theodore Bloom all week. Between the flight back, the mourning, and the new curfew, she hadn't thought about him at all.

*I should've thrown him into the Swamp myself.*

She'd imagined it before. A spell like *Follow the Leader* to make him walk, the brute force of a levitation spell if he tried to resist. She pictured the Wolf plucking him out of existence before he could crawl back over the barrier, and when they finished with him, the Haunting would end in a blast of flame, the whole Swamp engulfed in it.

But as hard as she'd tried, Jailah could never place herself in the picture. Theodore Bloom was sent, and he was taken, but she never saw the hand that led him as hers.

Now she could do it without a second thought.

Mathew knocked again.

"It's your room—you can come in!"

He poked his head in. "I know it's not really my place, but it's totally cool with Trent and me if you just camp out here. Iris, Thalia, and Logan, too."

Jailah looked at his reflection in the mirror. "Sweet of you, but not showing your face at a funeral is basically screaming that you're guilty."

Mathew's expression went bleak. "This isn't your fault."

Jailah shook her head.

"But. You were right. We voted incorrectly."

She turned to him now, slinging her purse over her shoulder. His face seemed much more dire than its reflection. "I should go."

Mathew knew better than to argue.

From the kitchen island, Trent looked up. "Jai, I'm so sorry."

She looked around. "Where is he?"

Mathew furrowed his brow. "Isn't he with you guys?"

"What? No, he's supposed to be here."

Trent lowered his gaze. "He's with Logan."

"Logan?" Jailah repeated incredulously. She'd been with Logan all week. She never said anything about Bloom.

Trent played with the strings of his deep blue Hammersmitt hoodie. "Sorry, I was covering for them, the lovebirds."

Acid rose in Jailah's throat. "I'm gonna be late." She finally walked out, her witchy senses buzzing like static against her skin.

⋯••❥ ✪ ❧••⋯

"Where the hell have you been?" Iris's voice was raspy, her eyes rimmed red.

Jailah shook her off. They were in the back row, the last of the Mesmortes witches who lined the Hill in plastic chairs. A storm raged around them, though a crafty witch had placed a *Sealing* spell over the gathering.

From Iris's other side, Thalia shot Jailah a scowl. "They've already done remarks. I thought you might've had something to say."

"Words are meaningless to her now," Jailah spat. "I've got a better way to honor her memory. Where's Logan?"

As Thalia and Iris shared a look, the baby witch slid into the empty seat next to Jailah.

"Here," she said, breathless. "Sorry."

Jailah kept her gaze forward. "Where were you?"

"You're both fucking late!" Iris whispered tensely. Anika shot them a warning look from a few rows up. Iris eased back into her seat.

Morgan came up to speak now. A crinkled piece of paper trembled in their hands.

Jailah understood their pain. *I know how you feel*, she'd whispered to Morgan at the assembly last night, her own voice getting thick. She wanted to tell Morgan that there were other ways to lose one, that severing your own tethered knot on purpose gave you all that pain and suffocating guilt, to explain that the empty ache in their chest would subside eventually, but they still might feel it at the most unexpected times. A punch in the gut during archery practice, a sharp pang in the pizza line, a choked breath in the middle of midterms. *You can move on, but you will never forget it.*

"I feel like nothing will ever be good again," Morgan said now, their little voice thick with tears. "I felt so lucky to find my tether. I know Jenna would tell me to get over it"—they hiccuped a laugh—"but I don't think I ever will."

"I can't believe it," Logan said under her breath.

Jailah thought of how she could respond. She thought of comforting words, calming words, something sweet to make it all better. Instead, she said, "You lied."

Logan turned. "What?"

Jailah met her eye. "I was just at Hammersmitt. Theodore Bloom wasn't there."

Logan said nothing. Jailah could feel Thalia and Iris tuning back in.

Up front, as Morgan started sobbing, Lilly helped them to their seat.

Jailah closed her eyes. "I can't do this."

Thalia reached over for her hand. "Come on. Let's go."

They slipped away and made for the cabin. The walk was quiet, except for the pattering of rain against the ground. Jailah felt like she was holding her breath. Once inside, Thalia began a brew of peppermint tea.

"Freddy León's parents might pull him out of Mesmortes," Jailah whispered, dazed.

"Seriously?" Iris wasn't dismissive, but she wasn't sympathetic either.

"Have you never thought about leaving?"

"No," Thalia and Iris said at the same time.

Jailah imagined Haelsford would be the last place anyone would look for Thalia. Iris's mother was born here, whatever the story behind that was, and she'd fostered a strange mentorship with the Roddin Witch.

*This town sucks you in.*

Jailah liked the way blankets of fog greeted her in the morning, the fresh smell of the river and dew, and how the moon looked bigger here. The past witches of Haelsford killed and died for this land, and Jailah felt like living here was accomplishing something. For them. For herself. If she could survive Haelsford, she could survive anything.

She turned to Logan. "What about you?"

Logan didn't hesitate. "I think about leaving every day."

Under different circumstances, Jailah would've tried to soothe away that insecurity. She said, "We're voting again. All in favor of ending the Haunting right now—"

Thalia and Iris immediately raised their hands.

Jailah turned back to Logan. "Where is Theodore Bloom?"

"Isn't he with Trent and Matty?" Thalia asked.

"No," Logan whispered.

Iris stood up so quickly that Maverick, who'd been napping in the corner, rose from his bed.

Logan exhaled sharply. "I think that he deserves to live."

Iris made a strange sound between a laugh and a sob. "Oh my god! I'm sorry, but *what the hell*? You don't even know him!"

"I know him better than you do," Logan said, raising her voice.

The air felt like the exposed end of a frayed wire. Waiting, just waiting to catch. Jailah didn't know when her hand had found it, but she was clutching her wand.

"I've known him for a long time," Logan continued defiantly. "I saw him in dreams after you told me the story of Haelsford, and I scryed for him. When we brought him back, you said you didn't know how it happened, but it had to have been me and the amplyfyr. I did it, Iris. Not you, *me*. I found him, and I raised him up. And since I'm responsible, I say that he gets to live."

Jailah put her hands up. "Back up, you dreamed—you *scryed* for him? Why didn't you tell us?"

Logan turned to Jailah. "I wanted to be a stronger witch before we went after the Wolf Boy. I don't know how or why it was so easy for me to see him, and I didn't want to come to you without an explanation."

"Maybe you were proxying," Iris offered. Even in her anger, her excitement slipped through. "Without even doing anything, maybe your magic latched on to the history here to lead us to him."

"Can she do that?" Thalia asked.

"She's a proxy. Her whole deal is that her magic can do things that defy every magical law there is." She stepped to the baby witch. "Logan, where is he?"

Logan swallowed hard. "You could force-feed me *alítheia*, and I still wouldn't be able to give him up."

Thalia narrowed her eyes. "Are you saying you don't even know where he is?"

Jailah dropped her head into her hands. She'd played this all wrong. *The alítheia wasn't enough. I should've taken his blood for a finding spell. I should've placed a tracking hex on him.* She looked at Iris, who was wearing a similar look of shame. Neither thought they'd *lose* him, and certainly not like this.

Jailah reached for the gentleness in herself that she'd buried. "Maybe Teddy isn't—"

But Logan wouldn't hear it. "Nothing you say will change my mind. He's a good person, and he doesn't deserve to die. We don't even really know that his death will end the Haunting!"

"Are you calling me a liar?" Iris's tone was calm, but Jailah could feel the angry heat wicking from her.

"I'm just saying that all we have is your interpretation of some book. There's no actual evidence—"

Iris cackled. "All right, Logan, you want to fuck him, Jesus, *we know.*"

Jailah closed her eyes. *Shit.*

Logan shook her head. "Why do you always have to be so horrible?"

"I'd take being horrible over the pathetic excuse for a witch that you are," Iris spat.

In twin movements, Jailah went to Logan, and Thalia to Iris.

"You are such a disappointment," Iris added, shaking off Thalia's plea. "I get it now! Like Donahue said, you're the anchor. You're just bringing us all down. We should've let you flunk out of your classes and run back home like you've wanted to every single day—"

Glowing fists clenched, Logan screamed, and Iris went flying through the cabin window, her body crashing violently against the glass.

Thalia rushed outside to Iris while Jailah was frozen there, her eyes locked on Logan, her hand over her mouth.

Logan looked down at her glowing hands. "I didn't mean to!" she choked out. "You know I didn't!"

*"The fuck, Logan?"* a furious voice questioned from outside.

Logan ran out first, wringing her hands in shame, and Jailah followed, feeling powerless. Logan controlling her magic should've been something for them all to celebrate. Instead, *this*. Iris stood shaking, blood trickling from a shallow cut on her head.

"Take a breath, Iris. Chill out, okay?" said Thalia.

But Iris cried out the beginnings of a guttural spell, and Logan put her hands up as Iris cut the air with her wand—

Jailah incanted a shielding spell. It was easy, freshman-level stuff. The ripple of Iris's spell hit an invisible barrier and dissipated. Iris glared at the two of them before raising her hand again.

A second spell never came. "Never mind," Iris hissed. "I shouldn't waste my magic on you. You don't deserve to be hexed by me."

Logan's lip quivered.

"This is stupid." Thalia stared straight ahead, not making eye contact with anyone. "You're both wrong! It was me. I brought back the Wolf Boy."

Iris narrowed her eyes. "What are you talking about?"

"The resurrection spell requires the blood of a murderess." Thalia's voice was unsettlingly even.

Jailah's gasp caught in her throat. *"Thalia."*

"It's okay, Jai. It's about time. This secret is way too big for one person to keep."

"Wait—" Iris shook her head a few times. "You—what? Killed someone?"

Thalia rubbed her eyes under her glasses. "It's a long story. Jailah can tell you—"

"Oh!" Iris turned to Jailah, pointing an accusatory finger. "You knew, too? So, what am I, then?"

"Not like you're an open book, Iris," Thalia said defensively.

*"Wow,"* Iris said incredulously. "Whatever. Forget y'all. I'll find the Wolf Boy by myself."

"No, you won't," Logan threatened.

"Or what? Try me again, I dare you." Iris twirled her wand. "This time, I'm actually ready."

Jailah thought anxiously for the right thing to say. "Logan made a mistake, okay? She's sorry—"

Logan sputtered. *"I'm* sorry? After everything she said?"

Jailah threw her hands up. "I was getting to it— Logan!" But without another word, Logan stomped off.

"Y'all!" Jailah started.

"I don't want to hear it," Iris seethed, waving her off. She walked away, too, but not before shooting them both a resentful look.

Jailah couldn't think of a damn thing to do. She'd lost Jenna, and the Wolf Boy, and now Logan, and maybe Iris. She felt like the world was fracturing around her and there was nothing she could do to repair the splits. She looked at Thalia. "What just happened?"

Thalia sighed. "Jailah, go home. Try to catch up on your sleep." She slipped back into the cabin and shut the door.

Up on the Hill, the procession started the long march to Haelsford Cemetery.

part three

# for all and forever

# 38

## iris

As a cold front took Haelsford, the body count grew from four to seven in the weeks since Jenna's death. A hexeating couple had flown all the way from California, claiming they had the cure for Haelsford in the blood of their veins. They offered themselves up willingly, and the Wolves were happy to comply. Then the widow from town who'd left her job, changed into a nice dress, and followed the voice of her deceased husband into the mucky, rotting land.

Too many had been lost. The baker. The frat boys. The second Mesmortes witch in two years. But life in Haelsford went on, as it always did.

The Haunting was nearly over, and as was tradition, they would mark the Wolves' nearing hibernation with the MidWinter Celebration. All six thousand residents would descend on Haelsford Fields for dancing, drinking, carnival rides, and elation. While Haelsford rejoiced, Iris couldn't find a thing to take joy in.

*Pretty tame year*, they said.

*Lucky us.*

*Low body count.*

What did it matter if Jenna was one of the unlucky ones?

It all made Iris want to scream. She spent January in a haze. Her grades slipped. Magic, both academic and everyday spells, had become frustrating. Practice and refinement in her witchery were necessities before, but every prick of her thumb seemed meaningless now. Nothing to work toward, no one to save.

The professors chalked it up to anxiety from being attacked by a Wolf, finding Jenna's body, and general teen-girl stress. The biggest part being the one thing she couldn't speak with any of them about. And she avoided those who knew. It was impossible to see Thalia, Jailah, or Logan and not think of how they'd failed Jenna. She'd never get over coming so close and failing so spectacularly.

After an endless morning of memorizing and reforming incantations, brewing potions, and finally determining the exact amount of toad's blood needed for the draft to cure sleepwalking—it was a strange time for Iris to enter the most mundane place she could think of: the café in Town Square.

The barista didn't look up at her from under his cap. "What can I get you?"

"Give me the sweetest drink you have," she said.

Mathew Beaumont did a double take and eased into a smile. "Hey." He looked her up and down. "It's been a while."

Iris sensed that she'd arrived on the tail end of a rush. His apron was covered in various chocolaty stains, and his forehead was marred with sweat. His hair was slightly longer, the dark locks starting to curl a little under his cap. When his eyes met hers, she was glad for the hitch in her chest. It was nice to feel something, even if it made her face all warm.

She tapped her chin dramatically. "I'm thinking an iced caramel macchiato, extra caramel. Like, use up the whole bottle. Don't be shy."

"Rough day?"

Iris felt the strange compulsion of desperately wanting to sob. "Rough month, really."

Mathew looked like he regretted his entire existence. "Right, of course. I'm sorry."

"Add a double chocolate muffin." Her heart pounding, she asked, "Do you get a break? We need to talk; it's important."

"I'm off in fifteen. And by the way, you can talk to me, even when it's not important." She didn't respond to that, so he added, "Do you want the muffin warmed up?"

"Yeah. How much?"

"Ah, don't worry about it."

Iris slipped a ten onto the counter. "Why do you even work here? I know you're loaded."

Mathew chuckled dryly. "My dad made me get a job last summer, and . . ." He shrugged. "I don't know. I like it here, so I kept coming back." He slipped the ten over to her.

Iris took a corner table and pulled out both her *Witchery in English Literature* textbook and her *Grimoire for the Good Witch*. She didn't want to look like she was just going to sit here and wait for him, even though that was exactly what she was doing.

Mathew brought over her macchiato and muffin, and she was thrilled that he had a line now and couldn't just hover around, asking pointless questions like *Are you okay?* and *How was your day?* She wouldn't have known what to say other than *I just want the world to swallow me up.*

Iris noticed someone watching her from the counter. She met the girl's eye, and the girl met Iris's, and neither looked too happy to be looking at the other.

Mathew peeked his head over the espresso machine. "This is my sister, Rebecca. Rebecca, this is Iris. She goes to Mesmortes."

"Becky," the girl said, her eyes trained on Iris.

To Iris's introverted horror, the Beaumont girl strolled over and sat across from her. Iris crossed her arms, her expression skeptical, but Rebecca smiled.

"What's that?" she said, pointing at the book but looking straight at Iris.

"A grimoire."

"Hm." Rebecca ran her fingers along the embossed text of the front cover.

It was unnerving, the feverishness in this girl's face and what was lacking in Mathew's. There were identical twins, and there were fraternal twins, and then there were Beaumont twins. Rebecca's face was his face, with a few girlish tinges. And his was hers, with a more cut jaw and slightly kinder eyes. It was clear, though, with just a look, that if there were ever an outbreak of hysteria, Mathew would be on the fringes trying to decipher it, and Rebecca would be running around in the middle, grinning, the cause of the whole damn thing.

She pulled a sleeve of bubble gum from her pocket and offered it to Iris. Iris looked at it as if she'd pulled out a two-headed rabbit.

Rebecca popped her gum. "So, you're the deathwitch. You and your friends are a hot topic for Matty and Trent."

"Necromancer," Iris retorted, ignoring the rest of Rebecca's comment.

Rebecca considered this for a moment. "Is there a difference?"

"I like one more than the other, Bex."

Finally, she dropped the smile. "Becky."

"I like Bex. It's witchier." It'd seemed like useless knowledge at the time, but Iris was suddenly glad Jailah had mentioned running into this girl at the Haelsford house, and her aversion to being branded a witch. She couldn't dwell on it—the thought of Jailah made her chest hurt.

Rebecca's smartwatch pinged. She glanced at it, then rose from her seat. "Hurt my brother, and I'll end you."

"I'd like to see you try." Iris grinned. "Only a fool with a death wish would threaten a witch. Are you a fool, Bex?"

"Are you capable of not making enemies of everyone you meet?" Mathew said, fuming from behind the bakery case.

Neither could really tell who he was addressing.

And in the strangest *fuck you* Iris had ever experienced, Rebecca squeezed her hand and smiled. "It was nice meeting you, Iris. Let's do this again sometime."

She left, and Iris looked to Mathew. "Your sister's a delight. Are you done yet?"

He looked to his wrist, though he wasn't wearing a watch. "Yep."

"Cool. Wanna go to the cemetery with me?"

----->🟊<-----

In some ways, Jenna Prim was lucky. She had a body to bury, at least, and the headstone bore her name. Understandably, Mathew looked like he was going to be sick. He clearly had not shaken the images of Jenna's Wolf-maimed body. Iris fixated on the celebration's Ferris wheel in the distance. Anger welled up in her chest again.

Mathew cleared his throat. "I ran into Thalia the other day."

Iris rolled her eyes. She should've suspected that Mathew would attempt some mending. "That's nice."

"She looked just like you. Tired."

"You sure know how to compliment a girl."

"Hold on now. I didn't say it didn't work on you, because believe me, it does."

She rolled her eyes but couldn't resist a smile. "Liar."

He laughed. "I feel like we haven't spoken in years, and I thought it was me, but it sounds like you guys are all—"

"Beaumont." She turned to him. "Can you not? It's an *us* thing; you wouldn't understand. This isn't something you can fix."

He stuck his hands in his pockets. "Oh. Understood."

Simultaneously, they turned back toward the slow-sinking sun, each hoping desperately for the other to speak next but each not minding the silence between them.

"What did you need to talk to me about?" Mathew said finally, his voice hoarse.

"What?"

"At Soma. You said it was important."

"Oh," she said dreamily. "Honestly, I just didn't want to be alone."

He moved closer. Their arms were touching. He dipped his head toward her. If she turned, her face would likely graze his, so she made herself totally still.

"Why does it feel like you just told me your biggest secret?" he whispered.

Iris smiled and instantly felt guilty for it, like spitting on Jenna's grave. She took a step back from Beaumont. "Maybe it was. Your turn."

"Okay." He ran his fingers through his hair. "I've always been . . . slightly afraid of witches. I know it's silly; you're not vampires or goblins or body snatchers. You're not looking for a fight. You don't want to leave me scarred."

"There are wicked witches."

"But some are gentle."

Iris contemplated this in agonizing fashion. "I am no gentle witch, Beaumont. I will not kiss your scars."

He touched the gold band in her braid. "Shame. I'm in such a dire need of kissing."

Iris let herself enjoy the thrill of his words. It was almost a nice moment. But Mathew's eyes sailed over Iris's head.

"Is that Logan?" he asked softly.

Iris turned.

They locked eyes.

The two witches stood this way for a few moments, quiet and still, neither wanting to give up the first *hi,* or wave, or *I'm sorry*, though those last words were on the tip of Iris's lips.

Suddenly anxious, Iris played with her red beaded bracelet. Just as she opened her mouth, Logan walked away.

The slight cut Iris, but she wasn't going to run after her. She turned to Beaumont. "I don't want to go to Mesmortes. Take me somewhere. Somewhere quiet."

He gathered up the books she'd left in a tidy pile on the ground. "Absolutely."

# 39

## logan

Logan didn't think that Iris would breach this void between them, but she still felt a pang of regret as she walked away.

*She kept her bracelet.* Logan had caught it glinting in the glow of the falling sun. Weeks without speaking, and Iris never took it off.

Jailah did reach out. Of course Jailah tried. But Logan was so ashamed of the last time she saw them that she couldn't bring herself to respond to her texts. And when Thalia waited outside her classes with a small plant as a peace offering, Logan made herself mean and hard and sprinted away.

Iris never so much as looked in her direction, and Logan was sure that they were both waiting for the other to leave her room before leaving their own to avoid an encounter. This dismissal stung most of all. Even though she could be sharp and closed off, Logan knew that Iris was the one who roped her into the Red Three.

It seemed so long ago.

Looking back now, Logan thought it would've made more sense if it had been Jailah, with her predisposition to kindness and love, or even Thalia, who might've seen Logan's inability to make a simple salve and thought, *Let me help this poor, weak witch.* But it was Iris she lived across from, and it was Iris who found her.

Just a few weeks after the semester had started, the overwhelming way of life in Haelsford became too much for Logan. She couldn't understand what others felt for this strange town and its horrible Swamp. *Homesick* was an inadequate word. It was strain; it was fear. It was knowing she didn't deserve the power that the earth had given her. Logan thought that moving to a mystical place like Haelsford would force her magic free. She thought she'd become stronger. Instead, she had spent two months waiting for the miracle ability to wield her wand like others could. Two months noting the way the professors' eyes never met her gaze, because maybe Logan just didn't have *it*. Two months passing the door across from her room and hearing the giggles and gossip and bursts of mischief. She was desperate to know what it was like to call this dreadful place home.

Logan was good at some things. She could perfectly recite spells over and over, could name the eighteen types of sparrow's nettle in her sleep, and knew the exact date that the notorious witch Olga Yara was hanged for her crimes against witchery. But put a wand in her hand, or ask her to perform without it? She was a waste of witchery.

One night, Logan was near tears outside her room because it was one a.m. and she'd spilled her strawberry frap all over the floor. She was sick of pricking her fingers and sacrificing to magic that wanted nothing to do with her.

Suddenly, Iris was there, looking menacing and divine. There was a red silk scarf over her braids, and her eyes were tired. She wore black pajama pants with little yellow moons stitched in them, her wand sticking out of the waistband.

And the first words that Iris Keaton-Foster said to Logan Wyatt were "Looks like unicorn vom."

Logan exhaled a shaky breath. She didn't need this embarrassment, not now, not ever, but Iris wouldn't leave. She just kept staring.

"Are you gonna clean that up?" Iris asked.

Tears pricked Logan's eyes.

"'Cause it's outside my door, too. And I don't want ants."

Logan contemplated what was more pathetic: getting down on her hands and knees with a towel, or attempting to clean up with a spell that would undoubtedly backfire and turn the frap into a bigger sticky mess. Her sob finally released itself. "I can't do this."

Iris squinted at her. "Can't do what?"

"Spell it away."

"Uh."

"I'm awful at magic, okay? I can't do it. I can't. I don't want to be a witch anymore."

Iris grimaced, like it was a personal insult against her. "Ever heard of a mop?"

Logan sighed.

"Don't sigh at me," Iris snapped, and Logan found herself standing straighter. "I'm not being bitchy. I'm saying, if you're just starting out, you can enchant a mop to do it for you. You don't have to spell it away." Iris wrinkled her nose. "Wait here."

Not knowing what else to do and curious about where this was going, Logan waited as Iris went back into her room, shuffled around, and came out with one of those easy-squeeze mops that she recognized from endless nights of infomercial watching. It was already soaking and smelled lemony fresh.

"Get out your needle, girl."

Two tears got away from Logan. She didn't move.

Groaning, Iris did it herself. When it was done, she gave Logan a hard look. "I swear to god, I never want to hear you say that you don't want to be a witch again."

A few weeks later, the Red Three came to her in homeroom.

*They only wanted you for one reason.*

She tried to foster that angry thought, but it wouldn't stick. Once Iris stomped off, Mathew trailing behind her, Logan doubled back. She'd come to the cemetery hoping that one look at Jenna's headstone would knock some sense into her, but she only felt shame and grief.

Logan desperately wanted the Wolf Boy to stay alive. He was the only one she had in this awful little town now. *But what kind of person chooses the death of her fellow witches for a boy?*

Someone touched her shoulder.

She turned and blinked hard. It was him, regardless of the unfamiliar face. Freckled, red-haired, with a crooked nose and big brown eyes.

Even his voice was different. "I've been looking for you."

Corporeal witchery wasn't really meant for this. A transformation of one's entire look wasn't supposed to keep for more than a few hours. Looks were meant to be altered, not completely overhauled. But Logan was a proxy, as awful as it was, and she'd used that damned amplyfyr. She hadn't touched it since Christmas, and even though there was a specific, destructive thrill to it, she'd succeeded at resisting its call. And yet, part of her wanted Theodore Bloom's disguise to fade, if only so she had an excuse to use it again.

Logan pulled him close. She touched her palm to his face and sighed in relief when his real look appeared. Hazel eyes, brown curls, cutting cheek-bones, precious lips. Sharp and soft all at once.

He closed his eyes, savoring her touch.

"I saw Iris," Teddy whispered. "Don't worry. She didn't even give me a second look."

Logan's heart quickened. "I saw her, too."

He raised a brow. "What did she say?"

"Nothing."

He gave a scoff, close to a laugh. "Of course. She would be so horrible."

"Well, I didn't say anything either."

"But you're not the one who should apologize."

Logan pulled away. Without her touch, Theodore's face morphed again.

He looked down at Jenna's headstone. "Did anyone figure out how the Wolves got her? Did she go past the protection?"

"She must have. That's the Haunting. People die."

He flinched. "Of course. I know that."

The tears that Logan had been holding back fell quickly now. Teddy reached out for her, but she angled herself away, unsure that she could say what she needed to say with him so close. "We have to end it."

"We do," he said quietly.

Logan couldn't read him because of the *Shade*, but his words were off-puttingly unaffected, especially considering Logan's loud sniffles. "I'm sorry. I'm so sorry."

It would be excruciating to go back to the Red Three with him next to her, even if she was doing the right thing by bringing him to the Wolves. That she'd even *considered* sparing him at the expense of Haelsford would be unforgivable. No matter the conclusion, she'd already done so much betraying.

"It's okay, Logan," Theodore said sweetly. This time she let him wipe her tears, his true image flashing with his false one when he touched her. He kissed her delicately, but Logan pulled away. It was no time to get even more attached than she already was, and his kisses had a way of muddying her senses.

"Do you want to go to the festival with me?" she choked out quickly. "We still have some time before . . ." *Before your death deadline*, she thought morbidly. "Before the hibernation begins."

Teddy smiled. "I can think of no better way to celebrate my last hours on earth, perhaps permanently this time."

Logan's phone chimed, and Theodore plucked it from her pocket. He said, "No phones, not tonight. Tonight, we celebrate the end of the Haunting. I'm going to devour my weight in ice cream."

Logan wiped her eyes. She had four hours before the Haunting ended, and she vowed that until then, she wouldn't think about the Wolves, or the Red Three, or the disappointment that she was as a witch.

*He chose me.*

And that would be enough for now, even if it wasn't for all and forever.

# 40

## thalia

The Wolves were always the worst during their last hours. The beasts howled morning to night, as if warning the town that their hunger was not yet satiated.

Thalia tried to tune them out. She'd promised Jailah that she'd help create a beautiful meadow in Haelsford Fields for the MidWinter Celebration. Though she and Jailah had spoken more than she and Iris or Logan, there was still a tension between them that felt off. But Thalia was hopeful that after the Wolves went back into the Swamp, things could go back to the way they were.

As Thalia pulled on a light jacket, the wind was knocked out of her. She doubled over as Maverick cried out from somewhere far away. She could feel his fear in her gut as if it were her own. Her familiar was in pain. He was alone, and he was scared, and he was calling his witch.

*I'm coming*, she thought, and rushed out of the dorm.

Her thoughts were wild as she sprinted to her cabin. Was it her father? Had Annex come for her? Had the Witchery Council finally discovered Bloom?

"Maverick?" she yelled, barreling through the door. Thalia could feel that his heart was beating *somewhere*, but not here.

Her hands shook so much she nearly yelled at them to stop. *Be calm.*

She blew away the dust from her cauldron and set to work on a spell that would truly make use of the Gift she was born with. She burned sage, holly, and devil's ivy, and dropped the smoldering bits into the cauldron. Each were the leaves of trees and bushes planted in various places around her cabin and in the forest.

The spell was called *Eyes of the Earth*. It was created by the mother of modern Greenery, Aurora Xie, who had been one of the strongest green-witches to ever walk the earth. It required no incantation. No wand movements. Only Thalia's blood and the need for vision that was not hers but of the seedlings, her kindred, the plants of the forest.

Her blood sizzled against the leaves.

The spell brought her sight. She could see the landscape of wherever the burning leaves were plucked from. Thalia was several places at once: here in the cabin, but also hiding in the devil's ivy by the river, and in the big holly patch close to the edge of the Swamp.

*Where are you?*

In a haze of double vision, Thalia saw the ash in her cauldron spark up suddenly. This was not a spell she was completely familiar with; her courses always skewed toward her healing powers. So when the marigolds that she'd left on Roddin's porch pulled her away, Thalia allowed her consciousness to drift, moving away from the woods and toward the Necromantic Emporium.

Thalia's eyes widened at the scene. The vision was out of focus, and she realized slowly that this wasn't a live shot, but rather a *memory* seeped into the soil of the plant.

The image of a brown-haired boy standing on Roddin's porch knocked the air out of her.

A voice screamed, *"Thalia!"*

She drifted again, and though the spell was disorienting on its own, she was unnerved by that voice, one that she knew, one that *couldn't* be calling her.

The spell brought her to a dark, wet corner of the Swamp.

Jenna Prim was on her knees, wand trembling in her unsteady hand.

*"Thalia, you'd be the one to find this. I did it—I'm talking to the plants, just like Fournier taught us."*

Jenna looked over her shoulder.

*"I—I saw a boy go into the Swamp, and I was tr-trying to stop him. But it's like . . . like he could control—"*

Jenna turned and saw something that the spell did not show, and as the magic broke and the world went black, her screams rang in Thalia's ears.

"Jenna!" Thalia cried out. As her vision cleared, she felt movement in her cabin. She yanked herself from the spell, grabbed her wand, and whipped around, pointing it at the center of the unwitch's chest.

"A witch and her wand, what a pretty sight," the Roddin Witch mocked. "Put it down. It's no use to you now."

Thalia didn't lower her hand.

Roddin stepped out of the shadows. Thalia looked at her for what felt like the first time. This was not a recognizable face. Her wrinkles were deepened, her skin less smooth. Roddin's hair was ashy gray, and her eyes, *her eyes*. Thalia never remembered them being so dark green or so sunken.

Roddin eyed the foliage sprouting through the walls. "You could grow forests. Your own Swamp. You could make monsters out of the earth, and this is all you've done," she spat viciously. "The dead girl could raise

heathens, and she does not. The powerful girl is more concerned with licking the boots of mundanes than her own greatness. Your proxy can't even
use her blessing!"

Thalia's throat tightened. "You don't have magic. You can't hurt me."

And yet, she lurched back with every one of Roddin's steps forward.

"You are not worthy to walk on the land we died to protect," Roddin
sneered.

Thalia stepped back until she hit the wall. "What the hell do you
want?"

Roddin's smile turned grotesque. "To *finally* give Haelsford what it
deserves."

Thalia shivered. Her brain sorted through the information she'd stored
away, pieces of a puzzle she never realized were meant to fit. "I know you've
been meeting with Theodore Bloom. I . . . I know who you are."

"You will *never* know me. Couldn't even use your mutt properly."

Thalia's chest tightened.

Something skittered by the door. The air smelled like oil and blood.

Thalia screamed a spell meant only for her father. *"Fall Like
Lightning!"*

The silvery blast soared toward Roddin with a burst of smoke. With a
sharp wave of her hand, the elder witch redirected the hex. A jagged hole
formed in the wall. Something howled. Outside, thick, heavy steps
approached.

Thalia stepped back. *"How—"*

"You and yours have disgraced my Hill. None of you deserve to live,"
Roddin hissed.

Thalia heard a low howl.

The Wolf burst into the cabin with a merciless sprint. The beast knocked her down. Her leg scraped against a loose floorboard as the Wolf pulled her from her safe house and dragged her toward the Swamp. Her throat went raw from her screams.

She wanted it to be quick, but everything was painful.

For the first time in forever, Thalia prayed.

# 41

## trent

Trent was highlighting exam dates in the Helios Dorm lounge when the spell snapped.

He jolted upward, the memory cutting through the haze of Thalia Blackwood's spell and drowning him with its urgency. It was so clear, so new, like it'd just been waiting until Trent shone a light on this dark corner of his memory.

A murderess's blood was the last ingredient to a resurrection spell. And Thalia played with his mind to make him forget it.

His heart hammered in his chest. Hands shaking, Trent called his best friend.

Mathew sounded out of breath. "Yeah?"

"You're at the stables?" Trent whispered, though he was alone.

"Yeah, with—"

"Stay there. I'll be down in ten."

Trent hung up the phone. It trembled in his fist.

Before setting out, Trent stopped by their room and rummaged for something in the back of the fridge. The jar was full of a sludgy black thing that smelled like vinegar and burnt wood. Every room had one of these jars—the school called it a precaution, only for emergencies.

*Yeah*, Trent thought viciously. *This is an emergency.*

He strapped his mother's dagger to his ankle.

# 42

## jailah

*Thalia, you better be in your goddammed cabin.*

Jailah walked up the mucky trail, choosing anger over fear.

Forgetting that she promised to help make Town Square look like a meadow for the MidWinter Celebration was *rude*, but Thalia missing her general floor meeting was just irresponsible, and it was something she wouldn't do unless she had a good excuse. Ten missed calls and fifteen texts was Jailah showing restraint. Everyone had become distant, and they hadn't been speaking as much as they used to, but the silent treatment was excessive.

*And if she's not in her cabin?*

Jai picked up the pace. She hoped the witch burners hadn't really come for her. She hoped Thalia didn't decide to just pack up and leave.

"Sweet T!" Jailah banged a fist against the door, the reverberations shaking the potted plants that littered the porch and all the little tendrils that curled against the wood. They were dying. Carefully, she touched one of the rough-looking plants, and the entire line of them fell away like crispy brown leaves at the end of autumn.

Holding a breath, Jailah threw herself inside.

There was blood on the floor, but that wasn't the worst of it.

Jailah knelt next to the bed and found a red clump of fur.

"No," she gasped. She slumped onto the floor, suddenly unable to keep herself upright.

Heart racing, Jailah gathered the still-wet blood from the floorboards with her finger.

*"Find Her,"* she choked out, waved her wand, and the blood dissipated into a smoky image. The finding spell showed Thalia curled up, shivering, eyes darting left and right out of fear.

Jailah knew exactly where she was.

# 43

## mathew

The first sounds of MidWinter trickled toward the Hill. Distant laughter, the mechanical screech of carnival rides, shouts of popcorn slingers. It was tradition that he, Rebecca, and Trent would head over after getting drunk on whatever bottle they could pilfer from the Beaumont wine cellar, then bet on who'd puke first after the Gravitron. It was mindless fun, and truly one of Mathew's favorite parts of the year. But he'd skip out, for this.

He was taking Ruby around the field, dizzy with the knowledge that Iris was leaning against the fence, *watching* him. The wheel of rope in him clicked and clicked, the most alive it'd been since the night Theodore Bloom was brought to life.

When he slowed down and pulled Ruby close to the fence, the horse bucked.

The witch smiled. "She's still not a fan."

"She'll come around," Mathew replied, dismounting. He took a few moments to catch his breath. "She's always stressed on the last day of the Haunting, and we have our first show of the year in a few weeks, so I've been working her pretty hard."

"Or maybe she just hates me," Iris said, reaching out a little. She pulled back just before Ruby snapped at the air with her teeth.

"Easy, girl," Mathew cooed. He looked back at Iris. She was staring toward the fields with a hard look. "You know, you shouldn't feel bad about not giving a person to the Wolves. That's a pretty horrible thing to do."

"There's only one Wolf Boy. This was our only chance, Haelsford's only chance, and I blew it." She rubbed her eyes with the heels of her palms, smudging the mascara and eyeliner. "I'm just so mad at myself."

Mathew splayed his fingers on the fence, dangerously close to hers. "Stop. Haelsford doesn't deserve you."

"Don't say things like that," she urged, venomous. "You'll end up following me into the Swamp again."

He shrugged. "Eh. I feel like I've already followed you into hell."

Iris's posture relaxed, and she laughed suddenly. Mathew sat on one of the lower rungs of the fence, close enough that his knee touched her thigh.

"Tell me what this is," he asked, fitting his fingers between the spaces of the buttons on his shirt.

She looked away. "It's hard to explain."

He moved closer. "Then show me."

Slowly, she placed her hand on top of his, inside his shirt.

"I feel it," he said, slightly wonderstruck. He moved his hand, leaving her fingertips pressed into his bare skin. He'd been scraped there, scarred from the night they almost died together.

"It still hurts," he breathed.

"It always will."

Iris retreated, but Mathew's hand caught hers, and suddenly, her words slipped out, almost breathless in relief.

"I am tethered to you, Beaumont."

And he couldn't think, he couldn't breathe, and before he could understand the sharpness in her eyes, he lowered his lips to hers—

"Beaumont!" she huffed, pulling away.

He stared at her, full of warmth, full of pain. Mathew's face dissolved into wonder and desperation. He didn't understand. *I am tethered to you* sounded as good a declaration of longing as anything.

Iris tripped over her tongue trying to correct this conversation. Her dark brown eyes were wide in a mixture of shock and excitement. "Shit, it's a magical thing. Wait, no, not like *magical*, but, uh, witchy! Witches have tethers, like pairs. Pairs that can change and influence and manipulate each other's magic. That's what happened on Hallowe'en! I don't know how, but you're mine."

"Oh." He touched his lip. "I just. I thought."

*I thought that was the moment.*

She couldn't stop staring at him. "People don't kiss me, and I don't kiss people."

The knot in his chest pulled taut, so hard it felt like an organ being pinched. It was painfully clear now that whatever warm and exciting moment had transpired minutes ago was long gone.

But then Iris took a step toward him. "Look, I—" She sighed, fiddling with the hoop on her right ear. "Mathew."

He looked up at her.

She opened her mouth but then looked away. "Um, Trent's here."

Mathew turned, forcing a smile.

But Trent had a fury in him.

When his eyes found the witch, he simply shook his head and threw a heavy jar of black at her.

Mathew watched in horror as Iris's face contorted with pain. She reached for her wand, trying to use her last breath to scream a spell, but all that came out was a strangled cry as she crumpled to the ground.

Heart racing, Mathew hopped the fence and kicked the jar away, but Iris's skin was already going sallow with the effects of it, the black smoke clinging to her like a cloud. He didn't know what to do. He moved to her, but Trent yanked him back.

Ruby bolted away in a frenzy. Another witch had approached, yelling something incomprehensible. With a few graceful swishes of her wand— the only graceful thing about the tear-streaked girl at the moment—Jailah flipped Trent into the air and pulled wisps of black smoke out of Iris's body.

"What are you doing?" Jailah yelled up at Trent, who thrashed aimlessly in the air.

Mathew knelt next to Iris. He tried to call this tethering thing between them, but nothing happened. He watched helplessly as Iris heaved, but as her expression grew angrier, he felt more relieved. He looked at Jailah. "Put Trent down!"

"He threw blackthorne at her!" Jailah screamed ferociously.

Mathew didn't know what to say.

"Murderers!" Trent called down.

That didn't help. "Jai, *please*!"

Jailah lowered Trent. She didn't draw her wand from him, even as he glared at her. Iris staggered upward, using Mathew as a crutch. Quickly, she lunged for Trent, but Jailah and Mathew stood between them.

"Explain yourself!" Jailah growled at Trent.

"One of you lot killed someone," Trent spat over Mathew's shoulder, almost desperately. He wasn't the same as he'd been just moments before, like the adrenaline in him had run out, and all that was left was this shivering boy who wasn't sure of what he'd just done.

Jailah and Iris exchanged a look. Mathew knew that an awkwardness had formed between them, but that look was one of soul mates, of conspirators, of partners in crime.

Trent continued relentlessly, "It's the last part of a resurrection spell! Theodore Bloom could only rise if there'd been sacrifice of a murderess's blood! And y'all messed with my mind to keep me from remembering that!"

"What?" Mathew said, turning to Trent.

Trent grabbed his shoulders and shook him. "Mate, you remember when I told you to stay away from them, right? You thought I was just freaked out from the resurrection? Well, Thalia came round and did some witchy woo-woo to make me forget!"

Suddenly, Jailah burst into tears. "He's right! It was Thalia. And she's gone!"

"Gone?" Iris sputtered.

"It isn't my story to tell, but . . . Thalia's name isn't Thalia, and she's from some town in Arizona. It's one of the last surviving bleedbays." She looked to Iris. "I'm sorry I didn't tell you."

Iris swallowed. "No—I—don't— You were being a good friend."

Jailah wiped her face, then turned to Mathew and Trent. "Thalia's parents didn't let her be a witch. She didn't have full control over her power yet, and there was some kind of accident." Her voice went sharp as she peered at

Trent. "She is a *murderess*, technically. But not on purpose, and they've been after her since, with her dad leading the charge, and she's missing, and I thought . . . I thought they finally found her."

Jailah reached into the pocket of her sunflower dress and pulled out a tuft of dark red fur.

"But Thalia wasn't taken by her family. She was taken by the Wolves."

# 44

## jailah

Jailah's head hurt from the crying. "Have you heard from Logan?"

Iris chucked her phone across Thalia's cabin. "She's not answering."

Jailah struggled to keep from bursting into tears again. They didn't have a piece of her—lock of hair, bit of blood—to do a finding spell.

Iris flipped through the beautiful, enormous book that she'd pulled from her chapel of death on the way over. "I *just* saw her a few hours ago. She's probably at MidWinter with everyone else. But Logan hasn't talked to us in weeks. I bet she has our numbers blocked or something."

"It feels so wrong that she doesn't know."

"By the time we reach her, Thalia will be back here, safe and sound, I promise." She paused for a moment and flicked her eyes up at Trent, who was pacing around the room, his head down, hands in his pockets.

Jai cleared her throat. "You got something to say, or . . ."

Mathew nudged Trent hard with his elbow.

He exhaled sharply. "Look. I fucked up. Massively. I know it's not an excuse, but I didn't think all that was going to happen, and I was scared, and . . ." He shook his head. "Anyway. I'm sorry, Iris."

Iris nodded. For her, that was as good an acknowledgment of forgiveness as anything. "For what it's worth, T shouldn't have altered your memories. She must've been feeling desperate."

"I don't understand," he said, touching the dead vine clinging to the wall. "How did a Wolf get in here?"

Jailah shook her head. "I don't know, but we have to go to the headmistress."

"No," Iris urged. "What happens when they start asking questions about *other* things? They can't find out about Theodore Bloom. And you said it yourself—Thalia never wanted her secret to come out."

"I don't care, I just want her to be safe!" Jailah was willing to give up everything for Thalia.

"I wouldn't be so against it if I didn't already have a plan!"

"We can't just go into the Swamp to get her." Mathew gave Iris a pointed look. "'Cause, you know, we tried that once, and it ended pretty badly."

Iris flashed them all a sinister grin. "We won't. Not *technically*." She ran her wand across the book's spine, whispering, *"Your True Colors."*

Before Jailah's eyes, the massive, embossed tome with gilded pages became a filthy little leather-bound book with oily black pages.

Her blood went cold.

It was the book that Vero had studied and loved, and wanted to build her witchery from. Jailah had told the Council that she'd never even seen it, and they'd believed her, because her reputation told them that they could. But she'd kept it and given it to Iris to hide in the chapel.

*The Most Wicked Works of Olga Yara.*

Jailah glared at Iris. "Why did you bring that?"

"We're going to cast one of Yara's Trinity spells: *Convergence*."

"You can't be serious!" Jailah snapped.

Iris was only amused. "Don't be dramatic."

Jailah said words she'd said once before, even as she felt drawn to the book. "The Trinity takes perfectly good witchery and corrupts it. Olga was a heretic, she was banished—she was hanged! We can't mess around with it!"

Iris took Jailah's hand and squeezed hard. It was like the past month never happened, and they were suddenly best friends again. "Listen to me. The Wolf Boy is a bust, and the Haunting doesn't end for another few hours. We can't leave Thalia in the Swamp for that long. This spell isn't like *The Culling*, I promise. Come on . . ." She pushed the book toward Jailah. "She needs us."

⋯•❯ ✪ ❮•⋯

The boys waited outside, partly to keep an eye out for a Wolf and for Logan, but mostly to give the girls some space. Jailah and Iris sat on the floor in the cabin, Thalia's standing mirror beside them. The wicked little book had an energy that tickled Jailah's witchy instincts and curiosity.

Jailah was feeling more like herself, the version of her that would put a plan in action, the one that would tear through heaven and hell and the Swamp with her teeth and nails to get her friend back. She lit a few of Thalia's candles. Primrose and vanilla, for comfort. "This is what we need," Iris muttered to herself. "Our own monster to save Thalia from the monsters of the Swamp."

CONVERGENCE. *To create a monstrous vision of a witch.*

In the diagram on the page, two witches held hands in front of a mirror, a golden figure shimmering between them. Jailah read the footnote. *Incantation must be said as one. Wands waved in time, in the shape of opposing helices.*

301

Tentatively, Jailah drew a helix into the air with her wand. Iris did the same, her helix spinning right to left in contrast.

Iris nodded. "Let's do it."

They pricked their thumbs. Jailah took Iris's hand. Together, they read the first lines—and then promptly stopped, each looking at the other in confusion.

"Uh, what just happened?" Jailah asked.

Iris blinked. "I'm doing the incantation."

"That's *not* the incantation."

"I'm reading the fucking words."

"Don't fucking swear at me!" Jailah pulled their clasped hands toward the book and underlined each word with her knuckle. "Read!"

Iris began again, but the words were still completely foreign to Jailah. *"Each hellmouth has a harbinger, a thread, a daughter of death, and in their darkness, they await—"*

Jailah shook her head. The words *she* read were of rivers and light and kings. *"A river widens at the bank, for a king and his lovely lass; here there is a drift, a longing, to take on each heart at opposite sides of the pass, they were called to see—"*

*"The reaper that is promised. May he stuff the hellmouth when hellfires of a culling have cleansed the earth . . ."* Iris's voice trailed off. "We have to say different things at the exact same time."

The incantation didn't rhyme. It sat uncomfortably on Jailah's tongue. There were no breaks, and she had trouble getting into the rhythm of it. "Is this a story or a spell?"

"Maybe it's both," Iris whispered. "Let's break it up into lines. Match my rhythm."

They started again, each telling a story—one dark, one light—their wands drawing helices in a slow, dreamy motion.

Jailah pictured the roaring river of the spell as she repeated her four lines.

*"A river widens at the bank for a king and his lovely lass."*

*"Each hellmouth has a harbinger, a thread, a daughter of death."*

*"Here there is a drift, a longing, to take on each heart."*

*"In their darkness, they await the reaper that is promised."*

*"At opposite sides of the pass, they were called to see that . . ."*

*"And may the reaper stuff the hellmouth when—"*

*"The hellfires of a culling have cleansed the earth."* They spoke their final line simultaneously.

In Thalia's mirror, a cloaked figure appeared on the grass, just off a river's edge. As it removed its hood, something like electricity sparked painfully in Jailah's arm. The image receded as she pulled away from Iris.

Iris clutched her own arm. "Ouch. What happened?"

"Did you see the river?"

Iris shook her head. "I see the Chasm, I think, and there's a throne, and it's *huge*, and there are all of these *souls* under it holding it up. They look like ants compared to this figure sitting there under a black cloak, just waiting and watching." Fear drenched Iris's words, but she straightened her posture.

"Who's under the cloak?" Jailah asked.

Iris bit her lip. "Death."

Jailah looked back toward the mirror, which only showed her reflection. *In mine, it's you.*

"You're there, too, like, watching this all happen," Iris added curiously. "You're wearing a crown. If I'm Death, then you must be King Jailah."

Jailah wiped her brow, newly satisfied. "Let's try again. We have to keep going; we can't break the spell, even if it hurts."

"Jai. I missed you."

She blew out a thick sigh. "I missed you, too."

They went to work, and this time, the image came quickly. The rushing river, the cloaked figure on the other side of it. Jailah pushed against that horrible pain and put on a sweeter voice, *her* voice, instead of trying to call with what she imagined was Olga Yara's own harsh tongue. Keeping in time with Iris's rhythm, she made the spell her own.

Jailah was in the river. It was cold and sharp, and she could hardly feel her ankles. Across the river, Iris, in that dark cloak, stepped into the water. Jailah could feel in her soul that she had to move farther in. They both did. It was the center, the deepest part that needed them.

She gritted her teeth against the pain and kept reading, even as the page suddenly presented new words to incant. *"For the king and his lovely lass, for the earth and for hell, a converging is a martyr's way of death—"*

But the landscape whined. Jailah could hear it, like wood cracking under too much weight. The world bent all around her, suddenly flimsy.

Iris squeezed her hand hard. *"A spinning devil at the earth's end, a converging is a martyr's way of death!"*

In the cabin, golden electric tendrils of light grew out of each girl, dipped into the mirror, and came out shimmering and warm above the alabaster borders.

In the river, Iris and Jailah became one shining girl. One beacon of light, one converged force of witchery. The light became a Witch. She did not breathe. She hummed and vibrated. Pure power. Pure light.

Jailah felt it all. The stunning specificity of the cabin, every speck of dust, every breath Iris drew, all the power flowing through this Wolf-ridden witchtown.

She gasped with fatigue. As the spell broke, the Witch evaporated, and Mathew and Trent ran into the room, concerned by the sudden burst of blazing light.

Jailah threw her head back and laughed. When she turned to Iris, she saw a different reaction to *Convergence*'s might. Where Jailah was thrilled with this power, Iris seemed apprehensive. "I can't believe it works."

"We can do this! We can send this *thing* into the Swamp for us."

"But I don't know how long we can keep it up, Jailah. It hurt at the end. We need more time to practice. What happens if we can't hold on long enough to find her?"

"I'll go, too," Trent interrupted.

With twin movements, Iris and Jailah snapped their heads to him. Jailah looked for humor in Trent's face, but his expression was serious.

"Trenton." Mathew fit fury and dread into those two syllables.

"You don't need to do this," Jailah urged.

"Don't worry. I'm practically invincible," he replied coolly. Trent Hogarth, always so worry-free. "Just tell me what to do."

Jailah didn't know what else to say, and she was grateful when Iris stepped in. "We don't know how this works, or how our normal spells will act in the hands of our monstrous Witch." Iris hesitated. "When we find Thalia, I think we can protect her, but if something goes wrong, if she's not herself, someone has to help her out."

It was a terrifying scenario, but Trent merely smiled. "This is like some James Bond shit, innit?"

"Except it's real," Mathew whispered.

She flexed her hands in and out of fists.

*Convergence* felt like fire. It felt like steel. It felt like she was balancing all the earth's energy in her palm. She was hungry for more.

Jailah ran her fingers over the ripped-up leather of the ugly little grimoire before slipping it into her pocket.

# 45

## trent

Trent stood at the edge of the protection spells, close enough to see into the murky mouth of the Swamp. He felt that gut-wrenching chill that he was sure only ever came before certain death.

He turned to Iris. She wouldn't sugarcoat like Matty would. "Tell me what to expect."

Iris looked at him, this boy who hid his fear in smiles where she hid hers in scowls. "I don't think Beaumont and I saw the worst of it; we weren't that far in. Just . . . remember that this is real, but you might see things that are fake. There was a second where I thought I heard my mom and dad."

Trent turned to the winds, his anorak fluttering. There'd always been rumors of things other than their terrifying Wolves lurking in the Swamp. Things that were worse. Things that would rip apart the mind rather than the body.

Iris wrapped her hand around his wrist. "We won't let anything happen to you."

He knocked his left boot against his right leg, the sound of his knife providing some comfort. "This'll be fun."

"You're a *strange lad*, Trent." Iris put on a horrible English accent that made him laugh.

"Ready?" Jailah asked.

Mathew and Trent weren't the type of boys who were afraid to show emotion in public, but Trent refused to hug him. "Mate, this isn't goodbye."

"I know." Mathew pulled him into a hug anyway. "Come back in one piece."

The girls sat before the mirror they dragged from Mesmortes. With the book open between them and without further prelude, Iris and Jailah dove into *Convergence*.

*"Each hellmouth has a harbinger, a thread, a daughter of death."*

*"A river widens at the bank for a king and his lovely lass."*

They chanted in sharp rhythm, punching out every syllable. They strained, clenching teeth and rasping their words. They held on to each other. Suddenly, Iris and Jailah entered a hush of unconsciousness, dark eyes replaced by full golden ones. Slowly, shimmering threads inched out of the girls' chests and into the mirror. They came out of the glass as linked chains.

Trent gasped at the sight. One moment, the Witch was Iris. Then Jailah. Her features were beautiful, her eyes were furious. She was born of constellations—shimmering and all-powerful. If Trent ever forgot the word *witch*, he might've used *goddess* to describe her.

With a ferocious sneer, the Witch stepped forward.

The air changed. The Swamp beckoned. It felt like a whisper against Trent's ear, something threatening and indecent poured into him by way of wind.

Trent said a quick prayer. *Keep me safe, like you always have.*

Carefully, he stepped into the cold.

Everything went dark, like the Swamp sucked all the light away. Even the moon dimmed above them, leaving the Witch as the only light. Every step forward was one darker, one quieter. The air held a thickness that was different from the usual Haelsford humidity. Trent touched his anorak, and his fingers came away with something slippery.

He held his hand up to the bright Witch and found his palms were dark red. It intrigued him in an odd way. He let the liquid run down his palms and into the sleeves of his anorak, cold and slick. The Witch wasn't affected. She only guided him into a thicket of bushes and tightly packed trees. The grass became muck. The water came up to Trent's knees, a green film coating the surface.

Immediately, he sensed the wrongness of this. The air was stifling now. The mud beneath him felt distressingly solid, like hands gripping him, bringing him farther and farther down with each step—

Trent screamed as something pulled him into the water.

His mouth filled up with the foul taste of rotting plants and bitter smoke. He thrashed for the surface, hoping to reach the Witch's grasp, but there was nothing there. It dawned on him like a stab in the gut that he was not the objective. Thalia was, and if the Witch could go after her and leave this mundane boy to rot in a hole of spoiling mud, then why wouldn't she? Why would she care, why would anyone, not *your father or your mother or your brothers or the witches or Mathew, for who would ever mourn an insignificant mundane boy*—

A flash of light, and Trent was yanked upward by the hand of the Witch. He heaved and spat mud. The Swamp *knew* things. If he was worried about it before, he was sure now. There was darkness in its core, in its roots, and Trent was running around as bait for his fears to be exposed. He wheezed, "Where *are* the Wolves anyway?"

The Witch said nothing. She only put her glowing hands to the ground. She pulled together rocks and stones and branches, forming a bridge in front of them. She walked on and Trent followed. They traveled deeper into the never-ending dark marsh.

*Maybe it's time to turn back.* The thought was a black spot in Trent's mind. Thalia was a witch. She could survive this. *A liar, too*, who'd used her power to manipulate him. The black spot was growing.

Birds, cicadas, mosquitoes, and squirrels cried out in the distance. They all hummed the same eerie cry of pain. But no Wolves. Trent listened again. The creatures weren't just humming a dark melody; there was something else. A chant grew out of the trees.

*Promised*, they sang.

Suddenly, the Witch stopped.

Trent squinted, searching for danger, but the Witch pushed him toward the closest tree. Fearing something that he couldn't even see, he climbed without question, figuring it was safer above than below. He barely kept his eyes open. Trent didn't want to know what he was climbing past or what he was climbing into. The whispers of the insects and animals were enough to send jolts of terror through him. He felt like he was a child again. When his mother turned off his lights and shut his bedroom door, he'd close his eyes tightly, not wanting to find something moving around in the dark.

At the top of the tree was a cradle of intersecting branches, forming a large nest of mossy wood. Trent threw himself into the middle of it.

From below, he heard the shrill howl of a Wolf. Trent peeked down. The beast slowly rose out of a bush, snapping its massive teeth.

The Witch was prepared for it. She whispered a deadly song, and Trent watched as the glowing goddess spun around and showed the Wolf her hands. Her palms emitted a blinding light that took a life of its own.

Something quick stumbled through the branches of Trent's hiding place. It took no care to quiet its movements, as if it needed him to know it was there, and that it was coming for him. Shaking, he crawled backward, feeling out the spaces between the branches that, if overlooked, could send him falling.

*"Baby?"* a voice screeched.

A horrific thing appeared before him.

The woman was broken. Her head hung limp from her neck like a doll's head that wasn't screwed tightly enough. Her limbs were thin and wiry, covered by loose skin mottled with decay. Lidless, swollen red eyes stared at him. Her desperate, jerky movements roiled Trent's stomach.

*This isn't real*, he thought, even as the specter before him felt so painfully and palpably true.

"Stop!" he choked out. "Please, I'm just here for my friend!"

In a cruel voice, she filled his heart with terror. *"You've been calling me! Here I am, baby!"* Her smile, terrible and gray, was a monstrous thing of its own. Stumbling forward, the woman opened her arms.

Trent recoiled sharply. "Stay away!"

Below him, the Witch screamed.

In one wild lunge, the wraith had him against the wood, and her fingers, pointed bones that felt like icicles, dug into his cheeks and temples. She had a devilish clutch on him. *"But you're mine!"* she cried. *"Mine! No matter who you were promised to!"*

"Promised?" Trent choked.

The birds sang the word again, mocking him.

Horrified, he forced the words out of his mouth. "You promised me to . . . to who? A witch?" The memory of a clever and haughty Thalia came to him. "A bloodpact?"

The soul screeched violently. It backed away from him, and though Trent wanted nothing but to be free of the spirit's grasp, he reached out.

"What did you do?" Trent spat out. As he stood to confront the figure, something shifted beneath him. He stilled, holding his breath.

With a blistering *crack*, Trent fell hard and fast through a tangle of wood. He would've collided with a boulder if he wasn't stopped midair.

"Trent?" asked a shaky voice.

A head poked out of the nest, wand raised above it. Thalia looked at Trent like she'd never seen him before.

He hadn't understood the size of the nest until now. The tangle of intersecting branches was built around the top of the tree, and he'd only been on one side of it. Thalia had been on the other end. She looked sick, her stringy curls matted on all sides, her face ashen and furrowed. Trent understood suddenly. Thalia used her greenwitchery for the nest but had connected to a land infused with dark magic, and the bond was eating her alive. A girl trapped in the Swamp had built herself a prison, to keep herself in and to keep things out.

As Trent lay there floating a few feet from the ground, she asked, "Where did we meet?"

"The library," Trent choked out. "What's your favorite kind of cupcake?"

"Coconut almond." Thalia lowered him.

Trent looked around and found the Witch in the distance. She wasn't glowing so much anymore. Golden wisps of witchery dissipated into the air. Each one opened up a little song into the night; it was muffled, but he heard the girls straining desperately to sustain the Witch.

The Wolf was there, quiet and unmoving. Trent thought that they couldn't die, but he wasn't about to lean in and check.

*Why aren't there more?*

Thalia floated down from the nest, cradling a sleepy dog with blood-stained fur. His front leg was wrapped in a bandage of dark leaves.

"What magic was that?" Thalia asked curiously, gesturing toward the bits of gold in the air.

"It was Jailah and Iris. We came to bring you home."

She grasped his hand suddenly, remembering something. Her fingertips felt rough and calloused against his skin. "And Logan?"

"No, she—"

"Trent, where's Theodore Bloom?"

He shook his head vigorously. "What? Who cares? We need to leave right now!"

Thalia's eyes went distant.

It seemed to happen in slow motion—Trent took a breath, peeled his eyes away from Thalia's sickly face, and followed her gaze.

Thick clouds of deep gray smoke billowed into the sky.

Mesmortes was on fire.

# 46

## jailah

The mirror exploded, sending hundreds of shards into the darkness.

Jailah threw herself onto the damp ground. Pain bloomed throughout her body. Every drop of her power, her soul, everything that she was, had been poured into this amalgamation of heretic magic, and when it broke in one blinding flash, it *hurt*. For a moment, all she could do was lie there.

Mathew touched her shoulder. "Jailah, are you okay?"

Jailah forced herself upright and blinked away the blurriness in her vision. Iris gingerly rose to her feet a few steps away. Just seeing her relieved Jailah immensely.

"Did you see Thalia? What happened to Trent?" Mathew asked urgently.

Iris shook her head. "There was only one Wolf. We . . . we fought it." She stopped, looking at her hands.

Jailah pulled herself to her feet. "We never saw Thalia."

Mathew turned from them. Even with his back to her, Jailah felt his pain.

"Trent really is invincible," he said quietly. "He wasn't joking. His mom literally watches over him."

Jailah and Iris shared a tense look.

"I swear, I saw it with my own eyes. Freshman year, he jumped off the Hammersmitt roof to show me—and gave me a heart attack—but he was totally fine. That's why he wanted to talk to her so badly; he wanted to know how she could leave him and still be by his side."

Iris rubbed her eyes hard. "Even so, what if she can't watch him in the Swamp? What if he and Thalia are both dead?"

"Iris!" Jailah cried.

"What? You're both thinking it!" Frustrated, Iris threw her hands into the air, and her eyes filled up with tears. "All of this is my fault! We should be at MidWinter right now, but I just had to end the Haunting! I pulled you all into this, and I pushed Logan away, and now Thalia and Trent are stuck in the Swamp, and we need to tell everyone what we did, and we'll be banished because of the Wolf Boy—"

Iris stopped unexpectedly. A voice called out to them, amplified by a weak spell.

"KILL THEODORE BLOOM."

Mathew did a double take. "Was that Trent?" He cupped his hands around his mouth. "Trent! Trent!"

"Wait!" Jailah shouted. "He's saying something else!"

*No. Not he.* Thalia spoke to them now, her voice distorted by the corruption of the Swamp. "AND STOP THE RODDIN WITCH!"

Immediately, Iris shook her head. "What?"

Jailah closed her eyes. She couldn't think while staring into the face of the Swamp.

"What?" Iris repeated incredulously. "The hell is she talking about?"

"I don't know," Jailah replied, somehow feeling calmer than her shaking voice implied.

"Is this a trick? Are they— Is the Swamp playing with us?"

Eyes still closed, Jailah could hear Mathew's uneasy footsteps. "Don't say that," he whispered. "No, they're okay. We just heard them—"

"But we didn't *see* them—"

*We didn't see them, so how could we really know?*

Jailah's stomach turned. She thought back to the night Bloom was reborn. Thalia had questioned the myth behind the Wolf Boy entirely.

*What do we really know?*

Slowly, she opened her eyes. "Iris, when did you first hear the story of the Wolf Boy?"

"What do you mean?" Iris snarled impatiently. "Everyone knows about the Wolf Boy."

"Yeah, everyone knows, but who told it to you? When I came for a tour, we stayed at Emily Odiene's B and B. She told me and my parents all about the Haunting. It was horrifying." Jailah laughed, something on the border of whimsical and distressed.

"My parents told me," Mathew chimed in. "The Wolves were like a scary bedtime story, but they always added in the Wolf Boy so Rebecca and I wouldn't have nightmares."

"And where'd they hear it?" Jailah asked.

Mathew shrugged. "My family goes way back."

Iris groaned. "Why does it matter?"

Jailah placed her hands on Iris's shoulders. "Think." She turned her thoughts over, not wanting to lose them. "We know that the Strigwach Sisters existed because their story has been passed down, but, like, we *also* have the writings of old townspeople that survived, like the Haelsfords, and the drawings of them—actual evidence."

"And?" Iris asked curtly.

"And we know the Wolves exist, because"—Jailah jabbed a finger toward the Swamp—"the Haunting Season comes every year. Now, what the hell do we really know about the Wolf Boy? Why do we believe in him?"

"Because it's all we've ever been told?" Mathew wondered aloud.

Iris lifted a hand. "I read Mathilde Strigwach's diary. She said—"

"She said he'd save us?" Jailah pressed on. "No. She said to *kill him*. If you wanted to trace him back, if you wanted to know who started the story of the boy who'd end the Haunting Season, who would you ask?"

Mathew added, "I guess, the oldest witch in Haelsford that I could find?"

He looked to Iris, whose eyes narrowed into accusatory slits.

"The Roddin Witch!" Jailah spat harshly. "She was there the night we told Logan about the Wolf Boy! Logan said she'd *dreamed of him*. She said she scryed for him! Where would you go to buy scrying glass, Iris?"

"No, she's not part of this!" Iris said, tears in her voice.

"Thalia just told us she was! And didn't you say she's how you met Madeline Donahue? You found her spirit in the Emporium, and she led us closer to Theodore Bloom!"

Iris shut her eyes, but a few tears fell anyway.

"What's your witchery telling you? Don't you feel it?" Jailah's witchy senses sizzled like static on her skin. "Something is *wrong* here."

A deep breath. A slow exhale. Iris scowled. "I have literally been under the Roddin Witch's thumb for years now."

"What are you saying? The whole thing is made up?" Mathew looked at the both of them.

317

Iris spoke as if the words pained her to say them. "We're saying—what if there is no Wolf Boy?"

"Then who the hell did we bring back?" Jailah hissed.

Iris drew her wand. "Jai, you need to find Logan. I'm going to the Emporium. If Roddin's behind this, I need to figure out what she's planning." She turned to Mathew. "Will you come with me?"

Mathew hesitated and looked toward the Swamp.

Concern grew on Iris's face. "I know you're worried about them—I am, too, but you can't stay here alone. Mathew," she pleaded, holding out her hand. "I need you. Come with me."

He nodded and took her hand.

Iris turned back to Jailah. "If you see Theodore Bloom—"

"Oh, I won't hesitate."

Jailah waited for the two of them to run off before she took toward the Hill. She navigated the dark, wet marsh with vigilance. She aimed her wand at every wind-rustled bush, always expecting a Wolf, even if she was behind the barrier of protection. As she approached the last dense thicket of forest before the Hill, a sound jolted her.

Logan sprinted toward her, red-faced. "Jailah! I've been looking for you—"

Theodore appeared as well, and Jailah raised her wand.

*"Jai!"* Logan shouted, but Jailah could barely hear over the blood pounding in her ears.

"Who are you?" Jailah spat, wand pointed at the boy. He was pale, his clothes plain, his hair damp with sweat.

Meekly, he raised his hands. "It's me, Theodore."

"I know a *Shade*, Bloom. That's not what I'm asking."

Logan sidestepped Jailah and put herself between them. "Put your wand away!"

"You can't trust him!"

"Huh? We came here to end the Haunting, to save Haelsford!"

Something crunched softly, a shuffle in the grassy land.

No one moved. Jailah had a strong sense that Theodore Bloom had a plan, and it did not involve saving Haelsford. She could feel it in her bones, even if Logan's instincts were too new or too bogged down by her love for him.

"*Sanguirremorr!*" Jailah screamed, hatred dripping on each syllable.

Everything happened at once in a blur of magic and violence.

There was a sound like static, and a plume of smoke burst into the air. When it cleared, Jailah saw that Theodore Bloom was still standing.

Her heart sank. *I had the perfect shot.* She was fast, and she was powerful. *How did I miss?* The truth made Jailah's heart drop.

Logan's wand was raised. She'd saved him with a protection spell of her own, a force field that made Jailah's spell rebound into the night sky rather than settling into the Wolf Boy's heart. A spell Jailah had once used to protect her.

Logan looked at her, dazed. "Why? Why would you—"

A Wolf lunged from behind Logan and knocked her down hard. Jailah had no time to scream because it only pushed the baby witch away to get to her.

Jailah levitated herself and wrapped her arms around a tree. Logan seemed hurt; Jailah watched Bloom lift her into his arms and take her away. Jailah's screams were drowned out by the howl of the mammoth below her. From this vantage, she could see the Hill in full.

319

Smoke billowed from the bright flame engulfing Laarsen House. Jailah gasped.

*Wolves.*

They were perched on a higher hill near the Cavern, where she'd never imagined they'd reach. *Iris was wrong. There is a Wolf Boy.* They'd just been so convinced that he had the power to stop the Wolves that they never considered he might use that very power to wield them.

*"I Need Tools."* Jailah felt the tree crack to provide for her. She pulled a bow and arrow from the wood, all splintery and raw, fit for her hands and the bloodlust she felt in her heart. She jumped down from the tree to meet the Wolf.

"Our magic could never kill you," she whispered as it circled her, bright red eyes locked on her nocked arrow. "Hexed fire wouldn't burn you. Our spells wouldn't make you bleed. But you're flesh and blood, ain't you? Same as me."

Its growl shook the earth.

Exhaustion weighed down on every inch of her limbs, but Jailah stood, sure-footed. "I might as well try, huh?"

The beast didn't allow her one last breath before it lunged at her, mouth open.

She aimed.

She released.

The monster only swallowed the arrow and charged on.

Helpless, Jailah screamed.

The earth screamed in response. Thick branches grew out of the dirt and impaled the Wolf from all angles, lifting it off the ground. The animal's ferocious growl of pain was so desperate, it might've even been sad.

She turned and saw Thalia and Trent, the two of them filthy and exhausted. Trent was holding Thalia's pup, and the greenwitch looked at her own work with dazed eyes, like she couldn't believe she'd just killed a Wolf.

Jailah could only laugh. "Bless you, T."

Thalia swallowed hard. "Jailah . . . It's Roddin . . . It's Theodore."

"I know. We heard you guys. I just saw Logan."

Thalia dropped her head.

"I've already made myself a promise that this night ends with us winning and the Wolf Boy dead. And you know there's nothin' in the world as reliable as a promise from Jailah Simmons. We're not dying tonight."

"And Matty? Iris?" Trent whispered shakily. "Where are they?"

"Back in town to get to the bottom of this."

"Jesus." Thalia sighed. "If we survive this, remind me to kill you for trying to take on one of those monsters by yourself."

"Don't you worry." Jailah half smiled. "I can be monstrous, too."

# 47

# thalia

Thalia Blackwood was done praying.

As she stood at the base of the Hill, she only had thoughts for vengeance.

Trent was still holding her precious Maverick and had taken to rocking the grimy dog like a baby. Trent didn't even seem to realize it, as his eyes were justifiably focused on the fire in the distance. Thalia was already endeared to him, but her heart grew softer.

She leaned down and touched her nose to her familiar. *We're okay. I trust him with my life. You can, too.*

She looked up at Trent. His usually neat curls were disheveled, and his skin was still covered in traces of filth. But his full lips curled into a sweet smile, big brown eyes looking down at her with amazement, like she was a wonder. "Are you talking to your dog? *Telepathically?*"

She let herself laugh. "God, you're such a mundane!"

With dirt-covered fingers, she brushed the Wolf fur from her skirt and squinted over at the pack of Wolves up near the Cavern.

"The hell they waiting for?" Jailah muttered meanly, gripping her wand.

"Maybe they just wanna see us sweat," Thalia replied, running up the rest of the way to Mesmortes.

Most everyone was at MidWinter, but a few witches were scrambling around the burning building, their frantic voices peppering the background.

"Oh, thank god!" Morgan said at the sight of them. "We set Laarsen House on fire!"

Lilly's voice was thick with tears. "We were trying to start fireworks! Like flares, since the alarms weren't going off!"

"Why didn't you get help?" Thalia asked, trying to take away the edge from her voice.

"No one's here! Everyone's at the festival!" Lilly cried. "Even in the infirmary, all the greenwitches are gone."

Thalia looked to Jailah and found anger where she only felt terror. "Is there a waterwitch around?"

Morgan angled their head to the dark-haired boy on the far side of the Hill, watching the flames with a helpless expression. "Danny Chen. Only a freshman, though."

Jailah nodded. "I got him. T, you good?"

Thalia was already removing her cape. "Yeah, I'm good."

Jai sprinted for Danny. Thalia flexed her fingers, a plan forming.

Morgan asked, "How are they inside the protection?"

"And where the hell are the bloody adults?" Trent fumbled for his phone, one arm cradling Maverick. "What's the emergency number again?"

"Six-six-six," Thalia said plainly.

"Fuckin' hell," Trent muttered. "'Course it is."

There was a burst of thunder, and the witches jumped. But it was

Danny Chen, his wand lifted toward the fire, Jailah's hands on his shoulders as she stood behind him. Rain fell from the sky and extinguished the flames.

The howls grew louder. There were ten Wolves visible, but Thalia had an itchy feeling that there were more to come. With a crack in the atmosphere, the first Wolf bounded down toward them. The others followed.

Trent's voice hitched with fear. "The call's not connecting."

The witches scrambled, but Thalia managed to pull little Lilly Han aside. "I'd say we've got five minutes until they're here. Get to a hollow room!"

Lilly faltered. "What are you going to do?"

Thalia said nothing. She simply ran toward the Wolves.

Time seemed to slow. Thalia bent down, groaning at the resistance in her still-sore limbs, and touched the grass. She called forward every part of her that had grown attached to this land. The crisscrossed mess of roots deep in the earth revealed themselves. They opened up, responding to the true call of her power.

This was her Gift of the Earth; she could feel deep into the earth and cultivate it with just focus and blood. With a twinge in her heart, she remembered Jenna Prim hovering around her station in Herbalism, watching her effortlessly pull up a cypress plant with a bit of blood. Her plan now would require much more magic and concentration, but she was prepared, angry, and desperate; three very dangerous things for a witch to be, especially terrifying if all at once.

This work required no incantation, but she felt like something needed to be said.

*"Bring Me a Wall."*

She pulled her wand upward, fat drops of sweat falling off her. It was like having two-ton weights attached to her arms. The clean earth here may have been more willing than the Swamp, but the task was so much greater. Thalia could see the beasts running down the surrounding hills from the Cavern.

Her body trembling, Thalia screamed out, *"A Wall!"*

There was a roaring crack. The first oak burst from the ground with an earthquake-like lurch. It was an enormous, beautiful thing, like a painting. The vivid brown of its trunk, the bright green of its lush leaves. A second one sprouted next to it, and then a third, and more and more until this side of Mesmortes was entirely blocked off by trees.

"Damn," Trent said from behind her. She hadn't realized he'd followed her.

All Thalia wanted was to collapse, but she needed to fortify every angle. She'd blocked the Wolves' most immediate path—forcing them to run around the border of trees rather than taking Mesmortes head-on. But she wanted to *stop* them. Slowing them down was just a Band-Aid on a head wound if Thalia couldn't protect them on all sides.

She turned to Trent. "I need your knife."

He didn't hesitate.

Thalia sliced open her palm. The pain spiked all the way up her arm as she released a cry. The blood flowed steadily from her.

The earth complied, satiated by this greater sacrifice. Six more trees erupted from the ground, blocking half the school in a semicircle of giant oaks. Trent dropped to his knees, steadying himself against the lurching ground.

"Go to the hollow room!" Jailah was suddenly behind Thalia,

screaming at Morgan and Lilly, who apparently couldn't stay away either. "Thalia!"

But Thalia was dazed, kneeling there in the grass. The howls grew louder. They were coming, faster than before, now twenty in view, maybe more, and then *here*, running up on her Hill.

Jai grabbed her arm and pulled her up from the ground. "You've done enough! *Come on!*"

Thalia's legs finally moved, and she was right behind Jailah, but she couldn't resist trying from here. She had to close the gap.

Jailah sensed this. "Thalia—stop—just—run!"

But Thalia was running backward, shouting at the earth. Another tree sprouted and took out three Wolves, though it was all twisted and smaller than the others. She focused, raising her wand. But she wasn't knelt down to the ground. Her connection wasn't quite as strong. The last tree that sprouted up was an ugly thing—stumped and bent over, and though it filled up the gap, it was still too small. Viciously, the Wolves forced themselves through the trees, the monstrous things clawing and biting at one another to get ahead. All that blood in the air made Thalia queasy, but there was no time to process this.

Six Wolves managed to break through. The biggest one was gunning for her. It nearly had its teeth in her waist when a bright pink spell hit its legs. The beast went down, stumbling over its own gigantic paws.

She had no time to fix the wall. The moment they were in the Mesmortes main building, she collapsed into Trent's arms. Whining, Maverick licked her face.

"Damn, girl," Trent said.

"I know, right?" Thalia mumbled back. "Who did that spell?"

Morgan smiled sheepishly. "Oh. Me."

"You did not just use *Legs Like Jell-O* on a Wolf." Jailah chuckled.

"Is that what you call it? I reformed it to *Super-High Stilettos.* It's the meanest spell I could think of." And just like that, they were all laughing.

It was brief. They could hear the beasts clamoring on the other side of the door. With a shaky hand, Jailah reinforced it. *"Iron for Wood."* She turned to the younger witches. "Who else didn't go to MidWinter?"

"Hardy and Layla," Danny said, standing up straight. "I think I saw Rowe Adler and Michaela DeWitt in Terrywood House."

"Round them up. Tell them to meet me on the roof."

"What can I do?" Trent asked.

"Get Thalia to a hollow room. Bramblewynn House is closest." Jailah looked at him up and down. "You should get some rest, too."

Though she was just about out of it, Thalia shook her head. "No, no, I have to help."

Jailah took her hand gently and healed the wound there. "You've done enough. Seriously."

Thalia took Maverick in her other arm. His heartbeats eased her. She looked to Jai. "What about you?"

"These doors are the only way in. It'll be slow, but they'll get through it." Jailah fiddled with her strange bow. "I'll be here when they do."

If it were anyone else, Thalia might've tried to stop her. But she had never seen Jailah look so wicked.

"Be careful," she said, and let Trent lead her into the courtyard and toward Bramblewynn House.

Her arm sloped over Trent's shoulder; Thalia touched her thumbnail to the tip of her middle finger. The spot itched, and when she scratched it, she felt something soft and sinewy.

There was a tiny sprout, three-clovered, and painted with a green so bright and saturated that it seemed fake.

Thalia tried to brush it away, only to find it growing directly from her flesh.

# 48

## trent

"Are you gonna fight me if I tell you to stay put?" Trent said, helping Thalia onto one of the hollow room's many sofas. He watched her adjust into a comfortable position. It was hard to look away from her after what he'd just seen her do.

She stroked Maverick's head. "I'm too tired to fight, but I'd still win."

He chuckled. "I'm gonna see you when this is all over, okay?"

"And then you'll tell me all about what you saw in the Swamp."

Trent froze.

"The Swamp knew things that only a few people know about me." She watched him carefully. "Like the boy I killed."

Trent nodded. He'd accepted this part of her. "Not to one-up you, but I think I might be a bloodpact baby."

"Shit. Firstborn son?"

"Fourthborn."

"*Shit.*"

Trent swallowed hard. "Thalia, what does that mean, exactly? I assume a deal was made, but . . ."

Thalia was failing at keeping the worry off her face. "A bloodpact is an unbreakable sort of deal. You ask a witch for something specific, something big, in exchange for something else. Could be as simple as money, or a new cauldron, or—"

"A child?"

Thalia sighed. "Maybe. Or maybe you were the contingency plan. Like, your mom offered up something else but vowed that if she didn't follow through, then the other witch could collect her fourthborn son, or something to that effect. But I don't know the terms here. It's hard to know for sure without asking the witches involved."

"I knew something was up. That's why I wanted to talk to her," he replied softly. That night at Roddin's seemed like forever ago. "I saw my mother in the Swamp. She looked like . . . I can't even explain it."

Outside, the Wolves howled.

"I can't stay here. I need to help Jailah, or *find* help. I don't know—"

"Do you forgive me, Trent?"

He pursed his lips, unsure of what to say.

Thalia ran her thumb over her fingers. "I'm sorry. I thought you were going to tell everyone my secret, and that I was going to have to run away again. I don't want to run anymore."

"You won't have to." Trent took her hand. "I wouldn't have gone into the Swamp for you if I didn't forgive you."

Her brow twitched. "That's it?" she whispered. "You forgive me? Just like that?"

"Of course."

He saw the relief fill her eyes. She reached out, grabbed his hand. "Be safe, Trent. Please, *please* don't get hurt."

His face grew hot, and he had the sudden urge to trace her jaw with his knuckles, to push the curls from her face and kiss her freckles. Her gaze bored into him, and she tilted her chin upward, as if daring him to.

But there were howls outside. Wolves on the doorstep. So, he only nodded. "No worries, love. Get some rest."

He left Bramblewynn House and took the brick trail back to the courtyard. For a moment, he stood in the middle of five stone buildings and thought of all the time he'd spent wondering what it would be like to be witchy and to come here instead of Hammersmitt.

Howls snapped him into focus. *Iron for Wood* sounded like a pretty legit spell, but Jailah seemed to think it wouldn't last against them.

*I'll be there to meet them, too*, he vowed.

In his peripheral vision, something shifted. A small nothing of a movement. A butterfly fluttering by, or a leaf falling next to him. Trent veered away from the main building and toward the one labeled MESMORTES FACULTY.

Inside, the lights flickered. The corridor was full of closed doors that belonged to different folks—PROFESSOR CHAPMAN, WITCHERY AND PSYCHOLOGY; PROFESSOR LANGLEY, ADVANCED PLACEMENT POTIONS. At the end of the hallway, a set of large double doors beckoned him.

LOUNGE.

"Hello?" Trent yelled, not sure if he wanted a response. "Anyone there?"

Then he heard it, just barely. A melody in the distance. It was beautiful and had an antique feel to it, like an old gospel hymn. And yet, there was something in the melody that sent a chill through him. He was sure it was coming from the professors' lounge, but the music never grew louder as he stepped closer.

Trent opened the door slightly. He saw a figure sitting, her head facing forward, her body swaying.

With a deep breath, he pushed the door open.

A blast of sound hurled Trent against the wall like a sonic boom.

"Agh!" he cried out, forcing himself up against the wind that blew out of the room. Trent planted his feet and struggled his way forward.

A circle of older witches sat around the room, transfixed by the record player in the middle of it. It was one of those antique gramophones, and it played that beautiful, bewitching, terrible music. The enchanted melody grew louder and louder, and he could feel it creeping deep into his ears, into his *thoughts*.

Trent swallowed. The Roddin Witch owned a gramophone. He'd sat right next to it when he asked her about the resurrection spell.

Trent kicked the damned thing over. The music continued.

The urge was building to stay, but he fumbled his way out of the room and shut the door hard behind him. His hands pressed to his knees, Trent huffed.

There was dark magic in the gramophone. Maybe something made for witches, and Trent had never been so delighted to be mundane. Or maybe it was his mum again, protecting him from something evil.

It didn't matter; he had to get back to Jailah. Trent was just a mundane boy, and he didn't know how he could help, but at least he had his own thoughts. Tonight, he hoped that would be enough.

He drew his dagger and headed for the main building.

# 49

## iris

"Roddin!" Iris screamed before she even cleared the porch steps.

She stopped short of entering the shop, frozen suddenly, her fingers resting against the worn mesh of the screen door. A wave of heat hit her, so fierce that she took a reflexive step back. Iris's hands flew up to her ears to drown out the noise of the screaming souls.

"What is it?" Mathew asked from behind her. He sounded distant under the noise, though Iris could feel him there.

"I don't know. The souls here are usually talkative, but"—she winced— "this is different." Iris forced herself through the door, heat pricking at her witchery.

The shop was different. Cleaner, maybe, though there were still cobwebs and dust. But the shelves were sparse and less chaotic. Things were missing. She looked up to the swinging trinkets above her, all the souls crying out to her to be released. They'd quieted, but were still swinging wildly above her.

"Roddin!" she screamed again.

Mathew wiped sweat from his brow. He looked around, one eye always on the front door, like he expected Roddin to walk in at any moment. He moved to the far end of the shop and pulled back the velvet curtain shielding the otherrealm tools. The shelves were empty of the enchanted mirrors and pieces of scrying glass that Iris knew used to be there.

Heart pounding, Iris pulled open the door to the prayer room.

It was empty. The round table was neat and the altar was nearly bare save for two tall candles, a sprig of sage, and a half-filled vial of something green and oily. She stepped over a few loose marbles on the floor and touched one of the candles. It was still warm.

Heat grew around her again, and with it came a sobering moment of understanding.

She bent down and picked up a green bead from the floor. Aside from the color, it matched that of her own bracelet.

A horrible sound grew from the shop, like a thousand scurrying mice scratching in the walls. Iris dropped the bead and hurried out of the prayer room.

There was Mathew, standing in the middle of the shop, dazed. He was staring above. Brow scrunched in fear or confusion, Iris couldn't tell. But his eyes were wide in wonder. She looked up to the source of the noise. The spirits were no longer crying out to her. Instead, the hooks' points were scratching at the ceiling, twitching wildly in their haste. And when they were done, when the shop was quiet, Iris realized that they were not scratching randomly at the wood. They were etching a message. Two words, carved over and over into the wood.

*Deathwitch.*

*Run.*

Iris decided quickly this was not the time to fuck around and find out. "Mathew," she screeched, already bolting for the door. *"Run!"*

But just as she reached the front door, the tether in her chest yanked her backward.

She turned.

Mathew had dropped to a knee, rooted to the spot by the Roddin Witch's hand on his shoulder, her fingers digging into his flesh.

"There you are, dead girl." Roddin smiled smugly.

Iris examined the elder unwitch with unease. She felt that blast of warmth again, like she was standing beneath a radiator. Sweat dripped down her face. "Roddin, why was—"

"That is not my name."

"Hold up, you mean you *don't* have the same name as the road out front?" Iris said, words dripping in sarcasm. "Then who the fuck are you?"

"You're being awfully flippant to someone offering to spare you."

Iris's annoyance swiftly became fear. "Spare?"

"From the Wolves. You are too powerful to waste." Her gaze brushed over Beaumont before returning to Iris. "You have your weaknesses, but you are young. I can rip them out."

Iris could only shake her head, unable to make sense of this. "What have you done? Why was Bloom here?"

"We were reminiscing." Roddin shrugged.

Iris's breath caught. The pieces were falling together slowly. When she looked at Roddin, she felt a strange pang of familiarity. Iris had seen her before, in the purple-tinged cloud of Theodore Bloom's memories. Her deep green eyes, the *resolve* behind them, the way she stood tall and fearless. Though she was older and frailer, her voice still held a commanding confidence.

She released a ragged breath. "Adelaide."

The elder witch smirked.

Iris's thoughts whirled. She was having trouble breathing under the heat and her growing anxiety. She had so many questions that needed answers, but all she could manage was one soft "What are you doing?"

Adelaide Strigwach's smirk became a dark scowl. "I am finishing the work I have waited a century to complete."

Iris glanced quickly at Mathew, who looked sick. His skin was white as a sheet of paper, his sweat soaking his hair and his shirt. "You've always hated Haelsford."

"*Haelsford,*" Adelaide spat, "hated us first."

"I know. I know that the Hunting killed your coven. I get it; I do. You want revenge, and I would, too."

Adelaide said nothing.

Iris sucked in through her teeth, detesting herself for being so thoroughly fooled. "There is no Wolf Boy, is there? It's a story you've been telling forever, making it legend. So, who is Theodore Bloom?"

"Some of the story is true. The Wolf Boy is real, even if he's not what you think. But it wasn't Mathilde who gave him power; it was me, and only because my sisters had grown soft-hearted for the mundanes. Creating monsters requires something dark and deep from within, and they'd decided to forgive." Every word from Adelaide's mouth roiled with that very darkness. "That is why the Wolves turned on us, because of their goodness. Well, I would have none of it, and I kept control of all of our sweet Wolves."

Iris hated hearing her talk like this, but she understood.

Adelaide curled her fingers into fists. "Do you know how my sisters responded? My own flesh and blood wanted to take my magic from me. Was I meant to let them? They tried to keep me hexbound. But they didn't get it all out of me. That's why I needed *you*." She flashed the faded pentagram on her wrist, one hand still on Mathew's shoulder. "Mathilde offered him love, but I offered him something greater. Witches like you and me, my girl, are stronger than others, death running through our veins. Who would choose love over life after death? Well, Bloom found it convincing. While my sisters were focused on me, I'd already given him the power of the Wolves. As long as his body is preserved, he can come back, and as long as he breathes, the Wolves bow to him. And *he* bows to *me*. You should've been there when he asked a Wolf to pluck that Mesmortes girl into the Swamp. It was *magnificent*. What was her name?"

Iris turned away, her eyes burning. "Jenna."

"Are you upset? You should thank me. You were allowed to walk away."

"Why even make me work to find Bloom?" Iris choked out. "You could've just given me his name or pointed out his grave."

"Oh, but I learned my lesson with the others. It works better when I take a step back, make you feel like you're working for it—"

"Others?"

"Did you think I've spent my life twiddling my thumbs until your arrival?"

Iris's heart hammered in her chest. She closed her eyes, but the tears slipped out.

"Sweet Amelia had so much darkness in her heart. She was hard to control, and when the Swamp called out to her, even I could not stop her. I thought I'd give you the pieces, let you put them together." Adelaide fluttered her fingers, like pulling strings.

*And I just fell for it.*

Finally, the curse of Haelsford's necromancers was revealed. The dropouts, the disappearances, the deaths by Wolves. Like Iris, they'd been wrapped into Adelaide's plot, and either fled town or died to get out of it.

This witch had been a mentor to Iris, with a wealth of knowledge that her professors refused to teach her, the books and artifacts, and their twin necromancer marks. And it was all a lie. Her name, her purpose. Her fondness for Iris. The betrayal took the air out of her. Her pentagram scar seared in response.

"Your powerful friend and your murderess greenwitch would not be so easy to convince, but that little proxy! So impressionable. I made her love him."

Guilt hit her hard. Logan and Iris, manipulated to the point of contempt for each other. As Adelaide relished her win, the pain in Iris's death mark grew so hot that she thought she was going to faint. Little spots flashed in her vision. Muffled voices called out to her.

*"Deathwitch? Deathwitch!"*

*"Let us out!"*

"But the amplyfyr . . ." Adelaide continued, her voice sounding thick like a wall was building between them. "I thought it would take you longer to find one. Thought I might have to make one myself. Do you know what goes into an amplyfyr, dead girl? The souls of murdered witches. I was curious to see how else you might use it, but you and yours constantly disgrace the witchery that binds you."

Iris had heard enough. She lifted her wand to Adelaide, who tightened her grip on Mathew's shoulder. "It's pointless," Adelaide said with wicked delight. "You cannot hurt me, not in here. No spell against me shall aim true. I could teach you such magic, if you let me."

Iris was hardly paying attention. The pain in her leg, the voices in her head—

*"Free us!"*

Mathew's eyes flicked upward suddenly, like he'd heard them, too. There was a prickle in her chest, the tether blooming between them.

Iris looked up. The hooks were spinning, each one a tiny pendulum ready to be called to. She could only call a spirit with a name and a face, unless . . . unless a spirit called to *her*.

Tears welled up in her eyes. The scar on her leg was electric with heat.

"What did you do with the necromancers that defied you?" Iris muttered.

For the first time, Adelaide's lip twitched.

She met the Strigwach's gaze once more. "All these years you've tried to have one naive necromancer do your bidding. I have a hard time believing that no one questioned you."

"They're dead," Adelaide spat.

Iris nodded. "Well, maybe I can't hurt you." She allowed herself a small smile. "But *they* can."

Iris jabbed her sacrificial needle into her leg.

A burst of light, a burst of pain.

The world around her slowed and blurred, except for the shimmering charms above her. Iris lifted her wand to the trinkets that trapped so many souls. *"I Call Upon You! Adelaide Strigwach's Victims!"* Her death magic warmed in her chest, filling her with a delicious surge of power. *"I Unbind You from Your Prisons!"*

It happened all at once.

From the hooks, a hundred trinkets shattered as if they were made of glass. Scores of spirits rushed from their trappings and surged toward their captor. Iris tried to see their faces—she felt like she owed them that, to acknowledge them and their pain, but they only rushed past her in blurs of black shadows and brilliant blue light. She felt the warm embrace of a hundred angry souls who wanted retribution and had waited months, years, decades for it. The air tasted sweet with their fury.

Iris licked her teeth, relishing it. She yelled over the chaos, "I grant you vengeance! Take it now!"

It was odd to see Adelaide Strigwach run. She seemed so much like a regular old crone, and not the almighty Strigwach Sister. She made it through the back door and into the garden before tripping over her own two feet and falling to the ground in a mundane display of clumsiness.

The souls converged around her, merciless. Adelaide screamed.

Every spirit that touched her skin left a mark. Angry red welts bloomed where pale wrinkled skin had been, and soon, there were more burns than flesh.

Iris could only watch. The angry righteousness she'd felt had dissolved into sadness. Even if she thought Adelaide deserved mercy, and she wasn't sure she did, the connection that the spirits had fostered with Iris was gone. She couldn't have called them off if she wanted to.

"Iris?"

She snapped back to Mathew, who was still in the middle of the shop on a knee. Relief flooded her senses. "Let's go."

As she took a step toward him, she heard an unsettling, high-pitched creak from above. She looked up, narrowing her eyes at the ceiling. Heat wafted down toward her.

She drew her wand. *"What Are You Hiding?"*

Iris was met with a furious green blaze, revealed as she pulled back the cloaking spell Adelaide had set. Her heart dropped. She understood now why the souls had screamed at her to keep her from walking in.

She turned back to the garden. The screams—both Adelaide's and the spirits'—had ended. The Strigwach Sister was gone, though her cloak remained. Had she run off? Had the spirits taken her? Iris couldn't be sure. All she knew was that the danger had only begun.

The elder witch knew Iris well. Adelaide knew she'd come here wanting answers, that she'd bring Mathew, and that, presented with the choice, Iris would never follow her dark path.

So Adelaide set it all on fire and invited her in.

# 50

## logan

Here she was again, standing outside the Cavern just like Hallowe'en night.

What Logan felt now could not be compared to what she felt then. She'd been afraid but eager to be welcomed by the Red Three, waiting for something to spark her witchery like a crack of lightning. *Fear* was too weak a word to describe *this*.

At the MidWinter Celebration, Logan had felt a chill, so sharp and so startling that she found herself wincing under the warm glow of the Wheel of Fortune. There had been magic in the air, something that her own witchery was responding to. It should've scared her. She knew the myth that souls that crossed the protection had been lured by something. But Logan knew that it was different. A gut feeling. It was her girls. So she'd rushed to them and found herself standing between Teddy and Jailah's wand.

The trip over was a blur. The air at the mouth of the Cavern trembled with a wave of distortion. In the distance, the Wolves howled. Her heart pounding and hands shaking, she felt an intuitive unease that this was all wrong. Was that her wand that went up as she blocked Jailah's spell? A shielding spell, recited from Jailah's own repertoire. And what was that spell she'd blocked?

*Sanguirremorr.*

Logan wished Jai was here, and Thalia and Iris. The four of them together. Maybe not infallible against whatever darkness plagued Haelsford, but at least she wouldn't be alone. But what was Jailah thinking? Logan had wanted to scream, *Stop, he's not supposed to die like this,* but then . . . then came the Wolf.

"What are we doing here?" Logan asked weakly.

"There's nowhere else to go," Theodore said. He still had her in his arms. The *Shade* was gone now, the magic finally dissolving without her re-upping the transformative spell. He was so warm, and he held her tightly. A part of her wanted to fall asleep like this: loved and safe, though her witchery screamed at her to leap from his arms and run without him.

Instead, she looked up at him. "We have to go back."

But farther into the Cavern they went. He moved like a snake in the dark, knowing just which way to go, and how to get through every tight spot. He was at home here.

"Put me down," she insisted.

"Can you walk?"

*"Teddy."*

With a furrowed brow, he lowered her. She bit back the pain that spiked up her knee when her foot touched the ground. Logan heard an explosion in the distance. The earth shook, like something within was newly alive, pulling itself out.

Teddy looked at her with desperate eyes. "You don't believe what Jailah said about me, do you? I mean, you haven't spoken to her, to any of them, in weeks."

She let out a pained sigh. "We agreed to end the Haunting."

"You asked. I said yes. But maybe I'm changing my mind."

"Please, I don't want to make you—"

*"Make me?"* Teddy sputtered. "How? With your magic?" He didn't laugh, but he was amused. When she turned away from him, he added, "If you leave, you might not come back." Logan almost didn't recognize his voice.

"What are you saying?"

"I'm saying that this is the only place where you're safe."

The shadows moved. From every corner of rock that surrounded her, there seemed to be life in the stone.

"They won't hurt you, not when you're with me."

Logan took in a breath, tasting blood and oil. "And why's that?"

"Because I've told them not to, Logan Phillip Wyatt."

How could she respond to that? The severity in his voice, the cruelty in his gaze? He delivered his words with an unkindness that he expected Logan to understand. The first time he ever said her name, it made her joyous and light and dizzy. Now she just felt sick.

His eyes scanned her without remorse. "Come on, just a bit farther."

Logan didn't move. "I never did see how Mathilde made you the Wolf Boy."

"I don't know what Mathilde did. All I remember is waking in the grave you dug up."

She shook her head. "You aren't the Wolf Boy, are you?"

Like a mask uncovered, Theodore's expression went blank, free of the meekness and apprehension he'd always worn. "I am," he said roughly. "You sacrifice your blood to the earth for your witchery, and I sacrifice mine for the Wolves. They aren't puppets, but they are trained to only obey me. They serve *me*."

"Yeah. For now."

Theodore stilled. "Kill the Wolf Boy, kill the Wolves?" he said, reading her thoughts. "Mathilde was always so dramatic."

Ahead, there was a break in the rock. The circular space was drenched in light, a fire burning in the middle of it. Logan choked on the stench of burning blood. Flames flickered in Theodore's lovely eyes. "Everything you knew was just a story woven to court you all to my side when the pieces were in place," he continued.

"Pieces?" Logan asked.

"A true necromancer was needed. A powerful one, one with the Mark. One that could be molded for this purpose."

*Molded.* With a wave of nausea, Logan said, "You know the Roddin Witch."

"Her name is Adelaide."

Logan closed her eyes, trying to make sense of this. "Roddin can't be . . . she's not . . ." Goose bumps lined her skin, that icy feeling returning. *The dreams. The scrying glass. None of it was real. That's why it was so easy.*

Who was *he*, then?

*Who the hell did I bring back?*

He noticed her apprehension. "You don't have to fear me."

*He's lying.*

"She had you on sevdys," she said. "You've never told us the truth."

"Adelaide and I had an understanding," he explained, unbothered. "My father took her and her sisters in, and I gave them the secrets they needed for our undoing. In return, I only asked to be spared . . . to *always* be spared."

*Can he really not fucking die?* Logan gave a sad little laugh.

345

He lifted a brow. "Adelaide is a deathwitch. Wouldn't you ask the same thing?"

"What, immortality?"

"Preservation in death. It was just as useful to her, really. She knew her sisters were going to try and bind her magic." He clicked his tongue. "Weak girls. They should've just killed her."

Logan took a deep breath. *This time, he needs to stay dead.* It wouldn't end the Haunting, but it was better that the Wolves served no master than serving him and Adelaide Strigwach. "What's the point of all this? To kill everyone?"

"To burn it all down and raise it up anew. Adelaide's plan, really, and I'm inclined to oblige her. You know how I feel because you feel the same. Haelsford isn't home to us."

"Aren't you going to kill me? Command a Wolf to tear me apart?"

"Some of it *was* real, Logan." He touched her gently, his fingers on hers. His eyes were gentle, lush lips beckoning. A small part of her still hoped that she was wrong about him, and she hated it. "Why do you think I've chosen to spare you?"

She pulled away. "Yeah, some of it was real, like my witchery only responding to you. I was scared when I had the first dream, but I felt important. Magical. *Chosen.* Of course I latched on to you. I made it so easy, huh?"

He dropped his voice. Made it soft and sweet. He lifted his hand and traced her cheek with his knuckles. "You've misjudged me. The other girls just wanted your ability to proxy. I want you because *I want you.* You know me."

He held his hand out to her. "We can watch Haelsford burn together."

She lifted her hand, her wand with it. "Call off the Wolves."

"You're the one who said I should want this," he replied plainly. The blood burning fire raged behind him. He shrugged. "You wanted me to live. You wanted to be mine, Logan, and now you are, as I am yours—"

"I'm not fucking yours!" she cried roughly. *"Sanguirremorr!"*

The spell, a flash of red light from Logan's wand, sent Bloom off-balance. He fell to the ground with a yelp of pain.

Logan had zero idea of what the spell was meant to do, but if it was good enough for Jailah Simmons, then it was good enough for her. She ran out of the nook and back into the Cavern, grunting from the pain in her knee. She stumbled over the hard rock and ever-changing slope. Logan focused on nothing but the witchy instinct that she was blessed with, the very one that she'd kept buried until now. It powered her through the dark, giving her something to fight for. When she heard his sharp voice echo through the Cavern, she didn't stop for her sore legs or her bloody knee.

*Screw the Wolves, and screw Theodore Bloom.*

The light at the mouth of the Cavern trickled in, and Logan homed in on it like it was a lighthouse and she was lost at sea.

There was a shift in the shadows. The smell of blood grew potent. Sensing something behind her, Logan twisted around and shouted, *"Mortif—"*

The Wolf bit down on her arm. She cried out. Her wand fell from her grasp and skittered away into the darkness.

Logan screamed, she focused, she felt a flame in her, and she directed it. She proxied.

*"Mortifoculo!"*

Light burst from Logan's hands. It hit the Wolf in the face with a sick, piercing crunch. Howling violently, the beast released her, its sharp claw catching her face. Blood and pain spread across her face, but she scrambled away. Only then did Logan realize that it was small. Still atrocious and terrifying, but a *pup*. She saw the marks that she'd left on the animal—her own blood on its fur, and thick black-red gashes where its eyes once were.

A blind Wolf pup was nothing to take lightly. Its sense of smell could still lead it to her. But the beast couldn't quite get around the tight, blustery way of the terrain without striking rock. Logan forced herself up and away as it struggled. Climbing up the final ledge before the Cavern's mouth, she found herself staring at his shoes first.

"Another of Jailah's spells?" Theodore asked cruelly. "It doesn't suit you."

Cursing herself, Logan met his eye. Blood muddled her vision.

Laughing, he yanked her upward and pulled her close. "You have to *want* it. Do you want me dead, Logan?"

She attempted to push him and run, but he was on her quickly, pinning one of her hands down while she managed to keep the other free. She clawed at his face, but aside from a few low curses, he hardly noticed.

Logan's plea came out in a muffled choke. *"Sang—"*

She fought and fought, but suddenly there were two hands around her neck.

"Why can't you just heel?" he screamed, tightening them.

"Why can't you just—" she choked out. "Just! *Just Die!*"

She didn't mean to do anything, but she found that the words fit well between her teeth. And the light that seemed to come from everywhere? Even better between his ribs.

Her magic was not a flame. It was a raging wildfire.

Growling, Logan pushed him off her.

A slick black hole formed in Theodore Bloom's chest. He laughed as he bled. "What did you just do?"

"You're dying," she whispered. "Again."

He tried to stand. He coughed a thick spray of blood. *"No."*

"No?" Logan mocked. Her throat was stinging and raw, but she liked how rough she sounded. "What was that, Wolf Boy?"

He reached a hand out to her, and Logan kicked it away. Her clothes were dotted with his blood and her own. Her face was slick. Her arm seared from the Wolf's bite. Logan waited there until he stopped breathing. She watched his hazel eyes go dark.

Limping, Logan made for the light, which shone even brighter now, like the moon was welcoming her back. She slumped against the Cavern entrance to catch her breath.

Behind her, something moved. Mostly for lack of energy, she didn't jump. She turned her head slightly and saw the Wolf pup.

Logan lifted her hand in an odd moment of reflex.

The pup heeled.

# 51
## jailah

Jailah Simmons was running on empty.

On the roof of the main building, she counted the witches unlucky enough to miss out on MidWinter. Three freshmen, two sophomores, junior Layla Marks, and Hardy Schrader, who really had no seniority in this moment.

For a second, Jailah wished that the roles were reversed. Who let her have this power? She was only seventeen, yet she was somehow responsible for these lives. But wasn't this what she wanted? Notoriety, if she survived. There were Wolves outside, their terrifying magic allowing them some headway on the *Iron* door out front, and more streaming in slowly through the gap in Thalia's wall of trees. The Haunting wasn't over yet. They couldn't just sit around and hope. But here she was now, in front of all these wide-eyed witches, and she had to put a plan into action. The Wolves needed to be put down.

As she'd instructed them to, Hardy and Layla brought their archery gear. Jailah still sported her makeshift bow. Something about it felt right in this moment.

Below, another Wolf trickled through the gap. They heard it howl.

Jailah said, "That's nine. There will be more, and they won't stop until we're all dead."

There was a shiver among them, but no tears.

"We may not be able to kill them, but maybe we can stop them until the Haunting ends." She nodded at Hardy and Layla. "You two lead. Focus on the Wolves getting through the gap, okay? Our spells seem to be hit or miss, but a sharp arrow?" She spun one in her fingers. "Aim for their legs, their paws, anything to keep them from moving toward the doors."

"They're fast," Layla whispered.

"Yeah, and so are you. You placed second at Southern Conference last season. They won't see your arrows coming."

"Where will you be?" Danny Chen asked quietly.

"Downstairs." They all gasped, but Jailah shushed them. "You and Rowe will stay up here, helping to direct the arrows. Lilly, Morgan, you need to find a way to warn people."

"No one's responding to our texts," Lilly said, trembling against the howls that started from below.

Jailah only shouted over the noise. "Then get creative!"

"What if we lose?" Rowe whispered thickly, her pale skin blushing red.

"I won't let that happen, and neither will you. Mesmortes witches don't bow to mundanes, or to the Swamp, or to Wolves. Remember that."

Jailah spun on her heels and shut the roof access door behind her.

The Wolves were throwing themselves at the front door. She heard the dull thuds grow louder as she made her way onto the second landing of steps. With every thud, every howl, she felt a new crack in her resolve. She'd hoped for an invincible rush of adrenaline, but all she felt was fear.

*I could die tonight.*

Reflexively, she considered every spell she'd ever learned, anything that might be helpful. Fire spells, shields, heart-stoppers—she never thought she'd have a chance to use *Sanguirremorr* twice in a night, not to mention *Convergence.*

She reached into her back pocket for that ugly little book. There was a crack below like thunder. Jailah's eyes darted to the door, then back to the book. She flipped through the pages hurriedly, feeling her time running out.

She settled on a curious page. Olga Yara had sketched a rather crude drawing of arrows piercing men.

"Black arrows . . ." Jailah's whisper trailed away as she read the terms, the incantation, the sacrifice.

*The sacrifice.*

Yara's spells were always painful. She favored great sacrifices for great magic, things other than blood. Jailah's heart seemed to race and drop into her stomach at the same time. She could save the school; she could save Haelsford.

But the price for this?

She looked through the spell again.

*Count your enemies, count them all.*

*Pick a limb; watch them fall.*

Jailah felt a sick sort of amusement at the crude rhyme, even as fear grew in her chest. She stuffed the book back into her pocket. She couldn't die tonight. She *refused.* If all else failed, she had the spell for a last resort.

From her vantage point atop the great stairs, Jailah could just make out the split in the door. That sickening aroma of blood seeped into the air.

She heard sniffing snouts and throaty growls, another crack, but something else, too. Whinnies and howls of pain. Jailah peered out of one of the massive windows lining the walls. Arrows were flying from above and landing in the beasts.

In the night sky, bursts of light made a message. Jailah grinned.

*SOS. WOLVES ON THE HILL. BEWARE.*

The final crack was a thunderous thing. Jailah wasn't ready for it. There was supposed to be a stream of Wolves, not a burst. Howling for her blood, they sprinted toward her.

Jai readied her bow.

Exhaled.

Loosed.

Her grip was shaky, but she managed a few hits. The arrows slowed them down, but Jailah knew that not even an endless supply could take them all. Every one that fell only cleared a path for two more, and now there were four breaking from the rest. Jailah scrambled furiously up the steps.

*"Break It Off!"* she screamed out, launching the spell over her shoulder.

The staircase behind her crumbled in an avalanche of stone, falling out from under the Wolves. She should've aimed for a spot farther away; the blast nearly knocked her off her own feet, her eyes watering from the dense cloud of dust.

*"Clear the Air!"* she cried just in time for her to see two Wolves launching over the crater that buried their brothers.

Desperation crept in. *"Hot Stuff!"* The incantation wavered in her throat, and the air only caught flame for a moment, a flash of orange rather than a brilliant rolling fire. One Wolf was caught with it and retreated with a howl of anguish. The other ran through the blaze, its fur catching fire, but it just wouldn't stop.

Jailah heard a voice then, breaking the bit of bravery she had left.

Lilly yelled, "Hey! Hey! Over here!" from the landing below.

"*Lilly!* No!"

But a Wolf meandered down through the rubble to meet her, its lips curled over its teeth.

Jailah ran so quickly to the ledge of the staircase that she nearly sent herself toppling over.

Lilly attempted to levitate the beast, but witchery had always been a gamble against the Wolves. It only lurched a few inches off the ground before regaining its footing and jolting toward her.

Howls drowned out Jailah's scream, but her incantation worked, and Lilly was blasted backward toward a far wall, but the Wolf—

It happened quickly. The Wolf should've been blown away like Lilly, but into the opposite wall. That was the spell, they were meant to act as like sides of a magnet. But the Wolf maneuvered away from Jailah's crosshairs just slightly, distracted by something in its view.

There was a screech in the air, and Lilly's falcon dive-bombed the Wolf, forcing it to lurch backward, right into the path of a small knife spinning through the air.

Shaking, Jailah racked her brain for something, something useful, *anything*, and all she could stupidly think of was putting Logan Wyatt's hair into barrel curls on Hallowe'en—

"*Do It Big!*" Jailah roared.

The spell hit the knife just as it hit the Wolf, and it became a sword, splitting the monster in half from head to tail. Blood and black flame burst from the beast's insides.

Everything stood still for a moment. She locked eyes with Trent, who seemed to have appeared from nowhere. He was drenched in sweat. "Did we just—" he whispered.

"Yeah," Jailah muttered, her tongue thick. *We killed one.*

Trent pointed up at her suddenly, his face screwed up in terror. "Watch out!"

She spun so fast, she got dizzy. Three Wolves had dislodged themselves from the rubble below. Each was injured—contorted, broken legs that they dragged forward, gashes in their flesh. One had taken a nasty hit to the head, but its remaining eye locked on her. Blood and bone and gristle. Jailah's stomach roiled at the sight of them.

Another attempted to lurch forward before stopping in pain and growling in frustration. Jailah felt a jolt of satisfaction; she could take them out easily.

That satisfaction swiftly turned to fear. There was one more Wolf waiting behind this mangled pack. She didn't think the Wolves considered strategy, but this one hung back while the others made their attempts. It was bigger than the rest. The leader of the pack.

Jailah looked around. She couldn't bring down the next landing without potentially hurting Trent and Lilly, and she couldn't run farther up the steps without leading the Wolves to the roof access door.

Abruptly, the half-faced Wolf ran for her, and Jailah's reflexive spell knocked it to the side so she could jolt out of the way. Another came and she slashed at the air with a *Knife*, lopping off its last good leg and sending it tumbling away, covering her in black blood. The third Wolf managed to sink its sharp teeth into her right forearm before she jabbed her wand into its eye in a rather mundane thrust of aggression. Pain seared up to her shoulder, but she was never more thankful to be a lefty.

She scrambled to her feet as the Wolves regrouped, circling her. Her gaze flicked to the leader, and she knew it was coming for her. She knew from the way the injured ones seemed to move out of the way for this one to finally take her out.

From below, Lilly launched an orange spell, maybe a binding hex, that missed.

"Don't!" Jailah yelled. "It's okay. I can—I can do this—"

The Wolf lowered its head and bolted for her.

Jailah put up her hands, head spinning as she tried to think. How many Wolves in all? At least ten. Twenty to be safe? She formed the image of them in her head, a pack to be put down.

*Count your enemies, count them all.*

*My right hand; watch them fall.*

She felt a searing sensation around her wrist, like a tightening, acid-laced string.

She whispered, too exhausted, too defeated to scream, *"Twenty Black Arr—"*

The Wolf was quicker than her tongue. It pushed her to the ground hard, sending her wand toppling over the landing.

Trent screamed for her. He seemed far away.

The Wolf drew its head back, mouth open. Sharp teeth. Red fur.

They might be the last things she saw.

Heart pounding, Jailah closed her eyes.

There was a howl.

A moment passed.

Jailah's breaths were ragged. Hesitantly, she opened her eyes and found the Wolf frozen, staring down at her, its crooked fangs stopping just short of her face. It wasn't any less terrifying; the Wolf was still atop her, heaving, pushing its mangled face toward her. But it stopped there, and Jailah was somehow *still breathing*. Jailah couldn't understand why.

The Wolf retreated, dragging itself off Jailah and ambling toward the doors. The others followed. She instantly clutched her wrist, thankful that the spell hadn't taken. She was left with a pale scar where her hand was nearly sacrificed.

Wobbly from the hysteria, she struggled to her feet. Lilly built a bridge over the stone and rubble, and there she was, running toward Jailah, Jang-Goon soaring overhead. Trent was pressed against the wall, mouth gaping in confusion as the Wolves passed him without acknowledgment. "Bloody hell'd you do, Jailah?"

Jailah pressed her hands against her chest. She savored the feel of her heartbeat, the warmth of her witchery. She waved away Lilly's hands; the baby witch was trying to get to her gashed arm. "Jai, *slow down—*"

She couldn't. Ignoring Trent's protest, Jailah followed the Wolves, all ignoring her. They bumped into her legs and arms as they calmly retreated. Jailah's heart pounded with the idea that they were heeding *his* call. Maybe she'd been naive. Maybe the Wolf Boy had more to do, and maybe she would still die tonight?

Someone came into view, but it didn't look much like Theodore Bloom. She squinted at the little figure that the Wolves passed on their way through the gap of trees and toward their Swamp.

"Hi, Jailah."

Logan was filthy—covered in dirt, scrapes, and blood. She smiled like she was glad but didn't want to show it.

Jailah gripped her bloody arm. Her laugh came out as a sob.

Logan threw her arm over Jailah's shoulder, and they watched the Wolves amble toward the Swamp.

# 52

## iris

The flames of the Emporium grew unnaturally quick and hungry, rolling up the high walls and devouring the wood.

Mathew was still crouched in the middle of the shop.

"Beaumont, this way!" Iris screamed.

He snapped to her, "Watch out!"

The rig in her chest pulled her away from the door and to the ground.

She fell hard, throwing her arms over her head. Iris didn't see the enormous wooden beam fall from above, but she heard it crash, felt it quake through the shop. Her pulse ticked faster. She lifted her head and found herself cornered by the massive pieces of flaming wood, blocking the garden door.

Scrambling to her feet, Iris pointed her wand at the barrier, but when she pulled her arm up with a spell to move it, something blocked her. A resistance in the air, like weights had been fastened to her wrist. She cursed. *Hexed fire.* She breathed in a lungful of smoke and heaved. The world tilted as she struggled against it, the air rippling with heat.

She reached out a hand to steady herself. She felt herself falling—

"*Iris!*"

She heard him, but not over the sounds of the collapsing shop. Just in her head.

*"To me!"*

Iris caught herself, one hand on the ground. With an angry push, she called her witchery against the heretic's magic and flipped the beam away from her. The effort brought her to her knees, but she forced herself to her feet and bolted toward her tether.

Mathew Beaumont heaved a furious cough.

"Come on!" she screamed over the whistling flames. She hooked her arm around his. But he wouldn't budge.

"I can't move," he huffed. "I'm trying—I *literally* can't move."

"Are you hurt?" she asked, but the moment it fell from her lips, she knew that it wasn't that simple. He was hunched over, his fists clenched as he tried to get to his feet. Her shoulders dropped.

Adelaide Strigwach had promised to rip out her weaknesses.

From the far side of the shop, crashes exploded in quick succession. The ravenous fire brought down half of the ceiling, taking two exits with it. Iris looked over her shoulder, toward the front door.

"Go," Mathew said weakly. "Go without me."

"Shut up! Let me think!" She flung out an assortment of spells, every hexfighter she knew. She could hardly grasp her wand from the sweat. Her entire body was drenched. She breathed in and immediately coughed.

"Now, Iris!" Mathew said, his voice a pained rasp.

Iris lifted her wand.

He grabbed her wrist. "If you don't go now, you won't be able to!"

"I—"

"It's fine, leave me!"

"I can't leave you!" she screamed back, a little angry, because *how could he not understand*? "You're my tether!"

And this time, she meant it in more ways than one.

Iris looked around for something. Anything. A last bit of hope to cling to.

She only found fire.

"Death in flames," she whispered to herself. She stilled. The words reminded her of a very different line about death, scribbled on the last page of Mathilde Strigwach's diary.

*Death favors those whose souls are lined with black.*

Iris touched the pentagram scar on her leg. A sliver of irrational hope grew in her.

Mathew's shoulders trembled. She lifted his head to drink in those teary blue eyes. She watched him struggle as he tried to push her away.

"Mathew."

He stopped.

"Sweet, dead Beaumont. Wouldn't you like to burn with me?"

She held his hand. Hellfire surrounded them.

*Favor me.*

Mathew gave her a questioning look. He opened his mouth to respond but only hacked a cough. Iris performed one last spell to make it easy for him. His head slumped onto her shoulder. She pressed her hand against his chest, savoring the feel of his heartbeat.

*I could be wrong*, she thought grimly. *This could be it.*

She tried not to dwell on Jailah, Thalia, and Logan, who had all filled her with a love that no one could ever match, or Trent, who she hardly knew but had grown so fiercely fond of. With a hope that refused to die, Iris recited Mathilde's words over and over in her head until she felt hysterical enough to believe it.

*Death favors those whose souls are lined with black.*

*I am touched with death.*

*Favor me.*

She squeezed Mathew's hand.

"*Favor us.*"

⸱⸱⸱➤ ✪ ⸱⸱⸱

Sitting atop a throne of souls, Death *pushed* Iris—hard, cruelly, and amused—toward the mortal world with a finger of dark red bone. Though Iris hovered in some odd ether between two worlds, she felt every bit of this cold, unrepentant violence.

Under a black hood, a mouth moved. It said two words:

"NOT. YET."

And the necromancer floated away, away, away.

Iris felt the magnetic call of her physical body. Just before it took her, she saw another soul drifting through the underworld.

"Wait!" she howled, reaching out for him. "You can't have him!"

And Death replied, "HE BELONGS TO THE DARK NOW."

"We are tethered! He is mine!"

She wanted hands to claw at the dark and force herself to stay. She wanted feet to plant against the current pulling her back. She was not done here yet.

His light flickered.

"Spare him!"

"NO."

*This is not a person*, she reminded herself. There was no rational thought here, no sympathies to play to. Still, she would try.

"I am blessed with Death, and so is he! You have felt it!"

Iris screamed. Death was around her, clawing at her skin, at her *heart*, so violent with its touch that she was sure it'd changed its mind about letting her live. Its cloaked body filled up the darkness, and she was just a speck in the palm of its bony hand. When it spoke, she felt the vibrations thrumming throughout her, seeping into every inch of her consciousness, drowning her out.

"WHAT WOULD YOU GIVE TO SAVE HIM? YOUR SWEET BLACK SOUL?"

"Hell *no*," she said, feeling her lips forming, only sort of there. She was becoming whole again. There wasn't much time left. "But I urge you to honor the desire of one of your children. His soul is tethered to mine, so if I am Death's daughter, then he is your son! There are so few of us touched with Death—wouldn't it be cruel to strike down one of your own?"

"THERE IS NO CRUELTY IN THE WAYS OF LIFE AND DEATH. THERE IS *ONLY* LIFE AND DEATH."

She heard voices on the other side. "Iris! Iris, oh god, wake up!"

Iris focused on Death. "I have rested so many tortured souls! Give me this one!"

The enormous skeletal hand cupped Mathew entirely. It spun thread in the air above him, pulling it from his chest. The thread looked like blood, bright red and shimmering, and Iris nearly cried out—

But then she saw the silver. It was cut into the red like lightning.

"WITCHBLOOD RUNS IN HIM. HE IS BOUND BY THE HARBINGER."

Iris didn't even attempt to make sense of this. She could only try to hold on to this world as it slipped away. The others were calling her.

"IF YOU WILL NOT SACRIFICE, YOU WILL BE GIVEN A PURPOSE."

"Purpose?"

The finger again, with little love and hardly a care, pushed her deftly through the worlds.

Her soul burned as she fell to earth.

Voices were all around her, muttering quickly.

And hands.

Hands all over, pulling her from still-smoking soot.

Her name.

They called again and again, even as her chest slowly heaved back to life.

"Mathew," Iris mumbled.

"He's—" Jailah's voice now, and it sounded like she was underwater. Iris strained to hear. "He's okay." Then, quietly, "God . . . *how are you two okay?*"

A hand, burning skin, rested atop hers. Iris blinked. Mathew met her eyes, and she sighed with body-trembling relief. Trent brought Mathew to his feet and pulled him into a hug. And though he couldn't have known what just happened, he looked at Iris with gratitude.

Logan threw her arms around Iris, her skin bloody and slick. Thalia, with a strained sob, held them both, and Jailah wrapped them all up, planting a kiss on Iris's forehead in relief.

"We're okay," Jai whispered. "We're all okay."

Iris squeezed back, even as a hollow voice haunted her thoughts.

*You will be given a purpose.*

# 53

## after

*Two months after the Haunting Season*

The witch girls and the mundane boys sat at the base of the Hill. The parents. The professors. The tourists. Everyone focused on the Haelsford Witchery Council as they levitated the final block of stone to complete the new Laarsen House. Morgan Ramirez cut the big red ribbon.

The boys fixed their ties. The witches held on to their top hats.

"Still can't believe we survived." Trent sighed.

"*Barely* survived," Jailah said. She examined the gold medal hanging loosely around her neck. The ceremony had honored her for her "bravery in protecting Mesmortes." It was a piece of the glory she'd always craved, but it didn't satisfy her the way it should have. She rubbed the scar that circled her wrist. She'd tried an assortment of spells and salves, but it wouldn't fade.

Jailah looked at her friends. Survival was something they'd once celebrated. But as each moment passed on from that night, there was an itch in them as a collective to get over it. Not to forget, but to move on.

Together.

That was how they would do it. Not a minute was spent alone. The Mesmortes girls took shelter in Helios Dorm, room 311. They moved the couches so that all six of them could sleep on the floor. Sometimes they chose Thalia's cabin, with Maverick snuggled between her and Trent. No one could stand the silence of their thoughts. Each one of them was a shield for another. None of them wanted it any other way.

The semester was almost over. They didn't have much time left. Logan would stay for summer classes, and Iris would cover Thalia's RA position. Thalia was going to meet with her mother and her aunt. She wasn't going to hide anymore. There was an internship here with the Mesmortes Witchery Council for Jailah, and she was ready to convince them to commute Vero's sentence. Mathew would spend his break in Europe with Rebecca and his mother.

Trent was determined to grill his dad about the witch that maybe owned his soul. He lifted his own medal. He didn't like it much—it was heavy and ugly—but his father was in town, which meant a photo op could present itself at any moment.

Mathew pulled on his collar. "I never want to *barely* survive anything ever again." He nudged Iris.

Iris, who had hardly said a word to him since the fire, ignored him. Actually, she'd said two words to him on that very night, delivered with that deliciously cruel sarcasm. *You're welcome.* She refused to elaborate, but he knew what she meant. He'd died, and somehow, she'd saved him. Whatever happened before he had woken up from certain death, it closed her off to him.

Silently, they watched the ceremony. None of the people up there knew the real story. The Wolf Boy, *Convergence*, and Adelaide Strigwach, still nowhere to be found. The people of Haelsford believed what they wanted to hear—a perverse spell of heretic magic by the Roddin Witch allowed for a break in the protection and the enchanting of the Mesmortes staff. Witchy terrorism, essentially.

"They'll be after us," Thalia said, sipping her lemonade. Her own medal was tied around her wrist. "I hear there's going to be an investigation. The High Witch of the Americas is sending a team. A big deal, if they're skipping the Florida Council and going all the way to the top."

"They won't find anything," Logan said. She could still feel the smoke on her skin. It'd been months since they'd descended into the Cavern to burn the body, but everything about that night still made her restless. They'd all been left with scars, visible and not, and Logan was left with a thin red mark that ran diagonally from the top of her right brow to the tip of her nose. Though the Haunting Season had ended, sometimes she thought she could still hear the Wolves.

Trent boldly grabbed Thalia's top hat and placed it on his head. "So"—he gestured toward the witches—"do we call you the Red Four now?"

Jailah shrugged. "That depends. Logan Phillip Wyatt, how do you feel about being drenched in fake blood?"

Logan blinked. "Uh."

"This is why we discuss costumes in advance now," Iris said, clearly salty.

Thalia rolled her eyes. "We all showed up as Carrie to the Box Chant party freshman year. Gotta love revenge by telekinesis; that's my kind of witch."

"That's where the name comes from?" Mathew asked, laughing. "A Hallowe'en costume?"

Jailah threw her arms over his and Thalia's shoulders, closing the circle between the six of them. "I wonder what they'd call us now if they knew what we did."

A wary silence fell over the group.

"What do we do now?" Trent whispered.

Iris shook her head. "We do absolutely *nothing*."

"Nothing?" Mathew replied.

It hurt Iris to look at him. She couldn't reconcile her acute fondness for him with the discomfort that she'd nearly died for him. She'd made no deals with Death itself—she was sure of that—but Iris still had a peculiar feeling that she'd bargained *something* for his soul. She didn't regret it but hated that he had that hold on her.

Finally, she met his gaze. "I'm so done with being responsible. Let the Witchery Council spin this how they want. Theodore Bloom is dead, the Season is over, and I'm bored, so who wants to go down to Hexagon, flash their medals around, and get drunk?"

Jailah snorted. "I'm in."

Trent clicked his tongue. "You lot are wild. Got finals in three weeks."

"You're joking, right?" Mathew said. "They're optional this year."

Trent squinted at him. "Your point?"

"I'm in." Logan brushed the wayward blades of grass from her freshly pressed uniform.

Iris grinned. "Good girl! Thalia?"

"I guess." Thalia nodded and then whistled sharply. Maverick ran from the fringes of the ceremony and into her arms.

Mathew raised his eyebrows at Trent.

"Oi. Fine."

Iris and Logan trailed after everyone, the two of them walking closely, their arms practically linked. Logan ripped the medal from around her neck. "Do you remember when we met? You cleaned up the frap I spilled in the hallway. You're basically the entire reason I could become a witch."

Iris shook her head. "You were always a witch."

"You know what I mean. After that night, I complained about myself a lot, and I even said I was quitting magic, but I never said that I didn't want to be a witch. Not those exact words. I didn't even *think* it." Logan flung the medal into a nearby bush. "Iris, do you feel that?"

A breeze passed over the Hill.

A few weeks into spring, and the stickiness in the air finally broke.

# epilogue

That night, a thunderstorm burst through the atmosphere, shaking Beaumont Manor.

Lying in bed, Rebecca had been thinking about who she was and what she stood for.

Mathew went on adventures. He ran with witches and undead boys and had broken free of the Boring Beaumont Curse.

Who was she? What had she done?

*Rebecca Beaumont*, she thought, *pretty and prim and proper.*

*Becky Beaumont, vapid teenager with a mean streak.*

Then she remembered a rich voice, one that teased and demanded attention.

"Bex Beaumont," she whispered to herself. "Witchier."

Sleep crept up on her, quick, dark, and with its hand around her neck.

When she opened her eyes at exactly 4:43 a.m., she found herself hovering above her bed, her body stiff and her skin hot.

She *screamed*.

A terrible burst of pain erupted at the base of her neck. A white-hot pentagram burned as a scar on her skin, right in the middle of her collarbone.

So much all at once. Fear and adrenaline and power and *magic*.

Wickedly, the newborn witch grinned, pumping her fists to make her blood flow faster.

Frances Beaumont ran into the room, her face dissolving quickly from terror and concern to furious dejection.

Bex Beaumont laughed as the thunder boomed.

# acknowledgments

If tween-Sophie knew that she would one day be writing the acknowledgments for her debut YA novel about a magic school, witches, and wolves, she would quite literally *faint*. This is a book! I will never get over this. First and foremost, thank you, reader, for picking up this story. I hope you found something to love in it.

To Mom and Dad, for giving me endless library trips and as many Barnes & Noble runs as we could swing growing up. I would not be a writer if I wasn't first a reader, and I have you to thank for that. And to Gabby, Greg, and Vlad, my sibling coven.

This book would not exist without the tireless effort, support, and guidance of Susan Graham, who made me realize what this book needed to be, who has been championing it for years, and who got me my first book deal. I know you don't like me to say *we did it*, but *we* did. Thank you! Special thanks to Laura Rennert for her continuing guidance and support.

I feel supremely blessed to have had this story be loved and cared for by Shelly Romero. I am so thankful to be supported as a writer (and as a human being!) by you. It feels like a dream, having a lifelong horror fan and paranormal YA lover work on this book. Your friendship and expertise during this process will never be forgotten. Thank you for everything.

Being published by Scholastic is the realization of a dream I've had since childhood. Endless thanks to Jody Corbett for picking up the reins on this journey; production editor Melissa Schirmer; publicity mavens Alex Kelleher-Nagorski and Victoria Velez; Lizette Serrano, Emily Heddleson, and the rest of the library and educational marketing team; and Rachel Feld, Shannon Pender, and Zakiya Jamal in marketing. Special thanks to Arianna Arroyo and Sydney Tillman for supporting this book from the start. To Thea Harvey and Stephanie Yang, I will never ever stop screaming about how y'all gave me the cover of my dreams!!! Lastly, to David Levithan, Ellie Berger, and the entire Scholastic sales team, thank you for everything.

Very special thanks to Danys Mares and Kieron Scullington for reading and helping me create and refine this inclusive world. Your insights meant the world to me.

To my writer coven: Maya Prasad, Linda Cheng, Candace Buford, Michele Bacon, Tanya Aydelott, and Flor Salcedo—thank you for the hours and hours of shoptalk, friendship, and support. I'll be forever grateful to Emily X.R. Pan and Nova Ren Suma for giving me my first start in YA, and for bringing us all together.

A massive hug to Aiden Thomas and Justina Ireland for their lovely words about this book.

To the many friends and roomies who were constantly exposed to my anxious brain at work—Kelsey, Rachelle, Rachel, Brisly, Yarelis, Allan, Chalice, Hyunjin, and Kristine. Sorry if I ever seemed like I was in my head a lot. In my defense, I was probably working out some plot holes.

And let me just go ahead and shout out myself. *Girl*. You did it.

# about the author

S. Isabelle is a reader, writer, and hoarder of books. After earning a master's degree in library science, she took that love of reading to youth librarianship. She is the author of *The Witchery* as well as the short story "Break" in the anthology *Foreshadow: Stories to Celebrate the Magic of Reading and Writing YA*. When she isn't throwing books at teenagers, you can find her binge-watching TV shows, drinking heavily sweetened coffee, or stressing over baseball. Visit her online at sisabellebooks.com.